THE CURSE OF THE BLUE SCARAB

A MONSTER MASH-UP

BASED ON *THE MUMMY* BY RICCARDO STEPHENS

JOSH LANYON

VELLICHOR BOOKS

AN IMPRINT OF JUSTJOSHIN PUBLISHING, INC.

THE CURSE OF THE BLUE SCARAB

October 2019

Cover and book design by Kevin Burton Smith

Cover art by Svetlana Rib

Edited by Keren Reed

ISBN: 978-1-945802-54-6

Published in the United States of America

JustJoshin Publishing, Inc.
3053 Rancho Vista Blvd.
Suite 116
Palmdale, CA 93551
www.joshlanyon.com

This is a work of fiction. Any resemblance to persons living or dead is entirely coincidental.

Who or what is responsible for the gruesome deaths of members of the secret society known as the Society of Osiris?

Doctor Armiston, an irascible, confirmed bachelor who believes in medicine not mysticism, is certain the deaths are only tragic accidents.

Members of the Society of Osiris suspect something more sinister is at work. They profess to believe an ancient curse has been visited upon their society. Handsome and mysterious Captain Maxwell requests Armiston's help.

Tarot cards? Egyptology? Spiritualism? Armiston has little patience with the superficial and silly pastimes of the rich, but he does love a good puzzle. Or could it be that he is more drawn to young Captain Maxwell than he wishes to admit?

Either way, Armiston must solve the secret of the cursed sarcophagus very soon, for Captain Maxwell is the next slated to die…

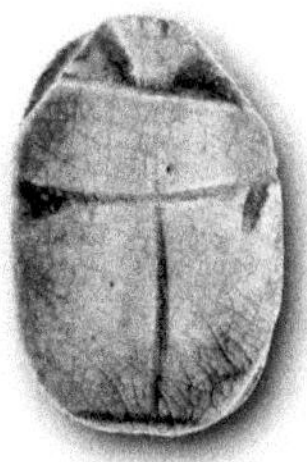

"Poor fellow," I said, and sat down again. "If he's dead, I may as well finish my breakfast."

The young man stared as though he could not believe his ears.

I took another mouthful of kippers.

"You damned cold-blooded c-cormorant," he said very angrily. "Will you come or won't you?"

I studied him for a moment. Too thin, nervy, and young. Younger than I had first thought. Pain and illness had taken their toll.

"Not unless you want me," I assured him, "but I'm ready if you are—and it seems you are." I took one final bite, rising and turning into the lobby for a hat, munching the last of my breakfast as I followed my visitor out.

I didn't mind his remarks, for though my attitude was both logical and practical, his sentiment was natural enough. I observed his awkward gait as he preceded me down the stairs. He managed to move quickly, which must have hurt considerably.

Instinctively I patted my hip-pocket, to make sure that my hypodermic case was there. It is an old servant, and reminds me of a good many odd things if I sit down to overhaul it. But the queerest had not happened when I felt its comfortable presence that raw February morning.

A taxicab waited at the street door, noxious fumes pooling into the damp fog. We piled inside and the cab pulled away at once.

Maxwell, as he told me his name was, said that he and another man had gone round to breakfast at the Albany, and had found their host lying lifeless on the ground.

"Poor Scrymgeour's man Seymour knew you," he said. "He gave me your address."

The name Scrymgeour was unfamiliar to me, and I could think of no patient named Seymour. I had a number of questions—beginning with why Scrymgeour's own physician had not been summoned—but it seemed futile to quiz Maxwell when I was about to see for myself.

My companion did not appear to be a talkative man. His profile was grim and withdrawn as he stared out the cab window. The hand clutching his walking stick clenched and unclenched in unconscious anxiety.

In a few minutes we reached the Albany. Maxwell paid the driver, and we hurried inside.

All was quiet. There was no sign of life. And by the same token, no indication that a death had occurred. The gas lamps made a valiant effort to challenge the chilly gloom of the day, but the soft light could not dispel the shadows lurking in the corners.

A long mirror at the end of the hall caught our reflection and for an instant created the unsettling illusion that our doppelgangers rushed to intercept us. I saw myself, a large man, neither old nor young, with a high nose, stern green eyes, and resolute jaw. The man behind me was shorter, slighter, and a great deal more alarmed. My companion and I merged briefly with our alternate selves and flashed past.

We hastened up the stairs. We had just reached the top of the dimly lit landing when a woman seemed to come out of nowhere, narrowly missing collision. Head down, face heavily veiled, she brushed past us with a breathy wordless apology and disappeared hurriedly down the stairs. I glanced after her.

"This way, Doctor," Maxwell urged, and we continued down the corridor.

Maxwell knocked at A14 and the door opened at once.

A cadaverous-looking specimen stood before us, and I recognized my former patient Seymour. His complaint had been a touch of liver, as I recalled, and in fact his gray and puckered face rather resembled a piece of undercooked meat.

Maxwell and Seymour exchanged a certain silent look. Without a word Seymour turned, leading the way.

These Albany suites consist mostly of dining-room, bedroom, bathroom, and kitchen, and a pigeon-hole for a servant. The three first are en suite, each opening into the hall or lobby. Seymour took us past the open door of the dining-room straight to the bedroom. Entering, one faced a high carved mantelpiece over the fire; and above the mantelpiece was the half-length portrait of a man in the dress of Charles the Second's time.

On the hearth lay a large, heavy man, his head turned a little over his shoulder, his face half-hidden. It was easy to see before handling him that his neck must be broken, and when I touched him I found he was not only dead, but cold.

Next to his feet lay wooden steps of the sort one uses to reach high book shelves. The right panel had broken off and the stool was overturned.

I glanced up at my companions. Maxwell met my gaze steadily, almost fiercely, as though waiting for me to make some objection. Seymour was staring at his fallen master.

I returned my attention to the unfortunate Scrymgeour. He wore evening-dress, and his face, the face of a man in his thirties, was strikingly like that over the mantelpiece. The resemblance was increased by a small pointed beard and by the dead man's pale hair being just a little longer than most men wear their hair in town nowadays. What troubled me was his expression. His dull brown eyes were protuberant, as though starting from his head in alarm. His lips were drawn back from his rather pronounced teeth in a grimace of horror.

Near his outstretched fingers was a speck of something blue. I touched the tip of my index finger to it and saw that it was only a bit of iridescent insect wing. It crumbled away at my touch.

A young fellow, whom I judged to be Maxwell's companion to this projected breakfast, joined us through another door than that by which we had entered, and bowed rather ceremoniously to me, without saying anything.

I began to like the situation less and less, though I could see nothing actually untoward in the case. More, it was the peculiar attitude of Scrymgeour's friends. They were genuinely shocked, as they should be, but they also seemed almost…fearful, and for this I could see no reason.

I became conscious of a strange scent, an undernote to the more obvious odor of death. What was it?

"Your friend is, of course, dead," I said, rising from my knees, "and he has been dead several hours."

"And will you be so good as to tell us the cause of death?" asked Perceval, the young fellow who had just joined us. He was fair-haired with wide, sable eyes like a calf's. He would have been about the same age as Maxwell, but of a softer and more conciliatory nature. Maxwell, unless I missed my guess, had seen military service. This young man had never faced a more dangerous adversary than a bill collector. His voice was pleasant, though high-pitched, his manner was polite almost to affectation.

"A broken neck," I said, "vulgarly speaking. More accurately, there's a separation of the cervical vertebrae, and probably complete rupture of the spinal cord."

"But would you kindly oblige us with your opinion as to the cause of the broken neck?" At Maxwell's warning look, he added, "I hope I'm not asking too much."

I looked at the young man, at the body, the steps, and the portrait.

"I cannot take the place of the coroner's jury, you know," I said. "The general appearance of things suggests that your friend was using the steps—perhaps examining that portrait—and that the steps broke, and the consequent fall did the mischief."

He offered an uncertain smile. "Quite so. That's what we thought. I'm greatly obliged to you for your opinion."

"But my opinion," I went on, looking at them both rather sternly, "isn't of the slightest value, except as to the injury. The police must be told at once, and things had better be left exactly as they are until they come. There will be an inquest."

"Is that absolutely necessary?" Maxwell asked.

"Absolutely, as you must surely realize. But the police will tell you," and I turned to leave the room.

I was thinking about the poor fellow on the floor, whose face was, I dare say, a good deal less grave and dignified then than it had been while he was alive. When death is sudden, in this case almost violently sudden, the victim is sometimes frozen in his final conscious or unconscious act, however ludicrous or embarrassing. The abject terror on the dead man's features was disturbing even to someone who had not known him, and I wondered if perhaps it was this that was so distressing his friends to the point of addling their wits.

Preoccupied with this thought—or at least that would have been my excuse had either challenged me—I made absent-mindedly for the nearest door which led to the room the second young man had exited in order to join us.

As I reached for the handle I heard the two friends say simultaneously, *"Not that door!"*

But they were too late.

The strange scent was much stronger in here, and I recognized it at once.

Bitumen.

The hair rose on the back of my neck, though there is nothing inherently terrifying about the substance.

The room smelled of other things too. Cedar and candle wax and musty linens, but the acrid smell of bitumen underlay it all.

I pushed the door the remainder of the way open, and my attention was immediately caught by the queerly shaped something propped against the far wall. It was the size of a small settee.

The next instant Maxwell reached me. He caught my arm. "This is only a dressing room, Doctor," he said. Though his tone was courteous, his expression was grim.

I glanced down at his hand, raised my gaze pointedly.

Maxwell stubbornly held my stare.

I saw the very moment the thought occurred to him—recognized it because it was the exact same instant the thought occurred to me. His eyes searched mine, and then he released my arm.

I said, "I was thinking that if I write a note for the police—I know the superintendent—it may save you trouble. I can write it here, I suppose?"

"No," Perceval said. "You can't." He threw Maxwell an impatient look and then turned to Scrymgeour's man. "Seymour, find the doctor pen and paper. Doctor, there's a writing-table right in here."

I ignored him, nodding at the heavy coffin-shaped container. "What's that?" I asked. I suspected I already knew what it was, though it was difficult to be certain in the poor light. I could see that it was made of dark wood and had been painted with exotic blue and gold designs.

"That?" It was Maxwell who answered. His tone was casual. Too casual. "That's a mummy case, with a Mummy inside. Poor Scrymgeour was interested in such things."

This was my first introduction to the Mummy.

I wish it had been my last.

CHAPTER TWO

An Unlikely Coincidence

"Doctor Armiston, you performed the postmortem examination of Paris Scrymgeour?" inquired the coroner.

"That is correct," I replied. "I was assisted by Doctor James Hardy."

"And it is your opinion there were no organic changes which might explain the expiration of Mr. Scrymgeour?"

I said sharply, "On the contrary. I believe the introduction of a broken neck rather conclusively explains the expiration of Mr. Scrymgeour."

The audience—for the inquest into the death of Paris Scrymgeour, a former resident of the Albany, resembled something along the lines of a music hall performance—tittered. Mr. Warrington, the coroner, turned the color of puce and banged his gavel for order.

Scrymgeour's mysterious death excited a good deal of interest, not least because he was related to several well-known people, and was himself rather an eccentric character. No fewer than three London papers detailed the more puzzling aspects of the case.

Not that the most puzzling aspects were revealed to the press.

But ludicrous rumors circulated. Scrymgeour had belonged to a secret society, Scrymgeour liked to dress up in the costume of the ancient Egyptians. Scrymgeour was an ardent supporter of female suffrage.

Having performed the postmortem examination, I was required to appear at the inquest and make my report. The only evidence besides my own was given by the three men whom I had met in the Albany: Maxwell, Seymour, and Perceval.

Captain Maxwell, late of the Royal Horse Guards, gave his evidence as though facing down an enemy cannon: face pale, expression set. Yet his account was innocuous enough.

The star witness was my former patient Seymour.

Scrymgeour's man stated that he slept in the house, but on the evening before the death he had gone to see *The Merry Widow*, and upon his late return had found the lights out—in the dining-room at any rate. He had "retired," to use his own word, without seeing his master.

When his master's guests arrived the next morning, he went into the bedroom and found the electric light on. He spotted the body lying on the hearthrug, cried out, and the two gentlemen joined him. Later Captain Maxwell went for the doctor, whose name and address he, Seymour, had supplied.

Seymour insisted he was not a heavy sleeper and would certainly have heard the sounds of a fall if the fatal event occurred after he was in his bedroom. The light might be switched on in the bedroom without his being able to notice it from the lobby. Therefore, he believed the accident had occurred before he returned from the theatre.

The evidence of young Maxwell and his friend Perceval was hardly more than corroborative of Seymour's. Both stated they had met up with Scrymgeour at their club on the previous evening and arranged to breakfast at the Albany. Scrymgeour had seemed quite well and in good spirits. He left the club about eleven o'clock—before they did.

As for myself, I was examined as to my visit and my post-mortem observations. The questions were routine, though I annoyed an inquisitive juryman, a druggist, by speaking of the victim as a "heavy" man, without having weighed the body.

Also no one had measured the precise height of the steps, and I declined to give a dogmatic opinion as to the height from which the fall of a man, say thirteen stone, would cause a broken neck. I suggested a hangman might be able to say, should the information prove absolutely necessary.

This resulted in another outbreak of titters from those in attendance, further incensing Mr. Warrington, who reapplied his gavel.

At this point in the proceedings, Perceval rose and asked whether he might be allowed to make a statement, which he thought might be useful in clearing up the matter.

Warrington agreed.

"Our dear friend Scrymgeour," Perceval began, "belonged to an honorable family, and had an amiable weakness. He delighted in genealogy and ancestral histories. He possessed several old family portraits; but his favorite was one of Sir Ambrose Scrymgeour, a soldier living in the time of the first and second King Charles.

"This remarkably lifelike portrait hangs in his bedroom over the mantelpiece, and poor old S. was fond of showing it to his acquaintances and hearing them comment upon the family likeness. I've known him to mount the steps already spoken of and dust the frame of the portrait himself, calling attention to various characteristics in his ancestor's face. I've given the matter great thought, and I believe it's only too possible that he was examining the picture when the steps broke and caused his fall."

This theory was met with murmurs ranging from approbation to disappointment, the audience no doubt hoping for revelations more in keeping with the denouement of a Fergus Hume novel. I had proposed this explanation myself, and yet listening to it in court…

The jury, after a certain amount of delay, due, everybody was sure, to the pedantic druggist, returned a verdict of death by misadventure, in accordance with the medical evidence.

Warrington himself did not appear altogether satisfied. Yet I left the place feeling that the verdict was common-sense, and sure that the druggist was a bumptious ass. Still, I had noticed one or two things which did not precisely square with the general evidence, although they did not contradict it.

For example, Maxwell and Perceval stated that they went by invitation to breakfast with Scrymgeour. Seymour also referred to this planned breakfast. But there was no breakfast laid, certainly not in the dining-room which we had passed on our way to the bedroom.

Were all three lying? Or was Seymour late with breakfast? Or were Maxwell and Perceval before time in their arrival?

Perceval's manner while giving evidence, and particularly while being questioned by the druggist (who obviously thought all men liars and rather wanted us to know it), was conspicuously unconcerned and matter-of-fact. But when he passed me on his way back to his seat, I was surprised to see by the light of a straggling ray of the cold February sun, that his immobile face was covered with little beads of sweat.

Maxwell too had seemed—for a military man—oddly shaken by both the death of his friend and the necessity of bearing witness.

In any event, the inquiry was closed.

There was, however, one further peculiar circumstance.

Following the inquest, I was making my way back to my surgery when it so happened that the traffic at Piccadilly Circus marooned me for a few minutes on the edge of the pavement. Losing patience, I made a dash for it, but I was stopped in midstream, between the two opposing currents.

A light, masculine voice spoke close to my ear. "Well, thank God we kept her name out of it. That's something."

"Yes. But the doctor, Armiston, is sus—" The second voice, deeper, huskier and, inexplicably, more familiar, broke off.

I turned and found myself staring directly into a motor-brougham. My fellow witnesses, Maxwell and Perceval, gaped back at me.

It was Maxwell who had been speaking until Perceval had him clutched by the arm. Maxwell's wide gray eyes fixed, as though hypnotized, on my own.

At that moment the traffic lurched forward. The blue brougham moved on; I had to leap for the pavement, and left them without a word or a nod.

But we had recognized one another—and I was more uneasy than ever.

CHAPTER THREE

A Night Summons

For a fortnight after the inquest my life in my flat over the grocer's shop was as monotonous as usual.

I had seen nothing during those two weeks of my fellow-witnesses, Maxwell and Perceval; but I heard something of them from my patient Seymour, the dead man's servant, who returned to me complaining of sleeplessness and palpitation.

Not yet having found another place, Seymour was still sleeping at the Albany, standing watch over his late master's things. More correctly, to use the old expression, he "lay" there, for he slept little. He complained of mysterious noises—whispers and rustlings—though he was alone in the suite. When he did sleep, he was apt to dream, so he told me, of being forced to enter his master's bedroom, knowing the ghastly thing he would find upon the floor.

I prescribed for him upon perhaps unorthodox lines—hot foot-baths and valerian and mint tea—and spoke of his master's friends. Maxwell, as I had learned from the Army List, had been in the cavalry and had the D.S.O. Seymour told me he was a "talented officer" and a "great traveler," but had suffered a tragedy in his youth. I assumed this tragedy was something more than the grievous wounding that had resulted in his being invalided out of the service, though Seymour did not—perhaps could not—expand.

As for Perceval… Seymour seemed quite shocked that I didn't know—nor care—about Charles Perceval's impressive lineage.

"Cousin, sir, to the Earl of Moy and Merricourt, and heir. A gentleman, sir, with a great deal more in him than meets the heye. A very delusive gentleman, if I may say so."

"You may not say so," I replied. "Unless you can support such a statement."

Seymour's thin mouth puckered primly. "Too much money, that's all. It's not good for a young sprig to have unlimited resources and no guidance."

"Where do you feel Perceval lacks guidance?"

His watery gaze slid away from mine. "Of course, I'm only going by the words of my own dear dead master."

Indeed. From what I could gather, Scrymgeour was another young man with too much money and not enough guidance. Still, I can't deny that, being curious by nature and a lover of puzzles, I wished to know more about both Maxwell and Perceval.

The affair at the Albany had stimulated my interest, and I was a little disappointed it had ended so prosaically.

But ended it had. Or so I believed.

I was talking to Seymour and Bird one evening when my bell rang, and Bird rose to answer it.

"Bearer awaiting reply, sir," said he, and stood to attention, while I read the crisp note he gave me.

There was a crest on the heavy paper, an eagle displayed, motto *Ad Solem*, and an address, "Dene Court, Sussex, S.O."

Doctor Armiston is urgently requested to meet Doctor Thorne in consultation at Dene Court to-night. The car will wait for him, and will be at his disposal for returning in the morning.

I knew nothing of Dene Court, or who lived there—certainly no patient of mine. Nor was I accustomed to such summons. However, I told Bird to put a change of clothes into a bag for me, and within a few minutes was down in the street, where a bottle-green electric-brougham stood with a chauffeur in gray livery.

"Back before lunch to-morrow, I suppose," said I. It was then about half-past eleven. "Good night, both of you."

As the car started I nodded to Seymour, who stood on the curb.

It might have been the electric light, but his face looked perfectly ghastly.

CHAPTER FOUR

The Mummy Returns

The road before us curved black and unrelenting as a mourning band. The March moon rode high in the arch of night, too far away to cast any real illumination, and the landscape took on a shadowy, unearthly quality.

In fact, it was so dark once we had passed beyond the lamps of the suburbs, I could not have testified as to whether we were en route to Sussex or the Moon.

I confess to a slight sense of foreboding.

First I speculated idly upon the reason which might induce people to send for me in particular as a consultant. I had no delusions about my small reputation. I seldom write to the medical journals, being well aware that what comes under my observation has been already noticed and recorded by others—and that the afflictions of dull common folk are rarely of interest to the ambitious learned. My patients were hardly likely to recommend my services to such personages as might reside in Dene Court. Nor would a family that sent a liveried chauffeur to fetch an undistinguished sawbones require the recommendations of the poor to whom I attended.

It was a puzzle.

After a time I recognized one or two landmarks and realized that I must be passing in the darkness through many places which had been familiar to me as a boy. I smiled sourly at the memory of the great things which at that time I had expected to do in life. I had surely been a fool at fifteen. But then, considering my current situation, it seemed I continued to be a fool at fifty—and there's no fool like an old fool.

The hour's journey was lengthened almost to three by fog, and was sufficiently dreary. I was far enough from the cheery frame of mind proper to the consultant, when we stopped before the great curved gates opening onto a carriage-drive.

By my calculation we passed through a leafless tree-lined avenue of about a mile before we stopped again in front of a large pile of buildings which stretched into the darkness on either hand.

No light appeared to shine in any window.

I threw off the warm rug and disembarked into a damp and clouded night that smelled of any number of cold and slimy things: wet grass, wet stone, wet frogs. My breath hung like white smoke in the air. Mist rose like ragged ghosts from the walk.

I was received by the stoutest butler I have ever seen.

He was a huge man, shaking like a jelly with grief. A ridiculous sight, had it not been for the conditions of my visit; but from his appearance I formed the worst possible prognosis of the case I had come to see. My heart sank and I knew my sense of foreboding had been justified.

I said nothing to him about that, of course, nor he to me. He directed a footman to take charge of my bag, and led me across a large empty hall, where a wood-fire blazed, to a smaller room where the table was laid for a meal.

Here he pressed me to take food, and asked me to excuse him, as there were things to attend to. A groom, he said, had driven to fetch the doctor who was to meet me, but they could not be back for half-an-hour.

Left to myself, I munched a biscuit and sipped a glass of very fine port, sitting in an easy-chair by the fire and studying my surroundings. Somber tapestries, ancient weapons, and gold-framed portraits of a particularly pugnacious-looking clan covered the walls. The women looked even more truculent than the men.

I sighed and ate another biscuit. The fire snapped and crackled in the grate.

Hopefully someone would come before I dozed off.

The house remained perfectly still, and no one else, rather to my perturbation, came near me. I remained quite alone with the defiant-eyed portraits and port until my confrere's arrival over an hour later.

Doctor Thorne was a smallish, hard-bitten man of sixty or so, with a tanned face and slightly bowed legs. His eyes were a flinty blue, his general appearance was distinctly horsey.

"Delighted to make your acquaintance, Doctor Armiston." He helped himself liberally to the port bottle. "You're an excellent fellow to have made the trip on such a night and with so little notice." He sniffed the port and went to stand beside the fire, resting one elbow on the mantelpiece and shaking his head at his own thoughts.

I felt that was a strange comment given that inconvenience is part of a physician's stock and trade.

"I'm happy to be of service. However—"

"A sad case!" Thorne interrupted—although I'm not sure he even realized I had spoken. He seemed to be thinking aloud. "To think that I've known him from the time he went into knickerbockers. A charming fellow, I assure you. One of our best families."

I've never known disease to make an exception for bloodline.

I said, perhaps a shade impatiently, "I'm afraid I know nothing whatever of the case. I've seen no one but servants since I came. What should I know about your patient before we meet with him?"

Thorne, who had been staring moodily into the fire, moved so abruptly that he knocked his wineglass off the mantelpiece. It smashed on the fender. The broken pieces winked like tears in the firelight.

"Patient!" he said. "God bless my soul, sir! The boy is dead. Was dead for some hours before we sent for you."

I stared at him, trying to comprehend. "Why then did you send for me?"

"Why? Well, the case is a curious one." He threw me a quick look. "Sad, very sad! And the hounds to meet here in two days' time. One of the best days of the season generally."

"A tragedy. Still—"

"Not certain if they'll be out again at all. Respect for the dead, you know. A most charming young fellow. Rode straight, and family of course greatly respected. All the same, hope they won't miss a day's hunting for me, when my hour comes."

"Why, sir, did you send for *me*?" I repeated, and rapped on the table to focus the old fool's attention. Thorne started.

"Yes, yes," he muttered. "There I go, rioting as usual till I'm whipped off. Disgrace to my profession. A mere hunting man." He threw me another of those glinting looks, and I began to wonder if he was quite the fool I imagined.

I waited in silence, and after a second or two he sighed. "Naturally you will have questions. Well, the boy is Hugh D'Aurelle. You know the family, of course."

I did not bother to hide my impatience. "I do not follow the society pages, Doctor Thorne."

"Don't—? Well! Daniel D'Aurelle is one of the richest men in England. One of the richest commoners, for he's refused a peerage, as more than one of his forefathers did. The boy was his only son—about twenty-two, and in every way a manly fellow. Lady Helene D'Aurelle, his mother, was ill last autumn, and wintered abroad with her husband. Hugh spent a good deal of time in town this winter, but he hunted here regularly."

"For God's sake, man. *Will* you get to the point?"

Doctor Thorne's tone grew nettled. "I'm getting to it as quickly as I can. The boy came down about a week ago, and, when I met him, told me that he would be here for about a fortnight. Two days ago he was riding hard to hounds, with a couple of friends who came down with him. Yesterday afternoon the butler found him lying dead. He had not been at lunch, but it was an understood thing that he and his guests acted independently of each other till dinner-time. They supposed he was lunching at a neighbor's house some few miles away."

"What was the cause of death?" I asked. "Is there some uncertainty?"

"None whatever!" Thorne answered briskly. "There's not a shadow of doubt about it. He overtaxed his heart two years ago.

He was in the Oxford boat. The run of two days ago was unusually stiff. Are you a hunting man?"

"No."

"Ah, well, you've missed one of the great pleasures of life; given a good scenting day, a good mount, and a country you know like a book. The first whimper of a trustworthy hound in covert—I know all their voices."

This time I did not interrupt his reminiscences. I had begun to form my suspicions.

Thorne broke off abruptly. "Poor Hugh. He'll never hear them again. Well! As I said, it was a hard day, and he rode hard, and we killed some fifteen miles from home. He spoke of stiffness next morning, and, undoubtedly, to try and work it off with heavy clubs was a fatal mistake."

"Heavy clubs?"

"Indian clubs. He was found dead in the *salle d'armes*."

He tossed the additional information out very casually.

I watched his face as I asked, "And why am I called in?"

"In the absence of his people, and to avoid any source of error or of gossip, an independent opinion seemed advisable. It gives me the pleasure of making your acquaintance." Thorne bowed pleasantly to me across the fire.

A preposterous story! And the most preposterous part of all was the idea that an uncelebrated London physician would in the natural course of things be brought in to sign off on the suspicious death of the son of one of the richest men in the country.

But I did not say so. Along with my skepticism, my curiosity had been roused, and I determined to discover what exactly was going on.

Accordingly, I returned Thorne's bow, and after a word or two more we went upstairs.

Passing along one of the chilly upper corridors, which smelled faintly of camphor and beeswax, we found Mott, the big butler, evidently on guard at a bedroom door. A candelabrum stood on a Chinoiserie chest, and its candles flickered in the draft. This made the butler's huge shadow go through strange changes; and indeed I think his fat body still shook with grief, though he made no sound, even when Thorne greeted him with a pleasant word.

Mott drew himself up to attention as we passed him, and stayed where he stood, making no move to enter the room with us.

Thorne told me that the man had served in the Guards, had saved the elder D'Aurelle's life in the Egyptian war, and had been the son's first teacher in boxing and fencing.

He may have told me other things, but by then my attention was on Hugh D'Aurelle.

Later I learned that in life the boy had been strikingly handsome, the very flower of English manhood. His portrait had been painted by no less a personage than William Powell Frith. But what I saw—what I could not fail to see—was a man who had died in agonizing terror.

D'Aurelle's clean-shaven face was a death mask of clenched teeth and starting eyes—not unexpected given the pain and fear he might have experienced in his final moments. What was *not* expected and *not* natural was the position of the body, frozen as it was in rigor mortis. He looked as though he had been struck down in the very act of crawling away…

From what?

The boy's muscular arms were outstretched, his hands spread like claws. His legs were drawn up, knees bent.

What made it worse—though I'm not sure there was a way to make it better—was that while fixed in this undignified and bizarre position, he had been placed in bed on his back and the covers drawn over him. He looked like a piece of statuary ready to be unveiled, and were the circumstances not so sad, they might have been macabrely comical.

I opened my mouth, but words failed me. I stared at my colleague. Thorne stared back at me without expression.

"I was shocked as well," he said. "Nonetheless I can find no indication that the boy's death did not result from heart-failure."

"Rigor seems unusually pronounced given the supposed time of death."

"Examine him for yourself."

I did exactly that.

I examined the body at length before returning to the corridor to ask Mott a few questions.

He repeated Thorne's story of finding young D'Aurelle in the fencing room the previous afternoon.

"Dead or dying?" I questioned.

Tears welled in the giant's eyes. "Dead. Stone cold dead."

In some indefinable way he reminded me of Bird, and I said more kindly than before, "All right. The lad was already dead. There was nothing more you could do. Was the door to the fencing room locked?"

"No, sir. Not locked."

"Can you describe what you saw when you entered the room?"

"The young master was lying on the floor. It seemed to me that he had been trying to reach the door. His arm was outstretched so." Mott stuck his arm out, fingers curled as though in desperate pain.

"You told the doctor the boy went there to work out his stiffness with the Indian clubs?"

"It was his habit, sir."

"Were the clubs beside the body?"

"No. They were back on the shelf. There was only this bit of paper." He proffered a stiff brown scrap to me. "I thought it might be a note, but there's no writing."

I took it curiously, smoothing out the crinkles. Was that parchment? No. Not paper of any kind. It was some kind of cloth. Muslin or linen perhaps. It felt dusty. No, it was coarser than dust. Sand? Salt? I sniffed it cautiously.

Camphor and a very faint odor of… What was that? Soda ash?

Natron.

Strange.

Still studying the scrap of cloth, I asked, "And what of these friends of Hugh's?"

"What about them, sir?"

"Are you sure no one was with him when he was taken ill?"

"He was alone, poor lad. The other young gentlemen went to the village for lunch."

"And where are they now?"

"They've since returned to London, sir."

I pocketed the scrap of muslin, asked a few more general questions, but there was no hint of dissembling from Mott. He seemed greatly shocked and genuinely distressed.

So too did Thorne, who I also chatted with a little longer. The doctor was eager to give all possible information—being anxious, he acknowledged, to avoid a postmortem in the parents' absence, if it could be honestly done.

I was not happy about the situation, but there seemed no just reason for doubting Thorne's decision about the cause of death. It was only too likely the boy had overtaxed his already strained heart, and that the final attack had occurred immediately after he finished his exercise. There had been no time to summon help.

Finally, I agreed to sign a joint certificate, giving heart-failure, due to overexertion, as the cause of death.

It was then between five and six, chilly and rather depressing, as it always seems to one who has been up all night. A bedroom was ready for me, and I am sure that the servants, of the old-fashioned type, would have offered me every attention. But I was conscious that my presence must be a burden on the distressed household.

Besides, I had taken an unreasoning dislike to the place.

I also declined Thorne's pressing offer of a bed at his place, and asked Mott, the butler, privately, whether he thought I could arrange with the chauffeur to take me back into town at once. It ended in my getting a quite decent breakfast while sundry preparations were being made; for Mott seemed to brighten up quite visibly at my suggestion. Indeed, until he conducted me himself to the car, I was rather puzzled at his haste to speed things.

Passing down the steps from the big hall door to the carriage drive in the ashen morning light, I talked to him, conscious all the while that like myself he seemed to feel some vague uncertainty about the cause of the boy's death. He didn't express it openly. Indeed, I knew if I pressed him, he wouldn't acknowledge it. Perhaps he only felt special responsibility because his master and mistress were away.

The flight of steps was high, rather reminiscent of those early pyramids, and in going down I looked on the top of the car.

My bag was there, and also a long, sinister-shaped object, partly muffled in rugs. The foot of the box stuck out several inches from beneath the wrappings, and I could see that it was painted in an alien gold and blue design.

"What in God's name is that?" I demanded.

Mott looked down too, began to stammer, but then the guardsman in him seemed to get the upper hand of the butler.

"'Twas an order I got from *him*," he said. "The damned thing was to go to town this morning, anyway. Twice this week he said, 'Remember, Mott, as I might forget, or be away, that the Thing's to go back on the twenty-fifth.'" Mott sighed heavily. "Well, go it shall, and it's me that's glad to be quit of it. Though if you ask me, I say it's too late."

"What is it?" I asked, but really I already knew.

"A blasted Mummy," said Mott.

CHAPTER FIVE

Wherein Something Happens

The black and gold hatchment over the front steps grew smaller and smaller, the drooping yellow and green flag at half-mast, damp and dull, swallowed by the morning mist as we departed Dene Court for London.

I uneasily fingered the bit of muslin in my pocket that I'd removed from the *salle d'armes*. Why had I taken it? I wasn't sure. Did I imagine it to be some kind of clue? Ridiculous. What were the chances that these two sudden deaths, one in Albany and one in Sussex, were somehow connected?

All the way back to town I pondered this question, my grim thoughts accompanied by the unsettling scraping and scratching of the silent passenger upon the roof, each time the car followed a curve in the road.

Every chilly draft that infiltrated the window frame seemed to carry the faintest whiff of bitumen.

What were the chances that in both households a Mummy—or at least a mummy case—should be present?

What were the chances it should prove to be the same Mummy?

Minus the dangerous fog of the night before, we reached Piccadilly in record time, and I decided to resolve these points as far as possible for myself.

While the startled chauffeur handed my bag over to Bird, who waited for us on the curb and has been too long with me to show or to feel astonishment at anything, I climbed to the level of the car-roof to examine its burden.

Yes—to all appearance this was the very same mummy case which I had seen a fortnight before. Though admittedly no expert, I thought the painted symbols of golden reeds and large blue beetles were both memorable and quite unlike any I had seen in a museum or private collection.

I'm too old and too skeptical to give way to imaginings, but in the smoky morning air of the city I thought I picked up a faint whiff of moldering decay.

Though I would have liked to examine the thing carefully, its suggestive shape was likely to arouse concern from prospective clients. I only settled one more point before climbing down. I looked for an address, and found it:

Professor Maundeville
21 Courtenay Street, W.
London

Over my coffee and a pipe that night I tackled the affair again. My thoughts were not pleasant.

Within the space of four weeks I had been called upon to certify two sudden deaths. Both had occurred apparently without witnesses. Those concerned were both young men, bachelors, well-to-do, of good social position.

Well, young men did frequently die.

In the first case the death seemed accidental, and the cause of the accident seemed obvious. The second case had been foreshadowed given certain conditions, namely overexertion and fatigue. According to witnesses, who as far as I could tell were unbiased, those conditions had been present.

Both cases, so far, might occur in any man's practice, but certainly not with the great coincidence that was left to be accounted for.

In each instance there was a Mummy in the house. Moreover, it was apparently the *same* Mummy.

While it is true that life is full of startling coincidence, that seemed an extraordinary one.

Further, whereas in the first instance I had been fetched because I was nearby and already known to someone present, in the second I had several hours' journey to make—and was an absolute stranger.

Imaginative or not, this troubled me.

I decided to know as quickly as possible whether the two dead men had been acquainted, or had had mutual acquaintances. I rang the bell.

"Where's Seymour?" I asked Bird.

"Gone to a music-hall, sir, to get rid of the 'orrors."

"What horrors, Bird?"

Bird's stolid features twisted into something like scorn. "Dunno, sir. 'E seems scared of something, and says 'e won't sleep alone in the Albany at any price."

"Well, keep him here when he comes back," I ordered, "but don't disturb me. I don't want to see either of you to-night. More coffee!" and then I was left to myself.

There is nothing like strong coffee, a fragrant pipe and undisturbed quiet to concentrate the mind.

That night I got nothing for my vigil except an attack of biliousness, and a certainty that I must interview the men connected with my Albany experience—Perceval and Maxwell.

I also reached the unpleasant conclusion that somehow I had been duped.

If I hadn't given in to my own undefined trepidation, I shouldn't have left Dene Court directly I saw that Mummy on the car. At the very least I should have returned and torn up that death certificate, refusing to sign without further investigation.

I had a miserable night.

It was the early morning when I fell asleep, and in consequence ate a late breakfast in a shocking temper.

I was in the middle of my smoked kippers and scrambled eggs when the front-door bell rang.

"If it's anyone to see me," I said to Bird, "I'm engaged and shall be all day. I won't see anyone but Seymour. If it's a patient, tell him there's a younger and better man at the bottom of the street."

By then I was convinced that the greatest Harley Street quack would be a better choice for a patient than someone as oblivious and cowardly as myself.

Nevertheless Bird returned in two or three minutes, and said that two gentlemen had insisted that they must see me, and were waiting in the lobby.

"*Insist!*" I repeated. "How much did they give you?"

Bird was so rattled, he mentioned half a sovereign before he knew what he was about.

"Return their tip and show them the door."

"They're gentlemen, sir," said Bird. "I believe one's an officer."

Apparently Bird was suffering a flare-up of dormant loyalty to his earlier life. "Tell your 'officer' what your orders are. I'm engaged," I snapped.

Bird saluted stiffly, went out, and returned.

"Gentlemen say they must see you, sir."

"Bird! Are you being deliberately obtuse?"

It was no use. In fact, I saw that I did not even have his undivided attention. Bird's gaze was pinned to the mirror over the mantelpiece a little behind my chair to the left, and he was grinning idiotically.

I twisted in my chair, and found that the two patients stood just inside the door.

Maxwell and Perceval.

My heart jumped and a strange flush suffused me as I met Maxwell's curious gray gaze. It was a reaction impossible to analyze, mixed as it was between pleasure and alarm—pleasure being the most inexplicable element. There was no reason for pleasure. Quite the opposite.

For a moment no one said anything. Then the situation struck me as being rather paradoxical, and I uttered a harsh laugh.

Maxwell's eyes narrowed. Otherwise neither man revealed thought or emotion. In deed, my two visitors remained perfectly solemn.

"Bring chairs, Bird," I commanded.

He obeyed with alacrity, placing the chairs before Maxwell and Perceval.

"Gentlemen."

My "patients" seated themselves with every aspect of self-possession.

I sat back and waited for them to explain themselves.

CHAPTER SIX

A PECULIAR CONSULTATION

"To begin with, we must apologize for this intrusion," Perceval said. "We realize our behavior might seem rather..."

Here he glanced at Maxwell as though requesting reinforcements. Maxwell continued to study me as though I presented a strategic problem he had not quite worked out.

I replied, "I see. Well, in any case I wanted to see you both. What do you want?"

Perceval explained that they had both come to consult me regarding the subject of their health. "Of which," he said, "we believe we have reason for concern."

Perceval, at any rate, looked remarkably fit, though both were as solemn as owls. My misgivings grew.

"My fee for each is a guinea," I said, and both, without saying anything, produced two guineas, and placed them on the table.

I inquired who wished to consult me first. "The other," I said, "can stay here till I send in for him."

They exchanged a look.

Perceval coughed politely. "We would prefer to consult you together."

I frowned. "That is not how an examination is conducted."

Maxwell said, "We don't request—or require—the use of your examination room, Doctor Armiston."

"I see." I poured out more coffee. "Most irregular."

I was inclined to say a great deal more, but decided it would be simpler to hear them out.

"What is your complaint, then?" I asked Maxwell.

He considered. His brows drew in a black line, he bit his lip. He looked like a schoolboy confronted with a difficult mathematical equation.

"Bad dreams?" Perceval suggested.

"Yes!" Maxwell agreed. "Bad dreams."

"Nightmares," Perceval added helpfully.

"Yes! Nightmares." Maxwell leaned forward eagerly as though getting into the spirit of things. "And I have the constant feeling that something is about to happen."

Perceval interjected, "A sense of foreboding. A feeling of doom."

Maxwell nodded.

I leaned forward and took Maxwell's wrist. He tensed, but then relaxed.

"What is it you fear is going to happen?" I inquired. He was wiry but strong. I could feel the delicate network of nerves and synapses flashing and firing as they went about their business beneath the blue-veined skin of his inner wrist.

Maxwell blinked into my eyes. His eyelashes were as long and velvety as a girl's and the irises were indeed gray and not some variation of blue. The sclera was a little red and his pupils were constricted nearly to pinpoints. "Oh, er, bad things," he said. "Death, I suppose."

"Horrid things," Perceval offered.

I said on the spur of the moment, "Such as mummies?" Beneath my fingers, Maxwell's pulse jumped from a cool and steady fifty-five to an agitated eighty. He withdrew his arm from my grasp.

"Why not mummies?" Perceval said. His voice was high and excited though he feigned amusement. "Ghosts and goblins and giant spiders too, I expect."

I said to Maxwell, "Show me your tongue."

He stuck his tongue out, again reminding me of schoolboy—and an impudent one at that. Perceval laughed.

I did not laugh. Maxwell's mouth was dry and his tongue furry. His breath had a certain sweetish smell.

"I expect that leg gives you a great deal of pain," I said.

Maxwell threw me a hostile look. "Not much."

"No?" I said. "Well, perhaps you've found a means of dealing with it."

He paled.

I turned to Perceval. "And what is supposed to be your trouble?"

"Oh, well, I find that I'm always restless and irritable. I can't sleep much and I'm never comfortable. I am anxious when alone and yet I can't bear company."

"That's why you brought your friend with you, I suppose?" I suggested.

He gave another of those light laughs. "When I'm alone I can't bear myself," he explained. "Besides, Captain Maxwell doesn't count, Doctor. We're old friends and understand one another; don't we, Max?"

Maxwell nodded, without troubling to say anything.

I overhauled Perceval in a general way, and then sitting back in my chair considered them both. They returned my gaze steadily.

"Well, Doctor?" Maxwell said at last, somewhat defiantly, in my opinion. "Would you say that either of us were in imminent peril of sudden death?"

I said dryly, "Having performed only the most cursory examinations, I wouldn't like to commit myself. Certainly not in another court of law. However, I see no outward sign of organic disease in either of you."

Perceval said, "You would be surprised to learn of either of us suddenly keeling over whilst playing cards or taking a stroll along the Strand?"

"Yes. I would."

This time it was Perceval who nodded without saying anything.

I said impatiently, "You've paid me for my opinion, and you've had it. I can only surmise that either you're suffering from guilty consciences, which for the time I leave to yourselves, or this 'consultation' is part of some elaborate charade for your amusement or the amusement of someone else. Certainly not mine, for I don't find this remotely funny."

They took this quietly, and merely sat looking at one another and seeming to consider. It is true that Perceval, who was much the fairer man, flushed hotly; and Maxwell clenched his hand, which lay on the table before me.

For a minute or so I waited to hear what they would say, but they said nothing.

At last Maxwell turned to Perceval.

"I suppose that will do?" he said.

"Altogether satisfactory, I think," Perceval answered. They both rose, bowed politely, muttered a word or two of thanks, and went away.

I never was more puzzled in my life. In fact, I was so non-plussed that I made no effort to keep them, forgetting my own questions entirely—or at least deciding it would be better to say nothing more, until I had time to think things over alone.

I sat and stared at the four guineas, still lying on the table, till some sound made me shift my gaze, and I found Bird watching with his usual expressionless stare.

I nodded at him to speak.

"Seymour is waiting to know whether you want to see him, sir."

"Is he? Good. Send him in."

Seymour came, looking very much upset, and I told him to sit down near me.

"I'm going to ask you several questions," I said. "Understand that I have no authority to make you answer them. You must please yourself. But if you answer fully and honestly, you may save yourself trouble. Will you do so?"

I watched him while he considered the matter, which he did for a while, biting his nails.

He was certainly unhappy, and looked as if he had not slept. His chin was blue and unshaved and he smelled of cigarettes.

"Will you answer my questions?" I asked again.

"I'd like to hear 'em first," he said cagily, but I understood what he meant.

"Very well. You heard where I was going two nights ago?"

"Yes, sir."

"You know the place?"

"Yes, sir."

"You were surprised?"

That man's renewed attack upon his nails set my teeth on edge before he replied he did not know.

"You don't know whether you were surprised? Odd. You looked surprised, at any rate. Surprised and frightened. Did you guess what was wrong?"

"I was afraid something was wrong," Seymour allowed.

I persisted. "Do you know what was wrong?"

"I know now, sir. I didn't then, of course. But yesterday I made inquiries at Berkeley Square—at the town house, sir."

"Did your master know this young D'Aurelle?"

"Yes, sir."

"Did Captain Maxwell and Mr. Perceval know him?"

Seymour sat gnawing his nails with indecision.

"They may have met," he said at last. "I don't say that they did or they didn't. It's not my business, anyway."

"And you think it isn't mine?" I suggested. "Would you be interested to hear that there was a Mummy at Dene Place? Or did you hear that too at Berkeley Square?"

Seymour turned a paler yellow than ever, and rising unsteadily said I must excuse him, but he didn't feel well.

He was staggering toward the door when I jumped up, got hold of him, and forced him down upon the sofa, otherwise he would have fallen. It cost me a good glass of excellent cherry brandy before he reached his normal shade of yellow again.

I had for the time to stop my questions, but I meant to continue my interrogation as soon as possible.

Fate, however, decided to play her hand.

CHAPTER SEVEN

THE SOCIETY OF OSIRIS

I saw patients most of the morning, but came in for lunch, as I was not inclined for chatter with men at my club. In consequence, I opened my letters by the midday post soon after they arrived. One envelope, over which I idled for a few seconds, was of thick rough paper, rather long and narrow, and was stamped in black with an odd symbol that resembled an Indian club.

Inside was a small sheet of rough-edged note-paper, and on that was printed the following:

You are invited to join the Society of Osiris. An emissary will call this afternoon.

The same symbol on the outside of the envelope was stamped in colors at the top of the paper. I realized it represented an Atef crown crossed with a crook and flail and not athletic equipment after all.

That was just as well, for I am not athletically inclined. I was also not inclined to the foolish pastimes of the rich and frivolous, such as Spiritualism, Spiritism, or Psychical Research, which I assumed this to be—though with an Oriental flavor.

People who believed in such nonsense, let alone formed a society for the purpose of expanding and exploring those beliefs, were gullible and weak-kneed individuals with too much time and too little education.

I could see that the invitation had not been sent by any intimate friend for the envelope was scrupulously addressed with a great many letters after my name, representing my membership in many learned and quite unimportant societies. I judged that my address had been copied from a medical directory.

I crumpled the card up, tossed it into my wastepaper basket, and settled down to lunch and my book, forgetting all about the thing.

Indeed, I tried to put all events of the recent days out of my mind, the better to approach the puzzle with fresh eyes when the moment came.

As I had no patients scheduled after lunch, and it was an unseasonably warm and sunny day, I decided to go for a walk.

A fashionable flower-shop sat at the corner where my street met Piccadilly. I was on the opposite side, but I crossed to get a sight of whatever blooms there might be. I saw some yellow and orange daffodils in the window, and while I was scrutinizing them, wondering whether I should tell the florist to send some across to my rooms, she took the whole lot out of the window, perhaps a dozen bunches, and showed them to a customer, a man. From the manner in which she set them aside, I inferred that he had bought the lot; and I glared at him discontentedly—and then recognized Maxwell.

He dictated some address to the girl, and then turning to the window as though to see what else might be there, noticed me, and at once limped out into the street.

"Doctor Armiston. I was on my way to call."

"I'm relieved to hear it," I said. "Though I'm not sure I've the expertise your case requires. You should consult a specialist, you know."

Maxwell looked completely taken aback—and then offended.

"You misunderstand. I've no wish—nor need—to consult you professionally. Will you step into the shop, or shall I meet you back at your rooms?"

"I don't meet patients in florists' shops," I said, "but I don't know that I care to turn back either—provided you mean to explain this morning's visit."

"I repeat," he said with a trace of hauteur, "I don't require your professional services. But if you'll be reasonable and listen to what I have to say, I don't think you'll regret it. Come into the shop."

My curiosity got the better of me, and I followed him inside.

The little shop was warm and smelled like springtime. Creamy roses and blue hyacinths were in full—and false—bloom. In a quiet corner away from the counter, Maxwell faced me and spoke, holding out a small card.

"You got, or will get soon, an invitation to join the Society of Osiris."

I took the thing, the size of an ordinary visiting card, and saw on it the small black symbol of the Atef crown. Only that and his name in pencil.

"I received it," I said.

His gray eyes met mine. "Will you join?"

"Secret societies are hardly in my line."

His mouth gave a sardonic little twist and he laughed. "No."

By any standards, he was an attractive fellow. Quite tall, even leaning heavily on his cane, and though too thin, well-proportioned. He was naturally dark-complexioned, and made darker by years of unrelenting sunlight. One could see the line of demarcation caused probably by the collar of a military tunic. His eyes were that light and startling shade of twilight, and his black hair was close cut and fine as Japanese silk. In profile, the fine, chiseled bones of his face reminded me of Etruscan or Greek statues. There was strength, intelligence and courage, but something not quite…regular. I judged him oversensitive, of a strongly nervous temperament and, despite his quite evident discipline, a frequent victim of his own sensual impulses.

I deplore these latter traits in a man, and yet, against my will, I was softened. "Why have I received such an invitation?" I asked. "What do you want of me?"

"I—we—think you would be a valuable addition to the society."

"How so?"

His grin was unexpected and engaging. "For one thing, you're an outsider. That's useful just now."

"Is it?" I said dryly.

"For another…" He hesitated, then seemed to come to a decision. "Scrymgeour's man Seymour mentioned that you've got something of a reputation as a sleuth."

"*What?*" I gaped at him.

"It's true, isn't it? You solved the matter of that char woman who murdered her husband by beating him over the head with a leg of lamb?"

I felt myself turning red. "Well, but. Well, I wouldn't make too much of *that*." The matter had done nothing to improve my professional standing. Not that I cared about that. "I had the advantage in that both husband and wife were my patients."

Maxwell shrugged. "You like mysteries, Doctor. Your bookshelf is filled with the works of Fergus Hume and Arthur Conan Doyle. You're good at puzzles—and we need someone good at puzzles."

"As of late, my aptitude for puzzles would seem to be overstated," I groused.

Maxwell's mouth twitched as though he found that funny but was too polite to laugh in my face.

I said, "And what should I gain from membership in this society as far as profit or pleasure?"

"Association with like-minded people."

"No. I doubt that."

Maxwell studied me. "May I speak freely?"

I raised a quizzical eyebrow, but he answered seriously, almost earnestly.

"I believe that you're a man of education and imagination. I think you're bored, even stifled in your present limited circumstances, and that a small adventure would not come amiss."

"You're a plain speaker, sir," I said after an affronted moment.

"As are you, sir."

"You've no idea what sort of man I am," I said. "Come to me again, if you can face placing yourself under the care of a physician. In the meantime, I shall be making more inquiries about *you,* Captain Maxwell." It was not tactful, but I was weary of fencing with him, and two people had already bumped against me in entering the shop.

Maxwell laid a hand on my arm, and an uncommonly strong hand I felt it to be. It was impossible to get away without making more fuss than I cared to make while the young person behind the counter kept an eye on us.

He said, "I believe I know this much about you, Armiston. If you understood what was at stake, you'd at least consider our invitation. I think if you refuse now, and get to know about it later, you'll regret it as long as you live." He added gravely, "That is, if you're the sort of man we take you to be. I can't tell you anything more unless you join."

I was nettled at his many assumptions. Nay, presumptions. But I can't deny I was intrigued too. Not least by the promise of getting to know the handsome and irritating Captain Maxwell better.

I said grudgingly, "Very well. I'll consider all you've said."

"Excellent." He was smiling again. I suspected he had broken many a heart with that deadly combination of boyish grin and steely resolve. "Come to the next meeting, for which you'll get a card—and after that we can speak frankly."

He gripped my hand very firmly, and went away without any more ado. I felt the warm pressure of his fingers for some time after.

CHAPTER EIGHT

HIGH SOCIETY!

The next day I found another cream envelope among my letters. Inside was a printed card, with the colored stamp of the Atef crown crossed with a crook and flail upon it:

> Your attendance is requested at the next
>
> meeting of the Society of Osiris to be held at. . .

Then followed the address of a great lady, and the time, 10 p.m.

I confess a frisson of excitement rippled down my spine.

On the date named for a meeting of the society, I had a note from Captain Maxwell, saying that he proposed to himself the pleasure of calling upon me at about 9.30 p.m., and of accompanying me to the meeting as sponsor.

It is embarrassing to admit I felt greater anticipation for the thirty minutes to be spent in Maxwell's company than I did for the evening's festivities, but that's the truth.

In any case, it was Perceval who arrived. He explained Maxwell had been detained until later by duty. I feared I knew what that duty was—Maxwell's taskmaster was a remorseless one—but thanked Perceval for his company.

His smile was tinged with irony. "I can't pretend to be as gallant a companion as Max, but at least I know the way."

Ten minutes' stroll was enough to take us to our rendezvous, one of the big houses whose fine grounds and high walls would delude anyone into supposing London to be miles away—were it not for the unceasing low roar of traffic outside those imposing barriers.

I shall resist revealing the name of our impressive hostess for the evening. While she was not in costume—to my relief, no one was dressed in costume—she wore a white diaphanous gown that somehow conveyed the spirit of antiquity while sacrificing nothing of contemporary fashion. She beamed graciously upon me from a height which seemed some inches greater than my own and said she hoped I would not find the poor little Society too frivolous.

Uncomfortably, I wondered how much of our discussion Maxwell had shared with his fellow members, but before I could disclaim their frivolity or my own pretensions to learning, she turned away to greet someone else.

"Come and let me introduce you to some of the others," Perceval said, with a finger on my sleeve.

We had crossed the room, and were now standing near a good-looking, gray-mustached man, who was pretty obviously a soldier, and whose face seemed familiar to me.

"Ah. We'll have to wait our chance," Perceval murmured. "Once the admiral and Maundeville begin arguing over the role of free will in the modern military—"

"*Admiral?*" I repeated. "Is that—?"

Perceval smiled at my shock. "You really do have us pegged for a confederacy of fools and fakes, don't you?"

I reddened guiltily. "Not at all!"

"Anyway, the other man is Maundeville. He was Max's and my tutor at Oxford. He's a charming fellow. Like yourself, a scholar and philosopher, completely without ambition."

I began to splutter at this description of myself. Perceval ignored me. "Maundeville is really the one who started all this."

Maundeville, I thought with a start. The name on the mummy case. The person to whom the Mummy was being returned following the tragedy at Dene Court.

"But I suppose you have questions as to what 'all this' really is? Let's sit here." Perceval led me to a settee close at hand, and not far from the big wood-fire.

The room we sat in was one of a suite of three. There was little furniture. Just a few chairs and settees in elegant dark wood and white brocade. The draperies were a deep red velvet. Two large fires burned at either end, and members sat and chatted in small groupings.

From our vantage point we were able to observe the two men in animated discussion. The admiral, who was unexpectedly short, but carried himself with an easy nonchalance, stood with his back to the fire, on a white bearskin, warming his coattails and listening to Maundeville talking with tremendous vigor and fluency, and with somewhat emphatic but not awkward gestures.

Maundeville was tall, muscular and vigorous. His clean-shaven face was well-tanned. He seemed never at rest while talking, and when he laughed, as he did once or twice, he showed remarkably good teeth. His hair was gray but very thick, and curled slightly though close cut. His face was full of good nature, and his blue eyes sparkled with lively intelligence. I decided I did not resent the comparison.

"What sort of club is this exactly?" I watched more people gradually drift into the drawing room. There seemed to me to be more women than men, and I was reminded of descriptions of salons during that period in French history before the Revolution really gained momentum and heads started to roll.

"I suppose in some ways we're simply a social club," Perceval admitted. "Perhaps the rest of it is merely an excuse for getting together with those who don't otherwise quite…"

Fit.

He didn't have to finish it. It was already obvious to me. This was an egalitarian gathering of members from vastly different strata of society, all mingling as though nothing could be more natural than that an Oxford don and vice admiral should debate such concepts as responsibility and guilt in the drawing room of a duchess, who was herself engaged in deep conversation with—unless I was very mistaken—the young owner of the fashionable flower shop situated at the corner of Piccadilly.

"We meet once a fortnight during the season, at the house of any member who offers to receive us. A list of such houses is kept, and they are taken in rotation. Our rules are very few. The essential one is that both our meetings and our membership are kept quite secret. No, a better word is private. No one may join except through invitation, and at least two existing members must agree to sponsor the initiate."

"Your friend Scrymgeour was a member of this society?"

His smile was approving. "He was."

"Where does Osiris come into it?" I inquired.

"Well…" Perceval cast me a sideways look. "What do you know of ancient Egypt, Doctor Armiston? Are you, by chance, a student of Egyptology?"

I said, "I've read Mr. Hume's *The Green Mummy.* I'm afraid that's the extent of my knowledge of mummies."

At the word *mummy*, Perceval winced ever so slightly. He looked about, hesitated a moment, and went on in a lower tone, "Maundeville is one of the foremost experts on Egyptology in this country. Possibly in the world. Believe it or not, at one time both Max and I considered following in his footsteps."

Captain Maxwell an Egyptologist! I must have shown my surprise.

Maundeville had bowed and turned away, leaving the admiral looking thoughtfully after him. Perceval took me to him and introduced me formally.

Sadly, I remember very little of that conversation—only that the admiral spoke to me with an informal friendliness, as though I were both an equal and a longtime associate.

"Maundeville is taking young D'Aurelle's death very much to heart," he said to Perceval at last. "Of course his hopes for this next expedition were pinned on the boy."

"We all feel it deeply," Perceval agreed, with what seemed to be a sideways look in my direction.

"Not perhaps the most intellectually gifted fellow, but a fine sportsman."

"Yes," Perceval agreed. "He had a wonderful seat."

"Well, he's none too pleased with me at the moment," the admiral admitted. "Maundeville, that is. I told him I thought he was too old to set off on another of these junkets and he ought to give the idea up."

"*Oh?*" Perceval said rather faintly.

"*Oh,*" the admiral repeated firmly and laughed at whatever he read in Perceval's expression. He then nodded to us, and turned to speak to a lady who was passing.

"What was that about?" I asked Perceval.

He grimaced. "Maundeville is afraid the Americans are going to take over the grave-robbing business."

I opened my mouth, but before I could ask the obvious question, Perceval cut me off with a quick, "You're now a recognized member and need no further introduction to anyone here. Will you excuse me for a moment? There's someone I wish to speak to."

"Of course."

The someone was a newcomer, a tall, fair girl—taller than any other woman in the room—and more conspicuous because of the heavy masses of copper-red hair in which emeralds flickered like forest fire. Her dress was shimmering green, and a necklace and pendant of emeralds hung about her neck.

I stood alone, watching Perceval chatting with the girl. Recognized member or not, I felt out of my depth.

"I'm afraid I stood you up earlier." A familiar voice spoke from beside me. "I apologize. I was unavoidably detained."

I turned to find Captain Maxwell smiling at me. Despite the smile, he did look genuinely contrite.

"It's of no consequence."

I *had* been disappointed earlier, but that's because I was a fool. And I was a greater fool for the way my heart jumped in happy surprise at the sight of him. Still, there was no denying that something about him stood out from all the rest. He was handsome, yes, but it was rather more than that. He was a forceful and appealing presence—and judging by the veiled looks of a number of ladies, I was not the only one who thought so.

Maxwell held my gaze quite sincerely, and I was forced to look away lest he see too much.

Neither of us said anything for a long moment. The unexpected thought occurred to me that he was uncertain of how to proceed—and not used to the feeling.

I decided to go to his rescue. "Now there," I said, watching Perceval speaking eagerly to the red-haired girl, "is a young lady who looks more like the ideal heroine in a romance novel than anyone I've seen yet."

"Romance novels? I thought you were a reader of mysteries, Doctor Armiston," Maxwell said with friendly mockery.

"Solve this one for me. Who's the girl?"

A flash of irritation seemed to cross Maxwell's face. He gave a short, unamused laugh. "What! You too?"

"Now, what the devil do you mean by 'you too'?" I wondered aloud. "Though I'm not surprised to hear that other folk agree with me. She's handsomer than any princess I've happened to look at."

Again his laugh was not entirely genuine. "Well spotted. She's an American though her father traces his descent from one of the Seven Kings of Ulster. I've heard him tell her she could meet royalty on equal terms. That is Miss Nora Hennessey, a third cousin of Perceval's."

While we watched, the girl left Perceval and went on into another room, bowing here and there as she passed.

Maxwell excused himself and limped over to Perceval, who was looking rather put out. Maxwell's appearance did not seem to cheer him any.

I had no further opportunity to observe them because I was joined then by Professor Maundeville.

"It's Doctor Armiston, is it not?" he said cordially. "Maxwell told me you might join us this evening. Delighted to meet a fellow medical man."

I was surprised to hear this, as my understanding was Maundeville's interest was in humans well past the aid of tinctures and tonics. I said so, which seemed to amuse him.

"I never practiced," Maundeville admitted, "but studied in London and Paris. I know a good many of the Vienna men too. Fascinating field, of course, but I…found I had no stomach for other people's pain."

We chatted for a few minutes. Maundeville kept nodding to men or bowing to women all the time we spoke. He knew everybody and commented on his fellow members with a friendly cynicism. I decided this was a man who understood human nature very well and forbore to judge. I liked him at once.

I think perhaps he felt the same for after a brief lull in our conversation, he said suddenly, "I believe you gave evidence at the inquest for poor Scrymgeour?"

"Yes."

"I'm a little concerned—"

He broke off as Maxwell crossed the room to rejoin us.

"Well, Professor, I suppose you're busy taking away our characters?" the younger man said with hard cheerfulness. "So I needn't apologize for interrupting."

Maundeville looked him over with a critical eye. "Burning the candle at both ends again, Hilary? I've seen you looking better, my boy." Without waiting for a reply, he turned to me. "It's time to prepare for this evening's talk. It's been a great pleasure, Doctor. I look forward to future chats."

He departed, and I turned a professional eye on Maxwell, this time taking note of his flushed cheeks and too-bright eyes. Sadly, not all of that vitality and charisma was natural.

"Are you enjoying yourself, Doctor Armiston?" Maxwell inquired, meeting my gaze steadily.

Upon consideration, I *was* enjoying myself and admitted it. "I'm still confused however, as to why I'm here," I told him. "If I'm to play sleuth, you should at least give me a clue as to whom—or what—you wish me to investigate."

"For the time being just observe and consider. It'll be very helpful to have your unbiased impressions of this evening."

"Very well." I still felt doubtful.

He smiled faintly. "You don't trust easily, do you?"

"Would I be of use to you if I did?"

Maxwell opened his mouth and then laughed. "Well, if you put it that way, no. I suppose not. Maundeville will be speaking soon. You won't want to miss that. I suggest you find a seat in the innermost room, by the fire."

He left me again, and I went slowly through the little knots of talkers in the middle room, recognizing more than one famous face and wondering what some journalists would give to be here in attendance, before passing at length into the innermost room.

It was about the same size as the outer ones, and a small string-band was playing softly. Though the instruments were the usual thing, the music itself was quite unusual. Folk music perhaps—and therefore probably Egyptian—but the combination of western instruments and eastern melody created something new and sophisticated.

Or so it seemed to me.

I spotted the American girl, Miss Hennessey. She stood beside the fireplace, staring down into the fire, with one green-shod foot on the fender, her elbow on the mantelpiece, her pretty chin on her hand.

I fancied she was listening to the fiddles and did not like to disturb her. I'm not sure what it was about her I found so interesting. Petticoats were not much in my line, but she was not easily dismissed. I found a seat nearby where I could observe her without being observed myself.

I watched the point of her small green shoe tapping the fender, and I noticed a long slender hand, with three fine rings on it, gripping the mantelpiece hard. I wondered what lay behind this display of nervous tension.

The room began to fill, and a few moments later Professor Maundeville appeared and began to speak.

"While it's true that there was significant distinction between the legal status of women in the Old Kingdom and their public or social status, we mustn't underestimate how advanced Egyptian society was in its regard for women as equal or superior to men. Whether unmarried, married, divorced—yes, my friends, *divorced*—or widowed, the legal status of Egyptian women was nearly identical with that of Egyptian men."

This statement was greeted with quiet applause.

Maundeville continued to talk about the role of women in that suffragist paradise of ancient Egypt for some forty-five minutes, during which I had much to think about, though little of it had to do with women, living or dead.

When Maundeville's talk ended, I rose and left the room. In the middle drawing-room Maxwell and Perceval converged quietly on me from different places.

"Well? What do you think?" Perceval asked.

"I think Maundeville is a fine speaker."

"Never mind Maundeville!"

Maxwell threw him a quick, rather irritated look.

I said, "May I ask a question?"

"Of course," Maxwell said.

"Was Hugh D'Aurelle a member of this club?"

Perceval glanced instinctively at Maxwell. Maxwell answered, "He was. Yes."

"I see. Now, unless there's any particular reason why I shouldn't leave, I'm going back to my rooms for a smoke."

"It was extremely good of you to come," Perceval said politely.

"Can we walk back with you?" Maxwell asked.

I declined their company, bowed to my hostess, who had clearly forgotten me already, and went away.

When I got back to my room I sat by the fire for some time.

I could hardly fail to miss the connection that two men had died while a mummy sarcophagus had been in their homes and that both gentlemen had been members of a "society" that devoted itself to the study of ancient Egypt.

It was a puzzle—and a worrisome puzzle at that. And yet the greatest puzzle to me was handsome and enigmatic Captain Maxwell.

CHAPTER NINE

I PROCEED WITH CAUTION

I was late at breakfast again, and was still sitting at the table at ten o'clock, turning over my letters and trying to choke off Bird, who was telling me—as if I hadn't heard the story many times—why he had joined the Marines. (It was, by the way, a girl. It nearly always is.)

Then the bell rang and Bird went out, and came back to say that Captain Maxwell and Mr. Perceval wanted me to fix any time convenient for an appointment with them that day.

My pulse jumped. *Ah ha! The game is afoot!*

But I was honest enough to admit it was not merely the thought of the "game" that caused me to brush hastily at the crumbs on my shirt and glance in the mirror to make sure my hair was not sticking on end.

"Put them into the consulting-room," I said, and joined them a few minutes later.

The two had seated themselves. Maxwell greeted me with a friendly nod and that quick grin. Perceval inquired after my health and apologized for the early intrusion.

"I can't help wondering whether you young fellows pester all your acquaintances as you do me," I said ungraciously, for I didn't like the fact that I was so pleased to see them.

"You're not so much older than us, you know," Maxwell said.

"I'm old enough to be your father."

He raised his brows in a display of unfilial skepticism.

Perceval stayed on point. "We wanted to be sure of catching you," he said. "We know your practice keeps you a busy man."

"It does. So you had best get to the reason for your call."

Maxwell began by saying that he wanted to clear the ground, and to do it he meant to speak quite plainly.

"It's not our intention to be rude. Indeed, our intention is complimentary."

I said mildly, "This sounds rather alarming. Proceed."

He laughed easily. I was beginning to look forward to that sound.

"You've told us you're a busy man," he said, "but our impression is your patients are not wealthy and perhaps even fail to pay you sometimes."

"We believe you're relatively poor," Perceval remarked.

Maxwell cast him a look of exasperation.

"The doctor appreciates the direct approach," Perceval said. "Isn't that true, Doctor Armiston?"

I conceded this was true.

Perceval said, "What my friend is hemming and hawing over is we think you might welcome a commission that would not require a great deal of time or effort on your part but would pay well. This is a professional matter, you see, and we want you to deal with it on that basis. We're comparatively rich beggars; aren't we, Max?"

"You are," Maxwell agreed cheerfully.

Perceval nodded and admired his boutonniere.

"What is the commission?" I asked.

Maxwell said, "It has to do with Scrymgeour, and D'Aurelle, and the Mummy."

I was expecting something along that line. I nodded noncommittally.

"You're already intrigued by our little mystery," Maxwell said, "but you won't get far solving it alone. Whereas we…"

He seemed to change his mind.

"Well, what?"

He said rather strangely, "We're too close to the thing. We must have help."

Perceval said, "You've probably already guessed Maxwell and I were at Dene Court when D'Aurelle died. We made them call you down."

He was wrong. I had not guessed. Not anticipated this at all. "You were both there? Why didn't you— Why did you—?"

I hardly knew where to begin. It seemed an extraordinary confession and seemed to set the whole case on its head.

Case? Now I was having delusions of grandeur. I was not even Doctor Watson, let alone the great detective Holmes.

Perceval said, "Why did we send for you? You were already mixed up in poor S.'s affair, and we felt you handled yourself well. Didn't we, Max?"

Maxwell assented.

There was an innocence to their arrogance, and I knew they meant this to be some sort of compliment. I restrained myself to a noncommittal grunt.

"What do you say?" Maxwell asked. "Will you help us?"

"What exactly is it you want me to do?"

Perceval smiled. I didn't quite trust that smile. "It's very simple really. We want you to hold yourself in readiness to go again to any patient whom we ask you to see, say during the next six months, and to take such hints as we may suggest for helping you to understand the cases. We propose offering you a retaining fee of five hundred pounds."

"*Five hundred...*"

"Guineas," Maxwell suggested.

"I forgot," Perceval said. "Of course, you doctors always count in guineas. I beg your pardon. Guineas it is. You mentioned that you've not studied Egyptology, but do you object to participating in the meetings of the Society of Osiris and getting to know better some of us who *have* been studying such things?"

I sat back in my chair and considered them both attentively before I answered. They were quite serious.

"I've no objection to expanding my learning on any subject," I said. "But you must realize how very odd this proposal is. On top of which, I know practically nothing about either of you."

This seemed to offend them both.

"It's not as though we're—we're—" Maxwell could not seem to decide what it was they were not.

"You'd know a good deal if you used your wits," Perceval said. "And you can learn more if you make inquiries."

Maxwell added, "After all, we aren't trying to *borrow* five hundred guineas, are we?"

"No." I allowed that. "But you must realize how…extraordinary this is. I'm still unclear what it is you expect me to do—let alone how this will help you."

"I give you my word," Maxwell said, "that if you stick to the job and try to explain certain things, even without succeeding, you'll most likely have earned the fee twice over before you've done. Perceval agrees."

To illustrate this, Perceval fished out a check book and began to write an order on Coutts.

I stopped him. "I don't deny that I enjoy a good mystery, but this is something different. You're suggesting—well, I'm not even sure what you're suggesting, and I'm not sure you are either. I can't promise anything definitely. But I'll consider your proposal and I'll take you up on your invitation to conduct my own inquiries into you both."

Maxwell began, "Oh, but that's not *exactly*—"

I rose. "And now you must excuse me. As you've mentioned, I'm a busy man with a living to earn. I can't spend the entire day chatting about mysteries and mummies. Not that we've yet spoken of the Mummy. It seems a strange oversight to me."

They exchanged quick, alarmed glances.

"Good day, gentlemen."

They didn't like it, but they had no choice in the matter and, with an effort at good grace, departed.

Now I'm old enough to have met blackguards in all ranks and classes; but wealthy blackguards of good family don't work in couples, according to my experience. So I hunted up the genealogist and *flâneur* of my club, and casually mentioned Perceval's and Maxwell's names.

Maxwell he knew slightly, and said he had been recommended for the VC, "and no one except the War Office quite knew why he didn't get it. Don't suppose the Johnnies up top know either."

I had my own thoughts on the matter, but merely looked politely interested in this information.

Perceval, my friend knew hardly at all. "Not easy to meet, either, don't you know. A trifle exclusive, like most of these quiet fellows with a peerage ahead of 'em."

The result of this tentative inquiry was that as far as the bona fides of these two were concerned, I was safe.

They had made no attempt to deceive me, and I could not see how their effort to retain my services could be viewed as bribery.

I decided to let matters rest until I had heard what more they meant to tell me.

A couple of days later I had a note from Perceval telling me that the Society of Osiris was to next meet at his house on the following Saturday evening at nine.

I sent a note to Perceval saying that I would be there.

CHAPTER TEN

Of Dreams and Desires

By now it was late in March, and the weather so bleak and damp that even a dull evening by one's own fireside at night was more tempting than any outside engagement.

Sitting at dinner the night of the meeting, and listening to Bird reliving his military exploits as he served me, I was tempted to let Maxwell, Perceval and the entire Society of Osiris go to Colney Hatch or the devil en masse.

It seemed to me, looking at Bird's pale, expressionless face while he carelessly referred to some highly improbable adventure with a former *mousmé*, that I was behaving like a complete and utter fool. I was too old for mysteries, too old for secret societies, and far too old and set in my ways for...well, improbable adventures. Especially when the improbable adventures I would have chosen were the kind of thing that could get a man locked up.

Or worse.

Nor was there the slightest reason for believing that my feelings—the very word made me uneasy—were returned. I could not but help remember Captain Maxwell's annoyance when I had praised the red-haired Hennessey girl—and all those bunches of daffodils he had purchased in the little flower shop.

I wondered at myself as I stood in the damp, waiting for the taxicab that Bird whistled up. I had been specially reminded of my age that day, because the post had brought me the prospectus of a new scheme for the assurance of income in cases of total disablement. I read the confounded thing attentively, and then discovered, at the end, that fifty was the precise age at which the company refused fresh clients.

Confound them. And confound myself for caring about such things!

Perceval lived in a tall, narrow house in Park Lane with bow windows, green balconies and a white-painted front. Every window box was filled with pink ivy geranium left spilling untrained and ghostly in the firelight from within.

My host received me in a room with too many paintings—most featuring scantily clad maidens fleeing lions and lustful Romans—too many cushions and a good many cut chrysanthemums like small blazing suns in quaint glass vases.

He was quite alone. On a white rug lay, as if posed, a fine black Persian cat.

"Am I early?" I inquired.

Perceval waved the idea away. "Punctuality was not an ideal of the ancient Egyptians."

"We are not ancient Egyptians," I remarked. "I'm surprised you haven't noticed by now. Where did you and Maxwell develop this mania for ancient Egypt?"

"In school. Of course our mania, as you quaintly put it, for the Old Kingdom is more about what that world represents."

"And what does it represent?"

"Everything this world has failed to deliver." He winked as though we were sharing a private joke, but I suspected the joke was on me.

I had not previously given overly much thought to Perceval, but now I was inclined to consider him from a revised perspective. His politeness seemed almost exaggerated, his dress over-careful, his tastes feminine. His relationship with Maxwell was patently close, and yet I did not sense a rival in him. They seemed rather like brothers.

In fact, I had suspected Perceval's affections might lie in the direction of Miss Hennessey.

"One seldom sees that," I nodded at the cat, "in a man's room."

Perceval looked at me with the faintest of smiles. "You don't keep a cat?" he asked. "Let me introduce Bhanavar the Beautiful," and, stooping, he took the animal in his arms, where she rested, purring softly.

"I had dogs when I was a boy."

"Ah! Dogs are different, and I won't have another. They die, and you are miserable; or you die, and they are miserable, and perhaps neglected too. If Bhanavar the Beautiful died to-night, I should be sorry that a beautiful beast was gone to dust, but I shouldn't mourn overmuch. If I died, she wouldn't miss me. Being a valuable beast she'd find a new master or mistress to-morrow. Neither of us would suffer in any case." He gave me another of those faint smiles. "What do you think of my philosophy?"

I thought it—and him—somewhat glib. But I didn't say so.

"You seem to have a fancy for them, dead or alive," I said, and nodded at a very fine tiger-skin that was stretched in front of a settee. "You didn't kill that, I suppose?"

"A present from Maxwell," he said indifferently. "He must have been pleased with me at the time."

"Isn't he pleased with you now?"

Perceval's laugh was curt. "No. He's not."

I would have liked to hear more about that, but members of the society began to arrive and Perceval slipped instantly and easily into the role of attentive host.

I became aware of a quickening of my pulse. I knew that Maxwell would soon arrive and I was looking forward—too much!—to seeing him again.

But the minutes passed and Maxwell did not show.

It was a smaller group than the previous meeting, perhaps fifteen or sixteen members in all. I recognized some faces, though not all. The last guests to cross the threshold were Miss Hennessey and Professor Maundeville, who arrived together.

I stood beside Perceval, who introduced me as a new member of the society to each guest as they entered the room.

I was introduced to these last two in the same manner. Maundeville looked surprised when he found me at Perceval's side, but said cheerfully, "Then you've committed to us? I knew we were kindred souls, Doctor!"

Miss Hennessey smiled with great warmth. "I'm delighted to meet you. I've heard a great deal about you, Doctor Armiston."

She had? From whom?

I didn't quite know what to make of that. In any case, no response was required for she turned to Perceval and said, "Has Hilary arrived yet?"

"He's not coming," Perceval said. "He sent a note saying he's under the weather."

Her face fell—I expect mine did as well.

I recalled that I had been hired in my professional capacity only a few days earlier, and when Miss Hennessey moved off, I said to Perceval, "What's the matter with Maxwell?"

"That's an interesting question." His tone was acrid.

"Is he genuinely ill? Does he require a physician?"

He gave me a long and uncomfortably direct look. "If he does, he certainly knows who to send for."

The knowledge in his eyes made me uneasy, but it was the sudden hostility that raised the hair on my neck. Perhaps I had been wrong in my earlier assessment of the bond between Maxwell and his boyhood companion.

I offered a bland and meaningless smile in return, and moved away.

I don't remember much about that particular evening. I think disappointment over Maxwell shadowed all. As before there was music and exotic delicacies—cakes and puddings made of dates and rice milk and almonds as well as ingredients I didn't recognize—and there was the frank and open exchange of unorthodox ideas.

At some point Maundeville read a paper about the significance of dreams in Egyptian religion and philosophy.

"The ancients understood that in dreams, our eyes are opened to the truths we cannot see in daylight. The priests and priestesses who interpreted these dreams were known as 'Masters of the Secret Things.' Indeed, the very word *rswt* means 'to be awake.' The hieroglyph for dream represents an open eye."

I say that he read a paper, but he had nothing more to help him than a half-sheet of notes and was clearly speaking from a wealth of knowledge.

It was not merely mumbo-jumbo, though. The professor also spoke of recurring dreams, of the curious stimuli which in certain cases have been obviously responsible for dreams, or nightmares, and of those in which the imagination takes one to heights of ecstasy, never in all one's days reached while waking.

I looked about me, and thought I could see the memories of old dreams in the eyes of half a dozen near me. What was it these people hoped to find in their study of—near obsession with—a long dead civilization? I couldn't understand it.

At last Maundeville finished his talk, smiling at the enthusiastic applause he received. He sat down and picked up the black Persian from where she slept on the white rug.

The chat became general as the other members shared their thoughts on trance, sleep-walking, and hypnotism. A few people offered up their own experiences, relating stories that were poignant, peculiar, or laughable.

All the time I noticed that the lovely Miss Hennessey listened, sometimes with obvious interest, sometimes with none, but rarely spoke. Yet it was clear she was deeply involved in the society. I found her affiliation the most puzzling. She seemed too much a woman of her own era and too…well, *American* to be drawn into this strange pining for a world that I believed was more fantasy than actual history.

Presently someone referred to the topic of second-sight, and to my surprise, Maundeville turned to Perceval.

"Tell them," he said, "of Maxwell's experience in Egypt."

"It's not my story," Perceval said, with uncharacteristic brusqueness.

"Oh, do tell, Charlie," Miss Hennessey cried eagerly, and after a little more coaxing, Perceval spoke, not very willingly, and with scant detail.

According to his friend, Maxwell had been one of a large hunting party while on a fortnight's leave. One night at dinner he noticed a curious appearance of mist about the man sitting opposite. Maxwell dismissed it as a touch of liver—or that he had taken more wine than he had intended.

He couldn't help noticing though, that everyone else at the table was quite visible to him.

The next night his vis-à-vis was more obscured. And by the third night the fellow was wrapped in what seemed like a fog, right up to his mouth.

"What happened next?" Miss Hennessey demanded.

"The next morning Maxwell learned the man had been stabbed by his native servant as he entered his tent after leaving mess."

There were several gasps—largely of delight, I suspect.

"Of all people, it *would* be Max," Perceval added wryly. "He doesn't even believe in ghosts. To this day he still says he thinks it was a touch of the sun."

"A touch of something," Maundeville said quite seriously.

CHAPTER ELEVEN

ONCE UPON A TIME

When the last of his guests had said good night, Perceval turned to me and asked if I would like to examine the stars from his box seat.

As invitations went, it was an original one, but mostly I wanted a hot drink and my own warm bed. I was tired of the Society of Osiris, tired of Perceval, and most of all tired of myself for wanting things I could never have—and would not be good for me if I *could* have them.

But it occurred to me that Sherlock Holmes—even Doctor Watson—never chose their warm and comfortable beds over any invitation, and I went with Perceval in a lift up to his smoking-room.

This was a fair-sized square room, with an immense window on one side. We were so high up above the rooftops and chimney pots that lying back among the cushions and looking out, I saw nothing but the glittering stars in a black sky.

The room was pleasantly warm, and the floor was covered with a heavy Persian rug in rich jewel tones of sapphire and emerald and ruby. There was practically nothing in the place but low divans and smoking materials of all possible kinds. The walls were of a silvery watered silk, and at first seemed blank. But while we lounged and talked I found that they were covered with the faintest possible suggestion of face and figure. They were alive with those delicate things you may sometimes fancy you see in a smoke-cloud.

Perceval told me it was the inspiration of a friend who often sat there with him. Scrymgeour's work, I found out afterward.

I was looking at this queerly hypnotic decoration when Maxwell was announced.

Until that moment I had been feeling sleepy and a little out of sorts, wondering when I might decently excuse myself, but suddenly I was alight with energy and interest. I sat up straight and brushed a quick hand over my hair.

As far as I could tell, Maxwell looked perfectly well. He lowered himself efficiently if ungracefully to the cushion-strewn divan and laid his stick on the floor beside him. "Hello, Percy. I figured you'd be up here." He nodded to me. "Hello, Armiston."

"Hello, Max. Feeling better?" Perceval greeted him coolly.

"Yes. Much. Sorry for earlier."

Perceval said with just a tinge of malice, "Armiston was much concerned for you, Max."

Maxwell smiled at me. "Were you?"

I felt that the room was suddenly too warm and my collar far too tight. But I answered honestly, "Yes. I was." I added boldly. "I am."

I half expected he would take offense, but in fact, there was something vulnerable in the quick look he cast me.

A pause followed before we turned at once to topics less dangerous but in their own way equally fantastic.

"Maundeville droned on about dreams and visions again," Perceval said. "He made me trot out that old chestnut of yours. The story about your pig-sticking party."

Maxwell groaned and then turned to me. "You must have a ghost story or two, Armiston?"

"In my profession the objective is to have as few ghost stories as possible."

Maxwell was amused. "Share someone else's ghost story, then. Percy did."

"Nurses have the best ghost stories," I said, which is quite true. I proceeded to relate the story of an elderly patient who, in the final days of her life, seemed to spend most of her time watching and conversing with an invisible presence, who she finally identified as her late husband.

In the middle of my story—which, admittedly, was not terribly thrilling—Perceval interrupted and asked if I had any objection to staying the night.

"Your man can send things round, you know," he suggested. "Then you can get straight to your bed when we've done with you. There's a room ready. Max, you can have a room too."

My curiosity was roused, of course, but it seemed a strange and sudden invitation, and I hesitated.

"Stay," Max said quietly, holding my gaze.

My face warmed. For a moment it was as though we were alone in the room.

We were not, of course, and Perceval said, "Max and I have learned a few things since we last spoke. We think it's time we told you about the Mummy."

That snapped me back to reality. I said, "Then I'll certainly stay."

Perceval telephoned instructions to the servants' quarters. I settled back among the large velvet cushions to smoke, opposite my two companions, who began to tell me about the Mummy.

"After all, I don't want to exaggerate the importance of what we've learned," Perceval said, in answer to a look of Maxwell's. "But the more you know, the better able you'll be to help us."

"It sounds reasonable enough."

"It all began with Maundeville," Perceval went on, "although he claims that his interest is altogether psychological. But it was a story of his that began the trouble. At least…it's not entirely a story. The Mummy is real enough."

"I'm afraid I don't follow."

Maxwell said, "Percy and I have known Maundeville since we were at Oxford."

"I told him all that," Perceval interrupted.

"Oh. Of course."

"I don't mind hearing it again," I said.

Maxwell smiled, and I was uncomfortably aware that he probably understood me all too well. "It's only that originally the society consisted of Maundeville and a few students."

"His favorites," Perceval put in. "Like Max. But then Max is everyone's favorite."

Maxwell ignored that. "But later it grew into something quite a bit more…larger and…perhaps meaningful."

Perceval yawned. "Speaking of meaningful, old boy, will you never come to the point? The fact of the matter is the society grew well beyond old Maundeville. In fact, he hadn't attended a meeting in years—"

"He was in Egypt!"

"What does it matter where he was? He was no longer a regular member of the society even if he had started the thing. It took on a life of its own. And speaking of a life of its own, who should show up one night just when we happened to be discussing the Evil Eye." Perceval's smile was sarcastic.

"The Evil Eye?"

"That's the sort of thing we had descended to, minus the great man's leadership."

Maxwell said, "Of course none of us had the slightest belief in it. The Evil Eye, I mean, except that we all agreed harm might be done to the superstitious through suggestion."

"You mean *you* had not the slightest belief in it," Perceval said. "Or claim not to. After the meeting ended, half a dozen of us men went to Maundeville's house for a smoke, and got him to talk about his discoveries. It was a bit like old times." He smiled at Maxwell and Maxwell smiled back.

"Yes."

"He showed us a few small things, and then someone—"

"Scrymgeour," Maxwell supplied.

"Maybe it was Scrymgeour, reminded the professor of the evening's discussion. He started laughing and said the Evil Eye was nothing compared to the curse that had landed on him."

I must have stiffened or started to speak, because Maxwell said softly, "*Now* you're interested."

It was the truth.

Perceval continued with the story. "According to Maundeville, he'd discovered a very old and very mysterious tomb while excavating a hundred miles or so east of Luxor. Now, all tombs are old and mysterious, so the fact that his men fled when they saw the markings on this particular inner chamber door is *perhaps* significant."

"What kind of markings were they?"

Perceval spread his hands. "No one knew at the time. A warning, of course. All the tombs are marked with warnings. But along with the hieroglyphics were paintings of blue beetles. *Scarabaeus sacer.* Egyptian beetles."

They were waiting for me to say something. I said cautiously, "Like the jewelry."

"Yes," said Maxwell.

"No," said Perceval. "Or yes. But no. The amulets you're thinking of are New Kingdom and this tomb was Old Kingdom. Or earlier."

"It can't be earlier," Maxwell objected.

"From an age of magic *before* history."

Maxwell groaned. "Don't say such utter rot."

Perceval laughed. "That's what Maundeville's men told him before they ran away. Maundeville had to open the tomb with a friend."

"What friend?"

"He's not part of this story," Maxwell assured me. "In any case, he's dead now. That's where this nonsense about the curse began."

"Am I telling the story or you?" Perceval inquired.

"You."

"I wish you could hear *him* tell it. It gave me the creeps when he talked about the sighing sand and the perfect silence and cold wind that rose up from nowhere, rustling their maps and sketches."

I was getting the creeps without any help from Maundeville.

Perceval's voice sank to something just over a whisper. "On the floor of the burial-chamber lay the bodies of four young girls in perfect preservation—though they crumbled away at a touch."

"Probably poisoned," Maxwell remarked. "You see a lot of that in the Orient."

Perceval ignored that prosaic interruption. "The sarcophagus was not remarkable except for its age and the firmness with which the stone was sealed down—that seal carried the blue scarab too. Now here's one of the strangest parts of the story. When Maundeville first tried to read the warning curses inscribed on the sarcophagus, he couldn't. The writing was too archaic. But when he relit his lantern—which had suddenly blown out—he could read the warning. It was written in the much simplified glyph of the New Kingdom."

They waited for my reaction. I said, "Then I can only surmise the poor light confused the professor for a few moments—perhaps because of the faked writing on the outside of the tomb."

"*Faked!*" they cried in unison.

"Of course. What other explanation can there be? The tomb was doctored to look much older than it was."

"Maundeville would know if the tomb had previously been opened. And had it been discovered, it *would* have been opened," Maxwell said. "Opened and plundered."

"What did the curse say?" I asked, unconvinced by his reasoning.

"A priestess of Khepri lay buried there and not to open the sarcophagus on pain of death. Inside the sarcophagus lay a wooden coffin with the figure of the priestess in her robes painted on it. The borders were painted with gold and blue symbols. Reeds and beetles. At each of the four corners of the coffin lay a canopic jar, and on the top lay a papyrus roll on which was written—also in hieratic script:

> "I am the last priestess of Khepri. Thou who
> hast disturbed me, a dead woman, and broken
> the seals, and weakened my Ka—behold my Ka
> shall follow thee, and shall see Justice through
> a woman; thou shalt know Hell before Death;
> and the hand, that broke the seals of Sleep and
> of Silence, shall bring Death to thee also."

"I'm paraphrasing, of course," Perceval added.

I didn't quite know what to say. For all its inconsistencies, it was certainly an astonishing—and effective—story.

Maxwell picked up the tale and I listened carefully, watching the shadow of firelight on his mobile face.

"When we asked what he'd done with the Mummy, Maundeville acknowledged it was actually there in his house."

"Here? He brought it home to England?"

"Yes."

"Wouldn't want the Americans to nab it," Perceval put in.

Maxwell continued as though there had been no interruption, "We pressured him, of course, and he finally agreed to show it to us. He got Scrymgeour and young D'Aurelle to carry the mummy case to the dining-room and place it on the table."

He stopped, looking uncomfortable at some memory.

The long and the short of it was, despite his guests' requests to open the inner case, Maundeville refused. And none too politely. He insisted that it was a job for experts and not ignoramuses.

The men sat around and smoked, and speculated about the Mummy: its probable appearance, its age at death, and other possibilities connected with it. It all sounded harmless enough to me, though perhaps Egyptian ladies were sensitive about these things.

Eventually Maundeville left the room to get another bottle—you would have thought a college don would know better—and two of the younger men set about trying to pry the lid off the mummy case.

"Which two men?" I asked.

"Scrymgeour and D'Aurelle," Maxwell said. "D'Aurelle was drunk and Scrymgeour…"

"Above himself," Perceval said coldly.

I asked, "How so?"

It was Maxwell who answered. "He thought he had gone one better than the rest of them—us—that night, poor chap!"

"What did the rest of you do when Scrymgeour and D'Aurelle opened the coffin?" I asked.

"They didn't get it open," Perceval said. "Not all the way. But close enough, I suppose, from the perspective of the supernatural. Anyway, there we all were, fighting over the thing, when Maundeville returned to the room. When he saw what we'd done, he nearly fainted."

Maxwell said, "That brought everyone back to their senses rather quickly. Maundeville was absolutely stricken at the destruction of such a valuable artifact."

"It was more than that. He was afraid," Perceval said.

Maxwell did not comment on that. "Scrymgeour offered to purchase the Mummy from him, but Maundeville wouldn't consider it. He said that every single person who'd had anything to do with it since it was yanked out of the desert had suffered very bad luck."

"Very bad luck as in—?"

"Death," Perceval said gloomily. "Disaster. Mostly death."

"Everyone except Maundeville," Maxwell said.

"And why is he immune to the curse?"

They both shrugged like the schoolboys they'd once been.

"It seems a little suspicious," I remarked, although really I couldn't see what benefit Maundeville would reap from killing off members of his own social club.

"Maundeville's theory is he's taken on the role of protector to the priestess. It's true that he took her out of the desert, but perhaps she wanted that," Perceval said. "He didn't open her coffin—clearly she *doesn't* want that."

"This is nonsense," I said impatiently. "Surely neither of you believe—"

"Of course not," Maxwell said. "But the thing is we were all rather the worse for wear that night."

"Drunk as lords," Perceval said succinctly.

"And we agreed that the best thing to do would be to-to dilute the power of the curse by splitting it up amongst ourselves. Since we were all partly to blame."

The candle flames jumped, and I shivered at a sudden cold draft from the window behind me. "What does *that* mean?"

They explained—sheepishly. It had ended in the small hours with a bizarre scene. The men joined hands round the table on which the mummy case lay and agreed to share equally the guilt of disturbing the slumbers of Khepri's priestess. To try to alleviate some of the otherworld ire, each man agreed to host the Mummy in his own home for a fortnight in turn."

I groaned, listening to this idiocy, but restrained myself to asking, "How did you choose the order?"

"Scrymgeour suggested we should decide by the Tarot. Maundeville is an expert on divination cards, and it was agreed that he should be the dealer. The High Priestess card was chosen to represent the Mummy."

I said, "I take it Scrymgeour was first to draw the High Priestess?"

"Yes. You know the rest," Maxwell said.

I snorted. "You think so?"

"Well, mostly. A few nights after Scrymgeour's funeral we all met again, discussed the matter, and again tried the cards. This time the Priestess went to D'Aurelle. And you know the result of that," Maxwell said.

"I know what followed," I allowed. "But you've got to remember *post hoc ergo propter hoc*. Still, it's a strange business. There's no denying that. How do I fit into it?"

"The business has to go on, of course," Maxwell said. "We want you to watch it and solve it, if you can."

"I can't agree that it's got to go on," I said. "The thing is brutal. You've no right to be playing tricks with a woman's body, whether she has been dead an hour or ten thousand years. *Why* should you go on?"

Perhaps I spoke harshly. A sharp and startled silence followed my words.

"Are we to take it you're contemplating backing out after having already given your word?" Perceval inquired haughtily.

"It should be obvious we consider this a debt of honor. Indeed, unless that's *quite* plain to you, I think maybe you shouldn't go further into the affair."

"I don't require your permission as to whether or not to go further," I said coldly, "but if you'd like to leave me to do so independently, you can."

Perceval opened his mouth to respond, but Maxwell, who had sat watching us both, spoke up.

"Stop there, both of you!" he said. "If you don't, you'll be saying more than you intend. Percy, we told Armiston he could speak frankly."

Perceval looked sulky but did not argue.

"Armiston, we've told you most of it. If the matter is too distasteful, then there's nothing more to be said. However, there's something more that might alter your feelings. What Perceval and I are really anxious about is that Miss Hennessey has got mixed up in this miserable business. That was a large part of our decision to bring you into it—and it's the best possible reason for keeping things quiet."

Miss Hennessey. I had wondered when she would make an appearance.

At that, Perceval leaned across and said he was sorry if his manner had been offensive, and that he agreed with me the thing was brutal.

I acknowledged that I might have been more tactful. "Now, what about Miss Hennessey?"

"She was first," Maxwell answered, "to find Scrymgeour after his death. No one knows that but Perceval and I. And Scrymgeour's man."

"What on earth was the girl doing there at that time of the morning?"

Perceval looked incensed all over again. Maxwell threw him a warning look. "As you know, Miss Hennessey is American."

"What has that to do with anything?"

"Only that she's very…impulsive, and is quite unable to understand the ordinary point of view, or, at any rate, to bother about it. She does not feel constrained by the normal rules of polite society."

"Nora is above reproach," Perceval said.

"Yes, of course." Maxwell looked a little impatient. "But that doesn't mean she won't be…won't suffer the reproaches of those more narrow in attitudes and of limited imagination."

"*Limited* imagination will not be the problem," I said.

"She was there to breakfast with Scrymgeour and discuss plans for a suffrage hike. They've had some success with them in the States. Miss Hennessey is an ardent supporter of woman's suffrage, and Scrymgeour felt strongly on the subject as well."

Perceval snorted.

"When Miss Hennessey arrived at the Albany, Seymour knew nothing of the proposed breakfast and said that it was past Scrymgeour's usual time for rising, but had strict orders not to go into the room until he was rung for. Miss Hennessey thought this was ridiculous. She knocked several times, uselessly, of course, and then opened the door herself. She found Scrymgeour lying dead. Immediately she sent word to Perceval who sent word to me. That's everything really."

I suppose that very few stories can seem absolutely impossible to a medical man who has been long in practice, unless they involve, or seem to involve, the supernatural. Even then one must keep an open mind—the only scientific attitude. What seemed supernatural yesterday is possible to-day, and will be commonplace to-morrow.

The role apparently played by the Mummy was the only part of this convoluted story I jibbed at. The vagaries of pretty, head-strong women—and the utter gullibility of susceptible young men, I was ready to accept.

Perceval, seated with his legs curled under him on a divan, blew a couple of rings and waved them aside before he said, "Max thought you ought to be told the entire story, because we don't know what may be important in the puzzle. But you can see it's a matter that calls for the utmost delicacy."

"On that point, we agree," I said with some asperity. "At present I don't see any reason not to believe everything you've told me. In fact, I'm beginning to think it's only *too* believable. What to do about it, I don't know. I'm afraid we shall have to leave it there for the evening."

To my surprise, they were agreeable to this and kept me entertained very well till I chose to go to bed.

CHAPTER TWELVE

AN ALLIANCE IS FORMED

The next morning, after breakfasting with Perceval—disappointingly, Maxwell did not make an appearance—I walked back to my flat.

Within a few yards of home I saw a man turn out from the door, a card-case in his hand, step off the curb and briskly cross the street.

Professor Maundeville.

I wondered why he had chosen that hour to call—apparently he had been leaving a card on me; but I watched him cross without trying to stop him. It happened that I had one or two people to see that morning, mostly in neighboring mews—coachmen's children and the like—and after that I wanted time to myself. The startling revelations of the evening before had given me a great deal to mull over. I watched Maundeville avoid a stylish motor with a jump, good-humoredly snap a word at the occupant, and then safely reach the opposite side. Unfortunately, he turned, saw me at my door, and at once crossed back again.

I waited, thinking that if he followed me up the stair, it might be some time before I could get rid of him.

"What a beastly morning!" he said cheerfully, directly he was within speaking distance. "It reminds me of how much I miss Egypt. How do you keep warm? Let us get a little farther in."

The wind certainly was cutting, though the morning was rather bright, and I saw that he was wearing a fur-lined coat.

If I put on a thing like that, I feel like a fifth-rate actor. It suited Maundeville's rather dramatic looks quite well, though.

He looked at me, and then up the stair.

"I left a card for you," he said. "I wanted to see you. But perhaps it's inconvenient to have me up now?"

A private door connecting the passage in which we stood with the provision-dealer's shop under my rooms swung open for a moment, and a gust of warm air, scented with coffee, cloves and, I suppose, a lot of other things, drifted past us.

"Gad! That's good." Maundeville sniffed with enjoyment. "If one only got a whiff of the mews mixed up with this, one could almost forget this brutal English spring. It smells of the bazaar and the caravanserai."

I was amused, though I wasn't yet prepared to tackle the problem of the eccentric professor who had started this whole contretemps.

"Isn't it said that our climate makes us what we are?" I asked him.

"Yes! And what are we?" he retorted. "A dull, pigheaded, self-satisfied lot."

He sniffed again, reminiscently, and with a regretful shrug, muttering a word or two under his breath, which I thought might be Arabic. He put the matter away from him briskly.

"Well," he said, "I see you're not going to ask me up the stair just now. Certainly it's not the right time to call on a new acquaintance. But we have friends in common and a shared concern for their welfare, I think. Will you dine with me to-night somewhere—say at eight? Medical men can afford to dispense with a little ceremony, can't they?"

I considered. If I were left to myself for the rest of the morning, and for the afternoon, there was no reason why I shouldn't dine out. I said so, and he nodded approvingly.

I watched him away, as I wished to follow the same direction alone and think things out. It seemed likely we should talk about the Mummy at dinner.

I considered what Perceval and Maxwell had told me the night before, and tried for a little while to build some theory thereon. I soon stopped that, though, for I hadn't much evidence, and I found myself suggesting theories which I could neither prove nor disprove.

But I ended that afternoon by hunting up a clean note-book, writing *Case Notes* on the cover, and jotting down facts as they occurred to me. I say "facts," but in the note-book I carefully separated what I had witnessed from what had been reported to me.

Then I locked the notes up before I dressed to go out. I didn't want Bird's studies of human nature to extend so far.

I never met with a better host than Maundeville. From the time I entered the hall of "The Scribes" until we lit our cigars before leaving, he was both entertaining and gracious.

What helped to make him a good host was no doubt the obvious fact that he was enjoying himself and wanted me to. He bubbled like a glass of champagne, was ready to talk or to listen, but kept an observant eye on the dinner and the service all the time.

Our oysters reminded him of pearl-fishing, and he told me that I must see one or two fine pearls he had bought at a South Sea fishery.

Sherry set him for a moment on Spanish affairs.

He ended what seemed to me a comprehensive criticism of the German Emperor, by sending his congratulations to the chef on the freshness of the salmon. It might have been taken that day, he said. Ice couldn't preserve that perfect flavor. And the chef sent back an equally polite message to the effect that M. le Professeur was right as usual, and that he happened to be able to guarantee that the fish was taken by a club member that very morning in Wales, and sent by express from the Wye. Maundeville nodded, and sketched for me a fortnight he had spent on the Wye, when he seemed to have been equally keen on angling and archeology.

Then he amused me with an account of his first day's fishing far up the Nile, where, as he put it, he didn't know whether to expect a rise from a hippopotamus or an alligator. He fell silent for a minute or two after that, staring blankly at the table. When he roused up again he looked about him as if wakened.

"Well, a hippopotamus steak isn't half bad if you're hungry," he said, "but neither is a Wye fish," and he chatted and made me chat till we reached the sweets. Then he suggested having coffee and liqueurs where we were, to avoid interruption in the smoking-room; but we found that, according to club rules, it would be still too early to light a cigarette.

"All this," he said, "makes a good excuse for finishing the evening at my place."

He beckoned to the waiter and scribbled a couple of messages for the telephone, then remarked, "Plain speaking is a luxury which can only be supported by an independent income—though a philosopher may manage it on a small one if it's a luxury he sets much store by."

"At fifty," I said, "one wants an occasional luxury."

"Fifty?" he looked me over; "I congratulate you. I should have taken five or six years off that. A wise man of fifty has tremendous possibilities. He knows what he wants. He knows what isn't worth bothering about. He has possibly half of an enjoyable life still before him."

I laughed. "I congratulate you on your youthful optimism. You can't be fifty!" In fact, I guessed his age was nearer sixty but his energy and intellect gave him a youthful air.

"Never mind what I am!" He waved that point aside with a firm brown hand. "Half of an enjoyable life, I say. See how the centenarians increase! Look at the *Times* announcements, and notice what a number of men are eighty, ninety, and over, at their deaths. Old sailors, old soldiers, old fox-hunting squires. How many of them do you suppose have given Life any scientific consideration? An occasional pill. Whisky, perhaps, sometimes, instead of port. That's about all; and yet they've lived. But I bore you?"

"Not at all!" I laughed. "You encourage me."

If that was not absolute fact, at least I was amused. It was impossible to be bored by a man so very much alive. I began to understand the sway he still held over his former students.

We had finished dinner, and he laughingly went on with his whimsical argument, stopping to crack a few filberts, which he did recklessly between his teeth.

"At fifty, too," he went on, "one's blood has cooled. One no longer acts on impulse. One concentrates more easily, achieves with less effort. A boy's illusions—"

He broke off and seemed to consider.

"—are replaced by a man's," I finished for him. "Different, often, but always illusions."

He was on the point of retorting, but checked himself. "Come," he said, "my tobacco will put you in a better frame of mind. I did something useful once for a tobacco merchant in Cairo, and I actually think he sends me pure tobacco. It's rather rash to rely on a man's gratitude, though, isn't it?—unless he is expecting something more of you."

"Who is cynical now?" I asked.

"I don't pretend to be anything else," he retorted. "I have faith in Nature, if you give her a chance, but not in human nature. Let us be going!"

He led the way down, softly humming an air.

A motor-brougham stood at the curb, and we entered it. We slipped away west, quietly, through a drizzle of rain which made the streets and pavements shine with reflected lights. Maundeville hummed as he went, in a soft baritone. But in less than ten minutes we stopped. He made me wait until a man, evidently watching for us, threw the house-door open.

"This rain," Maundeville said, "is soaking. But it's soft, and really means spring. It's a west wind, I'm sure I can smell the buds bursting in the country lanes," and he ran up the steps humming again. A minute later I was lounging before a wood fire, while Maundeville discoursed learnedly on liqueurs, of which an embarrassing variety stood on the table with Turkish coffee and Egyptian tobacco.

The room, lighted more by the fire than by a couple of shaded electric lamps, was very comfortable, and warm in color. The walls were dark red, and the large rug covering most of the polished floor was dark red and blue. There were half a dozen paintings of desert scenes on the red walls; beautiful things they seemed to me. Maundeville, when he saw that I noticed them, told me they were the work of one man, a corporal in the Foreign Legion.

There were a few foreign weapons and singular odds and ends of foreign manufacture, hanging here and there about the mantelpiece and between the pictures.

"Many not worth tuppence," Maundeville explained, "but they're all reminders of interesting times."

I crossed the room to look more closely at one picture of a night scene in the desert, lit by a camp-fire, and then went back to Maundeville, who was now jibing gently at the members of the Society of Osiris and their eccentricities.

"These coteries remind me of some Japanese boxes," he said. "You open one, and there's a smaller inside. You open that, and you find a smaller still. You go on opening if you've nothing else to do, and you find the boxes getting smaller and smaller, till at last you reach the smallest—with nothing in it."

"Nothing?" I said, with no particular intention, but Maundeville looked at me attentively.

"Nothing, I think," he answered. "If you spent a while opening the Japanese boxes and had a nightmare the night after, you couldn't swear that the nightmare was let loose from the innermost box."

"A fanciful idea."

"Is it?" He considered me. "If I only knew how much I could say to you without breaking one of our idiotic promises!"

I had no idea how to answer that, so I didn't try.

He said suddenly, "Have a look round the house! I've some more pictures upstairs, and a sort of a little museum or curiosity shop in the back room there," and he nodded at a door in the far end of the room.

He led the way out into the hall while speaking. There the chauffeur, and the servant who had let us in, sat by the fire, rising as we passed up the stair.

"Am I keeping you?" I asked Maundeville.

"Not you! What suggests such a thing?" he asked.

"The motor is waiting."

"Oh, Pierre always hangs about till eleven or so when I'm at home. If you got tired of me and went away early, I might take it into my head to go somewhere for an hour or two. I've no special occupation to keep me in this week. But there's nothing to take me out either, as long as you'll keep me company."

He led the way up a broad stair, switching on a light here and there as we went. It seemed a large house for a bachelor to occupy, and I said so.

Maundeville laughed, but I detected a note of something like melancholy. "I fear I must settle for being married to my work. I've left the other too late."

"It's surely your choice?"

"There speaks a contented bachelor."

I *was* a contented bachelor. Mostly. My living was sufficient to my needs. My household well-ordered and comfortable. I knew where to find good conversation when required. And yet... I was frequently bored. And lonely too.

I did not wish for a wife. Had never wished for a wife. But I would have liked a steady companion. A partner with whom to share my life. Though marriage vows were not for such as myself, I would have once been willing to love and to cherish through sickness and in health, whether richer or poorer, till death us did part.

"It seems to me many a woman of intellect and refinement would appreciate all that a man like you has to offer," I said.

My host shrugged. "Even the most educated and sophisticated females seem to prize youth and good looks above all else."

I didn't argue as I believed he was likely correct.

There were rooms on both sides of the hall, and the main stair opened at the first floor onto a little gallery hung with a good many pictures, and containing one or two bronzes. In spite of Maundeville's taste for archaeology and antiquities generally, all the paintings seemed modern, and a large proportion of them French. He stopped to point one out here and there, and then threw open a door at the gallery-end.

"There are no pictures in here," he said. "I think bindings are sufficient decoration, don't you?"

He switched on a couple more lights. The room was rather long and narrow. A wood fire burned at one end. In the center of the floor was a heavy round table, with writing materials, a typewriter, and a few scattered books and magazines. Near the fire was a high desk at which one could write standing. The walls seemed paneled with dark wood, but it was hard to tell, for they were practically covered with books, and the air was scented by leather and morocco bindings.

I stepped in and looked about me, envying the man his money for the first time. Here one could read or write in absolute comfort. The carpet was like moss, the walls of the old house were solid, the windows were double; there was a leather-covered door inside the one that opened onto the gallery. The noise of the West End was unheard.

"May one explore?" I asked, stretching out a hand, and Maundeville nodded.

"A mixed lot," he said. "I've no one's tastes to consult but my own."

I took down the first book my hand fell on. Sir Richard Burton's *Book of the Sword* on one shelf, his translation of the Arabian Nights on another. Given the rumors concerning Burton, and Maundeville's own comments on bachelorhood, I wondered…

The three or four shelves nearest to the high desk seemed crowded with books on Egyptian, Greek, Roman, and Indian antiquities, great books, profusely illustrated with photographs and drawings; and the one or two which I opened had autograph inscriptions in French, Italian, or English by the authors.

I said more than half seriously, "When we get outside you had better search me—though evening-dress fortunately…"

"My dear fellow!" He laughed heartily, and I suppose touched a bell unobserved by me, for the man-servant at once showed himself in the doorway. It was as though he had waited in the gallery outside, just as he had waited in the hall downstairs.

"Bates," Maundeville said, "this is my friend Doctor Armiston. I hope he is going to use the room often. You'll see that he is comfortable when he comes."

The man looked at me for a moment and bowed. He disappeared before I had got over my surprise.

"He's an expert at tea and coffee," was Maundeville's only answer to my thanks. "Try him! The beggar doesn't get half enough to do," and he led the way out into the gallery again.

"Here's another room," he said, throwing open another door, "but there's nothing to see in it."

The room was almost empty, except for a large easel with some covering over it, a throne or dais, a few empty frames, and canvases turned to the wall.

"You paint," I said. Of course he did. The man did everything.

"A little. I use the room quite as much for the foils," he answered carelessly. "My bedroom's in there," he nodded at another door. "That's about all up here."

He led the way downstairs again, past his man and the chauffeur, who were still by the hall fire.

Leaning his shoulders against the mantelpiece in the dining-room, he looked thoughtfully across at the door which he had already pointed out before going upstairs.

"Are you going to show me your museum?" I asked.

He smiled at that. "You've read my mind. I was wondering…" Then he roused up. "Well, why not?" he added briskly, and leading the way down the room, took me in.

A ghostly fragrance met my nostrils. A blend of ancient spices, the very scent of history. Cassia, myrrh, cinnamon, and always the underlying note of bitumen.

Electric lights showed a room perhaps twenty-four feet by eighteen. In the middle, littered with papers, was a large plain deal table, over which lights hung.

A papyrus roll lay there, and one or two well-worn books. The only one I happened to pick up was the *Egyptian Book of the Dead*. On the walls were a few large photographs. One I happened to recognize as the Taj-Mahal; others were of ruins, pyramids, one of a Sphinx; others again of interiors, perhaps sepulchral chambers, taken, I suppose, by flashlight.

"That only reached me yesterday from Orkney," Maundeville said, nodding at a flint arrow-head. "Now, given the remote possibility of a thing like that being absolutely shielded from exposure—this one lay among bones in a stone coffin—how long could a bloodstain remain on it?"

While talking, he moved slowly on, but I suddenly halted.

Standing upright against the wall was what I had suspected I might expect to find there—a mummy case. And yet, happening as it did, to be in a little recess between bookshelves, I came upon it with a start.

I stopped dead, and Maundeville presently turned, and seeing me stare at the thing, watched me just an instant. "Yes, I thought you would be interested in that," he said.

I saw, by the curious blue beetle design on the front, that it was the same coffin I had once climbed to the top of a motor to examine.

Maundeville came slowly back and stood looking at it with me. "Have a good look at it if you care to, and then we'll go back to the other room."

I looked it over carefully, more from curiosity than because I expected to see anything very illuminating.

"I can see where someone attempted to open it," I said.

He smiled faintly. "Come, come. I know you've had the whole story from Maxwell and Perceval. Maxwell told me he was going to ask for your help."

Clearly my detective technique needed work.

"I think it's an excellent idea having a fresh pair of eyes examine our little problem. Especially given that those eyes are not clouded by mysticism or even academism."

"Maxwell does not seem prone to mysticism or academism," I remarked.

Maundeville said almost sadly, "His eyes are clouded, though."

I looked sharply at him, but he had turned away. "My idea is to burn the whole thing soon," he said. "It will go up like a torch, but we will open and examine it first, if you like. I'd be delighted to have your help."

"That will certainly draw her attention."

"I imagine I have her attention. Have you finished? Let us go back, then. You can come in here and look at it again some other time, you know, if you want to."

He led the way back into the room we had first sat in, pushed an easy-chair to the fire for me and put a box of cigars at my elbow.

"Now," he said, stirring up the logs, "I wonder how much I may tell you about Scrymgeour, and D'Aurelle, and that thing you've just been looking at."

I prefer a pipe, but these were the finest cigars and not a treat to be missed. I picked one out, pierced it, and lit up. "I'd certainly appreciate any insight you have to offer."

Even if he knew no more than did Perceval and Maxwell, if he chose to chat freely, he might speak of something they had overlooked or forgotten.

He helped himself to a whisky-and-soda, and said finally, "The question is, if you don't mind my asking, are you going any further? I don't assume any right to be answered, but if you chose to answer, and said no, then we could drop a queer business altogether and talk of something more amusing. If you said yes—that, for example, you intend to join in a foolish experiment for which I'm partly responsible...I might suggest further consideration before you commit yourself."

He waited for my answer, but I was waiting for him to finish his thought. I felt sure there was more to come.

He said, "If you understand, then I'm speaking clearly enough. If you don't, then so much the better. We can drop it."

"I think there's no room for misunderstanding," I said. "But I've seen your Mummy twice before, and, as far as I'm concerned, I'm committed to the venture."

Maundeville nodded, and his good-tempered, clean-shaven face looked concerned, but he evidently wasn't surprised.

"It seemed likely," he said. "Well, you're in it with the rest of us! Those two fellows haven't broken the letter of the law, at any rate, by bringing you in. Perhaps they thought it the surest way of keeping you quiet."

"The letter of the law?" I inquired.

"Oh yes. There are laws in the spiritual realm just as there are in the corporeal. You're bound by the same promises as the rest of us now, you see. Such an easy thing, to make a promise!" He lapsed into silence again, lying back in his chair, his cigar forgotten and burned out.

"Are you saying you believe in this curse?"

He said softly, "Oh yes. There's a curse all right."

He roused himself and sat up briskly.

"Well, I am sure it's no use giving you vague warnings," he said. "Even if I could make them definite and credible, which I can't, you're not the man to draw back."

"No, I'm not," I said.

"And after all, there are great advantages to us if you come in," he went on, as if thinking aloud, "though myself I would have warned you what you're getting into. Ugly scandal at the very least, and what doctor can afford that?"

Until he put it into words, this aspect had not occurred to me. He was completely correct—and it was an alarming thought. My profession might bore me sometimes, but better bored than destitute.

Watching me, Maundeville said, "Young men believe themselves and everyone else indestructible. From the perspective of the Society, this is an excellent move. Your profession has trained you to solve puzzles and problems and you're not likely to have any bias. It could be worse."

I laughed.

To my surprise, he laughed too. "I'm sorry. I'm prone to thinking aloud. It's a rude habit. Well, we'll talk the situation over again as soon as you've something to report."

Would I be reporting to Maundeville? I wasn't sure myself.

After my cigar and a final whisky-and-soda, I rose to go, complimenting him again on his library.

"Use it! Use it!" he begged me. "Let me find you there some afternoon pretty soon, and we'll compare notes about this insane affair. Have another look at that too." He nodded toward the door behind which the Mummy stood. "I'll remember to put on the top of the case my notes about the inscription."

"Do you know anything of her history?"

"A little. It's disappointingly without romance."

"Isn't that the way of it?"

"All too often, I fear."

We passed out into the hall. An ormolu clock informed us it was then after one o'clock in the morning, but the chauffeur and valet still waited by the fire, and Maundeville insisted on sending me to my rooms in the car.

The rain was still drizzling down in the glistening, almost empty streets.

CHAPTER THIRTEEN

MISS HENNESSEY EXPLAINS

I spent my free hours the next day shuffling the loose bits of paper on which I jotted down my occasional ideas about the Mummy, and looking through the rather more coherent notes in my case book.

I decided that I would not relate my visit to Maundeville's to Perceval and Maxwell. In fact, I resolved to be chary of repeating to any one of the Society of Osiris what any other might say—deciding to apply this rule even to Maxwell and Perceval.

And all the time I was frankly uneasy at being mixed up with the business at all.

Why hadn't I sent these fellows to the devil, said distinctly what I knew and what I didn't know, and let the coroner and the police have a free hand?

Of course I knew part of the reason I had not done any of these things—and that recognition irritated me all the more.

So I was not at all in the bland mood suited for an afternoon call upon a young lady, when late in the day I walked into Cadogan Square.

I was taken upstairs to a little boudoir where I found Miss Hennessey and her *dame de compagnie*. Tea was brought in immediately after, and Miss Hennessey seeming unexpectedly nervous, I found myself talking the most amazing society twaddle to the gently twittering Mrs. Vavasour. Her very name brought to mind Dundreary whiskers and my mother's crinolines.

Some unnecessary admission on my part shook her confidence sadly. She left the room with a puzzled air, and for the first time I heard Miss Hennessey laugh. I was not at all sure whether the laugh was against me or Mrs. Vavasour or both; but it had a very pleasant sound, and I did nothing to discourage it.

"I know the role you're playing in this matter, Doctor Armiston." She was smiling, but there was a hint of anxiety in her gaze. "My cousin Charlie Perceval and Captain Maxwell have instructed me to be completely frank with you. I *want* to be frank for I have two dead men always on my mind, always before me, sleeping or waking."

"You!"

"Yes. Me. For God's sake, help me, that there may be no more."

I leaned back in my chair and considered her critically. The afternoon sun was shining straight in upon her. It lit up the coils of red hair, and shimmered upon her face and neck. She was a picture of youth and vitality. Two dead men on her mind! The idea was absurd.

Even so.

I said carefully, "I feel I should warn you that whatever my personal feelings, if I became aware that a crime had been committed, I would feel obliged to report my findings to the authorities."

I stopped, and she looked at me very distressfully, though one could see that she was doing her best to keep cool. I dare say I didn't feel any the less sympathetic because she seemed to me extraordinarily beautiful, and much too proud a young woman to ask for anyone's advice in general.

"They told me I could trust you," she said dolefully, but very quietly.

"I don't know how they could tell, but so you can," I replied. "You can trust me not to trade upon your ignorance. Tell me what you can about your trouble, and I think I can tell you where to go for the best advice."

She sat looking first at me, then away from me, as if still in an agony of doubt. One could not help being very sorry for the girl.

"Remember, I'm old enough to be your father," said I.

"Yes," she said quite simply, "you're old enough to be my father, and that makes it easier, but it's still very hard." She sat looking at me with a little frown for a few seconds.

"The beginning of these things," she said presently, "was when I saw you first in the Albany, on the morning Mr. Scrymgeour died."

"I've heard your cousin and Captain Maxwell's account of why you were there," I said. "I should like to hear your own."

"I know. I was at the Albany because of a letter that I got the night before from Mr. Scrymgeour. Some months ago he made me an offer of marriage, which I declined. That night he wrote saying that in case he died he would like me to know that his feelings had not changed, and that he had left me most of his property."

"You went round before breakfast to thank him?" I suggested, with some attempt at irony. Really, one must not believe everything one was told, just because the teller happened to be a beautiful woman.

"No, of course not. Paris—Mr. Scrymgeour—was a dear friend as well as a political ally. In fact, after I had refused him I liked him better than ever, because of the way he behaved to me. Well, that letter troubled me. It sounded so…dire. I suppose the knowledge that he was keeping that horrible Mummy in his room added to my feelings that something might be wrong. I couldn't sleep; and between seven and eight I suddenly made up my mind to go and make sure that all was well. I'm often out round the Square before breakfast, and as I had a couple of books Paris had lent me, it seemed a plausible excuse to visit."

"You went alone at that hour of the morning to the home of an unmarried man!"

She blushed, but it was with anger not shame. "Is there any danger in going from Cadogan Square to the Albany between eight and nine in the morning?" she asked. "You're a prude, Doctor Armiston. Yes, I went alone. Mr. Scrymgeour's servant told me he was not up yet, which was unusual. I made the man knock at his door, while I waited on the stair. But when he came back saying he could get no answer I grew frightened. Call it a woman's intuition. I insisted that he must open the door, and because he hesitated, I knocked, then threw the door open myself and looked in." She closed her eyes for a moment. "The door was the one opening directly onto the lobby, and at once I could see Paris lying on the rug."

"Aside from the broken step, did you notice anything else amiss?"

She shook her head.

"Did you smell anything?"

"Death." She shuddered.

"Go on."

"When my cousin and Captain Maxwell arrived, we talked it over and they said there was bound to be an inquest and—because of that letter—it would be better all around if no one knew I had ever been there."

"Seymour knew."

"Who? Oh, Paris's man. Yes. Anyway, Hilary—Captain Maxwell—said he would go for a doctor and that I had better leave and say nothing."

"Why didn't you?"

"I did. But when I had gone some distance I found that I had left my muff behind." She colored again. "I'm a great reader of the novels of Anna Katharine Green. I know a great deal about clues. I saw I must retrieve that incriminating muff. I met you after I had fetched it."

I sat and considered the matter. "But did your friend say he thought he was going to die?"

"He didn't say so. But he told me that sitting there as he did sometimes at night with the Mummy so near him…he couldn't help thinking of his own mortality. He thought he was wrong to have made a joke of it. Of *her*."

"He believed in the curse?"

She bit her lip. "No. He was not superstitious. I think he simply regretted his behavior. He knew what I thought of it. To desecrate, to make a bet on the body of a dead woman, who had done all she could to make sure of being left in peace! It was a coarse thing to do. A callous, cruel thing."

"How did you find out about the Mummy?"

"From my maid through Mr. Scrymgeour's man. Even before Mr. Scrymgeour's death, word of their ridiculous, sacrilegious pact had spread. I told them, my cousin and Professor Maundeville, what I thought of such foolish and disrespectful antics. I was sure there would be trouble of some sort. And I was correct."

"Maundeville is most to blame," I said. "He's old enough to know better, at any rate. He's responsible for the Mummy being here."

"I can't agree. The professor is so used to Mummies and tombs and mysterious antiquities, he didn't realize how foolishly the rest of them would behave," she said quickly. "Besides, he tried to stop the thing, but the others, Mr. Scrymgeour especially, told him it was a point of honor that they share in the curse. They will continue on now, even after poor Hugh. And they will die, one by one, until someone figures out what *she* wants."

CHAPTER FOURTEEN

MAXWELL

Three or four days after I had called on Miss Hennessey I decided to avail myself of Maundeville's invitation. I went to his house on Courtenay Street, only to meet Captain Maxwell on the doorstep.

He greeted me courteously enough, though I think he was not altogether pleased to see me. He looked sallow and unwell.

"I'm afraid Maundeville isn't home," he informed me.

"That's all right. I'm going to bury myself in his library for the afternoon." When he did not respond, did not appear to even hear, I added, "Perhaps I'll commune with the Mummy. She could surely answer a question or two if she chose."

He did not answer my smile. "I didn't realize you had become such close friends."

I presumed he meant me and Maundeville and not me and the Mummy.

"I doubt if I'm counted amongst his close friends. Which makes his generosity all the more remarkable."

"He can be very generous," Maxwell agreed. "He can also—" He broke off, biting his lip and closing his eyes. The knuckles of the hand clutching the head of his walking stick whitened.

"My dear boy," I said quietly. "Will you not allow me to help you?"

His lashes lifted. His eyes looked almost black with bitterness. "I've had all the help from doctors I require." He raised his hat in brusque farewell and hobbled painfully down the steps.

I was chilled by the undisguised loathing in his voice. I stared after him and then turned and rang the bell.

Once ensconced in Maundeville's library, I did my best to forget Maxwell's uncharacteristic hostility. In fact, I did my best to forget Maxwell himself—which was the only sensible course open to me. Especially since I was quite sure Maxwell did not spend time thinking of me.

I roamed about the room trying to get some general idea of the books there. Remembering what Maundeville had said on the subject of middle age, I was amused to see that he had several books dealing with the prolongation of life. There were the works of Metchnikoff, Brown-Sequard and others, with one or two scrapbooks of press-cuttings relating to centenarians. That particular shelf ended with works on occultism, and I wondered whether Maundeville classed the two subjects together, and whether he considered both seriously or otherwise.

I passed on to other shelves, dipping into a book here and there, and I was deep in one on Egypt, most beautifully illustrated with drawings and photographs, when Maundeville's man, without asking if I wanted it, brought in a tea-tray.

The result was that I stayed on, without seeing anything of Maundeville, until about eight o'clock. Passing down the stairs I met the servant again, and asked whether I could go into the museum without disturbing Maundeville. He said that his master would not be home at all that evening, and that his orders were to admit me whenever I came to any room I wished.

He switched on the lights in the museum for me, and I sat there perhaps a quarter of an hour looking idly at the mummy case, and speculating vaguely about it and its contents. Every now and again, the scent of camphor and cedar reached me, like the very peculiar perfume of a woman just out of my range of vision.

I considered the blue beetle paintings running up and down the peeling case. What did they signify? Maxwell and Perceval had spoken of Khepri's priestess. While I was not up on my Egyptian mythology, even I had heard of Osiris, great god of the dead, and his sister-wife Isis. Who was Khepri?

Intentionally I did not try to think hard, but just looked at the case and let my brain work or play as it would.

As I was strolling absent-mindedly out of the room I kicked against something hard, and nearly fell. Looking down when I had got my balance, I saw that I had come on a large tortoise, which was half-hidden under a table.

In the hall I spoke of this to the man, who was lounging there, saying I hoped I hadn't injured the beast, for I had really kicked it severely. This provoked the only smile I ever saw on Bates's solemn visage, but he merely said he thought the thing could stand more than that, and very likely had stood more, since he had heard his master say he knew it to be older than any man.

I told him to let his master know of my visit, and went home to dinner.

I dined alone that evening, still preoccupied with my thoughts of Maundeville's museum and that mummy case. When Bird brought in coffee, he mentioned that I had left most of an uncommonly well-cooked sole, and had let a cutlet grow cold before I began it.

I apologized absently and lit my pipe. Though I knew it was ridiculous, I could not quite shake my unease. I kept imagining that Mummy waiting there quietly in the darkness, till it should go out to find another host. The painted face was heavily malignant, and sitting alone in my room I could not get rid of it, although I knew quite well that it might not be a recognizable likeness of the woman whose body it covered.

Unless a man is a poet or novelist by trade, to have an imagination at fifty is merely ridiculous, and I felt this acutely. But even knowing myself to be ridiculous, I could not seem to get past the curiosity of two such long-enduring things as a Mummy and a tortoise residing together in a London house. I kept imagining the tortoise slowly crawling about in the darkness of the museum, the Mummy looking down on it with blind eyes.

Really, it's no wonder that I didn't do anything except fancy ridiculous things that evening—and my restlessness was made worse because of that miserable Purveyor beneath me. His trade was increasing and he had lately started an extra-sized coffee-mill, which worked at night, grinding coffee for the next day's sale.

When the grinding began it lifted me clean out of my chair. A Twopenny Tube under the floor couldn't have been worse, and it went on continuously for a solid hour. I sent Bird down to remonstrate.

But all doors were locked, and of course the rascals were wrapped in their own thunder.

The next morning I still had a headache.

I let myself in after interviewing my miserable and completely unhelpful landlord, and I found Maxwell limping up and down my consulting-room, surveying my bookshelves.

I was glad, though very surprised to see him, not least because he had seemed to so thoroughly despise me and my whole profession the previous afternoon. I was glad too to see that his color was better and his eyes clearer. He offered a quick uncertain smile.

"You read German?" he asked.

As opening salvos went…well, if I hadn't known him better, I'd have said he was at a complete loss for what to say to me.

"Enough."

He offered another of those tentative smiles. "Did you find what you were looking for at Maundeville's?"

"I wasn't looking for anything in particular."

"No?"

I thought he was perhaps nervous about coming to the point of his visit. He was a proud man and this would be a difficult and painful confession for anyone.

To give him time, I said, "It's a wonderful library. I could get lost in there for days."

"Yes!"

"The museum is interesting as well."

"Yes," he agreed, but with less enthusiasm.

I prodded delicately, "Did you perhaps wish to consult me on…some matter?"

He grimaced. "I want to apologize. I was appallingly rude yesterday."

I hadn't expected it and was genuinely touched. "It's all right. You weren't well."

"It's no excuse. You've been so very decent about everything. What I wanted—thought you might—that is." He stopped dead, drew a quick breath as though steadying himself, and made the plunge. "Would you dine with me to-night? Or have me to dine with you?"

"*Dine* with you?" As I had been expecting a completely different reason for his call, my surprise was only too evident.

Maxwell colored. "Yes. Whichever you prefer. I don't care which."

"Well, I—"

"I want to talk about that wretched Mummy. It must pay another visit soon. Have you been thinking of it?"

He was flushed and speaking too quickly, but I realized that was nothing more than embarrassment. In fact, I almost wondered if the mention of the Mummy was an afterthought. No doubt wishful thinking on my part.

"I could hardly help it given I was looking at the thing only yesterday," I said. "I nearly broke my neck over a tortoise at Maundeville's."

"Ah! Methuselah. Lively company, isn't he? Maundeville claims he's older than the one at St. Helena, and that's known to have been almost as big a century and a quarter ago as it is now."

I said, "That comes, I suppose, of having a low temperature and a slow circulation."

Maxwell grinned. "Does it? Well, there's a bright side. Methuselah won't burn out, will he? He doesn't let himself go. He isn't overly enthusiastic about anything, and doesn't let his worries get the best of him either. There's something to be said for a steady pace."

Was he making some joke at my expense? I couldn't be sure. I said curtly, "For example?"

"Oh, well…" He looked vague. "We can discuss it over dinner, I expect. That is…you haven't actually agreed yet. Will you dine with me?"

I wanted to so much that it alarmed me. I had enjoyed my meal with Maundeville, but the thought of that meal had not made my heart skip either before or after. I was far too old and staid a man to be feeling rattled simply because a boy twenty years my junior invited me to dine.

I said, "You must dine with me, of course. But I must look at my engagements first. I think it only means making dinner a trifle late."

He looked relieved. "Excellent. Your man looks competent for anything. A steak and a bottle of claret, eh?"

I was on the point of agreeing—ready to show that Bird's resources went further—when I suddenly remembered the infernal coffee-grinding. I expressed my feelings on the subject freely, and Maxwell listened sympathetically.

When I finally shut up, he said, "How irritating. So you'll be my guest to-night after all?"

By then I felt like a complete fool. "Certainly," I said. "I look forward to it."

He gave me the name of his club and I practically turned him out, as I had lost all patience with myself and my particular affliction, and had two or three patients yet to see.

* * * * *

I found the place in a quiet back street some three minutes' walk east from Piccadilly Circus. A gilded sign in the shape of a banyan leaf hung over first-floor windows.

The Banyan was not a club, but an eating-house, with rather a special clientele. It was run by a retired quartermaster, who somehow made his little pile in India. The man spoke Persian and Burmese and worked the house with Indian servants. He catered to Anglo-Indian tastes. It was the first place I was given a spoon for my curry.

According to Maxwell, men had been known to come home cursing India and all its ways—and yet turn up at the Banyan within a month. He said he went there principally to keep up his Indian vocabulary, but the fowl-curry, the chutney, and the fruit were all excellent and well worth the visit.

Though Maxwell was not a sophisticated raconteur like Maundeville, he was good company and sincerely charming. In fact, he was disconcertingly attentive. It was quite a heady thing to have his complete and unadulterated concentration. I could see no reason for it.

"How did you happen to become a physician?" he asked curiously as I finished a long involved story that even I could see no point to.

"My father was a doctor," I said. "One of those good old-fashioned country doctors who shepherded his flock in and out of this life for nearly the length of his own. He was greatly loved by everyone who knew him, and I thought that would be a wonderful thing. To be able to take away pain and suffering. And to be greatly loved."

It was the truth, but it was more than I had meant to say.

"It *is* a wonderful thing to be able to take away pain and suffering," Maxwell said after a moment.

"Yes. What I failed to understand was how difficult it would be when, no matter how hard you try, you can't manage it. Or when your best effort fails to save a life. It's a dreadful thing to have a child die in your arms."

Maxwell's somber expression no doubt matched my own. I said hastily, "Happily, most of my practice amounts to lancing boils and handing out headache powders."

He laughed. "I doubt it."

"Oh, it's quite true. I'm not complaining. The grand career I imagined for myself would have been contrary to my own nature. I like a quiet, comfortable life."

He stared at the ale in his glass. "You never married?"

"No, no," I said too heartily. "No woman would have me. Congenital bachelor, I'm afraid."

Maxwell's eyes flicked up. He met my gaze and offered a faint, enigmatic smile.

It was not easy—in fact, it was impossible—to get him to speak of himself. Nor did he broach the subject that had inspired this tête-à-tête until at length we settled in a quiet corner of the smoking-room.

"Now," he said with a sort of grim cheerfulness, "we're fortified and steadied by an excellent dinner. We shall take a common-sense view of the matter before us."

"The matter before us?"

"Your continuing involvement in this case."

"I'm…not sure I follow."

"It's quite simple. To begin with we have poor Scrymgeour and D'Aurelle. Both died suddenly, and apparently alone. You knew neither of them, but you certified one death and countenanced the certifying of the other although I believe you thought both those deaths were suspicious."

I stared at him, unable to believe my ears.

"I believe you feel you're partly responsible—since you certified those deaths—for the fact that there has been no further inquiry. I think, too, that you joined the Society of Osiris because of those deaths, and that you have those certificates on your conscience.”

“What the devil are you talking about?” I exclaimed. “I certified what I believed to be true.”

“Would you sign them now?” he retorted. “I know you acted honestly at the time.”

“Of what exactly are you accusing me?” I asked very coldly, very quietly.

Maxwell met my stare without flinching. “It’s the truth, isn’t it? Your interest in this matter, your involvement—”

I said, “My involvement is simply one of academic interest. You and your friend have presented me with a mystery, and I mean to solve it. That is all.”

He nodded as though satisfied, though his expression remained uncharacteristically austere. I thought his eyes held an unnatural glitter, and I prepared myself for more unpleasantness. Even so, his next words were startling.

“In thinking over those two deaths, we must consider points of difference and of similarity. Both these poor fellows were bachelors, and both had independent means.”

“You believe their deaths are connected by something other than the Mummy?”

“I do. Perhaps you don’t know where their property went?”

“Well?”

“Miss Hennessey.”

I think I gaped at him. Not at the information itself, but the fact he had essentially accused the poor girl of murder.

I said as much, though I tried to keep my tone neutral. "Then you suspect Miss Hennessey of somehow engineering their deaths?"

It was Maxwell's turn to look astonished. "Nora? Of course not. I bring up the matter only because you're a bachelor too, though not so well provided as they were with this world's goods. You're an older man also."

I laughed. He was rude and ridiculous, but I don't suppose he realized that—or cared. "True on all counts, I'm afraid. Furthermore, I'm an observer, not a participant in this little misadventure of yours. So if your concern is for my safety, you may rest easy. I don't believe either Miss Hennessey *or* the Mummy are after me."

"I think you should retire from the case, all the same."

I stared. He appeared to be quite serious.

"What's brought about this change of heart?" I inquired. "You weren't concerned for my safety five days ago."

"Five days ago you weren't taking tea with Miss Hennessey or having dinner with Maundeville. I—we—didn't then appreciate the fact that there might be risk to you." His throat jumped as he swallowed. He looked genuinely worried. "Enough people have died, Armiston. I wouldn't like something to happen to you on our account."

"You and Perceval have decided this between you?"

"Er...yes." It was such an obvious lie, I almost laughed. I was too offended to find the situation humorous, however.

"I see."

"It's not that we're unappreciative."

"No. You've expressed your appreciation most originally."

His brows drew together. "We should never have dragged you into this matter. That's the truth."

"Possibly not. But you did—I won't say *dragged* me because I joined the expedition willingly enough—invite me, and there's no going back now."

"Of course there is."

I shook my head. "I told you both before that I did not need your permission to continue my investigations. Such as they are."

He leaned forward, saying with quiet intensity, "You *must* stop, Quentin."

I was so surprised he knew my Christian name it took me a moment to collect my thoughts. "Shall I tell you what I think this is?"

"I'm telling you what it is!"

I shook my head. "I believe you've recently learned the cards are about to be drawn again. I believe you're convinced that this time you'll receive the Priestess. And I believe that you're afraid that because of my…" I didn't quite know how to phrase it without making matters more awkward than they were. I settled on, "…respect for you, I may act rashly and come to harm."

Even in the muted light I could see he flushed and then paled. "I don't think any such thing."

"I hope not. I hope you don't think I'm such a fool."

"I don't. Of course I don't." He looked stricken.

"However great my…respect for you, I'm not a man prone to rash or incautious action. I'm not the dashing hero of a romance novel. Frankly, you would be better suited to such a role than I."

He opened his mouth, closed it, and swallowed. "I wasn't suggesting—"

"Let's consider the matter closed. You've said what you needed to say, and I've given you my answer."

"Very well," he said stiffly.

Shortly after, Maxwell and I parted. I think he couldn't escape fast enough.

I spent some time later that evening in looking over my notes and adding a few more.

The end result seemed to be mere exasperation. I had no theory worth the name, although I considered Maxwell's idea that something more than the Mummy—or even the Society of Osiris—connected the victims to be an intriguing one. I surmised from his theory that he too had made Miss Hennessey his beneficiary, and that alone was surely proof I was no detective, for I had imagined… Well, it didn't matter.

After my dinner with Maxwell, I was inclined to believe that if ever I discovered a clue, it would lead merely to a mare's nest. I jeered at myself as an elderly busybody, with a talent for interfering unduly with matters which didn't concern me, and for which I had no capacity.

I stared at the fire and listened to the distant roar of Bird's snores. He could give the grinding machine in the shop below a run for its money. How I envied him his stolidity—which at the same time was most exasperating. I don't think a dozen Mummies could rob him of a minute's sleep.

I, on the other hand, spent another restless and aching night.

CHAPTER FIFTEEN

MEDITATION AND THE MUMMY

Grrrakka kkakkakkakkakkakkakk akkakkakk kkakka akk GRRRAKKA KKAKKAKKAKKAKKAKKAKKAKK AKKAKKAKK KKAKKA AKK grrrakka kkakkakkakkakkak-kakk akkakkakk kkakka akk

As if sleep was not difficult enough, for three evenings after my dinner with Maxwell, the cacophony of the confounded coffee-mill drove me near to distraction. Either I forgot to go out, or I came in too soon. The thing was additionally annoying because it was so ridiculous.

I finally mentioned the matter to Maundeville, when I met him one afternoon in Piccadilly, and he very kindly took up the question at once with his usual energy. We went to his house, and he demonstrated outside and under the library and museum how perfectly sound had been cut off.

It was done by double doors and double windows, with a very thick fibrous material, something between wadding and felt, worked in under the flooring, and between the opposed ends of joists. The patent was his own, plotted out in the first place, he said, for his own comfort.

I spoke to my landlord and persuaded him that the work would improve his property without expense to himself, and the job began at once—the whole flat being done, one room at a time.

Maundeville dropped in three or four times when passing, to see, as he said, that the British Workman didn't spoil the reputation of his patent; and at his repeated invitation I made pretty free use of his library during the eight or ten days that my flat was under treatment.

Bird kept a fish-like but vigilant eye on the workmen, remarking that in times past he had often done sentry-go while his ship coaled. This present operation, I gathered, was not so arduous or so dirty.

One afternoon I went to Maundeville's to consult his library—more particularly the pile of books, always increasing, in the museum. We were both interested in some really reasonable and well-conducted correspondence contributed to British and foreign scientific magazines at that time, on the phenomena of Life and Death, Growth and Decay. There was something new by Metchnikoff, which Maundeville wanted me to look at.

Near his door I met Perceval and Maxwell, coming away. They said he was not at home, and Perceval suggested that we should all go to Park Lane for tea.

After the painful dinner with Maxwell at the Banyan, I was determined to keep my distance. I excused myself, on the grounds that I wanted at once to run through this book, which I understood Maundeville wished to pass on to some correspondent of his, and I happened to mention the author and the subject.

My young friends were not impressed—but then *being* young, that was only to be expected.

Maxwell said sardonically, "It sounds like a losing battle. At the Service Clubs men with field-rank sit drinking sour milk, and talking hopefully of not being too old at eighty. The subs watch 'em, and take too many nips, to keep their spirits up."

"You may see it differently when you're my age," I said.

To my astonishment, he quoted from the Psalms. "They will still yield fruit in old age; They shall be full of sap and very green."

"And yet if no one wants to pick the fruit, it's all moot."

I was sorry I spoke for he looked confused, and after all, he was attempting to…well, that was the trouble. I had no idea what he was trying to do. Nor, I imagined, did he.

"Maundeville is an institution," Perceval remarked. "He'll never age. He can safely forego the sour milk, green fruit and stick to his whisky-and-soda."

"Unless the Mummy has other plans for him," Maxwell said.

"True." Perceval chuckled, but that ended the chat.

They might—and did—chaff now and then about the Mummy. Standing in Piccadilly's bright April sunshine, the pavement gay with the ridiculous women's hats of that season, the gutter absurd, too, with sandwich-men advertising the latest musical comedy, one felt the Mummy was altogether out-of-date.

And what could more beneath contempt than that? Still, mention of *her* always suggested unpleasant memories or vague possibilities—and was always enough to throttle any ordinary conversation.

I nodded to them and went inside—my business at Maundeville's house not being affected by his absence.

Bates was in the hall. I greeted him with the understanding that his master was out, and went straight to the museum.

For an hour or so, I read, but then grew fidgety. I rather wished I had gone to tea with Maxwell and Perceval. All else aside, they were engaging and entertaining companions and I had grown rather accustomed to spending time in their company. I felt younger when I was with them. That was the truth.

Methuselah, the tortoise, seemed almost restless, and kept moving about the crowded room. Now and then he distracted my attention by the faint rattle of his carapace on something against which he blundered. I sat and watched him for a time, wondering whether any sense of spring really stirred him; for that afternoon was quite warm, and all along Piccadilly flowers were being hawked in the sunshine.

The tortoise's wanderings brought him at last against the mummy case, and there he stayed quiet at the feet of the painted figure whose black eyes stared across at me, seeming to follow when I moved, as painted eyes will.

I wondered whether the malevolent portrait bore any faint likeness to what lay beneath. I wondered what *did* lie beneath now, and decided to suggest to Maundeville an experiment with X-rays, which could, of course, be repeated any number of times before the Mummy was exposed to light and air.

As a trio, this Mummy, Methuselah, and I, suggested some grim comedy to my mind. Here I sat reading and researching in hopes of discovering a modern elixir vitae, while quite well aware that the better and greater part of my life was of necessity past, and nothing particular done in it.

Here was Methuselah, who certainly had the secret of pro-longed life, but who could not yield it to me, or tell me if he found it worth having.

And looking down on us both was the Mummy, dead but incorruptible.

The wisdom of the Egyptians could keep everything but life in the body. Even hate seemed to have survived in that shell—and with it, deadly revenge for those who disturbed it.

I shivered at these thoughts. This room did not get much daylight, and though electric lamps were plentiful, I had not troubled to switch them on. I sat there in the shadows, staring at the mummy case and considering yet again the little we knew of its history.

According to Maundeville, her name had been Nefertiabet and she had been a princess as well as a priestess. Well, I thought that was probably Maundeville embellishing the story. But the story of the princess-priestess was otherwise without romance.

Princess Nefertiabet had been a difficult sort of female. Nature had compensated her lack of looks and charm with what appeared to be a very fine brain. She had chosen to apply that brain to the study of and devotion to an ancient and rather obscure—even in her day—god by the name of Khepri.

There was very little information on Khepri, and what there was seemed to indicate that he was associated with both creation and rebirth—or, more exactly—*metamorphosis*.

Not merely change. *Transformation*. To be transfigured.

The caterpillar becomes the butterfly. But not all transformation is for the better. The king becomes a despot. The damaged cell becomes a tumor.

In Nefertiabet's case, the princess became a priestess and created her own tiny cult based on a minor deity who was usually represented as a scarab beetle. The cult and all its secrets died with its high priestess.

That seemed to be that. A powerful but strange woman who had devoted her energies to the pursuit of something no one else understood or cared about.

Well, there were worse ways to spend a life. Provided she had been happy and satisfied in her work—but no. Studying that gaunt, painted visage, I did not think Nefertiabet had been happy or satisfied.

What had she longed for, yearned for, that had continued to elude her until her dying day?

What did she want now?

That was a silly question. What did any of us yearn for at the end other than well-deserved rest?

I had given a great deal of study to the question of whether there were any possible means by which the dead woman could ensure that those who troubled her rest should suffer for it. I did not consider the possibility of "supernatural" power, and I believed it had to be more than the power of suggestion. These young men were not particularly suggestible.

As far as I defined a possible source of danger, I thought of it as something like a poisonous exhalation, set free from the case or the Mummy on exposure to the air, and affecting those who stayed long near it.

For example, I fancied it was a part of this insane compact that the Mummy should be in its host's sleeping-room at night. Now, could that conceivably so affect a man's vitality as to cause fatal syncope? It seemed most unlikely; but then no more likely solution occurred to me. The answer to the riddle, indeed, if there were a riddle and an answer, was, if I may put it so, likely to be unlikely.

In my ordinary matter-of-fact state of mind the Mummy often seemed a chimera, a phantasm, and the deaths of its two hosts mere unpleasant coincidences. But on these quiet, lonely afternoons, watching it in the shadows, somehow it took on an air of menace.

Utter nonsense. I got up from the books, impatient with my fanciful thoughts, and decided to quit the room, since in it I couldn't use my wits to any practical purpose.

Part of my unease was no doubt due to the really superior sound-proofing qualities of Maundeville's patent. The museum was as quiet as a tomb, barring the slight occasional noise made by the tortoise's slow movements.

I compared this with my own flat, now at the workmen's mercy, and it occurred to me that I would go upstairs, and determine whether the library and the studio, both facing north, while the museum faced south, were equally silent.

I loitered for a few minutes in the library, which was empty and undisturbed by any echo, and then I passed on to convincing proof of Maundeville's success with the studio. I had entered the room before I realized that others were there already—and before they knew I was near.

Standing in the doorway, I stuttered a clumsy apology, so much taken aback that I didn't know whether to bundle and go at my quickest, or wait to hear whether my excuses were accepted.

There were three people in the room—Maundeville, Mrs. Vavasour, and Miss Hennessey.

CHAPTER SIXTEEN

"SHE IS FAR FROM THE LAND"

It was Miss Hennessey whom I saw first, and who first saw me. She was sitting upon a throne, as I fancy artists call the raised platform on which a model poses, and was bent forward listening to Maundeville. His back was turned to me as he stood at an easel, painting while he talked.

Mrs. Vavasour was placidly occupied in knitting some fancy-work, and near her was a tea-table, with a tray, cakes, cups, et cetera. My clumsy entry broke the spell of cozy domesticity. Miss Hennessey naturally changed her pose, and looked over Maundeville's shoulder at me. He wheeled about, to see who had disturbed her, and Mrs. Vavasour dropped her knitting and raised her glasses to peer at me.

Maundeville was the first to speak, and greeted me as though I were not only welcome, but expected.

"*Ben venuto!*" he called out, coming to meet me. "Just the man we wanted. An impartial critic!"

"I was told you were out," I exclaimed. "It's true that was some time ago, but I heard nobody."

Maundeville beamed upon me and cut short my apologies. "You give an unsolicited testimonial to my invention!" he said. "Of course you heard nobody. Can I help being pleased to see you? Don't run away! You've met Miss Hennessey, I remember. Doctor Armiston—Mrs. Vavasour. Have you had tea?"

I said Bates had offered me some, but I had refused.

"Oh, you've been among the books?" Maundeville went on, picking up a brush again. "Now, Miss Hennessey, there's a good half-hour of light left, and I know that a spectator won't trouble you."

While Maundeville fiddled with his palette, I looked across at Miss Hennessey, trying to decide by her face whether she wanted me to go or to stay. She smiled as if she had no objection.

"We've now been caught in the act," Maundeville said airily, stepping back a little from his easel and looking to and fro between it and Miss Hennessey. "We can't humbug the doctor, I'm afraid, Miss Hennessey, and we can't execute him. I propose swearing him to secrecy, after owning to everything."

"Honestly, I haven't looked at the easel," I said, "and I don't want to be told anything. I promise to forget."

"Uncomplimentary to the sitter and the artist," Maundeville declared, getting back to the canvas. I could only see the edge of it as I sat near the tea-table.

"Oh, but you must see the picture, Doctor," Mrs. Vavasour added. "It's lovely."

"The fact is…," Maundeville spoke in slow disconnected sentences while he painted, "…you have lit upon a terrible conspiracy. Look a little more downward please, Miss Hennessey!" Maundeville gave all his attention to the canvas, while I chatted to the old lady, or rather listened to her, and tried to unobtrusively observe Miss Hennessey.

She sat on a stool, one elbow on her knee, her chin on her hand. She wore a low-cut dress of green silk and bohemian make. A little pattern of shamrocks was on it in another shade of green. Emeralds were in her red hair and about her neck.

Placed as I was I could not see much of her face, but I saw the curves of cheek and chin, youthful neck and rounded arm, and I was reminded again of how very beautiful she was. I had known her to be good-looking, but this was something more. No wonder every young man associated with this affair was besotted to the point of bequeathing her his estate.

Meanwhile Maundeville was hard at work, sometimes talking a little to Miss Hennessey, often merely looking at her intently, putting in a touch here and there on the canvas, his mouth pursed in consideration, his quick eyes roving, sometimes discontentedly, sometimes with a look of satisfaction, from sitter to canvas and back again. Even in this room, with its big north lights, evening was now coming on. But he worked away, anxious, one supposed, to fix and finish some particular pose or expression.

He threw down his brush.

"I've done!" he said. "You can come down from your throne."

Miss Hennessey, stirred, slowly rose from her seat, and taking the hand Maundeville stretched out to her, stepped down onto the floor. She moved across to the tea-table, and held out her hand, greeting me in her forthright manner.

I repeated my apologies for having come in on them.

"But you're going to justify yourself," she said. "Professor Maundeville wants a critic." She half turned to Maundeville, who had dropped into a chair in front of the easel and sat looking at his work.

His mood seemed unusually serious, for him, and he neither spoke nor paid us any attention for some few minutes, but sat quite still, all his thoughts concentrated on what he had done. His head was silhouetted against some piece of white stuff that hung on the wall beyond him. His close-cut, thick gray hair didn't hide the fine shape of his head. His well-tanned face, rather prominent aquiline nose, and bold chin, stood out finely against the white background. Undoubtedly he was a modern scientific man, but sitting there he didn't give one that impression.

"Are you an artist?" I asked Miss Hennessey softly. "If so, there's a sitter for you in your turn."

She looked intently at him, but shook her head. "It's beyond me," she said. "What would you call the picture?"

The Fall of Kings, I thought. "I don't know," I said.

"Nor do I." Something in her voice made me turn to look at her as she moved toward Mrs. Vavasour.

Just after that Maundeville stirred, took a last long stare at his work, and then joined us.

"You may as well have a look," he said to me, and all of us moved across the room and stood in front of the picture. Maundeville lounged by the side of the easel, facing us, perhaps to judge by our faces what the verdict was.

I was certainly very much astonished by what he had done.

In the picture Miss Hennessey sat on the stool she had used on the throne, facing us directly, but with her eyes downcast. One hand half held a harp, the other hand fell at her side.

It was as though trouble had swept over her while she played, and left her stranded. In the background was nothing but a few shadowy faces—mere ghosts. The red hair was beautifully done, the loneliness and melancholy of the figure were wonderful, unearthly.

I couldn't help thinking Maundeville had a more sympathetic nature than I would have given him credit for to be able to create something so lovely.

"Well, what do you think about it?" he asked.

"I don't know. She looks…far from the land." I was not even sure what I meant by that, but it must have pleased him for he smiled upon me in the best possible humor, even though my opinion on the average picture isn't worth two pence.

As the two ladies were leaving the studio Mrs. Vavasour suddenly remembered that she had left her purse on the tea-table. I moved to get it, but was forestalled by Maundeville.

Halfway between the table and the doorway where the ladies waited, he startled us with an inarticulate cry. He jumped at the girl like a cat across the remaining space between him and the doorway, the force of his onset driving Miss Hennessey into the gallery outside. Directly he had struck against her he half stumbled, half threw himself sideways on the floor, and at the same moment a bust, which had stood above the doorway on a small bracket, fell with the bracket, grazing his shoulder, and smashed on the floor.

He lay for an instant, then rose, looking very white and shaken.

I went to him, but he waved me off.

"I'm all right. See if I've hurt her," he said to me. He dropped onto a settee close by the door, and put his head down between his hands.

Outside in the gallery Mrs. Vavasour, rather like a ruffled hen, was quite needlessly begging Miss Hennessey not to be frightened. The girl had been flung against the wall on the opposite side of the gallery, and was sitting on the floor half laughing.

The coils of her red hair had got loosened, and hung about her face.

"Are you hurt?" I asked.

"No," she said. "Will you give me a hand?"

I helped her to rise while Mrs. Vavasour chattered and fluttered about her, twisting her hair into order.

"Something fell, didn't it—and he saw it coming?" Miss Hennessey leaned against the wall and looked through the doorway at the debris on the studio floor. "Where's Professor Maundeville? Was he hurt?"

We found Maundeville sitting where I had left him. He rose with a laugh when he saw us, though he still looked extraordinarily pale.

"I have to thank you," the girl began, "I do, very heartily." She looked upward, and evidently realized then that the bust had fallen from a considerable height.

"It might have been pretty bad, I see," she said quietly. "I'm very much indebted to you, Professor Maundeville. I hope you're not badly hurt. Please sit down again!"

Maundeville sat down, but did his best to treat the whole matter lightly.

"If you're sure you forgive my way of speeding a parting guest," he said, with a whimsical smile, "I'll try to forgive myself. Oh yes, I'm all right—only frightened."

"You're not looking all right," Miss Hennessey persisted.

But Maundeville refused to answer seriously. "Without attempting to put a valuation on your imperiled brains," he said, "think of the damage to my reputation for hospitality!"

The girl studied him doubtfully, but Mrs. Vavasour now joined in.

"We must leave the professor to rest after his heroic effort, my dear." Adding with a certain stiffness, "You must remember you've had a very bad shaking too."

It was obvious the dear lady somehow thought the affair should have been more decorously managed. The girl and Maundeville exchanged amused looks.

"A very bad shaking, I'm afraid," Maundeville agreed. "I was shockingly rough. I can only plead inexperience!" We all laughed, even Mrs. Vavasour, though she did so with some uncertainty.

The ladies said good-bye again, and this time got clear off, and I with them. Maundeville saw them into their carriage. I left him on the curb, watching them away, and though he persisted that he was all right, he still looked very pale under his tan.

CHAPTER SEVENTEEN

MANY-SIDED MAUNDEVILLE

I went round the next morning to ask after Maundeville, and found him much the same as usual, trying some chemical tests for alkaloids in his museum. He was unwilling to say anything more about the accident of the previous evening.

"I've been busy this morning," he said, "and couldn't go out. But I sent Bates round with my card to inquire for Miss Hennessey. Mrs. Vavasour allows she is apparently none the worse for her fall. Indeed, they had intended to do me the honor of calling to ask after my welfare, but Bates told them I was engaged."

"He ought not to have let me in." I looked around for my hat, but Maundeville stopped me.

"This is mere mechanical work just now," he said. "Besides, you're different. With ladies one has to be more punctilious and less honest. They won't accept a divided attention, will they?"

I admitted I knew very little about women's vagaries.

"They're queer creatures," he said thoughtfully, examining his test-tube. "Even a woman as frank and straightforward as Miss Hennessey seems always to have something up her sleeve."

"I believe she's very much preoccupied with Woman's Suffrage. Perhaps it's her armband."

He grimaced. "That's the diversion of a wealthy unmarried girl." He returned to the subject of test-tubes and alkaloid, and talked of nothing else till I grew ready to leave. I was meeting a journalist friend of mine in the Strand.

"Perhaps I'll walk with you part of the way. I could use the fresh air. You'll call later to inquire for Miss Hennessey, I suppose?" he suggested.

"I didn't mean to. Why should I?" I asked.

"Why shouldn't you? You know that she had a shaking last evening."

"I knew at the time that she was none the worse," I said. "Besides, you've told me so just now."

Maundeville began to laugh. I was not sure if he was laughing at me or himself, but I suspected it was at me.

The morning was fine, and we walked away down Regent Street and turned into the Haymarket.

Although I was ready enough to have Maundeville's company, I hadn't much to say.

In recent weeks I had been forced, or at any rate tempted, into unhappy comparisons. First with Maxwell and Perceval—fellows much younger than myself—and now with Maundeville, who was probably a decade older. The latter comparison was frankly the most painful. Maundeville was learned, accomplished, witty, playful, and debonair. Everything I had once aspired to back when I was the age of Maxwell and Perceval.

Worse, he seemed younger, more vital, and more in step with the world than I. No. He seemed even a step *ahead* of the world.

I admired him, but I also envied him. I was under no illusions that I had made a great success of my life, but until I had come into contact with the Society of Osiris, I had not considered myself a failure. Now, comparing myself to Maundeville—and how could I fail to do so?—I felt humiliatingly aware of all I was not—and would never be.

"You're very quiet," Maundeville said suddenly. "Are you put out with me for some reason?"

"No. Put out with myself—" At which point I became truly put out with myself for I remembered that I ought to have had another document in the packet of papers I was carrying.

Since no conveyance was handy, we took a shortcut by back streets to my flat, Maundeville observing and commenting as we went, as was his wont.

He was just speaking of the grace of movement shown by a bare-legged girl of ten or so, who slipped ahead of us with her news-sheet and bundle of morning papers, when the child came to grief.

A fellow with a scarred and tattooed face, looking like a foreign sailor, lounged suddenly across her path. She ran straight into him and knocked a pipe out of his hand. It clattered and broke on the pavement. He stared at her for an instant, then struck her heavily on the side of the head.

She fell in the street with a scream, and I, being nearest the gutter, managed to drag her by her scanty skirts from the wheels of a passing lorry.

By the time I had straightened myself again the man was sprawling. Maundeville had knocked him off the pavement into the street, where he lay stretched for a few seconds as if stunned, and then raised himself on one elbow.

The fall of the child had stopped the near traffic, and the fellow was safe enough. He staggered to his feet an instant later. I saw his right hand go to his side, a woman shrieked from a window above our heads, and he ran in at Maundeville.

The child was still hanging a dead weight on my hands, and I could do nothing, but Maundeville seemed quite able to take care of himself.

Something in the fellow's right hand flashed toward Maundeville's throat, but he slipped to the left, at the same time striking the man's right arm with his own right. Twisting forward, he caught him at the back of the neck with his left hand, and his left leg with his right hand. He fell on one knee and seemed to toss the rascal forward.

There was a ferocious crash as the man's head slammed against a plate-glass shop-window, and then he lay still on the pavement.

At once there was a crowd, but Maundeville pushed quickly through it, reaching the child, who pushed out of my arms to stand upright.

"She's all right, isn't she?" he asked. "Here, child! Could you run if I gave you half a sovereign?"

The child looked up, considered an instant, then nodded, casting a glance about her.

"Here, then! Cut when you see your chance. Here's my card. Come to-morrow and let me see you're well."

"But—!" I began, reaching for her again.

The girl stooped and bit at the coin, and slipped free. I could not keep my hold. Someone stumbled against me, and the crowd was pushing and shouting all around. The child, a small eel of a thing, in any case, had disappeared altogether.

Maundeville's back was toward me, and presently I saw he was pushing to the shop doorway, where a policeman stood over the beaten man, who was now sitting up and staring stupidly about him.

"'E tried to knife the gentleman," cried a shrill voice in the crowd. "I seed 'im!"

"Nonsense, surely not," said Maundeville. "I think the lady's mistaken, Constable."

"I seed the sunlight on it."

"A bangle, I think," Maundeville suggested. "The fellow wears one."

The constable looked and found one, but wasn't quite satisfied. At this a second constable, who had come up, searched the lascar's clothes, and found nothing except a coin or two and some sort of an amulet.

"The fellow's sobered," Maundeville said, "and the child's more frightened than hurt. Why, where's she gone?" He looked about him, but naturally saw nothing of the girl. "Well, that shows she's none the worse, and I refuse to prosecute. I'll give the chap a lecture."

He spoke sharply to the lascar for a minute or so in a foreign tongue that the man quite evidently understood, for he answered humbly enough.

"Better let him go, I think," he ended. "Come along, Armiston. We shall be late."

He drew me away, and after a moment's consideration, the policeman let his man go.

Maundeville chatted blithely on, until we reached my rooms.

"You had better take a look at my shoulder," he said then, and I turned on him and had his cloak and coat off in a jiffy. There was a grazing wound over the insertion of the deltoid on the right arm, and the shirt and silk vest had stuck to it.

"Then there was a knife." I dealt with the wound briskly.

"The bangle had a sharp edge presumably," Maundeville suggested gravely, and then began to laugh. "It didn't occur to those muddle-heads to search me." He drew a long sheath-knife from an inner pocket and held it up for my inspection.

I gaped at him. "Why the devil would you conceal that?"

"We should have had to attend at the nearest police-station to-night, I suppose, and the police court to-morrow morning." He smiled. "We've neither of us time for that. Better give that scrape a good antiseptic scrub, I expect. No doubt the fellow has used that knife for everything from cleaning fish to cutting hashish. He reeked of both."

"You're mad, Maundeville. He might have split your belly open."

"Nonsense. My fur cloak saved me." He smiled ruefully. "It also made me devilish slow."

CHAPTER EIGHTEEN

I Am Invited to a Card Party

The next night Perceval wrote asking me to dine with him at Park Lane.

I refused. If I went, I knew Maxwell would be there, and I remained determined not to see him unless it could not be avoided.

Perceval's man, a haughty, pasty-faced individual, who brought the invitation, took back my refusal and thanks. He shortly returned with another note, in which Perceval wrote that it was very important he should see me, and begged me to make an appointment with him for any time after dinner that suited me, either at my flat or his house, as I pleased.

When I found that he really wanted me, I was rather disgusted with myself for having refused his invitation. However, having done so finally, I sent word that I would look him up at about nine. As my reward I had a shocking bad dinner alone at the club, and cursed the Mummy several times that evening though it could hardly be held accountable for my present grievance.

After all, what did that grievance really amount to? Bored with my own affairs, I had allowed myself to become overly interested in the affairs of others. And when those others had rebuffed me—however courteously—I had reacted like a hurt child.

Obviously I was becoming—had, in fact, become—a fine specimen of the crusty, curmudgeon bachelor.

As I walked to Park Lane I wondered whether a little real hardship or danger, instead of these petty grievances of mine, would not do me a world of good.

Well, I was soon to have plenty to occupy me.

Perceval was sitting alone in his dining-room, with fruit and decanters on the mahogany before him. He rose to welcome me, took me to a chair placed ready near his own, and thanked me very warmly for coming.

Really I liked the young fellow more and more, in spite of his affectations and over-formality.

"I think," he said at last, "that if you don't mind, we will have the decanters brought up to the smoking-room. Not only will there be less risk of eavesdroppers up there, but also I always fancy myself more reasonable nearer the stars. Nothing," he added, smiling, "seems to matter quite so much up there."

"Eavesdroppers?" I repeated the one thing that had really riveted my attention.

"One should never take discretion for granted."

True enough.

Accordingly, we mounted to the smoking-room, and it being late we found a few stars overhead, and a great many twinkling lights below.

Perceval poured us drinks, threw himself down on one of the divans, and explained abruptly why he had pressed for my company that evening.

"I feel I should warn you that to-morrow night we intend to have another deal of the cards. This gives you time to consider what position you intend to adopt." He leaned back in his chair, watching me curiously.

"I need no time," I said. "I shall insist upon being one of your card-party. Unless you intend to prevent me from joining it."

He made no reply to this announcement of mine for some time, but lay back in his chair staring out at the sky.

"No," he said at last, "we have no such intention. It's only fair to point out that neither Maxwell nor I believe that our bargain requires you to go so far."

"I suppose not," I said, after some consideration. "The terms of our bargain have always been rather vague. I'm doing as my conscience dictates."

"There's always satisfaction," Perceval said, smiling, "in finding that one's first impression of a man is correct. You will continue to be obstinate—I'm inclined to say pigheaded—even to your own disadvantage, and at a certain amount of risk?"

"Of course."

"I've no idea," Perceval went on gravely, "of trying to influence you in this matter one way or the other. You know as much about it now as I do—more, perhaps. But I want to remind you, before the cards are dealt, that you accepted our conditions—the conditions that bind us all. Whoever gets the Priestess accepts it without calling in outside help to avoid the consequences. Any public inquiry would inevitably end in Nora—my cousin's—name being dragged in."

"I understand. I've already agreed."

"It wouldn't matter if her part were known as it really is. There's nothing discreditable about that to any of us—and least of all to herself. But the mere truth wouldn't suit either the newspapers or their virtuous readers at all. Imagine the placards and the headlines for yourself. That view of the matter will never occur to her, so it's our business to protect her interests."

"You and Maxwell are in agreement on this." It was not really a question, but he answered at once.

"Of course."

"Meanwhile, you're running an equal if different risk," I persisted. "What if you get the Priestess? Maxwell seems to have some idea that he'll be next. Suppose it's you?"

"Has he?" Perceval looked surprised. "Well, he might be right. Or you might be right. Anyway, what I wished to tell you is I've decided to propose marriage to Nora in order that I might be better able to look after her. I believe Max intends to do the same."

This was an unpleasant jolt, though I suppose I should have expected it. "How on earth can you be sure? Has he told you so?"

Perceval looked at me with some amusement.

"Maxwell and I have known one another," he said, "from the time we fought together over our toy soldiers. He's closer to me than any brother could be. We don't need to tell one another everything. We'll both propose. Nora will likely refuse me, as she has refused me before—and a dozen or more other men. She will accept Maxwell—unless she thought that she put him in danger by doing so."

"What on earth do you mean by that?" I asked.

"How could she put him in danger?" asked Perceval in surprise.

"No. That she will accept his proposal of marriage."

"Oh." Perceval's smile was tinged with scorn. "Nora has almost a schoolgirl regard for Maxwell. All those adventures in sunny climes, you know."

"She must not marry him," I said. "That would be a great mistake."

Perceval's brows drew together. "What do you mean?"

I had spoken instinctively and said too much already. Maxwell was not my patient, but even so I could not reveal his tragic secret. Not that it could remain secret for much longer, if I knew anything of such cases. I shook my head.

The thing was a double disaster for not only was Maxwell unfit for marriage, there were two very decent men in love with and only too eager to marry Miss Hennessey, if she could only look past the heroic fantasy of Maxwell. Perceval was a charming and wealthy young man. Maundeville was equally charming and had already risked his life for the lady once and I had no doubt would be willing to risk it again.

Perceval continued to frown, but all he said was, "This is very ominous, Doctor. You alarm me. Is there something amiss with Maxwell? I know he's not been himself for some time."

"No, I expect not," I said.

When it was clear I would not continue, Perceval said, "Then we may assume you will be one of to-morrow's card-party? You won't change your mind? We won't think any the less of you."

"I won't change my mind," I said. "If I thought there was great risk to myself, perhaps I would keep clear. I don't know. But it's all rubbish. I'm coming to prove it. Tell the other men that they must admit me, or I'll somehow make it hot for everybody."

"Oh, I don't see why anyone else should object," Perceval said. "Max is the only one with the wind up. I'll see to it and let you know if there's any difficulty. Only remember! The same considerations that bind us must be binding on you. You must take your chance with the rest, and whatever happens you must keep it to yourself."

"I know. I agree."

It seemed there was no difficulty and no one did object, evidently. The next morning I received a note from Perceval stating the time at which the cards were to be dealt at Maundeville's house.

The matter was now settled. I was to be a guest at the deadly party.

CHAPTER NINETEEN

THE HIGH PRIESTESS

I hate the east wind.

An unhealthy, smoky exhalation, gusting up from the bowels of the city, rustling the ivy and knocking the flower boxes with a spectral hand. I could feel the east wind breathing down my neck the whole length of my walk to Maundeville's that evening.

I had to wonder at myself. Was I not tacitly lending support to this insane enterprise by attending this confounded Mummy meeting?

And yet, I could not talk myself out of going. Would not have considered it.

As it was fixed that those concerned should meet at five, and settle the matter without any elaboration or delay, I reached the house about a quarter before the hour, and spotted Perceval and Maxwell coming down the street together. I waited for them.

Maxwell greeted me courteously. He looked weary, as though his natural vitality had been somehow extinguished. I returned his greeting coolly. I was long past being angry over his rude comments at the Banyan, but I had faced some difficult truths and knew it would be easier for myself in the end if I maintained a complete and professional distance from him.

Perceval, dressed as usual point-device, in gray, had a very fine yellow orchid in his button hole. When I said something about the east wind and the vindictive hag about whom we had met, he refused to consider either, and begged me to give my attention to the orchid, as equally curious and far more beautiful.

The door was opened to us then.

Bates showed us into the little museum, where Maundeville was ready, with a young fellow to whom I had not spoken before, but whom I remembered seeing at my first meeting at the Society of Osiris.

He was tall, dark, thin, and looked decidedly consumptive. He spoke excitedly to Maundeville, but broke off abruptly at our coming, and crossed the room to very closely examine the mummy case, which stood in its usual position against the wall.

We chatted for a few minutes, and then Maundeville looked at his watch.

"Five minutes to the hour," he said, "and we agreed to be punctual. Who else is to come? Only Lethredge, I believe? Well, we must give him five minutes' grace, I suppose, but, I think, no more."

I said nothing, but the other three men agreed to this at once—even hurriedly, I thought.

A couple of minutes later Bates brought in a letter for Maundeville, who opened and glanced over it, then turned to Bates.

"Let the messenger wait," he said, and then, directly Bates had left the room, "Listen to this!"

Dear Maundeville,

I was schooling a polo pony this afternoon. He crossed his own legs and broke one of mine. I can't well join you. Put a chair for me and deal to that. Keep the messenger, and let me know by him whether I'm to have the honor of entertaining the Lady. It might break the monotony of my cure—or make it unnecessary!

Yours,
Guy Lewthredge.

"Well," he added, "I suppose we must do what he asks. What do the rest of you think?"

I gave no opinion, being quite ready to let the others settle as they chose. Maxwell nodded his consent. Perceval, considering his orchid, yawned slightly, apologizing for doing so, and said he imagined poor Lethredge to be within his rights. The other young fellow protested hotly, arguing that the meeting should be postponed until Lethredge could attend in person.

"Votes are against you," Maundeville said, and the young fellow stopped arguing to cough.

A pack of brightly colored cards lay on the table, and Maundeville took it up, and then went to the door with it in his hands. "I nearly forgot," he said, "a Frenchman is to bring me a letter of introduction some time this afternoon. I'll make sure that Bates keeps him."

He spoke to Bates at the door and came back.

By now we had seated ourselves round the table. I happened to be with my back to the Mummy.

Maundeville took a chair opposite to me, and next to him was an empty seat for the man Lethredge.

"Now," he said, briskly shuffling the cards as though it was any ordinary playing deck. "I'm going to speak plainly before I deal. I'm sick of this business. I'm ready to end it and declare all bets off if you fellows are. The joke has gone far enough."

Maxwell looked at him oddly and said nothing. But I understood him. He believed—as I did myself—that there was no stopping the thing at this juncture. Talk was useless.

Perceval concurred. "It has gone too far to stop."

The other, his name was Steyne, looked incensed. "I hope I've as much pluck as D'Aurelle and Scrymgeour. I'm going to see it through."

I said nothing in my role as looker on.

"I'm in your hands altogether," Maundeville said politely, "only I don't like it. Indeed, I protest against it. But if you choose, of course, I'm tied."

"Let's waste no more time, then," Maxwell said.

Maundeville shrugged. "Cut, please!" To my surprise, he pushed the deck across to me.

In answer to the surprised looks, he said, "Cards are queer things. I've dealt each time before. Let us ask Armiston to do it to-night for a change. I'm sure he won't refuse, will you Armiston?"

The rest turned toward me, no one speaking, and I hesitated. I had an intense objection to taking such an active part in a transaction which I thought altogether detestable. I was there with the hope of putting an eventual end to it, and I certainly did not wish to have a hand—literally—in bringing danger to any man there.

At the same time, this way I could be absolutely sure the deal was honest and aboveboard. I can't deny that when Maundeville had walked to the door holding the deck of cards it had crossed my mind that he had opportunity to tamper with the cards.

"Very well," I said, "I'll deal if I may do it in my own way. How do you do it, Maundeville?"

"I begin with the man on my left," Maundeville said. "I deal slowly, and each man is free to turn up his card if he chooses, directly he gets it. I don't suppose any one of us cares how it is done. You hold the Major Arcana. It contains only twenty-two cards."

"Only be quick about it," Maxwell said.

"Very well," I said, "I hope the holder of the card won't blame me. Don't touch them, please, till I've finished the pack." Beginning with Maundeville opposite me, I dealt next to the empty chair for Lethredge on Maundeville's left, and so round.

I dealt in a dead silence. The cards seemed to scrape off the desk with a sinister whisper as I placed them around the table.

A loud rattle behind my chair, where I knew the mummy case to be, caused me to jump and look over my shoulder.

Maxwell made a breath of sound too soft to be a laugh.

To my disgust, it was only Methuselah, the tortoise, blundering against the wooden case in the course of his wanderings. What had I imagined? The Mummy was opening her case to step out and join us for a game of cards? I muttered at my own silly nerves and went slowly on.

In those few seconds I noticed all sorts of trifles, all my senses seeming powerfully stimulated.

I heard young Steyne breathing quickly, I smelled Perceval's Turkish tobacco. I saw that Maundeville, leaning back in his chair, looked straight at me, drumming noiselessly on the table with his fingertips—and that Maxwell looked straight at him.

The cards dealt before the empty chair slid and scattered a little, though I never had heard falling cards sound so heavy before. Perceval had to draw his heap together to prevent them from getting mixed with those for Lethredge.

I was determined not to hurry, but I seemed to deal those twenty-two cards through all time. When the pack was ended I sighed, and watched while the men picked up their hands, wondering to which of them I had given the High Priestess.

"Trump!" murmured Perceval, and held up the High Priestess.

Maxwell started to speak, but stopped himself. He looked stunned.

Perceval began to settle the orchid more securely in his buttonhole, while the rest of us stared at him in silence.

It was he who spoke first, passing his cigarette case across the table to me. He asked Maundeville at the same time what hour on the following day would be convenient for handing over "the Lady" if he sent round his motor to fetch her.

"Send for the thing when it suits you," Maundeville said. "But to-day is Thursday, and I happen to remember you talked of spending the week-end in Hampshire. Now, as far as our wager is concerned, you keep strictly to its terms if you send on your return."

"That's very nice of you," Perceval said. "I meant to wire, telling my friends that an unexpected visitor prevented me from keeping my engagement. But I know they'd be annoyed. I think, do you know, Maundeville, that I'll accept your interpretation of our agreement, if you're sure it doesn't inconvenience you—and the Lady doesn't object."

The Lady made no demurral.

So it was arranged that he should send for the Mummy on the following Tuesday, and Maundeville suggested a move out of the museum into the dining-room, where he said there was tea for anyone who cared to have some.

Meanwhile Maxwell had been sitting quiet, saying nothing since Perceval had shown the High Priestess. He was frowning at the little stack of cards before him. As far as his face expressed anything, it seemed to show bewilderment.

Why had he been so sure the High Priestess card would fall to him?

As for myself, I felt guilty and unhappy that I had dealt the card to Perceval, but did not know how to express my regret.

Perceval was the first to pass through the double doors which ensured quiet for Maundeville in the museum. Steyne followed him, talking querulously in a high-pitched voice about his terrible luck. Maxwell followed—and I followed Maxwell.

CHAPTER TWENTY

MAXWELL IS SURPRISED

Maundeville pushed a chair up without another word and began to fumble with the kettle of boiling water and the tea-caddy. It was quite obvious that his mind was elsewhere. I counted eight spoonfuls of tea going into that teapot, and then I just put a hand out and moved the tea-caddy. I wanted a cup myself, and I didn't want my nerves jangled more than they had been.

My action roused our host. He looked at me, blinked, and paid more attention.

Perceval made a casual remark or two to me, and then softly, "I shall be back in town on Monday night. Can you come and give me a thorough overhauling?"

"Why?" I asked. "Do you feel ill?"

"I feel all right," he said. "My point is that I want you to certify me as sound before I take in this blessed Mummy—or else to know definitely what other cause might account for any trouble after she comes."

This seemed a wise precaution, and I agreed to it. "Fix your own time," I added, and he smiled whimsically at me.

"Dinner at eight," he said. "You wouldn't come two nights ago, but this is a professional engagement. Besides, you can hardly refuse me any reasonable request just now. I might accuse you of being responsible for my position."

He meant it as a joke, but it stung all the same. "I did what I thought best," I said. "I wanted to be quite sure that pure chance decided the matter. I didn't like the job."

Perceval laughed outright.

"You surely don't think I'm such a fool as to hold you responsible?" He was grinning. "I know why you agreed to deal. You've always looked with suspicion on the whole lot of us. Now I suppose you'll allow that I, at any rate, am not a criminal."

After we had our tea we said good-bye to Maundeville, and the three of us, Maxwell, Perceval, and I walked toward my place together.

All at once Maxwell stopped and looked across the street.

"I'm going through the park," he said abruptly. "Look me up directly you come back from Hampshire, Percy."

Perceval stared. "What's got into you?"

"Nothing. I want to think."

"Since when can't you do so in my company? If you know something, speak up."

Maxwell shook his head. "It's clear I know nothing. I would have been ready to lay odds that I knew the man who would get that card."

"Thank you for the compliment!" I retorted. "If you thought you knew, I suppose you were sure *I* did."

"Sounds like that, doesn't it?" Maxwell allowed quietly. "I ought to have considered before I spoke. I was wrong, anyway, you see. Good-bye, both of you. Mind you keep fit, Percy." He crossed the street.

Perceval watched him go, and then turned to me.

"Don't think too badly of Max," he said gravely. "He doesn't believe for a moment any of this is your fault." He made a dismissive noise. "Ready to give odds that he knew who would get the Priestess, was he!"

I gave Perceval a sideways look. "If that's true, it suggests that Maxwell believes human intelligence lies behind these deaths."

"That's a very big if, Doctor. Even if Max did believe such a thing, it doesn't mean it's true. We all know whoever receives the High Priestess card can expect the same fate as poor old S. and young D'Aurelle. The only variable would be the order in which that fate befalls us, wouldn't you say?"

Remembering Maxwell's comments at the Banyan, I said, "I don't suppose there would be any purpose—motive—in one of you eliminating the others?"

He chuckled. "You mean have we perhaps made wills leaving each other our fortunes?"

I felt foolish at his evident amusement, but persisted. "Have you?"

"No. Well."

"Well?"

"I've no idea what arrangements Maxwell may have made. His situation is complicated. Maundeville lost the financing for his next expedition with D'Aurelle. That was a great blow to him."

I tried to approach from another angle. "Miss Hennessey is a rich young woman, I suppose?"

Perceval burst out laughing. "Now I understand. Maxwell shared his dark suspicions of my dear cousin with you, I take it? Let me set your mind at ease. Miss Hennessey is a very wealthy young woman. She doesn't require Scrymgeour's fortune or D'Aurelle's. In fact, D'Aurelle had no real fortune to speak of as he had not yet received his inheritance."

"Ah. True."

Perceval was still chuckling at the idea of Miss Hennessey as a murderess.

"After all," I said, "the curse does state that Nefertiabet will find Justice through a woman."

"Yes, but I didn't take it to mean she'd bring in reinforcements. She seems well able to manage the thing on her own."

We left it there, Perceval still amused but trying belatedly to hide it for fear of offending me further. I remained more perplexed than offended. I could not bring myself to believe some supernatural agency was arranging for these young men to meet their deaths, and yet it didn't seem reasonable or logical that a human agency should be behind it.

Perceval reminded me I had promised to dine with him on Monday night, and we parted ways.

I stayed in my flat that evening, in spite of the workmen's half completed jobs and the demoniacal coffee-mill. Bird had the night off and had gone with Seymour to seek boisterous—or more likely bawdy—entertainment.

They were not gone five minutes before someone rapped on the outer door. I rose to see who was calling at this hour and silently vowing if it was anything less than life or death, I'd send them directly to young Doctor Leyton down the street.

It was not a matter of life or death. It was not a patient at all. Maxwell waited in the greenish light. Or perhaps that was the color of his face. He looked rather…peaked.

"Sorry," he began, but then seemed to run out of conversation.

"This is unexpected," I said, which was not much better an effort.

"May I speak to you for a moment?"

Considering how buoyantly he and Perceval had sailed in and out of my quarters previously, I was a little surprised by this diffidence.

I nodded, stepping aside. I followed Maxwell as he limped through the lobby.

"There's a fire in the sitting-room," I said. And then, reluctantly, "Would you like a drink?"

"No. Thank you."

We entered the sitting room and he came to a halt, standing beside the leather sofa. His expression was troubled. "Armiston… I feel I must—ought to—explain myself. Especially after this evening."

I sighed. He was so…correct. He made me feel both geriatric and unfair. "It's all right. I don't really think you were accusing me of stacking the deck against Perceval."

If anything, he lost color. "I know perfectly well you only became involved in this matter because Percy and I dragged you into it."

"I know that you know. Now do sit down. It's ridiculous for us to stand here as though we're waiting for our seconds to arrive."

He didn't smile. Didn't move. "The things you said at the Banyan were quite true. I did believe the High Priestess would come to me this time. I did believe you would try somehow to interfere. Because I did believe you…" His eyes seemed dark and troubled as they met my own.

"Cared for you?" I suggested gently.

I watched the color rise in his face. He did not look away. "Yes."

"Well then?"

"You're wrong though as to the reason for my concern. I'm not—I didn't—whatever you may think, I wasn't—"

I honestly had no idea what to make of that confused rush of words. It only then occurred to me that what I had always assumed to be taciturnity was in fact largely…shyness.

That opinion was instantly revised, however, when—words having failed him—Maxwell crossed the space between us and his hard mouth came down on mine, pressing fiercely against my parted lips.

I say parted, but in truth I was gaping at him.

His free arm circled my back, pulling me tight, and a strange sensation came over me. Though I was the larger man, I felt as though my limbs were melting against his muscular legs and thighs, the hard bulge of his body imprinted against my own with a shocking, unfamiliar intimacy. My cock answered in a painful surge against the restriction of my trousers.

This was the thing I had longed for my entire life and never known until now. It was exciting and terrifying at the same time. My vision dimmed, the blood drummed in my ears, and I forgot that I was standing in my own sitting-room, forgot about the coffee-mill grinding away beneath our feet, knew only this strong, passionate young man taking my mouth with wet, hungry kisses that made my knees shake and my heart clamor.

His lips moved from mine to my jaw, nuzzled beneath my ear, which sent a jolt of electricity zinging straight to my cock. He lingered for a moment, then trailed those moist, plush kisses down my throat. I groaned helplessly at the weird, wonderful feelings sparked by this erotic exploration. I couldn't believe what was happening to me.

At the same time I hoped it would never end. I felt quite desperate for what would happen next.

Maxwell's mouth roamed hungrily over the hollow of my throat, the pulse beating madly at the base of my neck, and then back to my gasping mouth. His tongue pushed against mine, and I opened to him instinctively. He sucked at me, our saliva mingling as he stole my breath away. His body strained against mine, and I could feel he was shaking too.

And then it was over. Just like that, I was free, staggering a little as he released me, steadying himself on his cane.

"So you see how it is, Quentin," he said, sounding a little out of breath himself.

It was perhaps the most puzzling thing he had said or done all night.

"I..."

As though his point had been made with an inarguable finality, this strange boy turned and limped from my rooms. I stepped back against the edge of the sofa and sat down, hard. I heard the thump of his cane all the way down the stairs until the sound faded into the night.

CHAPTER TWENTY ONE

PERCEVAL IS PHILOSOPHICAL

On Sunday morning I visited a friend of mine, who had a couple of surgical wards in one of the London hospitals. There was a case he wanted to show me.

We were touring the Male Ward when I recognized the tattooed face of one of the patients huddled beneath the rough gray blankets—the lascar whom Maundeville had upset so scientifically near the Haymarket.

"What's wrong with that chap?" I asked Sparratt, nodding toward the fellow's bed.

"Nothing but a very bad shake and a fracture of the surgical neck of the humerus," Sparratt said. "For a day or two I thought there might be a fracture at the base of the skull. The ruffian must have got a most awful wallop. He'll have been under the influence of bhang or some other of their concoctions at the time. I daresay it lessened the shock, but it obscured symptoms."

"How does he account for his condition?" I asked.

"He doesn't. He can't, or won't."

"I know someone who might be able to help you." I was thinking the story of Maundeville's trouncing of the ruffian would make a good yarn to give Sparratt over one of his Cubans presently.

"He'll have to be better than the brightest man I know," Sparratt retorted.

"And who may he be?"

"His name's Maundeville." Sparratt was moving across the ward to the lascar's bed. "I don't suppose you've met him, but he has the gift of tongues. He tried to talk to the chap the other night for me. Couldn't make heads or tails of his gibberish."

This certainly took me aback. "What happened?" I asked finally.

Sparratt was grimly amused. "I think Maundeville's attempts to communicate scared the fellow, to be honest." Sparratt looked at the shoulder-splint while he talked. "Still, it was worth a try."

An initially amusing situation now seemed quite different. I was tempted to explain the case to Sparratt, but decided against it.

Sparratt finished with his patient who showed no sign of recognizing me, and led the way back to the balcony, where we talked of other things.

On Monday evening I dined at Park Lane with Perceval, and later I overhauled him thoroughly, as he had wished—as thoroughly, in fact, as though I were acting for an insurance company with which he wanted to insure heavily. I found nothing wrong with him that I considered of any serious importance.

He pronounced himself in agreement with me, though mentioned that as a boy he had been troubled a good deal with asthma. The attacks were now only occasional, and ordinary stramonium cigarettes always relieved them.

I don't recollect that anything else of real importance was said or done that evening. Perceval, who seemed altogether at his ease, got me to witness his signature of three documents, which I did, together with his butler.

I cannot say that I myself was so unconcerned. I referred to the Mummy more than once. I remember asking him to believe that I had sincerely been doing what I thought best for our investigations when I agreed to deal the cards, and told him how much I regretted that the High Priestess card had fallen to him.

By this you may deduce that I'd had more than usual to drink that evening.

Perceval listened patiently, blowing rings of smoke across the room while I talked. We had gone after dinner to the queerly decorated smoking-room at the top of the house, and we were facing a gorgeous sunset, which Perceval pronounced more worthy of our attention than the Mummy.

"My dear Armiston," he said at last, leisurely stroking Bhanavar the Beautiful. "I'm about to run the risk of boring you with references to my affairs and my sentiments, so forgive me. All that I intended to ask this evening was a medical examination, and that's done."

"I'm here to listen to anything you choose to tell me," I told him. I felt this keenly. I had grown quite fond of Perceval over the past weeks. Perceval and Maxwell. In some ways they seemed inseparable.

He thanked me formally, but lay back in his long chair petting the cat for some moments before he said more.

"Understand," he said at last, "that I recognize my personal feelings and opinions to be of no importance except to myself. I do not often, I trust, inflict them on anyone. Just now, however, I believe you may be glad to hear them.

"First of all, with reference to your having dealt me the High Priestess. I said before and I repeat emphatically that I understand your motive in agreeing to deal. I approved of it then and I approve of it now.

"Just now it seems advisable to speak quite plainly. To be frank, I've no great liking for life as I find it. This is a matter of personal taste, personal idiosyncrasy, personal losses, and some disappointments. I don't say that life is unendurable, but I feel no terror at the prospect of quitting it."

I must have looked the genuine shock I felt for he paused, picking his words with care.

"Circumstances for which it would be ridiculous to blame anyone," he went on, "have prevented my life from being truly happy for several years. For a time I believed that matters might arrange themselves—but no. I was mistaken. Life, therefore, while quite endurable, as I have said, isn't a thing I cling to at all. I'm ready to drop it—just as I drop this cigarette, which isn't drawing properly."

His manner was so quiet and composed that I was at a loss for how to respond.

"This attitude does you no credit," I said, and even I couldn't help feeling as rebuttals went, it was pretty lame.

Perceval smiled at me, with no sign of irritation.

"Naturally you see it that way. Being in the business of keeping others alive, the man of medicine is bound to value life extravagantly. One can't depreciate the value of the commodity one deals in."

"That's because it's a precious commodity. It can't be restored or replaced," I pointed out.

His eyes sparkled with amusement. "Ah! Who assures you of that? You're speaking from theory not practice, aren't you?"

"Well, but—but—"

"I'm going to try another cigarette from a different box." Which he accordingly did, and, having lit it and satisfied himself that it drew satisfactorily, he looked at me again with a somewhat whimsical smile.

"In some ways you're a very conservative fellow, Armiston. But I think that can be put down to your profession, not your nature. Anyway, if things go wrong with me, from a medical point of view, while the Mummy is here, remember what I've told you. Waste no time in grieving about me, or in blaming yourself. Each death must logically make the problem easier to solve."

I nodded, silently staring at the walls with their mysterious and obscure suggestions. I did not like what I was hearing. And the more reasonable he was, the less I liked it.

"It seems to me you've more cause than most men to think life worth living," I commented at last. "I don't understand why you should be anxious to quit it. We all think ourselves sick of things at times, but we don't give in, and soon we change our opinion about it."

"Try a canter before breakfast, and a tonic?" he suggested. "Against the Mummy? Come now. Let us suppose that I'm the spoilt child who can't get the moon and won't look at anything else."

I was afraid I knew only too well what he meant, and I had no comfort for him. Or myself.

He said after a time, "But listen, Armiston, do me the favor of assuming that I mean precisely what I say—and no more. I didn't say I was anxious to quit life. I'm not more sick of things in general than I've told you. If I come to 'grief' in the next fortnight, don't let anything persuade you that I've been fool enough to settle matters for myself. I can't imagine any conditions under which I should commit suicide. I'm certainly not going to do it out of pique."

"When we last talked the matter of the Mummy over, you had no theory. Or at any rate you gave none. Have you any now?"

"Not really," he admitted. "I remain unconvinced that any supernatural agency is at work, but at the same time, I can't come up with any convincing motive for a human agent to target the members of the society. If any idea occurs to me that's really reasonable, I'll let you know at once." He smiled with surprising warmth, even affection. "Now let's drop the subject!"

CHAPTER TWENTY TWO

PERCEVAL ENTERTAINS THE MUMMY

I left Perceval blowing smoke rings and gazing at the stars.

He had told Maxwell that I was going to overhaul him, and Maxwell had asked me privately to let him hear the result, so I went straight to Maxwell's quarters, to tell him of my chat with Perceval while it was fresh in my mind.

That's what I told myself anyway, but the truth was I was longing to see Maxwell again after the bewildering encounter in my rooms. My feelings for him were foolish, of course, even self-destructive, for there could be no happy or healthy outcome to my attachment.

I was not pleased to find Maundeville with him, and Maxwell didn't appear overly delighted either. The professor was arguing hotly against any further experiments with the Mummy. After I arrived, he went on with his argument, calling on me to back him up.

I said little, for I honestly felt that, fantastic as the notion had been, and in very dubious taste, it couldn't decently be dropped at its present stage.

This was precisely Maxwell's argument. As a matter of fact, he didn't argue. He merely stated his opinion, and listened with weary patience while Maundeville made sarcastic comments on people who knew they were in the wrong, but were too pig-headed to acknowledge it.

"I'm not going to back out just now," he said, when Maundeville finally stopped. "And it isn't simply that it doesn't square with my notion of playing the game, as you suggest. Two men have died."

"That's my point!" Maundeville cried.

"Besides, how do we know that we *can* stop it. If this curse is real, it doesn't require a deck of cards to deliver its justice. Didn't you tell us that the man who opened the tomb with you died soon afterward?"

"Yes," Maundeville said reluctantly.

"Well then? If Nefertiabet is determined to do her worst, we'll have to find another way to stop her."

"The infernal thing goes to Perceval to-morrow!"

Maxwell's face darkened. "Do you think I don't know that? For Percy's sake, I should be glad enough to cry quits. But he won't hear of it, and I happen to agree with his reasoning. Our notions don't bind you, though, Maundeville."

"What does that mean?"

"Only that if I thought as you do, I suppose I should chuck it at once. Why should you go on? Indeed, honestly, I believe it would be safer for you to stop."

He said this with some emphasis. Maundeville noticed it, bridling.

"I may not be a young man, but I'm not lacking in courage."

Maxwell gave a funny smile. "No. But then you don't appear to be running the same risk as the rest of us."

"But that's my very point. I'm arguing for an end to our bets, for the reason it seems plain that I don't run the risk falling to the rest of you. I've reminded you before that the Mummy has been with me for weeks, yet I'm none the worse. I can speak plainly because of that."

"Your certainty on that score seems a little puzzling." Maxwell's gaze was hard and unsmiling.

For the first time Maundeville seemed to grasp what was being implied.

He paled a little. "Very well, my dear boy! That closes my mouth." He glanced at me. "Armiston is witness that I've done what I could to stop the Mummy's visits." He lit another cigar and puffed away in agitation.

I was a little surprised when Maxwell ignored this display of injured feelings. "What do you think of Perceval?" he asked me. "He's fit enough, isn't he? He won't mind your telling us."

"Oh, he's fit enough," I said.

"Healthy as a horse," Maundeville said. "Always has been." He corrected himself. "He had a mild case of asthma as a boy. I believe he still uses those confounded stramonium cigarettes."

"What's your objection to the cigarettes?" I asked.

"He smokes strong ones, and I think the quality varies."

That was a reasonable observation.

I wanted to stay but Maxwell said awkwardly that he had another appointment, so Maundeville and I left together.

Maundeville refused to talk of the Mummy as we walked, saying he was altogether sick of the subject. He thought he would cremate the thing, he told me, so that no more foolery could be possible with it.

I did not bother to point out that he had said the same thing weeks earlier and still showed no sign of getting around to striking the fatal match.

"Do it," I said.

He stared at me in astonishment.

"Yes. I'm quite sober. I think you should torch the thing. I'll be glad to help you."

Maundeville began to splutter. "That's hardly the scientific view, Armiston. The Mummy is a valuable artifact, after all. I have no real right to destroy a valuable piece of history."

"Not even to save the life of a friend?"

He stared at me. "You can't be serious! You, a man of science."

"I'm also a man of medicine. It may be that the power of suggestion is mostly to blame here. The High Priestess serves as a focal point of superstition and fear, and the natural biological weaknesses we all possess do the rest. D'Aurelle's heart-failure is a perfect example. The weakness was already there. His anxiety—"

"What utter nonsense! I can't believe what I'm hearing." Maundeville seemed genuinely appalled, and left me without further discussion.

The days went by and, to my great relief, Perceval seemed perfectly all right.

Disappointingly, I saw nothing of Maxwell, but Miss Hennessey came often, openly anxious about the results of the Mummy's stay with her cousin.

She gave no reason for making me her confidant, but begged me to keep her informed about him, and arranged to call daily for my report. I couldn't help noticing that she always asked after Captain Maxwell as well.

Of course I did the same with her—and was forced to conclude neither of us saw much of Maxwell these days.

On the days I could not report in person, there was to be a note left with Bird for her. But somehow on most mornings I managed to be in at half-past ten. Bird, who fancies himself a regular ladies' man, gave things an extra polish. I know he ran up a pretty bill in my name for cut flowers, and he stuck a flaming Japanese sunshade in my grate, without asking whether I liked it.

I grumbled to Miss Hennessey about it, telling her I was sure she was the cause, and straightway she took the first chance of praising the blessed thing before Bird. It was the only time I ever saw Bird blush.

He seemed to think that on the occasions of her calls there must be no possibility of interruption, which only goes to prove that no man can ever truly know another. For all the years Bird had been with me, he failed to understand one of the most basic things about me.

Or perhaps he did understand, but believed Miss Hennessey offered a solution.

If so, he was not the first to come to this conclusion. In the days since I'd dined with Perceval I had come to believe he too had considered Miss Hennessey a solution. Miss Hennessey clearly had other ideas.

And continued to have them.

Maundeville came once while she was there, and I found afterward that Bird had declared I was "not at home," and had stuck to it in spite of some argument on Maundeville's part.

Maundeville laughed heartily telling me the story, but I know how easily rumors can be started. I let him know the real purpose of her visits.

"Ah! I had no inkling she was so interested," he remarked.

"Naturally. Perceval's a cousin," I reminded him.

"Of course. A third cousin, I believe. Well, that should console him, eh, what? I know he's fond of her too."

"I suppose so." I didn't see the point of romanticizing their attachment for I knew she'd already turned him down. More than once.

"Now, now. Youth cleaves to youth. Hardened bachelors like you and me would only find young women inquiring about our health a nuisance. Isn't that so? Well, we must look after Perceval, if only for her sake."

"We're trying to do so—aren't we?" I asked him.

"I can't say I've done much," he admitted. "Maxwell put my back up with his insinuations. Though what he was insinuating I've no idea. No, the fact is I've had one of my fits of incredulity. At times I've forgotten about our bugbear altogether. Then I've remembered it only to laugh."

"I can't find it a source of humor."

He pulled a face. "No, and I suppose the thing must be getting on Perceval's nerves. I'm sure he wants cheering up, and I'm ready to help. Let's take it in hand, you and I. Turn and turn about."

"If he needs cheering up, I'm willing to try, though I hadn't noticed anything dismal about him."

"You haven't known him as long as I have," Maundeville reminded me. "He doesn't moan or whimper, but he's getting hipped most infernally. We'll take him in hand, you and I. Maxwell too. The three of us in turn."

He had seated himself comfortably in my favorite easy-chair, and while he talked his very keen blue gaze roved all about the room. I've never seen eyes with more life and energy in them than Maundeville's. He considered the copy of *The Opium Habit* by Horace B. Day lying on the table next to Bird's floral decorations—roses, that morning—that made the room sweet.

"How is Captain Maxwell?" I asked, for I had not seen him since the evening he had lied about having another appointment.

"As well as can be expected." He met my eyes and shrugged. "Come, Armiston, we both know Maxwell's secret. Though I don't suppose it can remain a secret for much longer."

He was perfectly correct, but to discuss Maxwell's tragedy, even with Maundeville, felt like disloyalty. I said instead, "How did he come to join the Blues? He doesn't strike me as of a militaristic nature."

"No." Maundeville's tone was pure acid. "He was a good-tempered, even a sweet-natured boy with a fine intellect and a lively imagination. There is some peculiarity with his inheritance, and it was at the behest of his uncle that he became a soldier. He did well enough until he was nearly blown to kingdom come."

It was too painful to think that Maxwell's sacrifice had been for nothing. I said, "Well, the world needs soldiers as well as scholars."

"I can't agree with you there. In fact, it's a contradictory attitude for a doctor, if you don't mind my saying so. If there were no soldiers, there would be no need for war."

It was the first genuinely silly thing I'd heard Maundeville say.

"And if there were no doctors, there would be no need for disease," I retorted, and returned abruptly to the original subject. "As for the three of us taking Perceval in hand systematically, that will need a lot of tact, or he'll turn restive. I don't believe Perceval will stand having three nurses."

"You think because I comment on Maxwell's decline that my tact isn't to be depended on? Well, perhaps you've some excuse. But think my suggestion over!"

Maundeville left before I had framed a satisfactory reply. I heard him complimenting Bird on his roses at the outer door.

After this we did manage somehow that one or other of the three should look in on Perceval, or get him out, pretty well daily.

In reply to my occasional questions, Perceval told me that the neighborhood of the Mummy did not trouble him in any way, day or night, except that his valet took a dislike to the thing and left suddenly.

"Said he could hear her whispering at night," he informed me.

"Whispering!"

I thought I detected a mischievous sparkle in his eye, but he said with apparent seriousness, "Yes. In her box. He swore he could hear her."

"What was she saying?"

At that Perceval laughed openly. "Always the pragmatist! She spoke in Egyptian, though how he knew that, never having been to Egypt! But I imagine something along the lines of *get me out of here*!"

When he could treat the matter so lightly, it seemed ridiculous for the rest of us to stand in the wings shaking our heads like a Greek chorus. Still, to have a definite arrangement about him with Maxwell and Maundeville suited me very well just then. An old friend of mine had been invalided home from India and was dying at Bath. I could do no more for him than any other practitioner; but he liked to see me and to yarn over old times. I used to go down once a week or thereabouts and stay a night—sometimes a week-end.

After I missed a visit to Bath the first week that Perceval had the Mummy, I got a rather reproachful message from my old friend. Accordingly I arranged to go down two days later for the week-end.

CHAPTER TWENTY THREE

WHAT HAPPENED TO PERCEVAL

As luck would have it, when arranging my visit to Bath, I'd forgotten that Maundeville had spoken of going to Paris for some conference of Egyptologists. When I did remember I went to Maxwell's rooms to suggest that he should keep an eye on Perceval while Maundeville and I were away.

I had seen almost nothing of him during the week Perceval played host to the Mummy. I knew this was no accident, and I respected his feelings on the matter—as far as I understood them. It was difficult, though. Those few kisses had given me a taste of what I had longed for since boyhood—and all but given up on.

At the same time, I understood only too well how difficult the thing was—how perilous to even contemplate.

And yet I couldn't *help* contemplating it.

It was raining when I reached Maxwell's. His man showed me into the sitting-room. I was too restless, too nervous, to sit still, so I wandered about, studying each and every object as though it offered insight into the heart and mind of Hilary Maxwell.

The room, which smelled of leather and good tobacco and the fireplace, was comfortably furnished and its shelves attractively crowded with books, sporting trophies, and other signs of his usual occupations. I pulled out a volume here and there, and discovered a hodgepodge of interests: the dialogues of Plato (to be expected), works on fencing, on cavalry training, on Egyptology, on medicine, on Persian verse. A book titled *The Beetle* by Richard Marsh caught my attention, but this turned out to be a novel.

The dark, solemn eyes of the sable antelope and tahr heads mounted on the wall seemed to follow me as I prowled the room. I had the uncomfortable feeling they knew something I should but did not.

The rain rattled against the window. Fat drops fell and flattened against the glass in pinpricks of unceasing sounds. The reflection of the flames of the fireplace danced on one side, and on the other the green slats of the shutters glittered and shone.

Maxwell did not come.

I moved from the window to the table strewn with feathers, silks, hooks, gold tinsel, scissors and other paraphernalia. He seemed to have been mid-fly-tying before my arrival.

My unease grew. Several more long minutes were ticked out by the clock over the mantel, but still Maxwell did not appear.

Finally he entered the room wearing a dark green dressing gown over his trousers. He was limping more heavily than usual and looked like a stranger. Dark circles surrounded his red eyes and he looked disheveled. Face pale and lined, hair too long and sticking up in tufts as though he had been clutching his head.

"Hullo, Armiston," he said too brightly. "You've been a stranger!"

This alone was so alarmingly out of character that it took me a moment to find the wits to reply.

"What's happened?" I said.

He didn't seem to hear me. Instead, he invited me to sit and, as if too tired to stand, pulled out a chair at the littered table and sat down heavily. His stick fell to the floor and I don't think he even noticed.

I began to tell him of my week-end engagement, and he listened and considered, saying nothing. He was trying to finish off a black gnat, but his long fingers worked slowly and with alarming clumsiness. Eventually he gave up and set the fly aside, leaning forward as though too tired to stay erect.

"I must think what I can do," he said at last. "Yes. I must think."

"It shouldn't be a challenge," I said—I'm afraid—acerbically. "You've only to make sure you check on Perceval while Maundeville and I are out of town."

He frowned. "Yes, but thanks to Maundeville, I've had leave to fish some of the best water on the Test, and I've made all my arrangements. Of course, it would be simple enough to drop it."

"Well?"

"Well." He looked up at me stupidly.

I felt a mix of impatience and pity gazing into his handsome but vacuous face.

"Will you not cancel your fishing trip?" I prompted.

He seemed confused. "Oh. But the fact is that I was particularly keen about going, and I've been telling Percy of it. If he finds me in town, he'll want to know the reason, and he won't be easily humbugged. He is getting restless about our supervision. Accused me of spying on him."

"What? When?"

"I…the last time I saw him."

"Which was when?"

He frowned as though this was an especially difficult question and rubbed his face. "This Mummy is on all our nerves."

"Now there you demonstrate a faculty for observing the patent."

He took no offense, and that in itself was alarming for I was deliberately—well, could not help at any rate—being quite rude.

"It would be easier if I had the High Priestess myself," he said.

"I doubt you'd be a match for her in your present condition. Why did you think the Mummy would come to you at Maundeville's?"

Another of those helpless looks.

He said earnestly, as though I had asked an entirely different question, "I fancied perhaps a couple of days' fishing would put me right."

"No," I said.

He blinked at me, heavy-eyed. "No?"

"It will take more than a couple days' fishing to put you right, and you know it as well as I do."

He opened and closed his mouth like one of the landed fish on this proposed trip of Maundeville's.

"I know your complaint, my boy," I said. "You're an addict." I rose and took his arm, easily overpowering his feeble attempt at resistance. I shoved back the silk sleeve, revealing the horror of his needle-scarred forearm. Maxwell stared down too, catching his breath as though the sight were a surprise.

I reached for his other arm.

"No," he muttered, and tried to fight me, but he had no strength. Despite the outline of muscle there was no power, no purpose to these limbs.

I stared down at the terrible tattoo of puncture marks. Groupings like black and lavender beads sewn into his skin. His legs, thighs and abdomen would tell the same story. Map lines leading straight to destruction of mind, body, spirit. This was a journey traveled over years, not the months I had hoped.

"An opium eater," I said wearily. The disgust was not for him, but rather for the poison that could destroy even the finest of men.

All the same Maxwell pulled his arms to his face—a desperate struggle to smother, to hold in, but there was no holding back that silent seizure of grief as he began to weep. I couldn't see his face behind the scarred barrier of his arms, but the broken sounds that tore through were like keening.

Too painful to listen to. Too painful to watch.

I gripped his shoulder. "Don't," I said. "Hilary, don't."

A stupid thing to say because what would one cry for if not a calamity such as this?

He bent over the table, burying his face in his arms. "Yes," he choked out. "An addict. A hopeless addict. I've tried to fight it. Again and again. You don't know. You can't know. There's no breaking free. Each time it comes back stronger than before."

None of this came as a surprise to me, yet I felt as though I had been punched, struck in the heart.

"You can't fight it on your own." I pulled up a chair, sat down next to him, tried to put an arm around him. He resisted, shaking his head, turning his back to me. "Let me help you. I'm not a specialist, but I do know something of this and I've been reading up on it."

"No one can help." His voice was thick and muffled. "I tell you I've *tried*. I can't go a week without it. I can't go two days without it. I did try."

I did try. I tell you this broke my heart. Even if I had been inclined to condemn, that would have disarmed me completely.

"Of course you did. You must have help with this. No one can win a war on his own. You must have allies, weapons, reinforcements."

He shook his head.

"Yes. Believe me. Your case is not hopeless." I didn't know if it was. I didn't care. I couldn't bear for him to be in despair.

"I'm glad you know. I'm glad it's over."

"It's not over."

He sat up, wiped his face, turned to me. His nose and eyes were red, his eyelashes spiky and wet. Yet all at once he seemed oddly calm, even dignified.

"After I met you, I thought perhaps this time I would have the strength. But I don't."

Instead of reassuring me, his sudden, absolute calm alarmed me.

I said, "Listen to me. I've been studying this disease. And it *is* a disease. This is no weakness of character, no lack of moral fiber. You have a disease. And I truly believe it's possible to break free of the drug. I don't say that it's easy, but it can be done. I've read of many cases where with the right care—nourishing food, rest, baths, and vigilant, tender nursing—even men enslaved for many years to the poison have made a full recovery."

He listened quietly while I went on talking, convincing myself with each word that I would be able to effect this cure—but clearly not convincing Maxwell. He didn't argue, didn't debate however.

"Let me help you," I urged.

"You have," he assured me with that eerie serenity.

He said that just having the thing off his chest was a great relief and the offer of support was a comfort and a kindness. But despite my efforts to persuade him to come and stay with me in Piccadilly so that he could receive treatment and care, he insisted he would go to North Hampshire to try to "pull himself together."

He would not be argued out of it and in the end I had to accept his decision—though I can't pretend it filled me with anything other than anxiety verging on dread.

Between Perceval and Maxwell I feared that Maxwell's danger was the greater, though I could not be sure.

Even so, I could not force him to accept my help.

The upshot was that Maxwell would fish the Test on Friday and Saturday, returning by the last train on Saturday night, and looking Perceval up at once, with the excuse of telling him about the result of the fishing. I was not to leave for Bath until Saturday morning—staying there till Monday. Maundeville had said he would take the night boat across from Newhaven to Dieppe on Saturday evening.

On Friday evening I occupied Maxwell's seat at the opera, sitting by Perceval, as for the last three seasons they had taken stalls together. We supped afterward and I went back with

Perceval to Park Lane, and stayed there a long time without having to manufacture any excuse for doing so.

When at last I found that the time was 2 a.m. and rose to go, I asked him to let me look at the mummy case.

"Making sure she's still there?" He was smiling, but somehow at that late hour the humor seemed forced.

The house was silent as he led the way to his bedroom. I don't remember much about the room, but a curtain of Eastern work hung on the wall. Perceval drew that aside and showed me the mummy case lying flat, with a pall of tapestry over it.

I bent to pull the black and purple velvet mortcloth off, and was startled when a black shadow sprang from it into the room.

"It's only Bhanavar," said Perceval quietly. "Since the moment the Mummy was carried into the house Bhanavar has been attracted by it."

"Strange."

"Yes. If she's shut out of the room, she hangs about the landing outside, and slips in at the first opportunity. If left alone, she lies curled for hours together upon the case, and even seems to forget her meal times."

"No doubt she's attracted by the faint odors still about the case," I said. "Some scents will draw cats long distances, I believe." What I said was true, but I found the account of the cat's behavior unsettling all the same.

"I believe the servants now object to poor Bhanavar as they do for the Mummy. To be sure that she doesn't suffer, I have to supply some of her meals myself."

To illustrate, he went outside to the landing, returning with a saucer of bread-and-milk. He called the cat and she bounded over at once with kittenish enthusiasm.

Meanwhile I studied the mummy case top to bottom, and of course found nothing fresh. I threw the tapestry over it again, and Bhanavar, when she had finished her meal, went back to her chosen bed.

The sight of the animal curled above the Mummy, just as Perceval drew the curtain across the alcove again, stirred my imagination and remained in my memory.

"The ancient Egyptians regarded cats highly, even worshipped a cat goddess," I said to Perceval. "Perhaps cats think as highly of the ancient Egyptians."

"The one's as harmless as the other, I fancy," he said, leading the way down through the stillness of the sleeping house. "We're agreed the whole thing is purely fanciful."

"You couldn't give me a bed here, I suppose?" I yawned widely. "I'm suddenly sleepy, and I'm sure there are no damp sheets in the place."

My dodge was only too obvious.

"I must be inhospitable for, I trust, the first time," he answered, with a little laugh. "I believe that for a few nights more I must have only one guest."

There was nothing else for it. I wished him good night, and went away down Park Lane, where only a policeman was visible, standing motionless on the edge of the curb.

Perceval saw me from the door, and the last sight I had of him was as he stood with upturned face, apparently watching a star.

As I tumbled into my bed to get a short rest before the early train for Bath, I thought of Maxwell and hoped he was sleeping easily, peacefully after a good day's fishing. Being outdoors in the fresh air and sunlight would help him a little perhaps.

I was afraid for him, though. I dreamed of that drawn curtain, with the knowledge of Bhanavar and the Mummy both sleeping behind it—only in my dreams Maxwell was trapped in the mummy case, clawing at the sealed lid.

In fact I did little but toss about until Bird brought me early coffee and shaving-water.

I managed to ascertain, however, by manufacturing an excuse for a message before leaving Paddington, that Perceval, who scribbled a reply from his bed, had apparently spent a better night than I. I sighed my relief—and then immediately wished I had arranged for some way to contact Maxwell.

From him there was only silence.

* * * * *

When I reached Bath I was very glad that I had gone, for my old friend's trouble had become acutely complicated during the previous night, and nothing more could be done, except to make his end as easy as possible.

He was conscious when I arrived, and pleased to see me; but he died that afternoon, and feeling myself useless, and a mere bore to his relatives, who were comparative strangers, I made the excuse of professional engagements to slip away up to town again immediately.

I drove straight to my rooms, with no particular plans made for the rest of the evening, but as I mounted the stairs I recognized Maxwell's voice from the landing above.

My heart lifted. I hurried the rest of the way, and found him at my door talking to Bird.

It's difficult to describe the relief—in fact, it was something closer to joy—I felt at hearing his quiet voice and seeing his familiar figure leaning on his stick.

"You're back then!" I said, and saw by Bird's surprised expression he registered that particular note of emotion in my voice.

Maxwell turned quickly. His gaze met mine without flinching. "Yes. I decided it would be wiser to return early."

"I'm very glad." I gripped his forearm with one hand, squeezed his shoulder with the other. Had Bird not been standing there watching in astonishment, I would have pulled him into my arms and hugged him tightly. "Very glad."

Maxwell's expression softened and he offered a half smile. I think he understood and was touched—as well as a little amused—at what I had feared. What he said was prosaic enough.

"I didn't expect to find you," he explained, "but I thought Bird could tell me where I might reach you."

"I'm glad you did. That you're here, I mean."

He drew a quick breath as if steadying himself. "If your offer of help is still open—"

I squeezed his arm again. "Of course. My dear boy." I glanced at Bird. "Of course we'll help you. Only commit yourself whole-heartedly to the course of treatment, and I know we can help you."

He was silent for a moment—and fair enough; it was nothing to be undertaken lightly—then he sighed.

"Very well. I'll put myself completely in your hands, Quentin. But first I want to check up on Perceval."

"I was planning to walk there myself," I said. "If Bird will take my bags, we'll go now."

"Er, of course," Bird said in the tone of one who has no idea what's happening—but suspects he won't like it.

I handed over my bags and we walked briskly through a fine warm May dusk.

Maxwell spoke only of fishing. In fact, seemed desperate to talk of nothing more serious than fishing, and I followed his lead. I felt instinctively that his plea for help had been made on the spur of the moment and might be withdrawn as impulsively.

But after a brief lull in the conversation, he said with a twisted smile, "Did you think I would do away with myself?"

"I was afraid for you," I said honestly. "I still am."

"I'm no coward. I know that's not the way out."

I glanced at his grim profile. "You understand this is no matter of cowardice or resolve? It's a disease. Like any other. You've contracted a disease, and all the determination in the world can't cure it. It requires proper treatment, medical care—it's only in your decision to seek a physician and stay the proscribed course that courage and resolve come into play. The rest is up to me."

He nodded, but did not answer.

We were within perhaps thirty yards of Perceval's house, when the door opened. A man stood for a second in the track of light streaming from the hall. Then the door closed, and he moved down the steps and away along Park Lane in front of us.

"Who's that?" Maxwell asked me. "Isn't it Maundeville?"

"You must have eyes like a cat. I can't tell in this light. Maundeville should be out of town by now."

"No. I believe it's him." He pushed on ahead of me. Presently I heard him call, "Hi! Maundeville!" and in a moment the man in front turned and came slowly back.

I saw that it was indeed Maundeville.

"Well, this is luck!" he exclaimed as I joined them. "Perceval has turned me out. Wants a good sleep, he says, and I was wondering what to do with myself for a few hours. I haven't got to read my paper in Paris till to-morrow evening, so we've been dining together."

"We were going to look him up," I said.

"Do! Do!" Maundeville agreed. "But I don't dare venture in with you. He gave me my *congé* quite distinctly. Perceval, dear fellow, is a man with whom I never feel free to take a liberty. It's different with you, though, Maxwell. Rouse him up. You're more intimate than I."

"I shouldn't be intimate long, if I took liberties with him," Maxwell said shortly. "It's not really late yet, though."

"Of course it isn't," Maundeville agreed, "We could all go in and make a night of it. I start for Paris too early to go to bed. Come along! We'll give that confounded Mummy a wake. A tantalus and a couple of siphons on the case will keep the Lady quiet, I think."

"Is it my imagination or is he a bit screwed?" Maxwell said to me in an undertone, as we dropped a few steps behind, but Maundeville heard him at once.

He turned to us. "So I am, dear boy, so I am!" he agreed. "No harm in that, is there?" and he moved toward Perceval's door again, and then stood looking back at us.

"If Percy's the least bit the worse for drink, he won't appreciate this," Maxwell said to me. "It's the sort of thing he couldn't stand at all."

"You might go in alone," I suggested.

"Yes. I think I will."

He knocked and after a moment was admitted.

Maundeville and I waited. Maundeville eyed me sardonically. "What a suspicious look on your face, Armiston. Of what do you suspect me? I've a notion to-night for translating Hafiz into English verse."

"Don't be a fool," I muttered.

After a few more minutes Maxwell reappeared. "All's well," he said brusquely. "In fact, he's sent me off with a flea in my ear. Shall we go somewhere we can talk? I know a place where we can have a private room as long as we want it."

For a moment Maundeville hesitated on the top step, a hand raised as though about to batter Perceval's door.

"Leave it," I told him. "If he doesn't want Maxwell, he doesn't want you."

"Where to then?" he inquired.

Maxwell said, "The Banyan."

"The Banyan!" Maundeville stood considering with tipsy gravity, and then began to laugh. Once begun he couldn't stop, and the street rang with his shouts.

"Oh, come along, man!" I implored him, and, each of us getting him by the arm, we hurried him into a passing taxi.

It was an unpromising beginning to a sort of Arabian Night's entertainment, but it ended all right once we reached the Banyan.

Maxwell and I drank something called Silver Fizz, which seemed to consist mostly of gin. I'm not sure why I drank so much, though I think I understood why Maxwell…teetering on the edge of a great precipice…did.

Maundeville stuck to spicy tea and was much as usual, only even more brilliant and amusing. Whether because of the tea or the cocktails that had preceded the tea, I don't know.

"When will the next meeting of the Society of Osiris take place?" I asked.

They both seemed vague, and I wondered if rumors regarding the Mummy had put a damper on certain people's enthusiasm for all things Egyptian.

We talked of many things, none of them serious. The Mummy did not come into it. Maundeville and Maxwell eventually got around to reminiscing about Oxford and the distant past. They painted quite a pretty picture of fellows sitting out of doors in the twilight, smoking and playing bowls and discussing the grand things they would do one day.

I might as easily have been listening to the melancholy recollections of Martians. But the truth was, I was hungry for every morsel of information about Maxwell even when those bits of information confirmed my understanding of how very different we were.

Finally Maundeville phoned for his motor, and took us to his own house, where we sat discussing all manner of subjects till he was told that everything was ready for him to go.

I don't deny that I was quite drunk by then. I think I was conscious of the great weight of responsibility that had descended on me regarding Maxwell's care. He, on the other hand, seemed more relaxed and lighthearted than I had ever seen him.

Maundeville persuaded us to see him off at the station, and wasn't very far from convincing me that it would be rather an amusing affair to see him on to the boat.

As it was, his motor took Maxwell and me back to my place. Once inside my quiet rooms, a certain constraint fell upon us. I was very conscious of Bird's snores echoing from down the hall as we divested ourselves of our coats and hats.

I smiled awkwardly at Maxwell. He smiled awkwardly in return. I was conscious that he was now my patient; and that truth necessarily, rightfully, put binders on me.

It had also occurred to me that some of his behaviors—even possibly the ones I found most appealing—might be attributed to his habitual use of the drug.

I saw him to the guest room.

"It's a bit bare," I apologized, seeing the bed and furnishings through his eyes. "That will be addressed to-morrow."

"It doesn't matter." He loosened his collar. His gaze met mine and he smiled.

The good grace of that smile spurred me into saying, "It does, you know. I want you to be as comfortable as can be." In fact, I wanted him to feel like this was a second home and not a sickroom.

He laughed. "I've slept on the ground rolled in nothing more than a blanket. Your guest room is a palace compared to some of the places I've bunked down. I'll be very comfortable."

I saw then that he meant it. Whatever his worries, they had nothing to do with curtains and rugs.

I said, "I'm very glad you're here, Hilary."

"I'm glad too, Quentin." I thought he would reach for me—I was trying to decide if I would reach for him—but neither of us moved and the moment passed.

"Good night," I said.

"Good night."

I went to my bed at an hour when a good many folk are beginning the day. For a time I listened to the sound of the settling floorboards and creaking beams, the distant sound of a clock chiming the hour.

I closed my eyes.

I knew nothing more until I was roused by being roughly shaken, while a distraught voice at my elbow cried:

"Perceval is dead! Wake up, Quentin. Percy's *dead*!"

CHAPTER TWENTY FOUR

BHANAVAR AND THE MUMMY

I sat up, suddenly wide awake. Maxwell stood at my bedside. He looked…harrowed.

I croaked, "What? What are you saying?"

We were not alone. Bird rattled at my blinds and let broad daylight into the bedroom. I put up a protective hand, wincing at the glare.

"Perceval's dead," Maxwell said. He sounded absolutely stunned.

I threw off the bedclothes and rose. He was already dressed, which I couldn't understand. Though his face was white, his cheeks and nose were pink with the cold, and I could smell the crisp scent of the outdoors on his coat. While he went on talking, I stood in my pajamas listening to him, trying to make sense of his behavior. Why had he slipped out? Did he not understand what he had committed to the previous evening?

"I can't believe it," he said again. "He was perfectly well last night."

I could hear the undertone of running water which Bird had turned on for my cold bath.

"Wait!" I pointed to a chair. "Sit down and begin again. You're sure he's dead?"

He nodded, seeming to lose his voice.

I nearly said, "If he's dead, we gain nothing by hurry," but remembered in time how Maxwell had come to my flat on the first occasion, and how I had shocked him by some remark of the same kind.

Instead, I took him by the shoulders and said, "I'm sorry, Hilary. More sorry than I can say."

He nodded and wiped impatiently at his eyes.

Bird reappeared in the doorway, and I told him to bring in brandy and a glass.

"Take a nip," I said to Maxwell. "I won't be a minute," and I turned into the bathroom, splashed into the cold water, and came out feeling that now I had my wits about me.

Maxwell was sipping a little brandy while Bird stood stiffly before him, holding the decanter. He somehow conveyed the impression of a sentry presenting arms to his officer.

What time was it? I checked my watch, lying on the little table beside my bed, and I found it was a quarter past nine.

"Make coffee and bring it in directly it's ready," I said to Bird. To Maxwell, I said, "Tell me everything while I shave. What were you doing there at this hour?"

"I couldn't sleep." The mirrored reflection behind my own was both guilty and rebellious. "I wasn't sure my coming here was the right decision. I decided to go round to Park Lane and have breakfast with Perceval. I wanted his opinion on the matter."

It was not what I wanted to hear, but I was glad for his honesty. "Have you told the police?"

"No," he said.

This alarmed me. "The servants will be disturbing things at Park Lane," I pointed out.

"No one is there who knows," he replied. "I locked the door and brought away the key and his damned fool of a man too. The fellow's down in the cab."

"Down in the… All right. Go on with your story." I interrupted him no more.

Bird brought in the coffee tray while he spoke.

Maxwell's story was that having arrived at the house in Park Lane, the new valet met him on the stairs and with much smirking confided that his master had been "carryin' on" the night before, and was sleeping it off.

Maxwell snubbed him sharply for his impertinence, although he knew it was accurate enough, ordered him to wait outside, and went in alone to Perceval's bedroom.

The blinds were still shut and the room was in semi-darkness. On going toward the bed, the first thing Maxwell noticed was Bhanavar the cat coiled at the foot, her black fur conspicuous on the white silk quilt, which was tossed in a heap. Perceval lay with his face turned away, and Maxwell moved quietly round the foot of the bed to the other side, meaning to go out again without disturbing him if Perceval were still asleep.

In doing so, he stumbled heavily over something on the floor, and only saved himself from a fall by catching at the foot of the bed.

At once he saw that his foot had struck the mummy case, tumbled upon the floor from its alcove. More alarming, the noise he made did not in the least disturb Perceval.

Maxwell moved up to the head of the bed, pulled away the pillows and rumpled bedclothes, and saw at once that Perceval was dead.

Here he stopped and struggled for composure. My instinct was to comfort him, but something held me silent. I watched him and thought his effort at control seemed genuine. Yet I was troubled.

"I called no one," he said, "and I told no one. I made absolutely certain that he was dead, and then I locked the door and came for you, bringing his man with me. I only told him as we came. I wanted no one in the room till we saw it together."

I nodded and drank a mouthful of hot coffee. Everything Maxwell told me seemed reasonable—at least from his perspective. I couldn't help thinking that the average citizen would have immediately called for help and then summoned the police. But then I was used to dealing with coachmen and shopkeepers. Maxwell and Perceval were of an entirely different class, and their priorities, even in such extremity, might be different from the ordinary man's.

By the time Maxwell had finished his story I was ready. Without further conversation I led the way out, and we went at once to Park Lane.

The door was opened by the butler, who had evidently not found anything wrong yet, and who stared at the valet, the unhappy third to our troop, as if he'd never seen him before.

"We're going to Mr. Perceval's room," I said. "You had better come up with us."

The butler looked from me to Maxwell.

"It's all right, Dale," Maxwell told him quietly. "Do as he says."

I went up the stair, followed by Maxwell, Dale and finally the valet, who dragged behind the rest of us, abject and pale.

Maxwell and I went into the room, leaving the other two outside on the landing.

The room was dark as dusk for Maxwell had not raised the blinds before leaving the room earlier.

He raised them a few inches, and bright morning sunlight fell first upon the black cat, which had coiled herself again at the lower end of the bed. Her eyes seemed to glow.

Then, as the blinds crept higher, I saw the spilled bedclothes and the vague outline beneath. The men in the doorway gasped, though there was really nothing they could see at that distance.

I went round the foot of the bed, and if Maxwell had not already warned me, I too should have stumbled over the mummy case. It lay diagonally between the bed and the wall. I stepped over it, brushing past a little table that stood by the bedside.

I drew back the bedclothes.

There was nothing particularly shocking in what I saw. Indeed, at a casual glance one might have imagined that Perceval had merely been tossing about in his bed before sound sleep had overtaken him. But looking more closely, I could be quite sure that he had been ill before he slept, and that he had probably risen from the bed after lying down.

Maxwell said nothing, but his very stillness conveyed stricken protest.

Of Perceval's death there could be no doubt. Nor that he had been dead several hours.

I turned back the bedclothes. One of Perceval's hands was closed in a half fist as though he held something. I started to lift his hand, drawing in a sharp breath as a very large, blue-black beetle trundled out from between his fingers.

I'm not quite sure what happened next because Maxwell suddenly lurched against my shoulder, and I turned to steady him. His eyes were closed, his face bloodless. He seemed near to fainting. In my haste to attend to him, I dropped Perceval's wrist, and the next time I looked, the beetle was nowhere to be seen.

In any case, all my attention was on Maxwell who was leaning into me, breathing unevenly against my neck.

"Steady, steady," I murmured. Looking over his head, I ordered the men in the doorway to bring brandy.

Maxwell was shaking his head. Not at the thought of more brandy, but in repudiating what we had just witnessed.

Though no entomologist, I knew an Egyptian beetle when I saw one—and I had seen many of them in books and art as of late.

"It's not true," he said.

"It's all right," I said. A foolish comment. Things were very far from all right.

I looked at Perceval's body again, but still didn't see the beetle.

The thing was quite large. Where could it have gone? Was it able to fly? I knew such beetles were not poisonous, even so the thought of it crawling around the dead man's chamber was greatly disturbing. These dung beetles, as they were called, were greatly attracted to the scent of excrement and laid their eggs in the same. That was really the least of their peculiar habits.

Such were my erratic thoughts as I helped Maxwell to a chair away from the bed and waited for the brandy.

"Come, pull yourself together," I ordered him, but despite my intent, I fear my voice came out as low and tender as a woman's. He seemed completely shattered, but far from striking disapproval in me, I was deeply touched by his need and felt only the desire to protect him.

Dale brought brandy, and I held the glass to Maxwell's lips. He swallowed, shuddered, and in a moment came back to life though his eyes were still black with horror.

"It's the shock of seeing his friend so," I told Dale, hoping to forestall any backstairs gossip.

He was staring at the motionless form on the bed. "We all feel it, sir," he whispered.

"Phone the police now."

He nodded and withdrew.

Maxwell had already pushed himself upright, although he seemed unsure where to go next or what to do.

As he seemed steady enough, I left him and returned to the bed, only noticing then that a pencil lay on the floor next to the bed stand. I looked about for any scrap of writing there might be and found a scribbling pad upon the little table.

There were some scrawled words, though I had to carry the pad to the window before I could make them out.

The message ran irregularly as follows:

Dear Armiston,

I said I would write if I suspected anything. Suspicion is not proof, and these suspicions are painful to entertain. Nonetheless, in the event that something does happen to me... M...

"What's that last word?" Maxwell asked from directly behind me, and I jumped a little not having realized he was so near.

He didn't seem to notice my start, peering down at the note.

"It's not complete." I squinted at the final illegible word. "It begins with 'M.' although it might be an 'N.' Or a crooked 'H'? No, I think it's an 'M.' I'm practically sure. The next letter is 'a' or 'e.' Or is that an 'o'? Hm. That dot might indicate an 'i.' Then it scrawls off. The previous sentence is not complete either."

"It looks as though he tried to write 'Mummy,'" Maxwell suggested slowly.

"Perhaps," I agreed. "But it might almost equally possibly be an attempt at Maxwell, or Maundeville. Or even Miss."

"Miss?"

I shrugged. "In any case, it's meant for me. I think we'll put it away and say nothing about it for the moment. One can always produce it later if need be."

The cries of a woman in hysterics now rose on the landing outside.

"Some fool has been babbling." I hastily folded the paper and put it into my pocket. "The murder's out."

"Murder!" Maxwell repeated. He was still very pale, the pupils of his eyes unnaturally huge. His shock was quite genuine. A man can pretend to faint, but there's no feigning biological reactions.

"Yes. Murder."

"By natural or supernatural means?"

"My dear boy. Think what you're saying."

His expression darkened. "Think what *you're* suggesting," he said softly.

True. He was right. This was an ugly and dangerous business. I said, "We must try to speak to the servants before the police arrive. Maybe we can get a few minutes more to look round."

He nodded, and we went to the door. The butler had returned and was waiting with the valet. There were also three women-servants, one being an elderly woman, who, I found, was wife to the butler and was a sort of cook-housekeeper, and two under-servants, one of whom was crying.

I frightened her into silence roughly enough, and bade the housekeeper and the other maid take her to her room.

"You had better come in," I said to the butler as the hysterical girl was led away, sobbing quietly.

With a gray face, Dale followed us back to the room. He began at once to speak to Maxwell.

"You'll bear me out, I'm sure, sir, that poor Master Charles hadn't the habit of it. I never saw him like that before. He could take his glass of wine and enjoy it, as you know, but always like a gentleman, and never what you might call really drinking."

"What do you mean, Dale? Who talks about drinking?" Maxwell asked him.

"It's best to be plain with you and the doctor, sir, if we can keep it from going further. Mr. Perceval had taken too much last night, Captain Maxwell. You must have seen it yourself. I needn't tell you he was as nice as ever. But there was something on his mind. Something to drive him to it."

Maxwell looked at him for a moment and then at me.

"It's true. Percy didn't drink to excess. He was a little worse for wear last night, but not…"

He trailed off and I knew he was thinking guiltily that he should have somehow recognized his friend's peril.

I had picked up Perceval's cigarette-case, which lay on the little table beside the bed, and I was examining the cigarettes. On one side of the case was "Dimitrinos," on the other three cigarettes marked as containing stramonium, a common remedy for asthma. On an ash-tray were two stumps, each of the stramonium brand.

I put back the case and the cigarette-stumps exactly as I had found them, and considered what Dale and Maxwell had said.

It wasn't my business to supply the papers with sensational copy, and I would do a great deal to spare Maxwell any pain, but I didn't see quite how to prevent it.

"A public inquiry may be necessary," I said; "I can't at present be sure it can be avoided. There's that man of Mr. Perceval's too. I don't believe any mortal power can keep that booby's tongue quiet. I suppose he has chattered already."

"Then you're wrong, sir!" the butler said, with sudden passion. "He's spoke to no one yet, but me and you and Captain Maxwell. He's had no chance, and he'll have none."

He moved as if to tackle the valet then and there, but stopped and seemed to sink back into himself with a sort of murmured apology to us, the quiet, conventional, whey-faced butler again.

Maxwell and I went on examining the room. Every time I lifted a cushion or throw, I expected to see that great blue-black beetle crawling along beneath, but it was never there.

The mummy case was the only other thing that seemed worth any attention. How had it got there from the alcove?

I said to Maxwell, "If people come in and see this thing lying about, it's sure to remind them of the Scrymgeour affair."

He looked grimmer than ever. "Yes. It will."

"Dale, can you stand it in your room till dark?" I asked.

Dale, like a good fellow, said he could stand anything that would help to keep his poor master's name out of the papers. So we moved the Mummy to his room, and then I sent a note to a police superintendent not far off, who was a patient of mine, telling him of the sudden death—asking him to meet me at Park Lane if possible.

He arrived shortly after the police Dale had summoned, which saved us a good deal of trouble. The superintendent was favorably prejudiced to start with, partly because he knew me and partly because the general surroundings didn't suggest anything to hide.

I told him, before Maxwell and Dale and the valet, that there was a possibility that death had been due to an overdose of stramonium contained in cigarettes, possibly aggravated by intoxication, and admitted frankly that our particular desire was to prevent the fact of Perceval's intoxication from being generally known. I suggested that the matter should be kept as quiet as possible until there had been time to examine and test the theory.

I obtained his suggestion as to the right course to follow, and told him that I would see that Maundeville, Perceval's companion of the previous evening, put himself in communication with the authorities as quickly as possible.

Nothing was said of the Mummy or of Perceval's scrawled note which was in my pocket. I mentioned casually that Maxwell had looked in briefly on Perceval before rejoining Mandeville and myself, but that he had been inside the house no more than ten minutes at the outside.

This was the danger point, of course. Maxwell had been the last person to see Perceval alive, and that placed him in a very precarious position, whether he knew it or not. But my friend the superintendent seemed to accept this information without mis-giving. Or at least did not openly question it.

Maxwell corroborated my comments, though declining to say whether he believed Perceval had been intoxicated. He said Perceval had already been in bed and was not prepared to receive visitors.

"You argued?" the superintendent inquired blandly.

Maxwell's smile twisted. "No. One could never argue with Percy. He threw a slipper at me. I left it on the bureau." He nodded at a red Turkish slipper resting on the dresser. "I told him I'd…see him to-day."

The valet gave evidence that his master came home "as drunk as a lord," and that he left him in his bed.

Dale testified, with obvious unwillingness, to the same effect—adding that he had never seen it happen before.

I reiterated the theory that small quantities of stramonium might act more powerfully together with overdoses of alcohol, and said that I would get authoritative opinions on that point.

The superintendent heard it all out and then dispatched the inspector to report accordingly.

Maxwell and I left and went straight to Maundeville's house, got his Paris address, and cabled him that Perceval was dead and he must return as quickly as possible to see me.

From there, Maxwell and I went to Perceval's solicitors and gave them all possible information about what had happened and what we had done—always excluding the Mummy.

Here there was more unpleasant news—at least from my per-spective. According to Perceval's solicitors, Perceval had left nearly everything he owned to Maxwell. I was greatly surprised at this, having assumed Perceval, like the other young members of the Society of Osiris, would have left his fortune to Miss Hennessey—especially given his stated desire to look after her. While I knew his feelings for Maxwell were somewhat complicated, this seemed to hint at an altered emotional state.

Of course there would still have to be the reading of the will, the solicitors hastened to add, but essentially…

Maxwell had a very strong motive for murder.

I didn't point it out, of course, and I'm not sure Maxwell understood the implication of this any more than he had grasped the delicacy of his position in being the last person to see Perceval alive. He seemed genuinely grief-stricken and operating by rote, following convention rather than exerting any conscious will.

However, after we left Perceval's solicitors, Maxwell insisted it should be he who told Miss Hennessey of her cousin's death.

I could do nothing but agree, but my existing concern grew even greater. I was convinced he had given up all thought of continuing his opium cure.

It was clear to me that when he'd left my house that morning he was already rebelling against the necessary restrictions and rules required for entrance upon the hard road of abnegation, already convincing himself his plight was not so serious, regretting the confession made to me before his fishing trip. Inevitably this new strain and grief would further weaken his commitment, further shake his confidence in both me and himself.

Also, by now he would have missed at least one dose of his anodyne—possibly more—and would be suffering the effects. It was very likely the moment he left me his first destination would be home and his syringe.

But one thing my study of the opium habit had taught me: there was no hope of cure unless the patient was one hundred percent committed to the battle ahead. So I told Maxwell I agreed his visit to Miss Hennessey was the best course and begged him to come afterward and dine with me that evening in my flat—even assuring him he need not promise more than that.

To my relief, he agreed. In fact, he even offered a small reassuring smile, his fingers brushing mine briefly as we took leave of each other.

It was a very long and tense day. I was heartsick over Perceval and terrified for Maxwell who I feared might be equally lost in his own way.

The hours passed without news.

Shortly before dinner was served, Maxwell arrived. To my great relief—and surprise—he carried a valise as well as several books, and I was reassured he still intended to pursue his cure. He looked absolutely ill, but gave me no details of his interview, nor did I ask for any.

"The Mummy has been smuggled back to Maundeville's," he told me after he had swallowed a few spoonfuls of the velvety smooth leek and potato soup.

"Good. Let her stay there until Maundeville burns it or donates it to the British Museum."

He made no answer to that, but after another spoonful or two, he said, "I didn't imagine the scarab? You saw it too. He was holding it. It was in his hand."

The horror was back in his eyes. I said quietly, "You didn't imagine it. I don't know what it means, but we both saw it."

He put down his spoon. "But that's just it. What *can* it mean? It's impossible."

"It's not impossible that a beetle got in there by some natural means. It's unlikely, yes. I can't argue with that. As for its equally mysterious disappearance, it no doubt fell under the bed or crawled beneath the mattress, which is why it seemed to vanish. Did you know that dung beetles can navigate using the Milky Way?"

Maxwell would not be distracted by the Milky Way or any other comforting nonsense. "He wasn't ill. I don't believe he had an asthma attack. And even if he did, why should he die of it?"

"You heard what I told the superintendent."

"I heard. Yes, it makes sense as far as it goes, but it doesn't go far. He *wasn't* ill."

"All right. He wasn't ill. And I don't believe Nefertiabet is reaching out from the grave."

He stared at me. "Then you do think it's murder."

"I said so, didn't I? I don't believe in ghosts or magic or curses. Or, to this extent, coincidence. If there's an agency at work here, it is human and it is diabolical."

"Do you think Percy knew this villain? Was he attempting to write the name of his assassin on that note?"

"I think for some time Perceval unwillingly entertained suspicions of one particular person. I believe something happened last night to confirm his suspicion." I added, "It doesn't automatically follow that his suspicions were correct."

Maxwell looked startled at this observation. It was the truth though, and something I had to remind myself of. Suspicion was not proof.

Of course it was possible Perceval possessed proof there had not been time to specify.

We were silent as Bird served warm poached oyster on a crouton drizzled with a creamy chervil sauce.

Maxwell, lost in frowning thought, took a bite and then another. He looked up. "This is very good," he said in surprise.

"Bird is a man of many gifts."

We spoke of other things until Bird brought in the mutton joint rolled in capers and anchovies.

"Maundeville will want to know if we're going to continue drawing cards," Maxwell said.

"I know. But...either way, you're out of it now." And I was very glad of that, though I knew this would be the first real battle between us.

He stared at me. "What? How so?"

"For the next four to twelve weeks—and it's more likely to be twelve than four—you'll be in the fight of your life. There's no room for any distractions, my lad. Your entire focus must be on getting well again."

He didn't like it and proceeded to explain his feelings at length—and then develop upon the theme rather colorfully. He was an excellent arguer, and if the thing at stake had been anything less than his survival, I'd probably have thrown in the towel twenty minutes in.

As it was I had to resort to unfair tactics. "If you're unwilling to accept my terms, Maxwell, I must decline to take your case."

He looked genuinely stunned. "You can't be serious."

"Never more so in my life. I know what's ahead of you, if you don't, and you must accept my word that you won't have strength for anything else. I can't help you if you don't have full confidence in me."

"It has nothing to do with confidence in you!"

I realized my misstep was about to lead to yet another argument. I said sternly, "If you wish for my help, you must agree to place yourself completely and unquestioningly in my care until such time as I may dismiss you as cured."

In the candlelight his eyes were the color of steel. He sat back in his chair and directed the full battery of his gaze on me. I stared back.

But I could see we were at an impasse. He was not going to agree. He was not the man to be cowed by threats, and he could not be bribed. So I resorted to unvarnished honesty, leaning forward and outstretching my hand in appeal.

"Hilary, listen. I care too much for you to risk failure. That's the truth. Your well-being is my first and only concern now. Maundeville and the rest of them can go to blazes." My face felt hot and red. I had never said those words—or anything like them—to anyone before. But I meant them. Every one.

The coldness left his eyes. The hardness left his expression.

He said gruffly, "You haven't known me very long, Quentin. I mightn't be worth the trouble."

I said boldly, "You're worth it to me."

He shook his head, looking away as though he didn't like to see all that was in my gaze. After a moment or two, his mouth twisted, and he gave a self-mocking laugh. He reached out, and we clasped hands. "Very well. We'll see if you feel the same in eight weeks."

We had finished our meal in peace and were sitting over our port when Bird brought in a wire from Maundeville saying that he would leave Paris that night for home, and would call on me the following morning or see me at his house, whichever I preferred.

I telephoned his man to tell Maundeville on his arrival that I would see him in my own flat.

CHAPTER TWENTY FIVE

MAUNDEVILLE CONFESSES

I was sitting alone over breakfast the next morning when Bird announced Maundeville.

He came in looking trim as usual, but very fagged.

"This is a very bad business, Armiston," he said, "a shocking bad business! How did it happen?"

"No one knows yet," I said. "No one but his servants saw him alive after you did."

He gave me a keen glance. "Maxwell looked in on him for a few moments."

"True. I'd forgotten."

Still watching me, he said, "Speaking of Maxwell, he appears to have disappeared. I stopped by his rooms and his man says he's out of town and can only be reached through his solicitor."

"I believe that's true."

"Are you saying *you* don't know where he is?"

I fenced, "Why me more than any other acquaintance?"

"Why? Because he and Perceval particularly befriended you these last months. You've been all but inseparable."

"I wouldn't say inseparable." This exaggeration made me wonder whether Maundeville was slightly jealous of my friendship with his former students.

"If anyone knows the reason for this mysterious behavior, it's surely you."

I am neither clever nor subtle enough for lying. I said nothing.

Maundeville eyed me as though evaluating the contents in one of his test tubes. He said suddenly, "He's here, isn't he? He's under this very roof?"

How could he know that? I didn't believe there was anything in my face to give it away. Somehow he had guessed.

His perspicuity alarmed me. Why? I had seen no indication that Maundeville was other than sincerely concerned for the welfare of his former students.

When I didn't immediately answer, Maundeville seemed genuinely astounded.

"He's your *patient*?"

I could see no advantage in dissembling. In fact, at this juncture I thought it would be better, safer—*safer?*—to appear to be completely forthcoming.

"Yes. He's attempting to undergo a cure for his opium habit."

He stared at me narrowly. I stared back. Suddenly he laughed. "Good heavens! If that's true, you've succeeded where I failed. I'd imagined no man had greater influence over Maxwell than myself. Well, you're to be commended."

I liked this conversation less and less, though I would have been hard-pressed to say why. Something in Maundeville's attitude made me uneasy. Again I had to wonder. Was it possible he resented my influence over Maxwell?

He said, "Is there any hope for him?"

"While there's life there's hope," I said like the pompous fool he no doubt thought me.

In fact, I was a little worried. Maxwell was not going to be an easy patient.

Before bed the previous evening we'd had yet another argument over the course of his treatment. Maxwell, having gone the full day without his habitual dose of opium, wanted to start his treatment by completely renouncing the drug, while I insisted that he must have his usual evening dose.

"The attempt to cure yourself by the entire and abrupt withdrawal of the drug is why you've failed each time before to break this pernicious habit. Our goal is minimum duration of treatment and maximum freedom of pain."

He had not been swayed.

Neither had I.

"The question isn't one of courage. It's of physical endurance. And I tell you now, you haven't the physical or nervous stamina to endure the course you're proposing. We must slowly, gradually wean you from the poison."

"I've tried this before. It's useless!"

"And you've tried the other before, have you not? And it was equally useless?"

I could see that reminder frightened him, and I didn't hesitate to press my advantage. "You've given your word to place yourself entirely in my care. Now you must live up to that word, regardless of how little faith you have in me."

That of course changed the direction of the conversation, as I meant it to. Eventually he consented to allowing me to inject him with his usual evening dose, and accordingly became calm enough to sleep.

I knew to-day would see yet another battle. Probably several battles, for the course he had agreed to was not an easy one. Not for anyone, but especially not for a young and proud man such as Maxwell. He still struggled with the notion that he had become utterly enslaved to the drug; still persisted in believing it was only a matter of determination and will to free himself.

"No wonder you cabled me," Maundeville muttered. "What a fix!"

"You'll be asked, I imagine, to say what you know about Perceval's movements the evening before last," I said.

Maundeville's pale gaze flashed to mine. "Of course! Of course! Who else can?" he agreed. "Although the truth is that the later part of the evening isn't much more than a dream to me—until I found myself back at that place drinking tea and talking nonsense with you and Maxwell."

"Back at what place?"

"The restaurant. The Banyan."

"When were you there before?"

Maundeville stared. "Why, man, we dined there! Didn't you know?"

"How should I?"

"Lord! I must have mentioned it. Or perhaps I took it for granted you knew. What a scandalous business! Honestly, I didn't know that we drank much. What do his servants say about Perceval?"

"They say he came home drunk and retired to bed."

"But that doesn't account for things, does it?" Maundeville asked fretfully. "A few drinks wouldn't kill a man. I was drunk myself. What on earth can I do, Armiston? I'm too tired to think. I can't have slept two nights ago, can I? And last night I crossed again, and I couldn't sleep then. Who could?"

"Have you had breakfast?" I asked.

"Not I," he answered. "I wired for my motor to meet me at the station and went straight to Maxwell's."

"Why?"

"Why?" He gave me a rueful smile. "Well, I suppose I thought Maxwell would know what you were up to. Anyway, I can't eat. Give me something to drink."

I gave him a cup of cafe *au lait* mixed with egg, and with a little brandy in it.

He sipped it quickly, and presently looked less harassed. He began to talk again.

"Your cable was handed to me just as I was going to answer what the fellows over there said on my paper."

"I'm afraid it upset all your arrangements," I said. "But for your own sake I felt you must know at once."

He gave an indifferent shrug. "What did the paper matter? They had said nothing worth reply. Have you a hypodermic you can lend me?"

"What for?" I asked.

"Just to put some life into my stupid brains, my dear fellow," he said. "I feel as if I were thinking through a blanket. My hypodermic case must be in my evening clothes." I gave him a syringe and watched in surprise as he took a tiny vial from his pocket. He turned down a sock and injected a few drops, fifteen minims, I think, of a colorless fluid, just above his ankle.

"Strychnine?" I suggested.

"No. My own formula."

"You carry it with you always?"

He did not reply, only stretched and shook himself vigorously, and insisted on washing out my syringe at once with hot water.

It seemed to me that already, whatever the reason might be, he showed much more vitality; but, of course, I had given him one sort of pick-me-up and he had given himself another. His face never had much color beneath its sun brown, and it was almost colorless still; but a certain firmness of flesh seemed to show itself. And his blue eyes looked less tired and lined.

"Poor Perceval!" he murmured. "Death in itself always seems to me a very unimportant thing when age has come. But he was young."

"Yes."

He roused himself and looked at me. "Help me to look at things from a practical point of view, Armiston. Can we save everybody trouble by just telling everything as we know it? Poor Perceval and I dined together and drank too much. I must own to that and keep back nothing."

"You forget the Mummy," I said.

"Man alive, what can the Mummy have to do with it? It doesn't come in at all!"

"I can't tell you," I said. "I don't say that it has anything to do with it. But sooner or later it will be remembered that Perceval found Scrymgeour dead not very long ago, and there was a mummy case in Scrymgeour's rooms. Whatever can be told will be ferreted out then. Servants talk."

"Well, what then? That won't be our fault," Maundeville pointed out, staring at me. "I rather inferred, Armiston, that you were keen to have the superstition exploded. Now's your chance. Indeed, I don't think it can be avoided. The case is in Perceval's room, and I suppose the police have seen it by this time."

"It isn't there," I said. "It was moved out of the room before any strangers were brought in. It's in your house now, I believe."

Maundeville goggled at me. "Well, then," he said finally, "shan't we just openly state the facts as we know them, and not hold ourselves responsible for other people's conclusions?"

I shrugged.

"There's only one other objection," he added thoughtfully. "Miss Hennessey's name may be brought up. I don't care for the idea of that."

"I don't believe she would wish that to influence us. Besides, how would her name come in?"

"Well, Perceval told me some time ago there was an understanding between them."

"He was not in love with her." I felt quite sure on that score. "Besides, she had refused him." I added, "Several times."

Maundeville was surprised. "B-but he told me so."

I shook my head. "I'm quite sure there was no understanding, however much he might have wished otherwise."

"On my soul, I didn't know that," he declared. "Poor Perceval—poor fellow!" He seemed greatly touched by this secondary misfortune of Perceval's. "Are you sure of that?"

"He told me so himself." As I observed him, noted his…let's call it regret…a dangerous impulse seized my mind.

I said, "I happen to know her feelings lie in another direction."

"What direction?" His brows drew together. "Not Maxwell!"

I said quickly, "Certainly not."

He continued to frown. "That accounts for what happened," he said, after consideration.

"For example?"

"Well, he was as quiet as ever, but it might explain his not noticing particularly how much wine he took."

"It doesn't account for your making the same mistake, does it?" I asked.

He smiled wryly. "Unlike Perceval, I have a reputation for being a man who enjoys his drink."

"That would fit, except I believe Miss Hennessey made her feelings known several weeks ago. It's puzzling that Perceval should drown his sorrows so late after the fact. How did he seem to you? Depressed? Angry?"

"As I said, quiet. More quiet than usual."

Neither of us spoke for a time.

Maundeville said, "I think a bottle of hock between us, and a glass of port, with a chartreuse with our coffee, and a whisky-and-soda later with our cigars will explain a great deal. We'll ask Samuels at the Banyan to hunt up the bills, and we'll look at them together."

I grunted something vague, for I had already meant to do that on my own account.

"We needn't say anything to outsiders about the drinking," I said, "until we see what turns up. We should have to say how extraordinary that was for Perceval, and the next question would be whether he had any particular excuse just now for breaking his usual habits. Then the Mummy or Miss Hennessey, or both, might be dragged in."

"As you like," Maundeville agreed. "I'm naturally not keen to talk about it. Still, if you or Maxwell choose to say publicly how things were, you must do so. Are you going to Park Lane this morning?"

"I must go this afternoon," I said, "but I've no business there this morning."

"Could you come round with me?" Maundeville asked. "I should like to go and see if anything useful suggests itself to me on the spot."

Now I detested the thought of having to be there that afternoon, and I was very loath to pay an unnecessary visit. But if Maundeville went, I thought I ought to go too.

I repeated that nothing necessitated my going, but that if half-an-hour would be enough for him, I could manage it.

We went together, Maundeville being silent and gloomy all the way, though he looked much less tired than when he had come into my dining-room.

I only remember one question that he asked before we reached Park Lane.

"How does Miss Hennessey take it?" he asked—and looked at me with obvious surprise when I said that I had no idea. I added an explanation that I had not seen her.

"Who told her?" Maundeville demanded. "Someone has done so, of course."

"Yes, Maxwell. But I know nothing of what passed between them."

Maundeville asked nothing more.

CHAPTER TWENTY SIX

WHEREIN MY SUSPICIONS DEEPEN

The morning was hot.

The bright May sunlight made the blinds drawn down over every window of the house in Park Lane all the more conspicuous.

In contrast, Perceval's bedroom was a light, airy space with two large windows overlooking a very pretty garden in the back. Both windows were opened wide, and a fresh and playful breeze wandered about the room, stirring the lace curtains and ruffling the petals of flowers in their bowls. Flowers were everywhere. On the mantelpiece, dressing-table, writing-table, wherever vase or bowl could stand. Some white blossoms were scattered on the bed.

They could not entirely smother the scent of decay, but otherwise there was nothing in the room to suggest death, until one's eye was caught by a certain rigidity of line under the bed sheet.

I looked around, annoyed at disturbing the peace of the room, and vexed with myself for having consented to come. Maxwell would be awake by now, and I wished to lose no time in outlining the difficult course of his treatment. The sooner he was prepared, the sooner we could begin.

"There's nothing to observe," I said softly to Maundeville. "You can see the room has been tidied up and everything put straight."

Maundeville agreed, but stepped across to the bed and laid a hand on the sheet. His nervous system must have been in most perfect order, since he showed no sign of disturbance at what followed.

As his fingers grazed the hem of the sheet there was a quick movement beneath it. The linen puffed as though Perceval was gathering himself to rise.

I heard Dale cry, "Lord, have mercy!" behind me, but Maundeville never moved. His hand was arrested for an instant, and then he turned the sheet further, and something black sprang up and leaped to the floor.

It was Bhanavar, the Persian cat.

I turned to Dale. "I ordered that animal was to be kept out of the room."

"It was done, sir. She must have followed someone in again."

"Why should she come here?" Maundeville watched the cat as though mesmerized.

Dale answered. "She had slept here lately, sir. She had a fancy for the—Thing that stood there." He nodded toward the alcove where the mummy case had been kept.

"The aromatics," Maundeville said to me, "possibly valerian. Who knows? I rather think that at one time valerian was supposed to ward off evil spirits. Perhaps the Egyptians used it. Where is she now?"

The cat had disappeared again while we spoke. Dale began to look for her under the bed.

"Never mind for a moment," Maundeville said. "We'll find her before we leave the room." He stood silently looking down at the peaceful face he had uncovered.

"Well, I'm sorry!" was all he said at last, as he turned away with a sigh. The sigh said it all. He might have said more and expressed less.

"Now for the cat. We must find her and keep her out."

"I'll speak to Simpson about her, sir," Dale said. "She's his charge, and he has nothing else to do now but gossip. I'll see to it."

But Maundeville and I were both possessed with the same intention of seeing the cat out of the room ourselves.

To find her was easy enough. Maundeville went straight to the little alcove where the Mummy had lain, and there she was, behind the curtain. But she was too quick for him, and darted under the bed. Dislodged from there, she ran up the little bed curtains and squatted at the top, spitting and growling in a fury.

The racket seemed indecent.

"Stop chasing her!" I said, "Bring milk or something."

Dale pulled a bell, and the valet came running up with a scared face.

"When was the cat fed?" I asked him.

"This morning, sir."

"Bring milk!" I ordered, and the fellow went away and fetched some.

Dale suggested that the animal didn't want to leave her dead master. But the moment the milk was put on the floor she came down, mewing piteously, and drank all she could get.

"More?" Maundeville suggested. More being brought, she took that too, and then set to work on her toilette before us all.

"A good appetite—after breakfast?" Maundeville suggested to the valet. "Your master would have sacked you on the spot if he had seen this. Dale, you had better kill the poor brute if no one is willing to look after her needs."

Dale said he would see to that, and picking up Bhanavar, ordered the other man out.

"Don't kill her," I said sharply. "The cat belongs to Maxwell now. Do nothing without his orders."

Maundeville stared at me in astonishment. "To Maxwell? How so?"

"The will has yet to be read, but according to Perceval's solicitors, the whole of his estate goes to Maxwell."

"To…*Maxwell*?" He recovered at once. "Well, they were always as close as brothers. I suppose it makes sense. A lucky break for Maxwell. Shall we go?"

I excused myself, saying that since I was there I might save time by making one or two arrangements before going.

"I don't know that I have seen anything worth noticing," he said. "The room, of course, has been put straight, as you suggested. But I'm glad we came, if only to feed poor Bhanavar."

When he had gone I turned to Dale, and told him to bring the cat to the window. He complied.

Two things about Bhanavar had caught my attention. When she was bolting about the room she twice missed her leap and fell, striking against the furniture to which she was jumping.

Again it seemed to me that in going to the milk she struck her nose. Of course, she was famished and very thirsty.

Directly Dale held her up for me to look at her closely.

I saw at once what was wrong. The pupils of her eyes were strongly dilated, and didn't contract even in the bright sunlight streaming directly in on them through the open window.

She was drugged.

I had hardly time to see this when she bit Dale, who naturally swore and dropped her, whereupon she bolted under the bed again.

While poor Dale alternately sucked his finger and prayed to be forgiven for such language in such a place, I stooped to see where the cat was hidden. I saw her, crouching at the other side and out of my reach, even if I was prepared to risk being mauled. But the sunlight shone on something else within reach, a glinting piece of gold, and I pulled it out and rose to examine it.

It was a plain gold locket, with a very thin, broken gold chain. I pressed the clasp and saw that the locket held a miniature of Miss Hennessey.

I was still studying it when Maundeville wandered back into the room and stood looking at me.

"I thought you'd gone," I remarked, managing—I hope—to hide my lack of enthusiasm.

"A thought occurred to me. It seemed brilliant at the time, but now quite escapes me." He smiled ruefully.

If there had been time for me to hide the locket, I should have done so, but I was sure he had seen it.

"I just discovered this." I held it out to him.

He took the locket to the window, and stood there looking at the portrait in silence for a minute or two.

"It's not a bad likeness," he said at last. "Where did you find it?"

"Under the bed," I said. "He must have dropped it there."

He glanced up from the painted face. "This seems to contradict your belief that Perceval had no particularly tender feelings for his cousin."

"I think he was very fond of her," I said. "The locket proves nothing else."

He said nothing for a time. "What will you do with it?" he asked at last.

"I don't know." I was increasingly bothered by his attitude, although I couldn't have said why. Everything he said and did was perfectly reasonable. Yet my unease grew.

"I suppose I should hand it over to Maxwell."

Maundeville considered this idea, looking at the miniature still.

"I don't think so," he said at last, handing it back to me. "It would be sure to pain him a good deal just now. Keep it for a while and think over the matter. It's safe in your hands, and you can give it to him later if you still think that best."

So I put it in an inside breast pocket of my coat, and we parted at the street door.

My meeting with Maxwell later than morning was as difficult as I feared.

In many respects his case was only too typical. He was twenty seven years of age—of the energetic yet at the same time delicate and sensitive nervous sensibility which is peculiarly susceptible to the effects of opium. His general health, apart from the inevitable disturbances of the drug, had always been excellent, and his constitution, under the same limitations, remained surprisingly vigorous. His habit, as in nine cases out of every ten, dated from the medical prescription of opium for the relief of the violent pain of nearly having his leg blown off. He was not aware of the drug then administered to him, or at any rate of the peril attending its use, and his malady was so long protracted that opium had established itself as a necessary condition of comfortable existence before he realized that he was addicted. When he realized his danger he had attempted, as so many do, to discontinue the prescription, but suffered so much distress that he voluntarily resumed it, without consulting his physician. As is inevitably the case, the drug gradually lost its power, so little by little he was compelled to increase it. Having begun with 1/3 grain powders of which he took three per diem, he was now taking 30 grains hypodermically per diem at the end of three years from his first dose.

I laid before him our battle strategy. Of course he demanded to know the odds of victory, and I told him the truth. It was impossible to know if he would get well or not. Everything depended on his strength of will. A desperate effort would be required and, while Maxwell was in other ways a man of restraint and discipline, opium enfeebled the will to such extent that the finest and most upstanding man would, in extremis, debase, degrade and dishonor himself to procure the drug were it withheld any length of time.

He was very quiet and did not interrupt as I sketched out how we would immediately discard the syringe and all future doses of opium would be given by mouth. We would slowly but steadily reduce his dosage—starting with a full three grains that day—and see how he adjusted. He did not interrupt as I spoke of sedatives, baths and massage.

I did not detail the difficulties ahead, only reminded him that he was neither a prisoner nor an inmate and was permitted to leave whenever he chose. Also, he could request more of any opiate at any time, but that it had to be administered by my hand. I promised he would never be pushed beyond the limits of endurance.

All of this he heard out in polite and attentive silence and then insisted that the entire supply of drug be cut off immediately as he didn't wish to waste any time in breaking free of the hold the poison had over him.

I resisted the temptation to knock him over the head with the nearest candlestick.

After all, that was the cavalry mentality. *Charge!* But this was not an enemy that could be vanquished by courage and will alone.

"Listen to me," I said. "How many times before have you tried and failed by that method?"

"I didn't have your help before."

"And you don't have it now. Not for that brutal regime. Not only is there no need for such torture of mind and body, it drastically reduces our chance of success."

"We don't have time to waste. I don't believe this…curse will end with Perceval's death."

Ah. Now we were getting to it. I said, "Hilary, last night you gave me your word. You swore to place yourself completely and unquestioningly in my care until such time as I pronounced you cured. Are you going back on your promise already?"

He flushed angrily and his mouth thinned to a tight line. "No. My word is good."

"I *will* hold you to it. You'd better speak up now if you don't believe you can—"

He snapped out, "I've told you I'll honor my promise!"

I nodded. "Then that's all that needs to be said."

We left it there, neither of us pleased with the other.

I had spent some hours of the bright spring afternoon at Park Lane with another medical man, making further investigations, the details of which perplexed even myself.

That evening I was intolerably tired and dispirited. The man who makes friends of his patients makes for himself just so many possible extra anxieties and heartaches—and I don't know that his patients are any the better for it either.

Maxwell and I said very little to each other over our dinner, and the silence was so unnerving that I even let Bird talk as he chose, and barely heard him.

I believe it was with the idea of bridging the gulf that had abruptly widened between us that after our meal I went to my bureau, and took the locket to show Maxwell.

He said he'd never seen it before and returned it to me.

It was the first time that I had really looked at the thing carefully.

The miniature seemed to me unlike most others—which generally tend to what I would call the chocolate-boxy, the insipidly sweet. There was plenty of character in this one. How an artist could get so much into a locket on so small a scale was a puzzle to me.

I got a lens to examine it.

"Who do you think Perceval had commissioned to do the thing?" I asked, studying the delicate brush strokes.

Maxwell shook his head. "I can't imagine him doing so at all. He wasn't sentimental."

"I believe most miniatures are the work of women. This lady must be original above the average. She's put life into the face. She has not been afraid of the red hair."

Far from that, she had emphasized it, and arranged it falling as a background all about the face and neck. The proud, refined face stood out boldly against a soft red cloud of it. It seemed to me that an artist must possess more than mere technique to do such a likeness. A certain appreciation, surely, of fine qualities. A certain sympathy.

I wondered what Maundeville would think of it as a piece of work. Maundeville had done her portrait.

As this thought passed through my mind, I looked at Maxwell. He gazed at me and I saw the same thought had occurred to him: Maundeville might even have done this for Perceval.

I said aloud, "But if so, why didn't he tell me when I showed it to him?"

"He knew you'd seen one picture already."

It was not really an answer. Or was it?

"But that's just it."

Maundeville knew I was aware he'd painted Miss Hennessey before. What was there to object to in that? I wondered, vaguely, with no great attention, staring idly at the bewitching face. Why shouldn't he paint her all day and every day if he was so inclined?

If he was so inclined...

It was then that my slow brain seemed to wake with a shock.

CHAPTER TWENTY SEVEN

I GO A-COURTING

The day after the inquest I was in better spirits, for I had decided on a definite plan of campaign, and was, I was sure, no longer fighting in the dark—but I'm getting ahead of myself.

At the inquest, Maundeville gave evidence that he and Perceval had dined together, and that he left him in his house in Park Lane, apparently perfectly well, except for a slight wheezing, for which—according to Maundeville—Perceval said he meant to smoke some medicated cigarettes before trying to sleep.

Simpson, the valet, took oath that he believed his master to be well when he wished him good night. He went out afterward, he said, to post a letter, and meeting a lady friend was longer than he intended, and did not know what time it was when he returned.

Maxwell told how he had checked on Perceval the night before but had been sent away and then how he found Perceval and fetched me.

I related what I saw—omitting the Mummy and the letter— telling the jury about the cigarette stumps, and also about the cat having stramonium, the same as Perceval. I explained to the jury in what way the stramonium had reached her, and I quoted a classical case in which stramonium cigarettes had been held to cause death. I added the theory that even a moderate quantity of alcohol might accelerate the effect of stramonium.

At this point Maundeville begged leave to address the jury. He said he now recalled some details of that evening, and that he remembered how Perceval, though he drank only moderately, ate even less, in fact, ate hardly anything. The stramonium, together with the alcohol, would, therefore, probably act with more power.

The young medical man who had helped me, merely corroborated my evidence, and was very pleased to be connected with the second recorded case of poisoning by stramonium cigarettes. He was, unconsciously I am sure, anxious to prove that to have been the sole cause of death. He had already asked my leave to offer an article upon it to the *British Medical Journal* or the *Lancet*.

The jury at once gave a verdict in accordance with the evidence, adding a rider about the danger of the unrestricted sale of drugged tobacco.

A mixture of frankness about some things, and absolute silence about others, had prevented much curiosity or suspicion.

My preparations for action the following morning when Bird came to pull up my bedroom blind, bringing with him a pair of new light-gray trousers, would therefore perhaps appear peculiar.

I had not slept much. In fact most of the night had been spent talking with Maxwell who, either because of the latest reduction in his anodyne dosage or the distress of the inquest, was unable to rest at all. He had walked up and down his room for hours, speaking at length of Perceval, and in those affectionate, humorous recollections, telling me even more of himself.

The sun was rising when he had finally consented to a very hot bath followed by a strong dose of bromide of potassium, which had the desired effect of putting him at last to sleep.

Bird informed me, "Folk judges more by the houtside of 'ats than by the hinside of 'eds—bein' heasier to see."

"Is there any reason I should especially care what people think of my houtside or hinside?" I inquired.

"Hisn't there?" He was being humorous, of course, but I could see he had a point—though perhaps not the one he intended.

After breakfast I went straight to a fashionable barber, and had my hair cut even going so far as to allow the man to put some stinking, oily stuff on my otherwise unremarkable locks.

Next I went to my hatter, who professed to barely remember me, and had a top-hat molded for me.

Since I was about to play the fool, I might as well look my part.

I lunched in my rooms and enjoyed the stupefied air with which Bird contemplated me while he waited table.

"You look very nice," Maxwell informed me. He was heavy-eyed and pale. I thought his lunch did not agree with him, though he made no complaint. "Are you going somewhere?"

I gave Bird a look of triumph, before answering. "It's a fine day. I thought I would call on Miss Hennessey. We've heard nothing of her since Perceval's death, and I'm a little concerned."

Maxwell looked slightly taken aback, but agreed it seemed like a good idea. Well, he did not go so far as to say *good*, but he did say it was an idea. He excused himself to lie down shortly after.

"I think I'll change my clothes, Bird," I said, lighting my pipe at the end of lunch. "Lay out some things for me to choose from, and see that my patent leathers are all right."

Bird went off in silence, and a short time later I went to check on Maxwell.

He was lying down staring moodily at the ceiling, but summoned a weary smile at my entrance.

I sat beside him on the bed and took his wrist, counting out his pulse.

"Not so well to-day?" I asked gently.

He shrugged. "It'll pass."

"We won't reduce the dose again until you've had time to adjust."

His eyes showed relief although he immediately began to protest. I heard him out, and said, "It only gets more difficult from here on out. You understand? If we lose the next battle, then all this has been for naught. We must go slowly and carefully."

"How much am I taking now?"

I hesitated, but after all, he was not a child. "Twenty grains per diem."

He flinched. "Still so much? I thought by now it would be lower!"

"In a very few days we've cut the dosage by a third. It's tremendous progress."

We were pushing harder than I liked, in all honesty. But he was right. It was still far too high a dosage and yet already his body was beginning to rebel at being deprived of its accustomed opiate.

If opium were not an anodyne, the terrible structural changes which it works on its victims would cause no surprise. It would be *felt* eating out its victim's life like so much nitric acid. Having used the drug so heavily for so long, every part of the poor boy's system had reconstructed itself to meet the abnormal conditions. If recovery were possible, he would have to go through a second process of reconstruction, this time without any anodyne to mask the anguish resulting from its decomposition, before his body could again tolerate existence of any normal kind.

"Is there anything you'd like? Can I bring you back something?" I asked. "A book? Something to tempt your appetite?"

He shook his head.

Shortly after, I left him and went into my bedroom where I found Bird standing at ease beside more pairs of trousers than I had thought I possessed.

I chose rather light-gray trousers, white spats, and a white waistcoat, a frock-coat—which I hate—and I worried Bird considerably before I found a tie which pleased me. In the end I made him fetch half-a-dozen from the nearest outfitter's, and I chose a gray silk one which Bird swore would hardly be fit to wear twice.

I ran it through a handsome tie-ring and considered the results critically.

"If it's a weddin'," Bird began uneasily.

I laughed. "It isn't," I assured him. "More like a funeral."

I made him brush my best hat for the second time, and choosing a swagger cane given me by an old friend, I set forth.

Bird, I knew, watched me from the door down the stair; and on crossing the street and turning sharply to look up at my windows I found Maxwell staring at me from there. I raised a hand in farewell and he raised his own in answer.

My first destination was Maundeville's house, which I reached soon after three o'clock. Bates told me that his master was in the museum, and I went there unannounced.

Maundeville was writing, and according to our mutual understanding he did not stop at my entrance. He merely looked up, nodded, and went on with his work, while I replaced a book which I had taken from the table several days before.

The Mummy, that harbinger of evil, stood in her accustomed place. I sat down before it, staring at the painted case and wondering, not for the first time, how far the malignant face before me represented what stood within.

Princesses in stories are always beautiful, but this was not my fancy. The expression of the painted figure on the lid was really heavily malignant, and it was difficult to imagine that the artist of three thousand years ago had been less prone to flattery than his brother of to-day. I imagined that he had made the best of his subject, according to his lights.

The dull, steadily staring eyes had a sort of hypnotic effect upon me, and though I could not have imagined it possible, I forgot Maundeville's presence for the time. When I remembered him again, I knew, without turning to look at him, that he was watching me.

I did turn at last, and we stared at one another in silence until he broke it.

"How is your patient?"

"I'm pleased with his progress. There is still a long road to travel, of course."

"Of course. He continues to live under your roof?"

"Oh yes. That was one of the rules he had to agree to before I would take on his case."

"No pleasure excursions allowed at all, poor fellow?"

"Not at this time."

"He can't be trusted, of course," Maundeville agreed. "But I would be willing to act as guardian and guarantee for a day's outing, if you think it would help him. I'm fond of the boy. Both Maxwell and Perceval were students of mine, you know."

"I recall. And eventually perhaps he will be well enough for the kind of outing you describe. But at this time he must focus on recovery."

Maundeville smiled. His eyes were cool.

"You puzzle me, Armiston."

"*Par exemple*?" I asked carelessly, returning to my contemplation of the Mummy.

"Well, just now you put on fine raiment, rather festive apparel, in fact, and then you come here and sit down to contemplate a thing of evil omen, as steadfastly as though that was your sole occupation for the day."

"Not an evil omen," I said. "More *memento mori*?"

"Meaning?"

"Life is short. 'Youth's stuff will not endure.'"

"Are we still speaking of Maxwell?"

"No. Maxwell is under my protection now and I intend to see he endures all right." I continued to contemplate the Mummy. "No, it is only that the Mummy has reminded me that life is short—in fact that 'in delay there lies no plenty.'"

"Ah." He smiled. "That's the conclusion of the whole matter, is it? Good luck to your wooing! How can I help you? Do I know the lady?"

I looked at my watch and rose.

"Yes, you know the lady. It's Miss Hennessey. Many thanks for your good wishes."

I left him and I can't deny that I was anxious about what I had started, knowing that it would end badly at the best.

But so long as it did not end badly for Maxwell, I would be all right with however it turned out. I went and sat in the Green Park alone, going over my plans to make the best of them, since my dull head could make out none better, and in the end I hung back so long that I had to take a taxi.

Once in the cab, curiously enough I didn't think at all about Maxwell or even Miss Hennessey and what I meant to say to her. Instead I sat wondering whether Maundeville was still in his museum.

I somehow thought he would be sitting looking at the Mummy, just as I had done an hour or so before.

CHAPTER TWENTY EIGHT

I TAKE MISS HENNESSEY UNAWARES

Miss Hennessey's eyes looked as though she were sleeping badly, though she smiled warmly. Even the deep mourning she wore for Perceval could not spoil her grace and charm. The creamy skin that sometimes goes with red hair showed doubly fair above the black ruffle about her neck.

She was alone in a room which I had not seen before, but which I guessed to be her favorite sitting-room. An oil-painting of a soldier on horseback hung on the wall opposite her low chair. It was a grim face and a thin, wiry figure, with a patch painted in over one eye; but there was an unexpected likeness between the rider and the girl sitting opposite, which made it impossible to doubt who he was.

In a glass case beneath the picture I could see a cavalry sword, with several medals ranged around it. On the writing-desk I noticed that the inkstand was in a silver-mounted horse's hoof. A well-polished pair of gilt spurs hung over the mantelpiece under two crossed rapiers, and below the spurs were a pair of long dueling pistols, all kept scrupulously clean.

The room was not like the average lady's boudoir. It comforted me by its suggestion of hardness, while I waited for tea to be brought in. I had determined not to announce my errand while there was any risk of interruption, and while I waited and pondered I must have stared, for suddenly she blushed, and her blushing bothered me so much that I gulped down some far too hot tea and made a desperate start.

"You should have your tea put in little bags," I said, "which can be lifted out as soon as the proper time is up. Otherwise the second cup is likely to hold less tea than tannin. I notice, of course, that this is very good China tea, with which there is much less risk. Still, one cannot be too careful of one's digestion and nerves."

Nervousness resulted in my voice sounding quite harsh and dictatorial, and Miss Hennessey looked more perplexed than pleased by this valuable information.

"I happen to speak of it," I added hurriedly, "because this miserable affair of the Mummy, and particularly the last step taken, is on my mind, and I find my nerves very irritable just when I want them steady."

She glanced down at her mourning, evidently with the idea that I referred to poor Perceval.

I blundered on. "No. What's past is ended. I'm thinking of the last move."

She had lifted a cup, but put it slowly down again—very slowly, as if forcing herself to concentrate her attention on it and to steady herself.

"The last," she echoed. "What more?"

"Haven't they told you? I thought Maundeville might have called."

"No. I haven't seen the professor."

"Then you won't know that they've dealt the cards again and that Maxwell has the High Priestess?"

I jumped to my feet immediately after and hurried across to her, cursing my own clumsy invention—for after one long stare of horror at me she had leaned back and fainted.

I threw open a window and got her to it, though I tell you frankly that she was no featherweight. I laid her flat on the floor and did what else I could, all the time feeling most horribly guilty.

It was quite different from attending to a mere patient. For one thing, I was responsible for her really serious condition. For another, I was all the time desperately afraid lest someone should come in upon us, and in everything I did I had to remember that I must make no noise.

I knelt at her side rubbing her hands, and whispering, "No, no. It's not true. I'm sorry, but I needed to be certain…" I was doing this when she opened her eyes again, and lay looking at me with the same fixed stare of horror which she had given me before she fainted.

"I'm sorry, but I had to be sure," I told her.

The color rushed to her face, and refusing any help, she rose and went slowly back to her chair, where she sat and looked at me apparently with mixed wonder and disgust.

For my part, I sat quiet and waited, feeling a complete brute, but telling myself that at any rate I had learned what I wanted to know, and that nothing else mattered much.

I was sure now of her feelings for Maxwell and that she would be willing to risk nearly as much as I to keep him safe.

"What do you mean?" she asked me at last. "Aren't you ashamed, Doctor Armiston? How could you be so cruel!"

I said, "I apologize again. There's not a word of truth in what I said. There has been no meeting, no cards dealt. Captain Maxwell is in no immediate danger, and I don't think he will be now if you'll give me your help. I don't know how I can manage without it, if I am to see this trouble through."

"How can I help you? What do you want of me?" Her confusion was genuine—and so too was her suspicion.

I braced for more trouble. "Before I tell you that, I want you to promise to be patient and to hear me right out."

"Very well, I promise. Be quick!"

"Another thing," I said slowly, "I want you carefully to keep in your mind two plain facts."

"What are they?"

I leaned forward to emphasize my points with a forefinger. I was terribly nervous, but determined not to show it.

"One thing is," I said slowly, "that I am a middle-aged man— quite old enough to be your father. Please remember that if I seem meddlesome."

"You're hardly in your dotage, Doctor Armiston!"

"The second indisputable fact is that I care sincerely for Captain Maxwell as both a patient—"

"Patient?"

"And…friend. It is for his sake that I'm about to propose what is bound to seem truly extraordinary. Possibly even offensive."

Her eyes narrowed. "I would risk a great deal to ensure any-one's safety with that horrible Mummy," she said at last.

"I don't know that I would," I said, "but I'm prepared to risk a good deal for Maxwell."

Interestingly, she did not question this, although I'm sure it must have struck her as odd.

"How can I help?"

I cleared my throat nervously. "To begin with…if for the next few weeks I seem to hang about you more than necessary, I hope you won't snub me in public."

Her brows shot up in surprise. "I don't often find it necessary to snub people. Why should I?"

"Well, perhaps I'm going to be more conspicuous than most," I suggested, "though I won't do more than I think necessary. Still, it would spoil my plans altogether if you showed me any marked coolness."

"But why should I?" she asked again, puzzled. "What are your plans?"

"Well," I said hardily, "the main point is to make people believe that I am in love with you, and next in importance, to let them believe that you haven't altogether discouraged me. That's all."

Her jaw dropped in a most unladylike fashion. "That's *all*?" she echoed. "Really, Doctor Armiston, I think it's quite enough!"

"More than enough too, I expect. But I can't help it. I believe my plan will work, and I'm not bright enough to think of any other that will."

"Work—how? What will it do?" she asked.

"Now that's sensible of you," I said. "I'll tell you what I think it will do. At the next deal of cards—and they all seem to think themselves bound in honor to go on—I believe it will bring the High Priestess—and the Mummy—to me."

For a moment she didn't seem to breathe. Then she whispered, "How?"

"Through Maxwell who is currently a guest in my home."

"You said he was your patient," she said slowly.

"Yes. But as to that…I cannot break Captain Maxwell's confidence. I can assure you that his life is in no immediate danger beyond the threat posed by the High Priestess."

"But if you're right and you accept the High Priestess into your home on behalf of Hilary, you'll be in awful danger," she pointed out. "What will you do?"

"Oh, leave that to me!" I said airily, having only the vaguest ideas on that point. "Forewarned is forearmed."

She looked at me curiously, and showed that she was very much of a woman after all.

"What are you doing it for?" she asked.

"There's a large fee depending on it," I said confidentially, "and I don't mind telling you I'm a poor man."

"If the Mummy kills you, you won't get your fee."

I said lightly, "I shan't want it, shall I? I shall be as well off as any other dead man. But I mean to live to spend it. And now let me go before I talk any more nonsense. I've said all that's necessary."

"I'm sure you're one of the strangest men I've ever known, Doctor Armiston," she said, as we shook hands. "Are you—will you assure Captain Maxwell there is no understanding between us?"

"I will assure him of that."

She studied me thoughtfully. "Where are you going now?"

"I think I'll go to Maundeville. As a man somewhere near my own age he may understand and sympathize."

To this she said nothing, and I never looked at her to see how she took my remark. But it took all the bravado I could muster to give me what I supposed to be the proper air of mild swagger on returning to Maundeville's house.

CHAPTER TWENTY NINE

WHEREIN SUSPICIONS DEEPEN… DEEPER

It was after seven o'clock when I left Maundeville's. Reaching home, I found Maxwell reading in my sitting-room. Or at least he was holding a book titled *Legends Of The Gods* and staring into space.

I was relieved to see he looked much better than he had after lunch. A little self-consciously I handed over the bunch of still dripping lilacs I had purchased from the corner flower shop.

"I thought these might cheer you up. A little breath of fresh air?"

"What? Why…thank you." He took them, looking both astonished and confused.

"It's early in the season for them."

"Er...yes." Maxwell smiled.

That sudden smile held the sort of affection usually reserved for someone quite a bit younger than oneself. The sort of look I imagine I generally bestowed on him.

I shrugged. "Anyway. I thought you might like them."

"I do. It was a kind thought."

I felt quite foolish, so it was a relief when he asked, "How is Miss Hennessey?"

"Grieving, I think."

His smile faded. He nodded. "I wish I could fix his death on someone more easily reached than a mummy."

I knew who he meant by "he" and studied him closely as I asked, "*Do* you suspect anyone of having a hand now?"

By now the solution seemed so obvious to me that I couldn't believe he hadn't reached the same conclusion. But then I had no long-standing affection for my suspect, whereas Maxwell was by nature loyal and warmhearted.

"How can I?" he answered impatiently. "Who'd do such a thing, even if he could? The only person who could possibly profit is me, and I would never..." His voice died out as though the very thought still winded him.

"I asked you," I persisted, "whether you suspect anyone—no matter how unjustly or ridiculously. You haven't answered me."

"I feel ready to suspect anybody—everybody," he said contradictorily. "I could suspect you if you'd been in it at the beginning."

"Well, as I wasn't, and as you brought me into 'It,'" I retorted, "you might speak out."

"I will directly I have the least justification for doing so," he promised, "but I can't fling accusations around with no evidence to back them. Especially when it means flinging them at friends. Besides, I've proved myself wrong once already lately."

"How so?"

"I could have sworn I was going to get the Mummy. How can I trust my opinion about anything connected with the matter after that? I hadn't the remotest notion of poor Percy's danger. Even after he got the High Priestess I believed he was safe."

"Why?"

"Oh, what does it matter? I was wrong, and there's an end of it."

"Is it?"

"Well, yes." He was watching me closely, as though waiting for me to object.

"Why did you believe the Mummy would come to you?"

The question made him uncomfortable. "I don't know. I just imagined it might."

"Because of Miss Hennessey's…tendresse for you?"

"Oh, well, that's putting it a bit strongly."

"She *is* fond of you. Perceval commented on it once."

His eyes narrowed. "Then was I not altogether mistaken?"

"I think the Mummy will certainly come to you next. Or would have."

"What does that mean?"

"I'm prepared to accept it on your behalf."

"*What?*"

"As you're currently under my care—"

He flushed. "Who knows that?"

"Maundeville knows the truth of your condition. He guessed long ago. Miss Hennessey knows only that you're living under my roof as a patient."

His expression grew furious. His eyes glittered like old silver in the firelight. "How dare you share a secret that was not yours! You promised me your absolute discretion. I *trusted* you. Well, Armiston?"

"Listen to me," I said patiently. "I repeat. Maundeville has known of your habit for some time. He guessed correctly that you were here and he guessed correctly the reason for it. I didn't attempt to deceive him because I'm happy for him to believe you're out of the game once and for all."

I regret to say this did little to calm him.

When he was finally obliged to stop for breath, I said, "As for Miss Hennessey, you can tell her anything you like. That you're undergoing a new therapeutic treatment for your knee, perhaps?"

His rage lost some of its luster. He said dully, "I suppose everyone will know eventually."

That would likely depend on the success of our cure. I withheld that thought and said instead, "Not through me or anyone in my household. I promise you. Now here's some news. What do you say to my telling you that someone has proposed to Miss Hennessey?"

He lifted a negligent shoulder. "That often happens."

"What do you say if I tell you that he has not been definitely refused?" I asked.

"Not Maundeville?" He seemed shocked. "Surely not Maundeville!"

"Not Maxwell!" Maundeville had said only a short time ago. Interesting how they both leaped immediately to the thought of the other.

"It happens not to be. But would that trouble you?"

His face was troubled. "No. I suppose not. I don't know. He's too old for her."

"Ah. Well, what do you say to myself? I'm not so old as Maundeville, but I'm not so young as you."

"You!" He looked at me with open and uncomplimentary amazement, and then grabbed his stick, rising from the sofa with a haste that must have wrenched his bad leg. He limped to the window and stared out.

"Then you're not pleased?" I asked.

"I'll say the correct things presently," he said over his shoulder. "You must do as you choose. She's a fine girl and possesses a fine fortune."

"Several fine fortunes at this point," I said dryly. "So you have no objection to me and Miss Hennessey?"

He turned on his heel and came back to me.

"Look here, Quentin!" he said stiffly. "I don't know what you're driving at, but you've gone far enough. I can't stand another word. Why did you bring me here if you were only going to—" He broke off and looked away sharply.

I shook my head. "Hilary, don't be a fool." I rose and took him in my arms. It was the first time I'd ever done anything so bold, but it felt natural. Shockingly so. I could feel his heat and hardness all down the length of my body. He was shorter, slighter, but the contours were right, and I liked that he was lean and solid, liked the feel of muscle and plane beneath my hands.

There was nothing tiny or fragile or pillowy to make one feel too large and clumsy and out of his depth.

Maxwell was a man and this was forbidden, but it felt like the most reasonable and right thing that had ever happened to me.

I held him tighter and realized he was shaking. Was that anger or emotion or something else? Those fine tremors brought out a fierce protectiveness in me. I couldn't stand for him to be worried or hurt for one moment longer.

I said against his ear, "Do you really imagine I'm in the market for a wife? However pretty or rich?" and had the satisfaction of feeling his body relax against my own. I liked the feel of him leaning on me, of seeking comfort from me.

"My only interest in Miss Hennessey is related to what you and Perceval asked me to attempt. You of all people should know that. I admit my methods are unorthodox, but the situation is unorthodox."

He drew back to stare at my face. "What has any of this to do with the Mummy?"

I pulled a rueful face. "I can't prove it—not yet—but I suspect it has everything to do with the Mummy."

CHAPTER THIRTY

THE MALAY COMES

The days passed and, although this must sound strange, I had never been happier.

Or in more danger.

Danger coming in all shapes and sizes, the most immediate threat was that of losing my heart for all time to Captain Hilary Maxwell.

Having lived so long on my own—not counting Bird, of course, who was as much a part of me as my doctor's bag—it would not be surprising if I'd had some difficulty adjusting to the constant presence of a stranger beneath my roof. In fact, nothing felt more natural than the sight of Maxwell across the breakfast table, or sitting beside my fire, or walking beside me down moonlit streets.

When I opened my eyes each morning he was the first thought that popped into my brain. And my last thought when I closed my eyes at night.

I suspected he would be my last thought when I closed my eyes for all time.

Granted, he was my patient and his case was complex, so part of my focus was natural enough. Most of it was not. Not by anyone's standards, unless possibly the ancient Greeks.

And yet it felt like the most innate and reasonable feeling.

I could never remember laughing so hard or talking so much. I had never considered myself lonely, but now I understood that a certain room in my heart had stood empty for many years. All the professional friendships and intellectual pursuits—all the puzzles provided by human nature—had not so much as turned the key in the lock.

Now that room had a tenant. And that tenant seemed to give warmth and life to what had previously been mere existence.

"Can you honestly say you didn't suspect me even for a short time?" he asked one afternoon as he read over the legal documents from Perceval's solicitors. His gaze was cool and curious.

"I could see you had both motive and opportunity," I admitted. "But I could not believe you killed your friend. No."

He said calmly, "Yet you believe another is capable of killing his friend."

"You are not he."

"Is that really an answer?"

I drew thoughtfully on my pipe. "Perhaps not. Well, call it my experience with human nature. I'm curious about something, though. Why did Perceval make you his heir? From comments he'd made, I fully expected Miss Hennessey to be his beneficiary."

"Oh." Maxwell made a face. "Perceval is—was—extremely practical. Miss Hennessey requires nothing in the way of material gain. Whereas I, in Perceval's opinion, have been 'ard done by."

The last words were in perfect mimicry of Bird—a gift of Maxwell's that, for some peculiar reason, delighted Bird no end.

"Hard done by how?" I asked.

"My father was the eldest son, but when he ran off with my mother, my grandfather disinherited him in favor of my uncle."

"Ah."

"My uncle never married and has no children of his own, so I'll eventually inherit the estate. It's no great matter. Though the situation always incensed Perceval." He smiled faintly at some memory.

"No great matter," I repeated.

"No." He shrugged. "My parents died when I was quite small. My uncle has been my guardian most of my life. We get along well enough. He was a military man, and it was his wish that I follow in his footsteps."

"I see." And I did. Many things. Things that made my heart hurt for a lonely little boy. One thing I had never lacked growing up was the love of a mother and a father.

Another occasion I asked—could not help asking, "The day we met at the flower corner shop you were buying bunches of daffodils. Were those for Miss Hennessey?"

"Yes." Maxwell threw me a quick, guarded look. "It was not a romantic gesture on my part. She was distraught after finding poor Scrymgeour—and then that D'Aurelle should follow so soon after. Perceval was worried."

I said carefully, "Perceval believed you would marry her."

"Yes. He did. I told him I would not, but he continued to think it would be best for all of us. Safest."

"Was he in love with her himself?"

"A little I think. Maybe. He was genuinely fond of her." He sighed, leaning his head back against the sofa and closing his eyes.

I could hear Bird in the kitchen preparing our lunch. I stroked Maxwell's hair back from his forehead. His hair was light and fine as gossamer, the dark strands seeming to crackle against my fingers. "You would be better resting, dear boy."

He smiled without opening his eyes.

Around this same time I was quietly, unobtrusively doing a great many things which led me even further out of my ordinary humdrum routine. I consulted fantastic books, met some fantastic folk, and acquired some fantastic and apparently quite useless information.

If a great deal of that was futile, I chanced across some things of importance I think can't be counted altogether a mere coincidence. I searched in so many directions, and kept my slow wits so constantly stirred to wakefulness, that I deserved some return.

One evening, leaving Maxwell to snatch what little rest he could, and Bird, I fancy, under the impression that I should dine at my club, I strolled away eastward, and entered the restaurant where the gilt banyan was conspicuous in the setting sun. It seemed to me that if I dropped in occasionally, I might, without showing any extraordinary curiosity, hear something of Perceval's and Maundeville's last dinner there.

Having dined, I sat over my port, and looked about me. Here Maxwell had brought me first; and in one of those little rooms at the back he had tried to warn me off from delving any further into the mystery of the Mummy.

Here Maundeville and Perceval had dined. At which table, and which of those soft-footed foreigners had waited on them? I sat sipping my port and speculating, until I remembered that I had an evening engagement. I went to pay at the desk, and stayed a moment to praise my dinner, which had been excellent.

"Captain Maxwell brought me first," I reminded my host, "and I mean to come back."

"So you did, sir," said he, "and I remember you came again later one evening with Captain Maxwell and the professor."

I agreed, and reminded him that Maundeville had dined there earlier that same evening.

He showed at once that he understood the reference.

"You'll be Doctor Armiston," he decided. "Of course I saw the report. Glad the Banyan wasn't dragged in. It couldn't have done any good, and might have taken away some of our best customers." His eye strayed to a far corner. "Yes, they sat over there."

After that, finding it inconvenient just then to accept invitations and bind myself for fixed hours, I chanced in at the Banyan some two evenings out of the next ten.

It seemed to me that all that spring season the prolongation of life became what I'm inclined to call more shriekingly fashionable than ever. To turn one's face to the wall and die decently seemed the last thing possible.

As for growing old? Unsupportable!

Advertisements of vitalizing agents, under suitably suggestive names, filled the columns of the daily papers, which on one page warned their readers against quackery, and on the next gave indecent details of wonderful and impossible cures for everything from thinning hair to thickening waists.

We marveled at the Bulgarian, who had apparently been a *médecin malgré lui* from time immemorial. We suddenly discovered that it was possible to live on rice and water—and then remembered that the mild Hindoos had done it before. We agreed that everybody ate and drank too much, and we supplemented our diet by concentrated foods and nerve-tonics. We all sighed for the Simple Life and to go Back to the Land. Duchesses did so, for week-ends, with the result that rents rose in the country, and the roses, particularly on Sundays, smelled of petrol and were covered with dust.

As for me, I took small daily doses of such poisons as meat, wine, tea and coffee, and tobacco, and continued to live.

To combine the wisdom of fifty with the dash and enthusiasm of twenty-five, might be a real advantage. I admitted as much to Maundeville, who confessed to me that he was still investigating these problems, and sometimes thought he saw glimpses of light on the possible way to success.

When I looked in upon him in his museum one afternoon, he told me that he had begun a graduated series of hypodermic injections upon himself, and he hinted at the lines of experiment.

"The thing really should not be left in the hands of charlatans," he said, "though Cagliostros will always flourish. Let me only get definite results—even if slight—to put before you, and then you and I might follow the matter further together. My knowledge is hardly up to date—and, besides, I need an honest man to verify results."

"You intrigue me. I shall always be eager to assist in any of your experiments where you believe my help might be useful."

"I have a wonderful physique," Maundeville said, as though stating the obvious. "I don't want to change that with any man. I only want to make sure that I keep what I've got—and why shouldn't I? Wear and tear can be minimized, and repair very much accelerated. But we must stick at it!"

He turned to his papers and test-tubes with frank dismissal. "Good-bye, my dear fellow," he said. "Ask for tea up in the library if you want to look at anything there."

But I said I wasn't going upstairs, and I went straight away. I found that I now much preferred to read at home than in Maundeville's library—and when I did visit I had begun to refuse the very excellent tea.

I was now welcomed, or endured, at the Banyan, so far that I could nod to the proprietor, and feel aggrieved if my corner was occupied. The second time I dined there alone I was shown to the little corner table where Perceval and Maundeville had sat, curiously observing the fast, solemn table attendant, who told me he was from Bengal, and had some little difficulty in understanding anything of my English, beyond the names of the dishes.

Chatting for a moment at the desk as I paid my bill, I asked the proprietor where these dozen or so hirelings of his lived. Did he board and lodge them?

He shook his head, and smiled at my ignorance.

"Half wouldn't live with the other half," he explained. "They get rice, butter, some other odds and ends, and the use of two rooms at the back. They do a little cooking there, and they smoke a bit. When I've done with them at night, they go out." He made a large vague gesture, which suggested a general scattering and disappearance in outer darkness.

"How do you get them?" I asked.

"Oh, they come, Doctor—generally from ships. One brings another, if there's a place to be filled. Most of 'em are old hands. If one means to go, the rest always know of it before I do. Then one introduces a pal, and I put him through his facings, or tell old

Abdullah to do it. Abdullah bosses them a bit for me, and makes a good thing of it, no doubt. But when I want to, I can talk to them in a way they understand."

"Rice, butter, odds and ends," I repeated. I was thinking of the popular debate on healthy foods. "That's plain living. They seem to thrive on it."

"They're better fed than they were at home, I'll be bound, and they save a bit. They do very well if they keep off arrack and bhang and opium."

"Can they get these things easily in London?" I asked him.

"Easily! Why, there's countrymen of theirs make a good living out of it. They have to be careful, of course, and they get nailed at times. But you see, the trade's almost altogether among themselves. So I think there isn't so much fuss made. Anyway, they get it. I sacked the man who waited at your table only a fort-night or so ago. He took bhang and turned nasty. I banged him." He smiled grimly at the recollection—or at his small joke—and was going to say more. But another client came to the desk, and he turned away.

I lingered, wishing to ask him a few more questions, when I saw an unusual sort of visitor come in and stare about him.

He was a scarred and tattooed fellow in dungarees. I could see the glint of earrings as he turned his head from side to side. Presently, he looked straight at me and started up the room.

I thought he was coming to me, and watched, rather surprised. But Samuels at his desk had been watching too. He stepped out quietly and met the man halfway, smiling good-temperedly. They spoke together for a moment, the other man in a quarrel-some loud way, Samuels nodding and apparently agreeing with everything.

It seemed to me that the man's face, clean-shaven, thin, unpleasant, was not absolutely unfamiliar. Samuels went on talking quietly, till the other appeared pacified, then put his hand in his pocket, half turned to his desk, and nodded toward a door near my corner, leading to the back premises.

After salaaming, the fellow went, passing close by me as he did so.

Presently Samuels came after him, jingling some coins as he went.

I leaned forward and stopped him.

"Who's that man?" I asked. "I seem to know him."

"Of course you do, sir," Samuels said—then corrected himself. "No, you don't, though. He was before your time. Unless the professor asked you to take him on for a job, as he did me. He used to wait at your table."

He moved to pass on.

"Stay a minute!" I said, quite certain now. "I do know the man. What's he here for?"

"He's here for what he can get, sir," he answered, "and I'm going to give it him—as soon as I can—and fire him out by another door. He's been on the spree and got left. I can't have my gentlemen put off their feed by anyone."

"I ask you a favor, Samuels. Let me come with you and speak to that man."

Samuels allowed himself a grin.

"D'you know Malay, Doctor? Unless you do, you won't get anything out of him."

"I know the true Volapiik," I said, putting my hand in my pocket, "and I can rely on you to know all other languages."

Samuels, with a sort of a grunt, gave way. The man whom we found in the back premises and who was certainly the Malay I had seen in a rough-and-tumble with Maundeville and afterward in hospital, seemed almost starving. The fighting spirit he had shown upstairs was fast oozing away. He wept, and Samuels explained that now he merely asked for food and a warm corner to eat it in. These he was finally promised for the night, and he groveled at Samuels's feet, talking vehemently, and shivering even in that Turkish-bath atmosphere.

Samuels said he was protesting that if he could only see "the professor," Maundeville would help him, and he wouldn't need to trouble anyone any more.

"I don't know that I care to turn him on to a customer," Samuels concluded, surveying his former employee with open contempt, "even though that customer brought the man here. He can wait table too, and he can cook more than a bit."

"Give him shelter to-night," I said, "and send him to me to-morrow afternoon. I'll perhaps do something for him. If I decide to let him have Professor Maundeville's address, that will be my affair."

And so it was settled.

CHAPTER THIRTY ONE

The Malay Goes

By now Maxwell's daily dosage had been reduced to four grains and he was having a very bad go of it.

I did not dare leave him for more than an hour or two at a time, and had to make sure that he was never entirely on his own in the house. His appetite was poor—much of the time he was unable to keep down what he did consume—and he slept very little. He suffered agonizing hemicranial headaches, neuritis and muscular weakness. In addition to acute generalized pain, his lame leg began to ache and throb as he swore it had not done for years, but only once did he break down and beg me to increase his dosage. His courage was humbling in the face of his sufferings, but all the courage and determination in the world could not alter the fact that he had slowly and systematically poisoned himself.

I had already faced the fact that a cure might not be possible and we would have to consider how to best keep him contented on the smallest possible dose. I devised several strategies for the future, but did not share my prognosis with him. As long as he had the will to continue, we would fight. The choice to surrender had to be his own.

In the meantime we used every means possible to ease his pain and sleeplessness. From the never ending hot baths, cold baths, and mustard "packs" to Bird's massage and my shampoos, my household—and even much of my practice—revolved around keeping our young guest as comfortable and calm as possible. I mixed tonics and sedatives and even resorted to ether when all else failed. Bird supplied a steady stream of beef tea and a milk and lime-water concoction he swore by.

Maxwell's own attempt to deal with his physical woes was to walk himself to a standstill—which sometimes meant a matter of minutes and sometimes meant hours—at any time of day or night. Because I could not allow him to make these campaigns on his own—not because I didn't trust him, but because he was often too weak to make it home without help—I usually accompanied him. With the end result that I was very short on sleep and had little energy or thought to spare for our Mummy.

I offer this as some explanation for the fact that my wits were perhaps not as sharp as they might have been regarding all that followed my aforementioned visit to the Banyan.

At breakfast the next morning, I asked Bird whether he had ever been in the Malay Archipelago.

"Was I ever, sir?" Bird was amused. "One of the prettiest little maids ever I met was a Malay. A headman's daughter, too. That's the way to learn anybody's lingo. Pick up with a girl o' the country, and you soon pick up her speech—leastways what's useful."

"Am I to understand, then, that you can talk Malay?"

"Like a native, sir," Bird declared hardily. "I won't brag—but that little girl used to say she never 'eard any man talk it like me before."

"Ah. Now that I can quite believe," I assured him. "Well, I've a Malay coming to see me this afternoon. He can't speak English—at any rate, hardly any—and you can translate."

Bird looked a trifle worried.

"It's a long time ago of course," he said, "and there's several dialecks. Some words, I suppose, though, is much the same all over," and he gave me various sounds which he said meant "love" and "drink," "money," "kiss," "knife," and so forth. "Other words'd come in conversation-like," he decided. "What is this Malay, sir?"

"He's a sailorman, a lascar."

"''E'll know all our swear-words, same as you or me," Bird said, "and that's always a 'elp if you want to get on terms with 'em. Besides, these lascars picks up a word 'ere and a word there, just like a marine," and he seemed serenely certain of his ability to equal the occasion.

I acknowledged that he did so when the fellow came—up to a certain point.

At his own suggestion Bird started by giving the lascar a meal in his kitchen, and I heard him catechizing the man about his voyages, and so forth. I'd given Bird no idea of what I wanted him to ask about.

He talked to the man in the sort of broken English with which soldiers, sailors, and a good many more are apt to address the foreigner—mixing this with words and sentences which I imagine were sometimes Malay and sometimes other Eastern languages. The man was now clean and bright-looking. His meal had apparently pleased him, and he stood to attention, looking a good-tempered, inscrutable sort of ruffian.

I told Bird to explain that I had remembered seeing him in hospital, and that I was a doctor, interested in the habits, customs, and particularly the drugs, of foreign countries.

Bird piled it on in broken English, with a few foreign sentences thrown in, and the man seemed impressed. At any rate, he salaamed profoundly, and, according to Bird, called himself a "hignorant devil."

I listened to them, lit my pipe and, as I smoked, considered what approach to take.

I told Bird to explain that I collected foreign drugs. For good specimens of pure drugs I was ready to pay, I said, if not too expensive—also for information about their uses. To make this point plain in case Bird's powers were not equal to it, I fished out some silver from my trousers pocket and separated a couple of half-crowns, putting them on the table, and jingling the rest in my hand.

The Malay waited, his eyes lowered to the coins on the table, a little smile just showing his teeth. Bird fatly impassive, sniffed discouragingly. I continued to puff away at my pipe, determined not to hurry matters.

"Tell him," I said to Bird, "that I understand he's a sailor and that I know he probably comes and goes between London and his own country. He might remember me and bring me some of his people's medicines. I'll pay him when he does."

Bird translated or paraphrased, and the man answered quickly. He, too, was talking a sort of pidgin-English, and I had an idea of his intention before Bird explained.

"Ses there's lots o' fine medicines in 'is place, sir, but bloomin' dear. He must take money back to buy 'em. Ses they're sort o' cash chemists over there. No pence, no pills." At the same time Bird protested strongly against any advance being made—

saying it was "too bloomin' thin," and I inclined to agree with him.

"In the words o' the song, 'D'you think that 'e'll come back?' sir. The odds is against it," Bird pointed out.

"What do they do when they're ill over here, or anywhere away from home? Do they always go to hospital?" I asked. "Don't they carry any of their medicines with them?"

"Ship's doctor, or ship's cap'n," Bird suggested. "Number one, Indigestion. Number two, Information. Number three, Rouser, and so on."

"Ask *him*!"

Bird asked, and the man first answered carelessly enough, then suddenly bestirred himself and began talking vehemently. His eyes brightened, his tattooed face changed, his voice rose, he almost chanted a long reply, while Bird stared in silence.

"Well, what is it?" I asked Bird, when he stopped.

"I can't quite make out, sir." Bird scratched his head. "'Is feelin's 'ave run away with 'is tongue, sir, I couldn't follow 'im. There's something 'e says is medicine an' meat an' drink, with a smoke chucked in."

The fellow was feeling inside his shirt, but drew out a little bag, empty, and showing it to me, shook his head.

"Stony," Bird suggested sympathetically, "and run out of 'is stock."

"He had money last night," I said. "He can't get the stuff here, perhaps. What is it?"

No! It seemed that he could get the drug here, though not so good. He gave a name I didn't know, and I rose from my chair, and went to the book-case. I took down two or three books: Taylor's *Medical Jurisprudence*, a Pharmacopoeia, and a Botany.

I knew precisely what I was looking for, though not under the name the Malay gave it. That name I could not find.

I said so, standing at the book-case with my back to them.

"Is it opium?" I asked Bird. "Tell him I can get good opium."

But no. The Malay knew opium, and preferred his own drug.

"Perhaps it would be of no use to a doctor," I said indifferently.

The man seemed to understand at once, and protested, "Much good."

"Oh, it doesn't matter!" I yawned elaborately. "If he thinks it worth his while to bring me a good specimen, I don't care where he gets it. Tell him so."

Bird told him, and the fellow said he would do so quite soon.

"Perhaps it's only used by Malays," I added. "I suppose he doesn't know a name for it in any other language."

Bird asked, and the fellow thought a moment and then gave me one word: "Bhang."

Bird jumped slightly and brought a hand down upon his thigh.

"Lord! Why didn't I think o' that?" he muttered. "What else got me Cells that time?"

"If he can get good samples of this bhang, or any other drug peculiar to his people, I'll pay him a fair price. If he's really hard up, and can get some of the stuff this very night, I'll give him something for his trouble and pay cash for the drug."

This man had waited on Maundeville and Perceval the night they dined at the Banyan, having been introduced by Maundeville. The drug used in the preparation of the drink "bhang" is *Cannabis Indica,* or Indian hemp, and its action is somewhat similar to that of stramonium.

The man's eyes lit up. He said he could, and would, get some if he had the money, and he gave Bird the name of a street in

Soho—the street, in fact, where I had first seen him. Then, while talking, he drew something else from his shirt. Outside this was a little bit of oilskin, then two or three layers of muslin, and then a little ball of yellowish, soft, putty-like substance.

He looked at it and at me with a good-humored smile that showed his beautiful teeth. "Very fine medicine," he said. "Much can do."

"What is it?" I asked. "What can do?"

But here his English and Bird's Malay failed altogether. They both became most amazingly stupid, and, indeed, the Malay seemed unwilling to talk more about it. He rolled up the little ball in its muslin, wrapped the oilskin outside, and shoved it back under the breast of his shirt.

It was not for sale, he said, and he could get no more till he reached home again. Perhaps he could bring me some another time, but not now.

But the bhang was different. He could get some of that and send it back by Bird, if Bird would go with him. And another evening he would come back and talk more about his people's medicines.

I handed Bird the money and told him to go, and to pay for the stuff when he had it in his hand. I also made the man comprehend that I was open to buy other drugs, and in any case would pay him a trifle to come again and tell me what he could of what I bought.

He promised, but suddenly objected that first he must keep another engagement.

"Where?" I asked.

It was at another *Hakim's*, and he fumbled in his pockets and produced a scrap of paper. I didn't know the writing at all—

indeed, it was a sort of printing hand. But I knew the address very well, for it was Maundeville's.

"Go with him to this address," I told Bird. "Wait about outside, but don't make yourself conspicuous. Then go on to Soho with him."

I turned to the Malay, repeated my promise about money for other drugs on another call from him, and I let them go off together.

I went immediately to check on Maxwell and found him awake, sitting before the fire and stroking Bhanavar. (Yes, perhaps the final proof of my besottedness was I'd introduced that damned black cat into my household as yet another comfort and distraction for our invalid.)

The fire had brought warmth to Maxwell's face and his eyes looked clearer than they had for a while.

"What was that about?" He was smiling a little as I sat on the sofa beside him.

"So you heard?"

"I heard. I can't say that I understood. Are you purchasing more remedies?"

"No. Or at least nothing I would use on you."

His brows rose. But what he said was, "I've been thinking we should reduce my dosage again."

I cannot deny I quailed a little at this, and my face must have showed it.

He said, "Such a tender heart must be a liability in a physician."

"It would be if I cared so much for all my patients."

He smiled, looking more like his old self, and put the cat on the floor. Bhanavar protested this treatment, but neither of us paid her any mind as Maxwell moved closer to me, putting his arm around my shoulders. I reciprocated, and so we were in each other's arms, gazing into each other's eyes.

Maxwell laughed softly, studying me. "Have you really never done any of this before, Quentin?"

I shrugged. It was nice like this. I liked holding him, liked being held. Would have liked to ask for more—but was equally afraid of overtaxing him either physically or emotionally. He was my patient after all and there are rules about these things.

"But you must have known the truth about yourself years ago." His eyes were bright and colorless in the firelight.

"Yes."

"I knew from the time I was a small boy. Percy knew."

"Perceval?" I had suspected this. I was an innocent only in practice. In theory I knew all there was to know.

"We weren't lovers. Not anymore. Not for many years." Maxwell was still smiling, but the smile had turned inward, was reminiscent. "He was my dearest friend." The smile faded.

I thought I should reciprocate his honesty with my own, but it wasn't easy. "I should probably tell you—that is, I fear I'm not like other men."

He flicked me a look that was almost teasing. "Well, no."

"No, I don't mean—I mean that while I've been aware of my true nature for most of my life, it wasn't as difficult as one might think to…to sublimate those feelings."

"Sublimate?" he asked slowly.

I felt cold inside having to confess, felt sure he would feel the disdain any red-blooded man must. "I don't—have not previously, that is—feel a powerful drive toward the…carnal."

I could see I had truly disconcerted him. "Don't you?" he asked uncertainly. "Not at all?"

"Not greatly. Not usually."

I could see he was worried by this, and I was sorry for it. It had worried me too when I was younger, although I had often thought, given my proclivities, it was also a blessing.

He was silent for a time. I studied his profile, afraid of what he must be thinking, but I could tell nothing of his thoughts.

Finally, he asked curiously, "Did you like it when I kissed you?"

"Certainly! Of course!" Yes. I had enjoyed that kiss and had thought of it many times since.

"You're not just being polite?"

It was my turn to laugh. "Do I strike you as being overly prone to politeness?"

He relaxed a little. "No. Since you mention it. And do you enjoy this?" He pressed closer so that I could feel through his trousers the half-arousal of his cock against my thigh. It gave me a warm, tingling feeling in my belly and made my own cock rise against the restrictions of my clothing. I would have liked to rub against him. I liked his thin, hard body and his muscular arms. And I liked his contrasts: the jut of his chin and the bristle on his jaw versus the softness of his mouth and eyelashes.

"Yes. I like that. I like to hold you. I'd like to touch you and caress you and have you do the same to me. I'd like to lie naked with you."

"I'd like that too, although lately..." He glanced downward in discontent.

Impotency being one of the inevitable effects of the drug. Nor could I give him comfort on that score. So much depended on his recovery—and he had not yet faced the worst. That would come when he stopped taking the drug altogether.

Assuming we got that far.

I said, "Bird will be gone at least another hour. Will you lie down with me?"

His smile was his answer.

I brought him to my own bed and was pleased to see him, brown and lithe against the white sheets, warmed and animated as he had not been for days. His eyes shone with pleasure as I leaned over him, taking time to rub and kiss his cock until it stirred into semi life.

"That's nice. I like that." And then as my mouth closed around him, his hips rocked up and he gave a little moan of "You don't mind?"

Of course I didn't mind. I loved him. Wanted to caress and cherish every inch of him. I can't deny it took a long time and a great deal of loving and cherishing with hands and lips and tongue and even the lightest scrape of teeth to finally bring him to a small spurt of sticky wet against my tongue.

He groaned, a sound that was part pleasure and part shame.

"What does it matter so long as it feels good," I whispered to him. "Did it feel good?"

He nodded, face buried against my shoulder. "Why are you so sweet to me?" he muttered.

"Now there's a silly question." I kissed his ear, which was all that was available to me, and his damp temple. He was breathing as hard as though we had performed some great feat of acrobatics. I kissed him again and again, and eventually he lifted his flushed face and fastened his mouth to mine.

The kissing was as nice as all the rest of it, though you might think a doctor would have some concerns about shared breath and spit. His tongue slipped into my mouth, and I could taste the exotic sweetness of the opium. I could have kissed him forever. He was my addiction.

"We must do something about this," he murmured when we finally stopped to gulp air. His hand wrapped around my jutting cock with startling familiarity.

"Yes. God. Do that."

He whispered hotly against my face, "Would you like to fuck me?"

The vulgarity was shocking, but what was more shocking was the fact I nearly came from hearing it said aloud.

"No," I said quickly. "That is, yes. *Yes.* When you're stronger. Now would be—"

He covered my mouth and rubbed his nakedness against my own, not seeming to mind as the hard thrust of my cock caught him here and there in sensitive places. The friction felt good and frustrating at the same time.

He rose up on his arms, grinding against me with a hard efficiency, and within relatively few strokes I was arching up into him and spuming like a bottle of champagne. He smothered my shout with his mouth, and I could taste his laughter—and something that was worryingly like tears.

I put my hands on his wide shoulders, conscious of the fine bones beneath the thin skin, and pushed him back, studying his face. His eyes had a glittery, blind look. "What is it?"

"I don't want this to be all there is."

"What? Was it not right? Did I hurt you?"

He shook his head fiercely. "I want there to be time for us."

I pulled him close, clasped him so tight I couldn't tell where his heart started and mine left off. "There will be. I promise you there will be."

I didn't know if it was true, only that it *must* be true because he wanted it and I would give him anything in my power.

I said against his hair, "*Was* it all right? I didn't hurt you?"

He gave a watery chuckle. "It was wonderful. I feel well for the first time in weeks."

Everything he did gave me pleasure, and it made me happy that I could give him even a little of that back. He seemed genuinely relaxed and contented as we lay together, and after a time he slept quite deeply, yet naturally.

To be able to take away his pain and give him peace even for a short while—that was the greatest satisfaction of all.

At about five o'clock I rose carefully, leaving Maxwell still asleep, and made tea. But for once, tea and tobacco could not keep me quiet. I alternately cursed my past stupidity and rejoiced that my eyes were opened, even though without credit to myself.

When six o'clock arrived, neither Bird nor the Malay having returned, I was too impatient to sit quiet any longer. I couldn't help remembering Bird's liking for a yarn, and no less for a glass. He might conceivably have turned aside for both, either alone or even with the lascar.

Other more serious things might have happened.

I looked in on Maxwell who was still sleeping peacefully. That sweet escape was too rare to disturb, so I locked the flat and went in pursuit of Bird.

I found that I had done him injustice. A seat under a tree, just outside the Square gardens, and perhaps eighty yards from Maundeville's door was where I found him. He was placidly smoking, and keeping a steady eye upon that door.

Bird never looks very wide awake, but I knew quite well that no one would go in or out without getting his immediate attention. When he spotted me, he rose and saluted.

I sat down, after satisfying myself that the windows of Maundeville's house did not give a view of the seat.

"I was wondering what on earth had become of you, Bird. If you had been worth worrying about, I should have been worried."

"Knew you would, sir," Bird admitted. "But your orders was to wait for the Malay."

"You don't mean to tell me he's there still?"

"I mean to tell you 'e 'asn't come out," Bird declared, "and this was the last of my 'baccy. So I'm glad you've come. I wasn't sure if you would."

"I suppose you've been asleep?" I said.

"Knew you'd say that, sir," Bird remarked, philosophically calm.

"Has anyone else come or gone?" I asked.

"Not a soul. The 'ouse has been as quiet as the grave." Bird proceeded to knock the ashes out of his pipe. "Shall we go? You're dinin' at 'ome, you'll remember, and it's time I saw to things."

Bless my soul, no! What did dinner matter?

I believe I said something to that effect, and Bird grunted, and stowed away his empty pipe, while I tried to think.

"Shouldn't leave the Captain too long," he pointed out when the thinking brought no immediate results.

What was I to do? I couldn't go in and ask for the lascar. I couldn't even go in and prowl about on the chance of meeting him there. I didn't want him to know that I visited the house and knew Maundeville. I didn't want Maundeville to see me meet him.

"No, we shouldn't. But this is really important, Bird," I said at last. "I should have told you so at the start."

"Pity not to, sir," said Bird. "Still, better late than never. And it wouldn't have brought the Malay out any sooner," he added, I suppose, for consolation.

"Perhaps there's a back way out," I said.

"There may be," Bird allowed, and then suggested that if I would watch the front with its area gate, he would go round and reconnoiter at the back.

He left and I smoked my pipe, with incongruous thoughts about Maxwell and the house I was looking at, and the nuisance of not knowing when I was going to get my dinner. Mixed with these was the feeling of a difficult stalk, and finding that my chance of a stag hung in the balance.

It was some time before Bird returned from the opposite direction to that in which he had gone. He seated himself with another of his characteristic grunts.

"There's a garden-door at the back," he said, and waited while I relieved tension by a few rancorous remarks. Then he added that no one had gone out that way.

"How do you know?"

Bird hinted that in his branch of the service men learned to use their eyes. Then, in the face of my exasperation, he condescended to details.

"There's cobwebs on the door. Lots of 'em." He added that a heavy thundershower, which I had paid no attention to while I had lain with Maxwell, had fallen while he and the Malay had traveled together. It had laid the thick dust in the little lane at the back of the house, and there was no mark of a foot near this door.

"Are you sure which door it is?" I asked him.

"Numbered, sir," was his answer, and that settled it. I sat and stared at the house with a sense of foreboding not at all in harmony with a fine summer evening.

I asked, "Is there any friend of yours who could watch this place and say nothing?"

Bird considered, and then suggested Seymour.

"You can trust him not to talk?"

Bird deliberated again, and then explained that Seymour had broken with the lady whom he had been taking out, and was, therefore, to be trusted.

"Find him," I said. "But first check on Captain Maxwell. Make sure he's all right and that there's something he can eat, if he's able. Then you and Seymour get a meal, both of you, and join me here. You may have an all-night job. The garden-door must take care of itself till you come."

It was only after Bird departed that I remembered I'd left Maxwell sleeping in my bed. The realization of my mistake left me feeling as if the ground had opened at my feet. I almost ran after Bird. But I recognized it was already too late.

Whatever would happen would happen.

I had over an hour of anxious smoking and useless watching before Bird returned, bringing Seymour with him.

I must have looked fairly stricken because he reassured me at once that he'd left Maxwell perfectly comfortable and reading his "'eathen book." Maxwell had instructed Bird to tell me all was well and not to worry about him.

Which I took to mean that Maxwell had woken safely before Bird's return.

I pulled myself together sharply and told them that I needed their assistance for a most serious matter that they had to watch the house, front and back, until the morning, and to say not a word of it, except to one another. They were to come and report to me, straight from there, at eight o'clock.

I went off and dined at my club, and about eleven o'clock I went round and looked them up. Seymour, at the front, reported that Maundeville had gone out alone in his car. Bird, at the back, had seen nothing.

I returned home and spent the night with Maxwell. We held each other quietly through the long hours, kissing softly and sharing the occasional sleepy thought.

He said at one point, "Did you know the ancient Egyptians believed sexual relations would be part of the afterlife?"

"Did they really?"

He nodded.

"Something to look forward to even in death."

He laughed.

I slept even less than he did. Not because I wasn't tired, but because I hated to lose even a moment of our time together.

At eight the next morning Bird and Seymour turned up together. Nothing more had been seen of the lascar. Seymour reported Maundeville to have returned in his car about 1.30 a.m. That was the whole of their account.

Bird got me breakfast, and then went off to his hammock for a nap.

For me that day chanced to be a busy one. I saw Life come, and I saw it go. Where one unwelcome mortal entered this world, likely to be unhappy and unhealthy from cradle to grave, another exited—and that a man younger than I, and much more useful.

Further, at Maxwell's request, I'd cut his dosage by another grain and by dinner time he was again in dire straits. I did the best I could for him, but it was not enough. It half killed me to see him twisting on that bed, tears in his eyes, asking me to leave him for a bit.

I was gloomy that night—and it did not cheer me any to consider the certain piece of work I had set myself.

Because of the original promise I'd made—and because I feared my other inclinations were only too obvious—I could not go to the police as any right-minded citizen does when he sees crime unchecked.

Perhaps it's the risk of practicing medicine and growing accustomed to the power of life and death that left me ready to take the law into my own hand. But what I contemplated frightened me too. After all, it was not just my risk. There was Maxwell and even, to some extent, Bird.

One thought consoled me. Until I got the High Priestess card, I believed we could all sleep safely. But once we had the Mummy as our tenant, trouble might come at any moment—night or day.

Therefore, it seemed advisable to control as much as possible when that trouble should begin.

CHAPTER THIRTY TWO

WHEREIN IT GETS MORE COMPLICATED

Five days passed without any developments, and I began to get angry. The old joke is that a doctor requires patience, but in this case to sit still and wait didn't suit my nerves at all. I fancy between me and Maxwell, Bird had a deuce of a time.

That said, Maxwell had adjusted to the two latest reductions in his dosage with surprising speed and was pushing hard for the final cut. This presented its own problems because if trouble came, I did not want it to strike when he was most vulnerable and Bird and I were preoccupied with his care.

I could hardly offer that as an explanation though—unless I was willing to give him the full story, and I was rather hoping to avoid that. Or at least postpone it as long as possible.

On the sixth afternoon my patience was exhausted. Maxwell and I had finished our lunch—pigeon for me and a few bites of omelet for him—when an idea occurred to me and I called Bird in.

"If anyone wants me this afternoon, I'll be at Professor Maundeville's house. I expect to be in at five, when I shall want tea."

Bird stood and looked at me, and then looked at Maxwell.

"Suppose you're not in by five?" Maxwell inquired.

"I intend to be," I said.

Bird rubbed his chin, a trick he has when not standing rigidly to attention. "Always ready to obey orders," he informed me.

"Are you?" I asked, with interest.

"I don't pretend to know the game," Bird went on calmly. "But you'll remember, sir, that there Malay."

"What about the Malay?" Maxwell looked from me to Bird.

"Went out at the garden door," I suggested to Bird.

"Maybe," said Bird.

Maxwell looked from Bird to me. "Are you saying that this Malay *disappeared*?"

"Very well, sir, I'll get a taxi." Bird directed a meaningful look at Maxwell.

"Gracious, man! What d'you take me for? A millionaire? What do I want a taxi for on a fine day like this, and for that distance?"

"Get the taxi, Bird," Maxwell ordered. "Quentin, you'll keep the cab waiting and if you aren't home by half-past five, Bird and I will be coming to look for you—and we shan't wait outside."

This display of high-handedness gives an indication of how much better he was feeling.

"Now what on earth do you mean?" I demanded, glaring at the both of them.

"I don't know, sir," was Bird's somewhat unsatisfactory reply. Without giving me time for a rejoinder, he went off and got a taxi.

I turned to Maxwell who looked rather grim. "What's this about?" he asked.

"A long story, Hilary, but I promise it's nothing to worry over."

In fairness, I don't suppose that would have reassured me either.

Maxwell said, "Then you're convinced beyond a shadow of doubt that Maundeville is involved in these deaths?"

"We already know that he is."

"As more than the mere catalyst."

I acknowledged this reluctantly.

"Then what are you playing at?"

"Suspicion is not proof, as you said to me not so long ago. And as we're on this topic, who, if I might ask, were you suspicious of at that time?"

His lashes lowered, but then he met my look directly. "Maundeville."

"Why do you suspect him?"

"Why? Because the Mummy belongs to him."

I sighed. "You see? It's not good enough. Not nearly."

He frowned, but he couldn't deny it. "What's your plan of attack?"

I smiled faintly. "I'm still formulating it. This is more of a reconnoiter."

"You should have a plan."

"I will. When the time comes I promise to get your advice on how to proceed. In the meantime, you have *your* orders, do you not?"

He made a face but nodded.

Bird saw me into the taxi, and told the driver that he was engaged by the hour, and was to wait and bring me back again—and I repeated the order when I reached Maundeville's door.

But I rang with a strong belief that I should find him at home, and did so.

His first invitation, making me practically free of the house, still held. I went straight to the little museum when Bates admitted me, and there was Maundeville busy with test-tubes, Bunsen burners, distilling apparatus and other instruments and appliances, which I had forgotten the use of or perhaps had never known.

To protect his clothes, no doubt, he had put on a frayed old college gown, and being, as I knew, always very careful of his white and muscular hands, he was wearing rubber gloves.

The handsome, keen, clean-shaven face which he turned to me, directly I opened the door, was paler than usual, and even, I fancied, a trifle thinner.

"Ah ha! The happy man," he said. "*Ben venuto*! But fancy straying in here on a June day. It's fine outside, isn't it?"

"Of course it's fine outside." I went to one of the bookshelves and took a book to carry away. "You were out this morning, I suppose?"

"I don't think so." He held a test-tube against a flame. "No, I think not."

"You don't know?" I asked curiously.

"I forget," he said a trifle impatiently, and stopping to compare the test-tube in his hand with a small stoppered bottle on the table, he began to heat the tube again.

"The Philosopher's Stone?" I suggested, "or rather the Elixir Vitae, I suppose."

"There's a variety of things here," Maundeville replied, without turning from his work. Then he exclaimed, "I can do no more. The rest can wait!" He put the tube carefully to stand in a rack and dropped into a deep easy-chair, leaving various gas-jets and spirit-lamps burning.

"Oblige me by pressing that button behind you," he said to me.

As I turned from doing so, I found that Bates was already in the doorway, and Maundeville seeming to take that for granted, spoke without changing his position in the chair or raising his eyes.

"Have a good fire at once in the dining-room, and heat up the pipes too. What meal is there for me?"

"Dinner, sir."

"Order it to be served. Are my clothes laid out?"

"Yes, sir."

"When you've told them in the kitchen, come to shave me upstairs. Oh, tell them to lay for two. Doctor Armiston dines with me."

"Too early for me, thank you," I said.

"Ah, yes! I've missed a few meals, I expect. But wait a little if you've time. I want to talk to you. You'll have tea, perhaps?"

"I'm having mine later, but I'll wait a little while if you want me to."

It would have been interesting to test the sort of dinner Maundeville could have waiting his pleasure and ready to be served in a quarter of an hour. Even at four o'clock I daresay I could have found it tempting. But apart from any other consideration, I have the old-fashioned idea that eating or drinking in a man's house implies certain obligations on both sides.

"Wait here," Maundeville suggested. "It'll be more comfortable while the servants lay the table, unless you care to go upstairs?"

I said I would wait where I was, and Maundeville rose, glanced about him.

"Put out those spirit-lamps and burners on the table," he said to Bates. "Leave everything else." He passed out through the door which Bates held open for him.

It was the first time I had seen him tired. I should have liked to hear from Bates what his master's hours and meals had been during the last few days. But I said nothing, nor did he, and after obeying Maundeville's orders he followed him without a sound. I never heard a door creak or a handle rattle in that house. I never saw or heard any servant but Bates and the chauffeur; and Bates moved as though he were on rubber tires.

I dropped into the chair Maundeville had left, glancing about without any expectation of seeing anything particularly instructive.

Alchemy was the interest of the moment obviously, and odds and ends relating to other sciences and hobbies were shoved away onto side tables and shelves.

Bates came back in a moment, noiseless as ever. Maundeville had noticed my taxi, and told him to ask if I wouldn't have the man paid and sent off.

I said no, that he was to take me elsewhere later, and Bates slipped away again.

I had not gone there with any intention of spying, but merely of giving Maundeville an opening—to draw him.

On the edge of the long deal table in the center of the room— the one he had been working at—I had laid my gloves and the book which I had taken from a shelf while we talked. It was a book on mummification techniques, and I thought I would look at it while I waited.

I fancy that Bates, in putting out a burner, must have slightly disturbed loose papers, sheets of memoranda, calculations and so forth, lying scattered about the table. At any rate, as I picked up the book I saw something else that I had not noticed before.

An inch or two of oilskin stuck out from under the other things. In such a place the discolored and rough material was noticeable, and I pushed the papers aside.

There, half opened, lay the packet which I had last seen in the hands of the Malay sailor—the outside oilskin wrapper, the inner covering of muslin, and the yellow putty-like substance enclosed.

Heart beating fast, expecting every instant to be discovered, I pulled a bit off the little ball, rolled the latter—fingers unsteady—hurriedly into shape again, wrapped the bit in a corner of my handkerchief, pushed back the papers and went to my seat as quickly as possible.

Maundeville's shave and change of clothing was a very speedy operation. Certainly in a quarter of an hour from the time he left me he came in again—in dinner dress now, though it was only about half-past four. He found me sitting in the chair which he had vacated, taking a note or two from the book I had borrowed. I told him I had found all I needed, and I returned the book to its place.

He looked much fresher, and announcing that his appetite was enormous, led the way to the dining-room, taking some vermouth from the sideboard before he sat down—at the same time laughingly declaring that it was altogether superfluous.

"I've received no invitations from the Society," I said as Bates put a cold fowl, with tongue, salad, and a pint of Irroy before Maundeville. "Am I out of favor?"

"Not at all. There have been no meetings," Maundeville said. "I've no time for them now and without my impetus, the others simply drift." He shrugged and then asked if Bates might open a bottle for me.

When I refused he told Bates to leave the cheese on the sideboard, and come when he heard the bell. "It's time—well past time—for another drawing of the cards, but I've been waiting to hear how Maxwell fares."

His blue eyes scrutinized my face.

"Not well, I'm afraid."

"Ah." He pursed his mouth. "Then the case *is* hopeless?"

"I fear so."

"Hm." His eyes were intent. "She—Miss Hennessey—speaks of him often."

Yes. She did. I heartily wished the woman would shut up about Maxwell. Her infatuation seemed most unbecoming for a suffragette and it kept Maxwell in Maundeville's mind. The last thing I wished.

"Do you see her regularly?" I inquired.

He chuckled. "Now, you mustn't be jealous. We're simply friends."

"Of course." I tried to look smug. I felt mostly uneasy. I did not trust Miss Hennessey to convincingly pretend to any special tenderness for me. In fact, in any contest between Maundeville and myself, I suspected *he* would have her loyalty.

He then drank half a glass of champagne, attacked the fowl with gusto, and said, "I have other news for you. My mixed serums promise well."

"How have you tested them?" I asked.

"Solely on myself. But in that way I've been able to exclude fallacies. Mostly. A certain amount of risk in these things is inevitable. How many clever fellows have openly worked for the elixir, or some modification of it, and openly failed? How many, more wisely, have brought good brains to the job and failed, and therefore said nothing! For the time, if you'll help me, you and I will be among the wiser ones and say nothing yet. What is it that's said about fools and bairns not seeing half-done work? If you subtract the fools and the bairns from our population, how many are left?"

"You and I, apparently," I said, with absolute gravity, and Maundeville, after looking steadily over his plate at me for a minute, laid down his knife and fork and laughed hugely.

"Forgive me if I say bluntly that now and then I find we have a good deal in common," he said. "Neither of us is a fool, Armiston, and so neither of us thinks himself omniscient or omnipotent. Still, we're a good bit above the average. If we had only met earlier!" He didn't say what would have happened in that contingency, but went on: "Now let's quit our noble selves, and talk of more important things."

"With all my heart," I said, looking at my watch. "I've been rather expecting to hear from you. But I must be elsewhere by 5.30 at the latest."

I thought for a moment that he was about to ask where I was going, but he did not. After all, he was never impertinently inquisitive, and besides, I dare say that he supposed he knew.

"Well, I mustn't make you late," he said. "It amounts to this. I've found a combination which is at any rate a strong whip to one's nervous system. For three days and nights now, working as I do best in long spurts with complete idleness between, I've eaten and drunk very little, and slept still less. Here am I enjoying my dinner uncommonly, and not now particularly tired."

"You attribute this to your treatment?" I asked.

"Oh, decide for yourself. I've done a longer spell than before with less effort and less fatigue. Ergo these injections being the one new factor, they are responsible for the new results."

"Most impressive. And what do you want me to do?"

"First observe the effects on myself! Decide whether the treatment is merely exhausting my store of energy at an abnormal pace, or whether vital force is being abnormally produced and stored. Then—" He stopped and looked at the clock. "You'll be late for your engagement if we're not careful," he said. "It will take you a quarter of an hour to get there."

Naturally he assumed that I was going to call on Miss Hennessey.

I nodded noncommittally.

"After you've watched me for a day or two," he said, "decide whether you care to test the thing on yourself. You and I are much the same age. It's an age at which, for certain possible gains, one can afford to run risks. One's stake in any case is not the stake of a young life."

"You forget," I said, "that I may value my life more highly than I did, say, a week or ten days ago."

"Do I?" He looked at me fixedly. "You value the possibility of another fifty years of potential youth higher still, I fancy. I should in your shoes, at any rate."

"You make a good case."

"I know." He gave me a cool smile.

I left him helping himself to cheese, while Bates decanted a bottle of very special port under his master's supervision.

When I reached home, Bird came to the door before I could use my latchkey. He looked distinctly worried.

All he said was, "Thank Gord! Another five minutes and I couldn't have stopped him."

"Hilary—Captain Maxwell?"

Bird nodded grimly.

He went to get my tea, and I braced for battle. Bird waited on us more attentively than usual, but asked no questions, and, of course, I told him nothing. Maxwell was an entirely different matter.

"You can't be serious!" he exclaimed when I had told him of Maundeville's proposal.

"Completely. Now have no fear. He's not going to attempt anything until the next draw of cards. And that's assuming we're not doing him the greatest injustice by suspecting him."

Maxwell seemed to suffer no qualms on the possibility of injustice to his old tutor.

"Of course he is. What do you suppose all that nonsense was about never speaking about the experiment?"

"That will relate to something planned for further down the line."

"They're bound to be connected."

"Naturally. But at this time there's no danger."

"You can't be sure of that!"

"My dear boy, I'm no hero. I assure you if I thought there was any significant danger, I would not proceed."

"I wish I might believe that."

"Of course you may believe it. What I don't understand is what role Maundeville himself believes the Mummy plays in all this. Is the priestess merely a bit of legerdemain? Or does he believe in the curse? Let me ask you something. Did Scrymgeour suffer from any hitherto undisclosed health condition?"

"You know he didn't. You conducted the postmortem examination."

"True. Let's put it another way. Had he dangerous habits or vices unknown to any but his closest friends?"

"Such as an addiction to opium?" Maxwell asked bitterly.

I did not allow my sympathy to distract me. "Since you've put it so plainly, yes. D'Aurelle had a weakness of the heart and Perceval a weakness of the lungs. What about Scrymgeour?"

"This is ghoulish. He was prone to overeating and suffered from dyspepsia and a peptic ulcer, I believe."

"Ah."

"What does that 'ah' signify?"

I said triumphantly, "And, as you now know, prolonged opium use damages the liver. So. What do canopic jars contain? The heart, lungs, stomach and liver of the mummified remains."

Maxwell shook his head. In fact, he seemed faintly amused. "Impressive, my dear Holmes. Except the heart of the dead Egyptian didn't go into a canopic jar. The heart was believed to be the seat of the soul and it remained within the body. You're looking for a fourth victim with intestine trouble."

"Oh."

Maxwell grinned at my disappointment, his own good humor restored. "Still. It's an interesting theory."

I sighed. I had many interesting theories—interesting to myself and Maxwell, at any rate—but they brought us no closer to solving our case.

From that time Maxwell insisted knowing in detail what my movements were to be when I left the house. Twice when I replied vaguely, he asked me point-blank if I was going to Maundeville's.

It was somewhat annoying for I was not used to having to report to the headmaster—or even the drill sergeant—he seemed to resemble on these occasions. But it was also oddly comforting. Not so much because I feared for my safety—I was quite confident that no one would make a move against me until the next draw of cards—but because it had been a very long time since anyone cared so much for my safety and well-being.

It was ridiculous too.

I couldn't help but be aware that our little interlude of domesticity was coming to an end. Once I cut entirely Maxwell's opium dose, we would know within a matter of days whether a complete recovery was possible or not.

If not, he would spend the brief remainder of his life as a hopeless addict.

If so, he would eventually regain his health and resume his normal life—away from me.

CHAPTER THIRTY THREE

PRETTY POISON

The evening after my visit to Maundeville's I visited my old friend Mortimer at Gray's Inn.

I was at Guy's with Mortimer, and though I'm only a general practitioner and he refused the chair in Medical Jurisprudence and Toxicology, we have remained cordial—perhaps because of our shared love of puzzles. Granted, Mortimer prefers to poke and prod at the riddles of chemistry whereas I'm fascinated by conundrums posed by human nature, but sometimes these two collide.

Straightaway Mortimer told me he disagreed with my inquest declaration about the Datura stramonium.

"There's only one case on record of poisoning through stramonium cigarettes, my dear Armiston," he informed me.

"I didn't say it was the cigarettes," I reminded him, "though I did say stramonium. I've changed my opinion on that too," I added.

"Ha! That's awkward for you. What are you going to do, then? Ask for a fresh inquest?"

"I'm going to do nothing," I said. "I didn't come about that. This is something different. Can you tell me what this is?" I held out my bit of putty, half uncovered in the handkerchief.

Mortimer took it from me, displaying the frayed sleeve-edge of what was certainly a disgraceful old jacket.

He held it to the light, sniffed at it, pinched it, and looked at me sideways, almost bird-like.

"I shall need to test it in various ways," he said, "and there isn't much of it. What can you tell me about it to start with? We might eliminate certain things, or get an idea to start upon. Where did you get it?"

"It belonged to a Malay sailor," I said. "I've some reason to think it's a poison."

"Oh! Very likely. Why don't you ask him?"

"I don't know where he is," I said. "He talked of going home."

"Hm. Naming it may be fairly simple," he said. "Come again to-morrow night if you like. I should have an answer for you. Don't go treating your patients with it meanwhile."

Between that night and the next nothing particular happened.

I cut Maxwell's dosage by a half-grain, which was less than he wanted but more than he could bear once it was done.

"We needn't cut so much at once," I told him that evening. "We can add a quarter grain and see how you fare."

After a day of it he looked spectral: gray-faced, hollow-eyed. "You don't think I can do it. You don't believe I can break free."

The accusation in his voice hurt. "I don't know. I know you can't take much more of this."

He said bleakly, "You mean *you* can't take much more, Quentin."

"Maybe," I admitted.

"I won't go on in this half-life. An opium eater. I've wasted years already. I'll die first." He spoke with a great and final calm, and I knew he was completely serious.

"Don't say that."

"Death is nothing," he said. "One goes to explore a new country—which is always interesting. Or being tired, one sleeps."

Sleep being something he had very little of these days. I said quickly, "Then we'll continue. The decision has always been yours. Whatever you choose, I'll support and aid you any way I can."

This seemed to calm him.

When I left him he was sitting in the bath gasping and gulping beneath the buckets of near-scalding hot water Bird poured over his head.

I returned to Gray's Inn and found Mortimer hunched in his favorite chair drinking his own poison, bitter black tea.

His greeting was characteristic. He didn't rise or even say "How d'you do?" but only announced one of the several names by which a certain poison is known. He leaned back and grinned at me.

While I was considering Mortimer's information, which I was certain would be accurate, he startled me by another remark.

"It would very much interest me to know," he said, "whether this Malay, to whom our identified poison belonged, was in the very least degree in touch with your Park Lane case."

"Why?" I asked.

"Hashish, Armiston. Hashish that time, *not* Datura stramonium. That's where you went wrong, as I think you know."

"Yes," I said. "I know." I rose to go, and as I did so I asked another question. "If I happened to get a dose of this stuff, what antidote should I try?"

His eyes narrowed in thought. "If taken by mouth, only a very large quantity would be injurious. But if *I* was unfortunate enough to receive a subcutaneous injection, I should certainly try a hypodermic of strychnine hydrochlorate—if I had time." He sat and considered the matter. "If I had time," he repeated softly under his breath.

"I'll keep it in mind."

"Do. But you know, I'm of the opinion, my dear Armiston, that this is one of those instances where prevention is very much better—and easier—than cure."

* * * * *

I don't pretend to be a man who thinks overmuch of his dress, but on the next occasion I visited Maundeville I believed it right to make my attire strike a rather more pronounced note. In fact, I tried to keep up the general impression of a man who has hope to live upon—and finds it an invigorating diet.

I suppose my face wasn't precisely as youthful or as bright as my apparel. But then the lover on probation must have anxious moments anyway, and may be allowed to show the effects. I was sufficiently rewarded when I saw that Maundeville watched me with increasing attention.

I avoided his house for a few days, and he soon dropped in to call, complaining that he had become accustomed to see me come and go, and that he missed me.

"Besides," he added, "I've reached the point in my investigations where I can't do without your help. Can't Cadogan Square spare you occasionally?"

I did my best to produce a fatuous smile and reminded him that I was only there on sufferance. Which was of course absolutely true.

"My dear fellow, don't be too modest!" Maundeville implored gaily. "Own that the lady listens more readily."

"Certainly sometimes I believe I shall win." I preened into the little mirror over the mantelpiece at the effect of a fresh pink rosebud and maidenhair fern in my buttonhole.

Perhaps I only imagined the momentary spasm that crossed Maundeville's reflection. At any rate, he congratulated me warmly and chaffed me lightly, and all in excellent taste.

"We must soon be choosing our wedding presents, I see," he said. "'Unto him that hath shall be given.'"

I recommended that he leave the question of presents until he had Miss Hennessey's assurance that the wedding was definitely arranged. Then, fearing lest I had not been sufficiently the coxcomb, I rang for Bird and rowed him for having put out a dark waistcoat for me, instead of a light one, and told him to go to the florist's, and ask if the flowers I had ordered had gone to Cadogan Square.

Bird's face was such a study that when he left the room I had no difficulty in laughing heartily enough, while Maundeville for a time became curiously silent.

I then asked him to excuse me, as I was due at Cadogan Square, said good-bye, making an appointment with him for two days later.

Miss Hennessey having kindly agreed to receive me whenever I thought fit to present myself, received me graciously and over tea questioned me at length on Maxwell's progress.

Two days later brought thunderstorms—several occurring beneath my own roof when I informed Maxwell that I was visiting Maundeville.

I found Maundeville in his museum. Two or three electric lamps were lit, and the shutters closed. The lights were well shaded, and the shadows were deep all round the room, the table alone standing out clearly. When I entered he was apparently doing nothing, but sat outside the lighted space among the shadows, with his chin upon his hand, and his face turned toward the Mummy, which stood in its usual niche.

What were his thoughts on that dark and crackling afternoon? Lately I felt that, however interesting or amusing Maundeville's conversation might be, what he said was not so important as what he kept to himself.

Apropos to nothing, he remarked, "I saw Miss Hennessey yesterday. She still has no inkling of the true nature of poor Maxwell's illness."

"I've not had the heart to tell her, coming so soon after the death of Perceval."

He nodded thoughtfully. "The fate of the opium eater is a living death, true enough. Any right-thinking girl would be naturally repulsed. She seems to believe he's undergoing treatment for his leg."

"Yes. Maxwell is in great anguish at the thought that the truth of his condition must soon be widely known. Understandably. So much so that I've volunteered to take his place at the next drawing of cards."

Maundeville looked as close to thunderstruck as I'd ever seen. "*You?*"

"Yes. Why not?"

"Well, but the—the curse is not yours to share."

I smiled. "Come now. Neither of us share in these superstitious beliefs."

After a moment he smiled. It was an odd smile. "No. I suppose not."

"I'm happy to do whatever I must to put my patient's mind at ease."

"Poor Maxwell." He was silent for a few moments. Then he shrugged. "Your compassion does you proud, Armiston. I'll speak to the others. I can decide nothing without their consent."

"Of course!"

He changed the subject at once and began to discuss his favorite topic, his experiments on prolonging life, and, of course, of youth and energy with it.

He talked on, quoting Pythagoras, Herodotus, Bacon, Horace, Juvenal, Galen, Aristophanes and Paracelsus, besides half a dozen of our contemporaries. Man had always shown his instinct to prolong life and to preserve youth, he said. And I could not fault his energy and passion on a subject that was frankly of interest to any man over forty.

Certainly I had cause to think more of youth and vitality these days.

Suddenly Maundeville stopped. He considered me for a long moment. "Supposing that, for the time in strict confidence, I give you a certain formula, or recipe, which I have used personally. Then I give you certain evidence of what I believe to be the direct results of my treatment."

"To what end?"

"That you might criticize my theories, analyze my concoctions, scrutinize my results. What I suggest is that you test my prescription practically upon yourself—if you have pluck enough, and then decide with me whether we can put our conclusions quietly, say, before the British Medical Association, as worth its consideration."

He stopped, waiting for my response. I had none.

"Good men and good work have been ignored and ridiculed by our liberal profession times enough," Maundeville said in a different tone. "The outside public, ass though it is, would recognize the results of such a bit of work long before many of our brethren. But if I'm right, I shall have the best possible way of silencing my objectors—I shall outlive them."

I laughed. To my own ears I sounded nervous, but I don't think he noticed.

"You, who are meeting the very personification of youth itself almost every day, will think it worthwhile—no, I won't advance the most selfish argument—you'll be pleased if you can do anything to keep youth youthful and charming as it is now, if only for a time. It would be a wedding present that emperors can't equal."

He had hit the mark more nearly than he knew for I did indeed have a young lover—though not the one he imagined—and I did indeed fear that the age difference between us, attendant with what I already recognized to be a certain lack of erotic vigor on my part—might ultimately drive us apart. Given the odds already against us.

He watched me closely. "Well? Do you care to see my formula and the different constituents?"

"Of course!" I said. "That doesn't bind me to anything."

"Except silence," Maundeville warned.

"Naturally, my dear fellow!"

He straightway launched into detail.

The stuff he worked with was an ethereal extract of certain animal organs, combined with large quantities of hydrochlorate of strychnine. The constituent to which he attached most importance was extracted from the cerebellum and medulla oblongata of the calf—these parts being chosen because of the important nerve-centers located there.

"And why the strychnine?" I asked, and his reply was that since one couldn't isolate the precise vital centers, apart from their surroundings, the extract contained forces which must be counteracted. For example, in experimenting one night with an unusually large injection he found that his pulse gradually sank to thirty beats to the minute. After that he combined strychnine. He found that no apparent effect resulted from taking large doses by the mouth, and he now always used a hypodermic syringe.

I listened while he explained these things to me, and then putting down the glass-stoppered bottle which held the completed fluid preparation ready for use, he picked up a note-book from the table, and showed me the entries under different recent dates.

For example, on the night of June 10 he had returned from a reception at about eleven o'clock, and after changing his clothes had walked thirty miles, returning to breakfast at nine, and going through an ordinary day's occupations afterward.

From the morning of June 12 to the evening of June 14 he had worked in the museum, with little food—he noted the precise quantities—and no sleep.

On June 16 and 17 he had taken no food, except coffee, with his ordinary quantities of cream and sugar, and had gone about as usual without any particular discomfort.

"You were always strong," I reminded him, watching.

"You're right. I was always strong, though I'm sure I could never endure fatigue before as I have lately. There's only one way to check my results properly. Experiment upon yourself, and see how far we differ, and how far results coincide."

I deliberated a moment, weighing the probabilities. By now I had proved to my own satisfaction Maundeville's motive in eliminating certain members of the Society of Osiris: he wished to eliminate all possible rivals for Miss Hennessey's affections. But it would be difficult to convince a jury of that motive without considerably more evidence than I had. Naturally I did not want to die in pursuit of that proof, but I continued to postulate that as long as the Mummy resided in Maundeville's museum, no danger would come to me or any other members.

But I confess it was more than the wish to bring my erstwhile friend to justice. His inadvertent reminder of the age difference between me and Maxwell—one of the many differences between us—had sparked a certain recklessness in my heart.

"Done!" I said. "Give me an injection now!"

For a few seconds Maundeville sat motionless. Whether I had taken him by surprise, or whether he too was deliberating over his actions, I can't say. Presently he rose.

"My dose is thirty minims," he said. "At starting, and to guard against any personal idiosyncrasy, I'll dose you with fifteen, and gradually increase it."

I said nothing more. I rolled up the sleeve from my left forearm, and watched him take fifteen minims from the little glass-stoppered bottle, which he proceeded to inject under my skin.

I confess that—having been such a fool—I should then have preferred to get away at once, but Maundeville insisted upon the necessity of sitting quiet for at least ten minutes.

I waited docilely trying to think whether—assuming I didn't die immediately—I would confess what I'd done to Maxwell.

Whether it was because the summer thunderstorm charged the hot air with electricity, or because of the injection I did not know. It might even have been mere imagination. But I seemed to creep and tingle all over, and all my senses were exalted. I even noticed Maundeville's newspaper crackle on the table as he passed it. The sound sizzled along my nerves like a whiplash and I told him so.

"Ah, yes!" he said, seating himself again, and pulling the newspaper to him. "That reminds me of something. It will serve to keep your mind from magnifying symptoms while you sit quiet. When you came I had just been reading the account of the Darnley murder. You've followed it in the press, I suppose?"

"Yes."

"The man's nerve failed him. He took so many precautions after the event that he roused suspicion. A little more patience beforehand, and a little more pluck after, and I think he'd have got clear."

The hair prickled on the back of my neck. I said nothing. He stopped and listened to the far-off crash of thunder.

"The rain is coming at last!" he said. "We'll be able to breathe better now. I like a good rainstorm, don't you? Let's open the window."

He pushed back the shutters, opened the windows, and switched off all except one light.

"Referring for a moment to poor Perceval's unfortunate death," he said, "I sometimes fear that we got on the wrong scent. Do you remember a little rough-and-tumble I once had with a lascar?"

"Yes," I said. My heart was pounding so heavily I felt it would smother me. I wondered if I had made a fatal mistake after all.

"I happened across the fellow again. He seemed to think that because I had knocked him off work for a time he had a claim on me." His lip curled in scornful memory.

"He couldn't enforce it," I suggested.

"Oh, no! But I hate bother, and it sometimes makes me do things that seem good-natured. I found he could cook a bit and wait table, and I got him a job pro tem at the Banyan. He waited on Perceval and me that evening, and now I wonder whether he doesn't know more about that evening than we do. I was a good-natured fool to suppose that a Malay ever forgets."

"Where's the Malay now, do you suppose?" I asked him.

"Shipped for another voyage, I expect," Maundeville said carelessly. "Samuels sacked him. We must do what we can to trace him again, but I was reminded of him while I read the paper."

"Why?"

"Oh, they say 'murder will out.' It's one of a good many fallacies which give the bourgeoisie a little ease, and perhaps sometimes frighten a neurotic criminal into betraying himself. The police know better, but of course they don't say so. Apart from a good many known murders unexplained, there must be many never recognized as murders at all."

"And you believe this Malay—?"

"We can hardly prove it without getting hold of the fellow, and that will not be easy to do. I don't believe he'll ever come back."

"You don't?"

"No," he said confidently. "If he did, he wouldn't betray himself. Mark my words, I don't believe we shall see him again. There's the storm at last!"

So it was. It broke a mile or two away, and rolled over the West End, the rain falling as if in the tropics, the lightning dazzling us where we sat, and the thunder shaking us in our chairs.

Maundeville rose as it drew near, and stood at the window watching it with tremendous enjoyment, until the storm rolled muttering away eastward.

"It must have done damage somewhere, one would think," he said vaguely, still gazing out the window as I rose to go.

"Yes," I said. "I imagine it did."

I went away and when at last I reached the wet and shining street outside, the pavement warm and steaming, the air shimmering, only then did I feel I could take a full breath.

CHAPTER THIRTY FOUR

I GET THE HIGH PRIESTESS

"You did *what*?" Maxwell exclaimed, when I related my adventures at Maundeville's. "Quentin, have you completely taken leave of your senses?"

"My dear boy, this is the most careful and calculated of risks," I assured him. "The danger is negligible."

"You say that to me when we both know what he's capable of!"

"But we don't know. Not for sure. We have no actual proof."

"There are other ways of getting it."

"But there aren't. Hilary, listen…"

Maxwell and I argued over my plan several times over the next days. I did not convince him nor, frankly, myself either. I knew quite well that I was playing with more than one kind of fire, and to tell you the honest truth, I don't think I shall ever quite get over the scorching.

The one element of danger I was unprepared for was to nearly be my undoing.

Those subcutaneous doses of Maundeville's had a power which I did not anticipate, and will not attempt to explain with any precision now. The strong doses of strychnine must not be forgotten, but I never knew strychnine alone to have such results. Somehow Maundeville had found a way to target his powerful extract to isolate and pinpoint those tracts of the brain that were most susceptible to the stimulating effects of his serum.

Whatever the cause might be, at the end of that June I felt remarkably well—and much more reckless.

I took daily doses from Maundeville, and was ready to push them further and faster than he would allow. I kept a record of various subjective and objective tests for comparison with his—but I also noted various facts of which I told him nothing.

For example, my sexual stamina had increased to such a point that I could not go a single day without some kind of release. So fierce was my appetite that I found myself seriously considering seeking the services of prostitutes rather than risk exhausting or even injuring Maxwell with my unappeasable hunger.

And though the idea terrified me, it excited me too. Beyond this new animal vigor, I felt a fantastic kind of confidence, even power in all my abilities. I felt that I could do no wrong. That my diagnoses were infallible, that my orders were absolute.

Also, and equally troubling, I began to view the contest between myself and Maundeville as an exciting game. I relished the idea of pitting my wits against his and utterly crushing him.

Not that he was deserving of sympathy, but that I was so utterly devoid of it—that I had seemingly developed a capacity for genuine cruelty—worried me.

I think Maundeville noticed the change in me too, for several times I caught him watching me curiously, as though he had found something to consider.

Once after the daily injection he turned from the table and put a strong hand on my shoulder.

"Tell me," he said, "if it's not indiscreet, have you gone quite out of your depth at Cadogan Square?"

"Over head and ears," I declared boldly.

"And the lady, Armiston? Honestly, I'm not asking out of impertinent curiosity."

"About the lady it's not for me to say." I believe I spoke with a certain arrogance, and his hand fell from my shoulder.

"You and I would have done great things together," he said moodily. "You're a bigger man than I thought. It seems a pity."

"Why 'would have done'? We'll go on."

"A man can't serve two masters—or mistresses." He turned back to the table. "But—yes, we will certainly go on."

He never again asked me about Cadogan Square.

I remember that same day I found myself nearly three-quarters of an hour earlier than Miss Hennessey would expect me, and I turned into my club. Every man there was complaining of the heat, and talking with greedy longing for August and the moors or the sea. I was surprised to realize I hadn't noticed anything oppressive about the weather.

One fellow asked me, "Where've you been for your holidays, Armiston?" and when I told him that I hadn't left London, and was too busy to go, he stared.

"That's something. Never saw you look so fit in my life!"

Indeed, as I went down the wide club staircase with two others toward a big mirror, I could see plainly that their faces were haggard and sallow compared with mine, yet I knew I was the eldest of the three.

I felt a surge of reckless joy in my power and authority over other men.

I believed I had done it for Maxwell, but Maxwell was the one who brought me crashing back to earth when I went to his room that evening.

For the past two weeks we had tried unsuccessfully to reduce his dose, but having come so far, we could go no further. It was a bitter blow. From 30 grains to half a grain was nothing less than heroic. But he was unable to adjust to such a low dose and his physical and mental distress was such that I knew the time had come to deliver the dreaded verdict.

"My poor boy, you've deposited so much improper material in your tissue that your life is not consistent with the protracted pain of removing it. You will have to take opium all your life. Further struggle is suicide."

We would raise his dosage to a sustainable minimum and take each day as it came. Whatever he did, his organs marched to death. He had to continue the habit which killed him only because abandoning it would kill him sooner—it became a mere question of time. The only way left to preserve his intellectual faculties was to keep his future daily dose at the tolerable minimum.

But when I opened the door of the sickroom I found Maxwell out of bed and in the process of packing. I froze in the doorway. He gave me a cool look and continued to fold his garments. And although he was clearly unwell, he did not seem as ill as he had that morning. Certainly there was no discounting that obvious strength of purpose.

"What's this?" I asked in alarm.

"It's time for me to return home, Quentin."

"But…" I found my legs uncommonly weak and had to sit down on the nearest chair. "What's happened?"

He gave me a long, level look. "There's probably a scientific explanation for what's happened. All I know is that you've changed. You've turned into someone I don't care for. Not as a doctor nor as a friend nor…" He drew a quick, shaky breath. "The other."

Having spent the afternoon on the pinnacle of self-love this felt rather like being struck by a thunderbolt and dashed to earth.

"I…don't understand."

"Nor do I. I've tried to make sense of this transformation. I can't. I wish I could blame it all on Maundeville's serum, but what drove you to take the serum? You mock and belittle Bird. You're patronizing and pompous with me. You speak callously, conceitedly of your power over Miss Hennessey. You refer to your patients as though they're little more than animals to experiment on. I could list a hundred instances of your inconsideracy and unkindness these past two weeks. There would no doubt be more, but you spend all your time at Maundeville's—or Miss Hennessey's, where I presume you've been most of this evening."

"But you know why that is," I protested.

"Yes. And that scares me more than all the rest of it." He did not look scared, though. In fact, having said what he intended, he did not even look angry. He appeared weary and resolved. "Have you read Shelley's poem 'Ozymandias'?"

"I—no."

"You remind me of that poem, Quentin. You are now more like those ancient Egyptian kings than Maundeville. Than even the damned Mummy."

I was the one who was frightened.

"But, Hilary—my dear boy, I'm doing this for you."

"No." He shook his head. "You're not. I don't know who this change is meant for, but it's not me. All the things I liked best about you—" He broke off as though too moved to continue.

I said, and I couldn't help feeling a bit indignant at this injustice, "*How* have I changed? What were these qualities you once saw that you no longer recognize?" I believed if anything, my courage was greater, my intellect intensified, my strength… stronger. I was in *all* ways a superior man to the man he had first—

"Your kindness and compassion," he said quietly. "Your humility."

I felt as though he'd struck me in the heart. As though all the wind had been knocked from me.

As his gray gaze met mine I realized several things at once. He was quite right about the injections. I was not taking them for him. I was taking them for myself. Pride—no, vanity—had got the better of me and I was attempting to…what? Cheat time? Turn back the clock?

Secondly, whether it was some after-effect of the drug, I had allowed my desire to outmaneuver Maundeville turn into an obsession. It was now as much about me besting him as finding justice for Perceval and the others. I wanted to win at all costs.

Or so I had imagined, until I understood what the cost might be.

Thirdly, and perhaps most importantly, I had arrogantly written off Maxwell's chances. I had settled on the idea of him as my own personal tragic invalid who I would nobly, magnanimously care for until the end, but Maxwell was not finished. He had not surrendered, he was still fighting the opium habit—my nerve had failed before his.

"Perhaps you're right," I managed.

His jaw clenched. "Clearly I am."

"But don't…" The words were so difficult! "Don't, Hilary. I'm an old fool, but I do love you. So much so, there don't seem to be words for the feeling. I can be again all those things you liked and admired. I *want* to be those things."

His face twisted as though I'd hurt him again. "You're *not* old," he said impatiently. "You're in the prime of life."

"It's easy for you to say." But I smiled at his indignation. He had fought as a soldier and traveled the world, and yet he really was in many ways still a boy.

"As for me, I'm growing older too," he said. "It isn't for your youth and virility I turned to you, Quentin. I liked *you*. I *love* you. The boy who tried to mend the injured birds and rabbits. The young man who felt too big and clumsy to attend those dances and teas. The grown man who was willing to take on this quest when Percy and I came to you, though I know you first thought we were either fools or villains."

"I never thought that."

He gave a little snort of amusement. "Of course you did."

"No. I thought you were both perhaps slightly mad."

"We were." He sat down on the side of the bed and rested his face in his hands. "Don't let Maundeville destroy you," he muttered. "Don't let him destroy us."

"He won't." I rose and went to him. "I promise. I've heard every word you said and I promise you things will change. I give you my word. Please. You mustn't worry anymore. It's very bad for you."

He raised his head, studying me. "You'll stop the injections? Will you give me your word?"

I put my arm around him and drew his head to my shoulder. "I don't know. It's really the best way I have of keeping close to Maundeville."

"One addict per household is enough, Quentin," he said, and the weariness in his voice made my chest ache.

"*Shh*. My dear. It will be all right. Now I understand the danger. Now I understand what to watch for."

His eyes closed, and I kissed his forehead. He felt warm. Feverish. "Come, get back in bed. I'll unpack for you."

Maxwell opened his eyes and sat up. "No. This isn't the only reason I must leave, Quentin. It's beyond cowardly for me to lie safe here and allow another deal of the cards when we both know where the danger will fall."

"Now listen," I said. "The fact is Maundeville is the man most in danger."

He eyed me skeptically. "That's the serum talking again."

"I promise you it's not. We're coming to the end of this mystery. Can you trust me a little longer?"

He stared at me as though I'd said something incredibly foolish. "Of course I trust you. I love you."

The next day, as expected, a note arrived inviting me to come for "cards" and tea on the following Friday evening.

I went, of course. Our party consisted of me, Steyne, Lethredge, and Maundeville. Maundeville explained that I was there in Maxwell's stead, and Steyne and Lethredge exchanged looks but did not offer comment.

Maundeville offered to deal the cards. No one objected.

At the third round I got the High Priestess, and sat looking at her painted, scornful smile with more trepidation than I had anticipated. It was a pleasant surprise to be congratulated over tea later on my sangfroid.

The only unexpected occurrence that evening was the freakish sandstorm that rose out of nowhere and peppered the taxi on the drive back to Piccadilly.

It left a certain bitter aftertaste of dust in my mouth when I arrived home.

CHAPTER THIRTY FIVE

THE MUMMY WALKS

The first piece of bad luck the Mummy brought was a row with Bird. Indeed, the row came before the lady.

I had casually told Bird at breakfast that I had a large case coming to store for a few days, and that it would be safest and most convenient to stow it away in a corner of my bedroom.

He was silent at the time, but when waiting on me at dinner that night—and a particularly nice dinner he gave me—he opened fire.

"About that there Mummy, sir," he said.

I was thinking about it, and I said, "Well?" and only remembered too late that he wasn't supposed to diagnose a Mummy before he saw it.

There was nothing to be gained by fencing about it then, so I listened as patiently as I could while Bird, in danger of becoming as presumptuous as he was verbose, did the heavy father and the familiar retainer of popular melodrama to perfection. The amount of information he had obtained rather surprised me; and the point of view which he tried to make me take was unexpected.

The core of his argument was that it wasn't respectable. "You and the Captain's single men," he said more than once. He went into the history of priestesses in general, hinting that, broadly (very broadly) speaking, they had at all times been no better than they should be.

"I've come on 'em," he said darkly, "'ere an' there." You'd think he was indulging in memories of past incarnations.

"Very well," I said when he stopped for a fresh argument, or perhaps to get his wind. "It might be best if you accompanied Captain Maxwell back to his quarters until the lady has departed."

This left Bird gasping as if I'd run him through with a cutlass.

"*Leave* you, sir?"

"Yes. The more I consider it, the better I like your idea. Maxwell should not be exposed to any potential…germs the lady might carry. And he certainly isn't well enough to be on his own."

"Leave *you*, sir?" He was still looking mortally wounded.

"Only for the fortnight our dusty guest is visiting. I couldn't do without you for long, you know."

He wasn't mollified. "You can't do without me at all," I was informed. Bird added darkly, "We'll see what the Captain 'as to say."

"Don't think about worrying the Captain right now," I warned him, and he could see I was deadly serious on that score. "You've been talking to Seymour. Is he here now?" and Bird acknowledged that Seymour was currently in the back premises.

"Very well. Give me my coffee, and bring him in when I ring." And I added that I didn't see the use of his cooking a good dinner for me if he meant to worry me into indigestion afterward.

I took my coffee leisurely, with my pipe, worried the matter over for a little, and then rang the bell.

"Bring a couple of chairs to the table," I said to Bird, "and a couple of glasses." I filled the glasses, and I told them both to sit down, which they did a trifle stiffly.

"Now," I said, "we're talking man to man. I won't say I'm going to tell you everything, for it isn't my business only. But what I do tell you will be the plain truth, and I expect to get the plain truth from both of you. Do you agree?"

They looked at one another, and at last Bird spoke.

"Man to man," he said, "it shall be God's truth as far as it goes." And Seymour muttered that he was agreeable.

"Now," I said, "I'm going to be plain with you as far as I'm at liberty to be. I can't tell you more because, like you, I find out things professionally that I can't talk about. But I tell you both that, as far as I can see, both Captain Maxwell and Miss Hennessey will be helped best by my keeping the Mummy here for a fortnight or so, and by your holding your tongues and doing what I tell you. Now, are you on?"

I explained the situation to them and sketched out my plan. I expect it was more the second glass of port they had more or less absent-mindedly swallowed than admiration for my strategy that led them to say they were on—and I closed the interview at once, handing each of them one of Maxwell's "Alma" to smoke in the kitchen.

The next morning the Mummy arrived at my door in its coffin-like case.

I stood and watched the thing being carried up. For the life of me I couldn't help wondering whether it or I would be carried down first.

The second piece of bad luck the Mummy brought—though perhaps it's unfair to blame her entirely—was that Maxwell, barely hanging on to his sanity by his fingernails, suddenly and stubbornly insisted that I completely cut his final dose of opium.

This I refused outright. He was already in a dreadful state, unable to sleep, unable to even rest for more than a few minutes, always pacing, always moving. I would dose him with bromides of potassium and sodium, hyoscyamus and ginger, but they had no more effect than water. We would talk long into the night while we walked up and down the empty streets.

"That bit of material you found at D'Aurelle's. Do you suppose it's a piece of bandage?" he would ask. Or, "The lid of the mummy case was slightly raised. Did you notice when you were in Perceval's room?"

His appetite was gone. He could just manage a little toast moistened with beef-juice and seasoned with salt and pepper or a mouthful of egg, but rarely anything more substantial. I gave him malt extract, wheat extract, and glasses of port to keep his strength up.

Given the precariousness of his situation, of course I refused his request.

He answered fiercely, "Then give me a pistol and allow me to blow my brains out, for I *can't* go on like this. One way or the other this torture *must* stop."

I stared into his red-rimmed eyes and understood no further delay was possible. The timing could not have been worse, but Maxwell had reached his breaking point.

"Very well," I said. "I promised at the start that you would set the pace. If this is truly what you want—"

Tears sprang to his eyes. "Quentin, for the love of God. *I can't go on*," he cried.

It half killed me to hear that note of desperation. I took him into my arms and kissed his tears. "Hush. I'll help you any way I can. You know that."

That morning was the last dose of opium he ever took.

With every hour Maxwell grew more restless and miserable, yet at the same time he seemed wildly exultant that he was finally free. As for me, I was quite simply terrified. I did not believe I was a good enough doctor to save him, and I didn't think I could survive watching him die.

Sometime near dawn the bromides finally took effect and he slept a little. I slept in a chair beside the bed and quite forgot that the Mummy was down the hall a little ways, having her own nap.

The next day was much the same, but Maxwell ate less and seemed weaker.

On the third day he could scarcely retain any nourishment at all. His entire system was near collapse. He perspired profusely and was in an agony of restlessness.

"I feel as though my leg were being ripped off," he told me. "Why does it hurt so much?"

I held his hand, and his grip was punishing. "I know it hurts. Your nerves were muffled with opium these past years. Now you're experiencing a kind of naked sensitivity. It will ease, I promise you."

He slept in fits and starts. Bird spelled me throughout the day and evening so that I could stay awake through the night when the danger would be greatest.

Maxwell talked with nervous energy between uneasy naps, his dark head tossing restlessly on his pillow. "It's funny to think of it now. That first morning, Quentin. I thought you very cold and hard."

I smiled faintly. "You called me a cold-blooded cormorant."

"Yes. In the taxi, though. I remember looking over at you a couple of times, and your eyes were kind. You looked sorry for me."

"I was puzzled, that's all. I thought you were quite handsome. Also *very* odd."

He laughed.

He was quiet for a time. I thought he was sleeping, but he opened his eyes and said suddenly, anxiously, "You won't give me opium again? Whatever happens?"

"No. Of course not."

"Your word?"

"You have my word."

This seemed to relieve his mind.

Before midnight he fell into a doze, then started awake. His eyes were wide and dazed.

"I thought someone whispered in my ear."

"No, dear boy. You were dreaming."

"I could hear her. The words were Egyptian."

I believe my heart stopped for a few seconds. "No," I said firmly. "You're feverish, that's all. You're having fever dreams. Here. Let me bathe your face. That's nice and cool, isn't it?"

He assented. I gave him a few sips of brandy and washed his hands and face, and eventually he fell back into a troubled doze.

Here I must confess my nerves weren't what I had thought. I believed I had made suitable provision for both my own and

Maxwell's safety, so when I had to go "off guard" it would be without risk to either of us. When Bird had to go out, Seymour was generally in his place. They both slept in the house, so we were never alone.

Nevertheless, I own to moments, even in broad daylight, when I would hear the creak of a floorboard or feel a shadow fall across me and turn quickly in my chair, expecting to find trouble at my back.

Even when I slept in my own bed, more than once I waked suddenly, sweating, to find that I was sitting upright, waiting for I knew not what.

That particular night, after Maxwell fell asleep again, a strange sense of panic came upon me. I became sure that someone had entered the house, and instead of getting up like a sensible man and going round to investigate, if necessary with a poker, I sat and listened, suddenly chilly, and with a queer crawling sensation over me as though my skin moved under my clothes.

Though I could hear nothing, I had a very distinct impression that this Something came nearer, and I felt quite unfit to meet it. Indeed, I felt as though if I even saw the door opening, I should go crazy.

Sitting there, with the sick-room lamp turned toward the wall making gray, uncertain distances of shadow, I began to sing. I am not remotely musical and have no idea what I sang. It might as easily have been one of Bird's sea chanteys or a church hymn. Or nothing at all. Perhaps I imagined I was singing while I sat there clutching the arms of my chair and listening for the sound of the door opening behind me.

Untroubled by my performance, Maxwell continued to breathe softly, steadily, the slight rise and fall of his chest the only sign he wasn't already a corpse.

Then this unformed horror went as suddenly and as silently as it came.

I rose, telling myself that I was a damned coward, and I carried my lamp round the flat, holding it up to examine every corner and nook. The odor of the mummy case seemed to have permeated the building, for I caught the faintest scent of bitumen as I walked from room to room. Or perhaps that was merely nervous fancy.

Nevertheless, I was not sure how far fancy was responsible for the notion that I saw light prints, of a smaller foot than mine, as though some dusty foot had walked the length of the runner in the hall that night.

The crisis came on the fourth day.

It was a hot, dry afternoon, and all the length of it Maxwell grew weaker and weaker. By evening he began to wander in his head, and by nightfall he was quite delirious. Neither conscious nor unconscious, his eyes followed the movements of some imagined presence from beneath flickering lashes. I needed Bird's help to keep him in bed, for he had a manic kind of strength in between bouts of torpor.

The room was so hot, I had to open the window. The night air was still, oppressive and yet it carried the snap of electricity. I could hear the sound of crickets, but in my imagination the insect chorus seemed to hum like beetles.

The hours dragged. With each chime of the clock, Maxwell seemed quieter and more gray. Watching him, my heart grew heavier and heavier.

Around midnight he nearly gave me a heart attack—and poor old Bird too—by rising up and shrieking, "She's here, Quentin! Look out. She's *right behind you*!"

I think both Bird and I dropped him onto his pillows to jump and turn, but no one stood in the shadows.

Bird swore fluently, begged my pardon, and whispered, "Is he goin' to die, sir?"

"Hilary? Can you hear me?" I bent over Maxwell. His hands were like ice, his pulse thready and faint. His blue-tinged lips moved soundlessly, forming the silent words *she's here* over and over.

I opened my mouth to answer Bird and found that I could not respond without breaking down.

I could save him. Even the smallest dose of opium would make the vital difference, prolong his life so that he might truly sleep and take nourishment. But then what? Maxwell would never forgive me for betraying his trust. And in a few days we would be back here again.

"No," Bird said all at once. "*No*. Not 'im! 'e's a fighter. 'E won't give up the ghost."

His confidence bolstered my flagging own. "No, he won't," I said fiercely. "In any case, we've had enough talk of ghosts for one night. Bird, bring me towels soaked in hot water. Plenty of towels and very hot water. Hurry."

I had never seen Bird move faster. He was back with a pail of steaming towels just as I finished giving Maxwell an injection of digitalis.

I pulled back the bedclothes. "Wrap his feet in the hot towels. I'll wrap his hands."

Once Maxwell's extremities were swaddled in the hot, wet towels, Bird and I began to rub his arms and legs, pushing blood to his heart. We rubbed and pummeled and massaged him until we were both sweating and red in the face. But the blue shade left his lips and his skin was warm to the touch.

I straightened my aching back. "I'm going to give him something to tone his stomach so he can swallow some nourishment. What is there ready, Bird?"

"Cold beef tea and milk."

"Just the thing. Put a little of the tea in a wineglass, and then come and help me."

I prepared a very strong dose of capsicum and mixed it with sherry and bitters. I woke Maxwell as best I could, and Bird helped me raise him.

Maxwell's head lolled against my shoulder.

"Here we go, dear boy. Just a few sips..." I gently massaged his throat, the base of skull, attempting to stimulate the vagus nerve. "One sip. There. That's it."

Maxwell obediently swallowed, and then his eyes flew open and he began to splutter and cough. He sat up and swore with surprising energy, even glaring at me.

"You needn't poison me. I'm dying as it is."

Why Bird and I should have found that so funny, I can't say, for it was only too close to the truth, but we were indeed laughing almost maniacally as I eased him onto the pillows.

"I know. I'm a brute. Now lie very quietly for just a minute. That's it..." I stroked his hair back, watching his face.

He swallowed unhappily a few times but was not sick. "So thirsty," he complained at last, huskily.

"Good. There's something here for you. It's nice and cool." I gave him a little of the beef tea, and he managed to keep that down as well. After five minutes or so, I fed him a little of the milk, and that was also a success. For the next few hours I alternated feeding him broth and milk until he finally fell into a deep and seemingly natural sleep.

When I felt his pulse again it was still too quick but strong and steady. I knew then the crisis had passed. Bird insisted he would watch the rest of the night—although by then the sky was lightening—and promised to call me if there was any change.

I slept like a dead man and didn't wake until late the next morning when I found my patient conscious and clear-eyed. Maxwell was as weak as a cat but insisted he was not in any great pain. He held out his hand to me, and when I took it, brought it to his lips and kissed it.

"Thank you," he said.

He laughed when I returned gravely, "Thank *you*," but I meant it with all my heart.

Up until the actual crisis when Maxwell's life had hung in the balance, I had managed to continue my investigations with Maundeville, doing a certain small amount of work in his museum. I got a daily hypodermic injection when he did, and kept a taxi always waiting for me at the door, regardless of expense, explaining that it enabled me to keep to my engagements elsewhere.

During the crisis I told Maundeville that it was impossible to meet him as Maxwell's health was failing rapidly. I was determined that he not turn his attention in that quarter, and judging by the odd glint in the professor's eye when he heard this news, I think my decision was a sound one.

"What a tragedy," he said. "Poor Miss Hennessey."

As I hoped, once I failed to keep our appointments, Maundeville suggested that it would serve our purpose if I took away several doses with me. I did so and was therefore able to cut the doses in half, to mitigate whatever untoward effect they were having.

Even so, on the ninth day after the Mummy had crossed my threshold—safely past the crisis with Maxwell—I began to be uncomfortably aware that all was not well with me. I had been in a bad quarter of the West End, and having a fancy to change my clothes before lunch, found a difficulty in tying my scarf. I fumbled with it for a minute or two before I realized my condition.

It was not long in passing off, and I had a healthy appetite for my lunch, but I broke my usual rule, which is not to touch alcohol until dinner-time.

That afternoon I looked in upon two or three friends, and called upon Mortimer, the toxicologist at Gray's Inn.

I wanted to see Maundeville, but he was not at home. I asked Bates when he would be back, but Bates could not tell me, though he knew that Maundeville was making arrangements to spend a week out of town.

"I'll write," I said, and after leaving the door, turned again and wrote my letter up in the library. I was looking at the somewhat scrawling calligraphy caused by the numbness in my right hand, when Bates, always attentive, brought up a tea-tray. But I declined this, explaining that I was not quite well, and I went away home, had an early dinner, and took to my bed.

Maxwell sat with me for a time, but he was still on the sick list himself, and I would not let him stay. If I could have convinced him to do so, I would have ordered him back to his own rooms, but I knew I'd be wasting my breath. I gave Bird and Seymour their marching orders however.

After eight o'clock I lay quiet, listening, and wishing vaguely that I had a better life-record to look back upon. It was just nine o'clock. I had heard my clock chime in the hall, when close upon the last stroke came the sound of swift footsteps.

Not Maxwell, then. And then too quiet for Bird or Seymour.

My heart was pounding so hard I felt quite sick—or perhaps that was the effect of the serum—but in any case I felt incapable of moving a muscle as I listened to those footsteps drawing closer.

My gaze rested on the Mummy case and then returned to the door.

The footsteps stopped.

Nothing happened.

I waited, feeling strangely, alarmingly weak, my gaze pinned to the blank and blameless surface of the door.

Slowly, almost cautiously, the knob turned.

CHAPTER THIRTY SIX

THE MURDERER EXPLAINS ALL

I opened my mouth but closed it again as Maundeville strolled into my bedroom.

He looked so normal—smiling and well groomed, in speckless evening-dress—I felt somehow foolish for my previous alarm. After all, *I* was the one who had set the trap—even if I did feel a bit like a tethered goat waiting for a tiger.

"What! As bad as all that?" Maundeville asked sympathetically, approaching the bed. "I expected to find you all right again."

"My right hand is still a trifle numb," I said, not taking his. "I thought an early night's rest would put me right. But how did you get in? I warned you that Bird would be out."

"So you did. So you did," he agreed, pulling a chair to the bed. "But sick friends mustn't be neglected for want of trifles like latchkeys. I consulted the constable now standing at the street corner, explaining the situation—a friend of yours, I fancy. Prudent man, to keep in with the force!"

"He couldn't let you in."

"No, so he said. So I assured him it didn't really matter, and that I could leave you till to-morrow. After we parted I remembered your staircase window, and I carried your defenses by escalading from the mews."

He stopped again and laughed softly. "Not a soul saw me," he said, "otherwise you might have had to bail me out. Now let me hear all about it. A medical man's fist is generally pretty bad, and your letter was shaky as well."

I again told him of the numbness, which I said was passing off. "I had better drop the injections for a few days," I said, "and then perhaps continue them in smaller doses?"

He considered this, rocking himself to and fro, and finally glanced at his watch.

"No, I think not," he said at last. "I'm due at the French Embassy to-night," and even as he spoke, leaning forward a little, I caught sight of the cross and ribbon on his breast. "But as your hand is shaky I'll give you a small dose myself. I had the same experience a few days ago, but with half-doses the thing went."

I lay quiet for a moment or so, and reminded myself that I had undertaken a job.

"Do as you think best," I said. "You'll see my hypodermic and the stuff itself, there on the mantelpiece."

"Right!" Maundeville agreed, rising and crossing the room. "May I shut this window, just till I go? I find the room quite chilly. Ah! There's our friend the constable, presenting a stolid back to us!"

He pushed the window up gently, and turned to the mantelpiece. I could hear him fiddling behind me with the things, but he was at an awkward angle.

"A small dose," he said, "will make all the difference."

I tried again to turn my head. Instead, I felt the startling burn of a needle driven in under the skin at the back of my neck.

I had thought I was ready for anything, but that caused me to cry out.

"You'll be quite comfortable presently," Maundeville said cheerfully in response to my protest. "And I have still half-an-hour to spare. Half-an-hour soon goes in your company, my dear Armiston." To my amazement, he returned to his chair and sat down.

He had hardly begun to talk again, however, when I felt an increasing difficulty in breathing. All muscular power seemed to be draining away as though I was being severely bled.

In spite of my determination to keep from panic, I was rattled. He had taken me by surprise in using the needle so much sooner than I had anticipated.

By now I was choking, and half rose. "Wh…what…have you…done?" I gasped.

He bore me backward as if I had been a child, and in a moment gagged me with a towel.

"A superfluous precaution, I believe," he said. "The deafening in these rooms is excellent. Now, my dear blockhead! A little increase of your dose has made your limbs as wooden as your head always was. You'll make an admirable listener, for you can neither contradict, nor get up to go away. No, no. Stop goggling at me. You're not going to die yet."

He sat facing me, in my own easy-chair, nursing his knee with clasped hands, one leg resting debonairly over the other.

"I defy anyone to say my methods of achieving my object are not in general most humane," he said pleasantly. "And why not?

I've had no more animus against those I've removed than I have against this hassock, which is rather in my way."

He pushed the hassock gently aside with the point of his small patent leather shoe.

"*You*, Armiston, are in a rather different position, and I cannot pretend to forget it. The other men were old acquaintances. Dear friends, in fact. *You* are an outsider. *You* pushed into what didn't concern you in the least." His brows rose. "Oh! You want to contradict that? My dear fellow, fussy folk always have an excuse for interfering. It isn't worthwhile ungagging you merely to hear arguments which I'm sure I know already, and which don't in the least satisfy my logical faculty. But I'm straying from the point. This flat is so quiet, thanks to me, and your chair is so comfortable. You won't mind my smoking, I'm sure?" He took out his cigar-case, but stopped to consider.

"I might be forgetful later, might I not?" he said. "It wouldn't do to leave my own cigar-end behind me, would it? I'm sure you won't mind my taking one of your cheroots."

He went away, and returned, smiling faintly, with one in his hand—and in the other he held the locket with its miniature of Miss Hennessey.

"You will have no further use for them, you know," he said. "I never grudged you a smoke when you honored my poor house—and I've let you keep this property of mine quite long enough. Now let us get on. So very pleasant not to be obliged to hurry. Where was I?"

Having lit one of Maxwell's cheroots and pocketed the miniature, he leaned back in the chair, and sent a smoke-ring or two eddying across the room.

"There are no draughts here," he said meditatively. "That's always a comfort. I hate draughts—don't you? Oh, I forgot!

Well, I'm sure you do. Now for my explanation, which I know you will appreciate."

He smoked for a few moments in silence and then said in an entirely different voice, nothing like his usual mellifluous tones, "You forced yourself in upon a little circle of friends that didn't want you. We laughed at you behind your back. *You* a member of the Society of Osiris! The idea is absurd."

As he spoke he gradually worked himself into a cold passion. I had never seen him in the slightest degree angry before, and it fascinated me. He crouched in the chair, gripping its arms, and looking as though he were holding himself back from me.

"By God," he said softly, "I have had patience. I have had miraculous patience." He sat muttering to himself inaudibly, his eyes staring into mine, the pupils contracted to pinpoints, for some seconds before he went on.

"But your real sin, the unpardonable sin, is that you aspired to the moon," he said suddenly. "It's not enough merely to wipe you out like the rest, for she lowered herself by raising you above them. The insufferable ridiculousness of it all! You have degraded her in my eyes, and you have made me feel a fool, a hoodwinked fool."

He sat quiet again for a minute or so, and the room was so still that I could hear my own watch ticking under my pillow.

Watching him as I did all the time, stretched out under his eyes, I noticed everything. I saw that the hand he raised to his mouth shook with passion, and I saw, too, that when he moved the cheroot, the end was chewed to bits.

"Well, what is your punishment?" he went on presently. "You're going to die, of course, but that's a mere detail. Since you've meddled with the affair of the Mummy, you shall hear how you and the rest have been fooled." He stopped and looked at his watch. "Plenty of time. Since you think yourself favored by Miss Hennessey, you shall hear what her future will be, and whom she will favor after you're gone and forgotten—like *that*."

He sent another vortex-ring rolling away, and watched till it broke and disappeared. He smiled at me.

"If it's too much of a monologue to please you, my dear Armiston, pray remember that when it ends I add Finis to your own story. That may make it seem less prolonged."

He thought a moment.

"Long ago I counted the cost. There were a score of men—boys, really—dangling about her, but most of them had no earthly chance, and I've left them alone—a case of the survival of the unfittest, my dear Armiston. There were just half-a-dozen who, for different reasons, seemed dangerous, and therefore safest to eliminate them. There are only two now after you—Maxwell has put an end to himself, it seems—and they will go in various ingenious ways, should it prove necessary."

He paused again and considered.

"I was not unfriendly," he said, quite seriously. "I was merely logical. They were in my way—I moved them out of it as gently as I could. Perceval…I regret. Perhaps he even suspected at the last. I can't be sure about that scrawl of his. But in any case, by that time he could have been only barely conscious, and must have been indifferent to his fate."

Here I could not help making a sound of protest. I don't think he even heard me.

"It was they themselves who suggested the Mummy as a stalking-horse, by their silly chaff and bravado. I had been waiting some time for an inspiration, and *she* appeared.

"Scrymgeour's case was child's-play. You see, I knew them all so well. Knew their habits. I paid him a visit one evening when

I could be sure his man was out. I told Scrymgeour I noticed a small tear in that ridiculous painting he thought so much of, and when he climbed onto the step-ladder, I jerked him off backward.

"D'Aurelle was known by his friends to have a marked tendency to heart trouble. I was at Dene Court, where we came and went very casually. My luggage went early to the station one morning, and I was supposed to follow on foot. I purposely met D'Aurelle, and agreed to show him an attack with the gloves which we had talked of. I struck him over the heart, and he collapsed. I was ready to be discovered, and to plead misadventure. I could have done the thing before a dozen witnesses without risk of detection. But no one saw it or knew of it, so I went quietly away, and it was never asked what train I went by.

"In Perceval's case you helped me. For that I suppose you should go painlessly. I do feel rather bad about the boy. I was so fond of him and Maxwell. Once. And after all, I don't want to be brutal, and I daresay you have acted according to your lights."

I felt increasingly strange as I listened to him, as though I were slipping in and out of my body. I could see Maundeville and I could see myself, slumped against the pillows, watching him beneath heavy eyelids. I knew I was in great peril, and yet it was very hard…to care.

"Hitherto I had dealt the cards—and someone else suggested it, mind you—so of course the High Priestess went where I thought fit. But the night you came I thought it would be wise to let the cards fall where they might. After all, it was only a matter of when, not if, for all of them.

"Perceval got the Priestess, and an overdose of stramonium—according to you. You will remember a certain Malay. What?"

That woke me up a little and he must have noticed, for he leaned forward to study me.

"Hm. I took care to deal again, myself, at the next meeting, and this is the result." He sighed and shook his head as though in sympathy at my plight. "In every case I've managed to adapt my means to the individual. You, my dear Armiston, in your new role of ardent lover, wanted renewed youth, and you were fooled by the hope of it. I won't insult your understanding by naming the drug which paralyzes motor-nerve endings and lays you where you are, with all your rather poor wits still about you. It keeps you quiet while I satisfy your infernal curiosity, and presently a stronger dose from your own hypodermic syringe will dismiss you.

"Your friends already know that you are experimenting with some new elixir vitae, and it will be obvious to all that you have pushed your experiments too far. I myself shall be forced to admit that I thought you were overdoing it, and that I warned you."

He smoked in silence for a time. "I shall have to make certain of Maxwell. I don't quite trust you there, Armiston. I confess to you frankly that even now I can't understand how you found favor while he was about. I know the lady's thoughts and ideals wonderfully well. I've studied her as I've studied nothing else. He was the man I feared most."

He laughed quickly. The sound raised the hair on my head.

"No," he said, "I never *feared* him. I never feared man or devil. But he counted most in my calculations. Well, it seems I was wrong."

He sat quiet again, hugging a knee, and to all appearance forgetting his errand. "Without women," he said, "it would be a pleasant, friendly world. I humbly think the scheme of Creation is open to severe criticism. But you may be better able than I to judge presently, and meanwhile I must take it as I find it—with its compensations. Each one of you removed is one distraction less for her, and one obstacle less for me."

How had none of us noticed he was absolutely mad? How had we confused insanity with charming eccentricity? Maundeville babbled on, singing Miss Hennessey's praises, which he mixed with reference to his recent experiments, and assertions of his certainty of a prolonged and active life, and plans for future murders.

"The theme is inexhaustible," he said suddenly. "There's no time for more. If you're as altruistic as you pretend to be, you'll be satisfied, my dear Armiston, that her future happiness is assured. That is the main thing. On the other hand, if your love is mere selfishness, you're suffering the tortures of the damned—and you deserve them all.

"Now, I will use your own hypodermic, and make an end. I expect to meet her at the French Embassy to-night."

He rose, went to the mantelpiece, and found my hypodermic case, complimenting me casually upon its spotless condition as he filled the syringe before my eyes with the undiluted solution of his preparation.

"We needn't sterilize it, I think," he added, smiling. "This will be about forty times above the normal dose. Despite my earlier display of temper, I've no wish to give you any physical pain. It will act at once."

He returned to my bedside, pulled the easy-chair closer, and sat down.

"You're a scrupulously honorable man, my good Armiston," he said, "and I've implicit faith in your word. Promise me, by closing your eyes, that you won't make any noise—which might conceivably be risky, though I don't think so—and I'll remove the gag in case there's anything you wish to say before going into the Unknown."

I closed my eyes, and without any further stipulation he removed the gag.

"Briefly," he said, "can I do anything for you afterward? Give me your instructions and I'll carry them out, as far as I can without risk to my own plans."

By now I understood how badly I had miscalculated. The only trap I had sprung was on myself, and I had likely destroyed Maxwell as well. Bird and Seymour had somehow missed Maundeville's entry and would remain waiting and watching until it was too late. In fact, it was already too late, for my drugged wits were too fuzzy to see any way out. In the end I simply whispered a word or two about Bird.

Maundeville nodded. "I'll see that your wishes are carried out. And now, farewell."

He bent over the bed, picked up a fold of skin from my forearm with his left finger and thumb, and was about to introduce the needle, when it was dashed from his hand. Maxwell's furious face appeared over his shoulder, and Maxwell's arm locked around his neck.

At the same moment I made a desperate effort and launched myself forward. We all fell together in violent struggle.

In spite of the amazement that convulsed Maundeville's face, it was characteristic of the man that he never uttered a sound. Twice he flung us both off, and I got a scar on my forearm that I shall carry to my grave. Though the first injection had been much weaker than Maundeville had intended, it was quite strong enough to make me of little help to Maxwell. And Maxwell, unfortunately, was still convalescent.

The second time Maundeville wriggled free, he dived for the window. Maxwell was after him in a flash, but Maundeville threw open the sash and jumped out.

Maxwell leaned on the sill, panting and cursing quietly. When he could rise, he limped back to me, dropping heavily to his knees.

"Dear God, Quentin. Are you all right? Did I leave it too late—"

I reached for him with still alarmingly leaden arms, and he gathered me into his own. We held each other tightly and said things then that were meant for no ears but our own.

CHAPTER THIRTY SEVEN

WHAT THE MUMMY CASE HELD

On the following afternoon, within a few minutes of the time fixed for the final meeting of the Society of Osiris, Maxwell and I drove up to Maundeville's house.

Bates opened the door.

In answer to my inquiry, he said that his master was not at home. "He told me, sir," Bates added, "that he would be back from the country by this time. He went out of town yesterday. He expected you to-day, and three other gentlemen whose names he gave me. They're here already. I expect he won't be long."

"I expect not," I agreed. "I've brought back Professor Maundeville's mummy case. Please take charge of it. Where are the others waiting?"

"In the studio, sir."

"My man and the driver will carry the case up to the studio with you." Maxwell and I stood watching while they lifted the Thing down from the roof of the taxi. We followed them up the stair when they carried it to the studio.

Maxwell was just telling Bird and Bates we should not want them any more when a bell rang downstairs.

"That may be Maundeville," said Steyne, who was gazing uneasily out of the window.

"He wouldn't ring at his own door," Lethredge pointed out. He was sitting on one chair, his leg in splints upon another.

"Better wait," I said to Maxwell, who nodded.

A moment later Bates opened the door widely, without knocking or announcing anyone, and the admiral I had met the night of my first meeting of the Society of Osiris came quietly in.

Bates closed the door at once again, and the admiral stood alone just inside, looking from one to the other of us, as if to see who was there. Lethredge made the effort to rise, but the admiral said a word, and he sank back again on his chairs. The admiral's eye rested on the mummy case, ranged over us one by one, and returned to the case again.

"I'm here uninvited, gentlemen," he said, "and for that I'm ready to apologize to our host when he comes." He paused a moment, and then pointed to the mummy case. "But before I go I must hear all about that."

No one answered, and after watching us, he asked when Maundeville was expected. "I assume," he added, "that this is a meeting of what one might call an inner circle of the Society, and that you're waiting for Professor Maundeville—possibly to arrange where that goes next. I understand that wherever it has gone death has followed. I have come to join your circle and help as far as I can in solving the puzzle."

There was silence again, and he stepped forward deliberately and took a chair which Maxwell offered. We looked at him, and at one another, and then Lethredge spoke out.

"I think, Admiral, I may say that when we began this business we did so in a fit of bravado, not knowing what we were in for. I speak frankly for myself, at any rate. Speaking for myself still, I say plainly that if I had known more, I would have had nothing to do with the thing. I advise no one else to be mixed up with it."

The admiral listened and gave him an ironical little smile.

"I'm sure Major Lethredge's advice is valuable," he said. "Too valuable to be given until it is asked for. This affair has gone much too far already. I am determined to have the mystery exploded, either as a senior member of the Society of Osiris, or in my other capacity, where perhaps I can bring greater pressure to bear." He paused a moment, and then added, "I am most anxious to be here merely as a member of the Society, who happens to have learned too much of this coterie to be kept out. Where is Maundeville?"

This time it was Steyne who answered from where he still stood, coughing, in the window.

"We've no idea where he is. We're waiting for him. With regard to this mummy case, those who wish can back out. For myself, I'm willing to take the Lady as my guest this evening, whether you help to solve the riddle or not."

"There's nothing left to solve," I said.

All except Maxwell stared at me, astonished, and the admiral eyed me with curiosity.

"If there's no further mystery," he said, "I suppose even I may hear all about it, without any breach of confidence."

"You've told us," I reminded him, "that you came to prevent further trouble with the Mummy. I've told you there will be none."

"This is Professor Maundeville's house, I believe," the admiral said, after treating me to another prolonged stare. "I believe I shall wait for him as long as you think fit to do so yourselves."

Maxwell said to me, "It's useless to waste more time in trying to extricate them from the results of their own foolishness. Tell them everything."

And so I did. Though not everything. I did not tell them of Maxwell's addiction or the truth of our own friendship. But I told them how I had first begun to suspect Maundeville. I reminded them of the three deaths—Scrymgeour's, D'Aurelle's, and Perceval's—each a host of the Mummy. I went on to describe the result of my own turn.

"I had seen Maundeville as a conjurer," I explained, "and when I believed him to be a murderer too, I annoyed him purposely. He dealt me the High Priestess as any cardsharper might."

I did not mention what I believed to be the first attempt on me…the dusty foot tracks in the hallway outside Maxwell's sickroom. Something about that night still left me feeling uneasy. But I told them of Maundeville's second attack and how he had confessed to killing three men before me—and his intention to go on killing, as necessary.

"If he's still alive," said the admiral, "this is a hanging matter, three times over. We have, I suppose, with no offence to you, only your word against his?"

"He's still alive," I said, "and what he will say I neither know nor care. I have one living witness." I nodded at Maxwell, who nodded back. "And one silent witness."

"What does *that* mean?" Steyne asked.

"Here," I replied, and knelt beside the mummy case. I beckoned to Maxwell for his help, which he gave, while the others began to protest. The rusted nails and cracked wood of the painted cover screeched in protest as we lifted it off to reveal the ghastly, partially mummified remains of…the Malay!

"What in the name of…" The admiral looked every one of his years as he turned to me. "What is this grotesquerie?"

"Another victim."

"And where is Maundeville?"

A floorboard creaked from just outside the doorway. "I believe this is our host," I said.

We waited in silence that seemed to stretch interminably.

Then Maundeville, still in evening dress, appeared on the threshold. He looked weary and pale but surprisingly composed as he studied us.

His gaze fell on the open mummy case, and something changed in his face. He smiled a bitter little smile.

"The Priestess won't like this, Armiston."

"I don't imagine she likes any of this, Maundeville."

His gaze fell on Maxwell. His lip curled. "As I suspected."

"Now, Professor Maundeville," the admiral broke in, "you must hear the charges made against you by Doctor Armiston."

"Do you imagine I'm unfamiliar with them?" He yawned. It was theatrical, admittedly, but it got the point across.

"Do you mean to say you don't deny them? *Any* of them?"

He laughed harshly. "Dear me, no. I've no doubt that Doctor Armiston was scrupulously correct in his accounting. Anyway, didn't I foolishly supply him with most of the information? Let it be a warning to you all against bragging."

"Professor, you admit to these accusations?" the admiral insisted. He seemed genuinely flabbergasted.

"All the main facts," Maundeville agreed, looking across at me. "You see, I still trust you, my dear Judas. Even now."

The admiral stared at him and then me. "I must own, I find it almost impossible to credit such statements. The thing is monstrous, and seems absolutely impossible."

"It's a wicked world," said Maundeville mockingly. "Which means that we don't all think alike, or, if we do, some of us are afraid to say so."

"If all this is really true, madness is the only possible explanation of his crimes," Lethredge said. "A criminal lunatic asylum is the only place for him."

"Madness! Crimes!" Maundeville jeered openly. "Merely words applied by fools to the unconventional before they try to stamp it out."

The admiral looked at him as if marveling, and then turned to Maxwell.

"You say that you were there outside Doctor Armiston's room. That you heard this man own to having killed D'Aurelle, Scrymgeour, Perceval, and saw him attempt to kill Armiston?"

"Yes, sir. I agree with all that Doctor Armiston has said."

"Armiston and Maxwell agree," the admiral said, speaking more particularly to Major Lethredge and Steyne, "and Maundeville admits. Yet, I confess, I find the thing incredible. What possible motive could drive the man so far, so low?"

No one said anything.

He turned to Maundeville again. "What was your object?" he asked, and even I, who knew, waited almost as curiously as the others to hear what he would say.

He shrugged his shoulders as if such questions were beside the mark. "They were in my way," he said. "I had to move them."

Beyond that he would tell nothing, though the admiral questioned him further, pointing out that a full explanation might decide what we did more favorably for himself.

"Who cares what you do?" Maundeville said carelessly. "Certainly not I. The fact that my game has been seen prevents my winning the stake. Nothing else matters."

"Why did you come back?" Maxwell asked suddenly. "You got away last night. You have contacts, friends, allies. You could have left the country quite easily. No one would ever have found you unless you wished it."

I wondered if there was a part of him that wished Maundeville had done exactly that.

Maundeville smiled almost affectionately at him. "For the same reason I've already given. Everything I care about is here. The game is up. There's no point carrying on."

I can't guess how long we might have gone on without actually doing anything, for we were startled by an interruption which I confess I ought to have foreseen and guarded against.

"Someone is calling here," Steyne reported from the window. "A carriage is stopping." Then a moment later, with a note of breathlessness in his voice, "Miss Hennessey is at the door!"

"The man will keep her out," suggested the admiral, looking to the rest of us.

"He will not," said Maundeville sharply. "Unlike the rest of you, Miss Hennessey is welcome here."

"Go out and stop her," the admiral ordered Maxwell.

"Wait!" Maundeville cried, and Maxwell waited, though he, at least as much as any of us, must have dreaded the girl's entry at such a time.

"You want to keep the meeting quiet," Maundeville said. "You fear what I shall do if she comes in. You mean to keep her out. I say she *must* come. If you don't bring her in, I have ways of letting my man know when I'm here, without opening the doors, and I'll use them. You can't keep anything private after that. Let her in for five minutes, and she'll go away quietly and willingly, without any suspicion."

"Why should we believe you?" Lethredge asked. "What do you want with Miss Hennessey?"

"Only to see her once more," he answered simply.

I suppose if anyone in the room had failed to understand Maundeville's true motive up to that time, he had no more doubt about it after that one sentence. The professor's face, voice, and manner when speaking of her were altogether changed.

"Preposterous," I heard the admiral mutter.

While we looked at one another, hesitating, an electric bell somewhere in the room began to ring shrilly. I don't remember that one ever jarred me so much before. I've hated the sound ever since.

"Remember," said Maundeville softly, staring at me.

"I believe him," Maxwell said. "I'm going to bring her in. Be careful that no one else makes her suspicious."

CHAPTER THIRTY EIGHT

EXIT THE VILLAIN

Maundeville limped forward to meet Miss Hennessey with his ordinary jaunty welcome. I don't exaggerate when I say he was easily the most self-possessed man in the room.

She shook hands with him and she bowed to the rest of us, eyeing the admiral with some surprise, and bowing to him with more ceremony. Perhaps she had hurried, perhaps she was excited. Her face was flushed, her eyes were bright, her black dress and big black hat set off her delicate skin. Though I'm no judge, I thought I'd never seen any female look more bewitching. Involuntarily, I looked from her to Maundeville, and saw how his eyes lingered on her face, while his little compliments and words of welcome stopped as though lodged in his throat.

There was an ominous silence all through the room. She noticed it at once.

"What is it? What is happening?" she asked. "Why are you all looking so startled? Is this another deal of the cards?" Her glance fell on Maxwell, and her expression changed to immediate and passionate relief.

"Then you're better?" she said quickly. "Oh, I'm so *glad*. I was so—"

She broke off self-consciously, glancing at Maundeville. He never took his eyes off her face. His laugh, a little too loud, a little too gay, broke the silence again. But when he took it upon himself to explain, there was no trace of excitement in his voice or manner. He seemed so much his usual self it was uncanny.

"We've been favored, as you see, by an unexpected visit from the admiral," he said smoothly. "He's found out a good deal about this silly business with the Mummy, and has persuaded us to stop it."

No one contradicted or added anything to this explanation. Miss Hennessey, after waiting a moment, perhaps for someone else to speak, accepted it.

"That's excellent. I'm grateful," she told the admiral. "I only wish you had heard about it sooner."

From the chair where Lethredge sat came a solemn "Amen," that made her turn and look at him, startled.

Then she saw that the Malay rested in the painted case, and remarked that she had imagined the Mummy would look quite different. That there would be wrappings and bandages, that this piece of driftwood almost looked *male*.

Now here was a strange little comedy of errors, but no one corrected her. In fact, we all took turns answering, each more idiotically than the last man.

Finally, mercifully, the admiral broke in. "This has been a charming surprise, Miss Hennessey, but we must ask you to retire. We have some business that only men can settle."

No member of woman's suffrage could take that lying down, and Miss Hennessey prepared to do battle, but Maundeville once more stepped in.

"Will you forgive me if I don't come down, my dear girl?" he said, and there was such warmth and tenderness in his voice that

I think that alone silenced her. It certainly silenced the rest of us. "I find I'm a little under the weather today."

He bore her expressions of concern and care stoically. "Armiston, I'm sure you'll be glad to take Miss Hennessey to her carriage for me." He stood in the doorway, his eyes fixed upon her, until she passed out. I closed the door behind us.

"What does it all mean?" she whispered, as we went side by side down the broad stair, watched by Bates, who stood in the hall below. "I feel horribly frightened, and I can't tell why. If I had stayed, I thought I should scream. Are you quite certain there's no more danger to anyone?"

"Our troubles are ended, I think," I said. "It's better that I shouldn't tell you more just now. You shall hear all about it someday. Now go, and remember there won't be the slightest danger for Maxwell anymore."

She then went quietly away, obviously unsatisfied with my assurance, and protesting that he was not the only one whose safety concerned her.

I waited at the door until the carriage had moved off, being determined to make sure that Bates had no chance of learning the whereabouts of his master until it was too late to provide aid.

I dreaded returning to the studio, but there was no choice about it.

Maundeville was in his favorite chair, smoking, and lecturing the others on the mummification process.

I think that was the final straw for me. "You've heard my accusations against this man," I said. "They're backed by Maxwell, and the man himself doesn't deny them. Is there the least shadow of doubt in anyone's mind?"

I made each one answer for himself in turn. Each said "No," and Maundeville himself said "No" when the others had spoken—jeeringly adding that he claimed a voice in the matter.

"You're infernally proud at having trapped me, Armiston," he said. "But if we hadn't worshipped at the same shrine, your poor wits would never have been sharpened. You've a lonely crabbed old age before *you*, Armiston!"

I glanced instinctively at Maxwell and Maxwell met my gaze. There must have been something in our eyes because Maundeville's jeering stopped abruptly. He stared from me to Maxwell with dawning realization and then began to laugh.

At this point Maxwell suggested the admiral had better leave us, and the others backed him up. But, after considering, the admiral refused, saying that it was too late.

In the end, he even took the lead to some extent in what followed.

"Here, then, is a criminal," he said, "with these deaths to answer for, and ready for more. What shall we do with him?"

"Call in the nearest policeman, and let him hang like any other," said Lethredge.

Maundeville turned on him.

"You blundering fool," he said fiercely. "Am I like any other? And is *she* like any other? Will you have her name tossed about through all the gutter-press of Europe? It's a pity your pony didn't break your neck as well as your leg. It's a pity I didn't deal *you* the High Priestess, though I knew she couldn't love such a fool."

One sees the ludicrous side of it now, but at the time I believe none of us felt anything except his blighting contempt. Maundeville was more like a scorpion writhing in fire than a human being—though the root of it all was human enough.

"Let's hang him ourselves," said Steyne, and took no notice of the taunts Maundeville flung at him. "We might shove him out this window, but it won't necessarily kill him."

"We can't let him live, of course," Maxwell said quietly. "One way or the other, the time has come. But we must do it… properly."

Maundeville seemed oddly impressed and made no attempt to interrupt.

The admiral said, "I absolutely agree with Captain Maxwell. Maundeville has to die. I will ensure it, even if Miss Hennessey's name cannot be kept out, and even if I must give evidence myself."

"Even if!" sneered Maundeville. "What self-sacrifice! What self-satisfaction!"

"Show some respectful," Major Lethredge said angrily.

The four of us drew round Lethredge's chair, leaving Maundeville to stand alone. I don't believe any of us were afraid of the responsibility. Our case was clear, and no one doubted what would happen if we appealed to the law. The admiral insisted upon being the one to tell him our decision, saying plainly that since he had pushed himself into the investigation, he was determined to take his full share of the responsibility.

"We have decided," he said to Maundeville, "every one of us, that you shall die. So long as that happens quickly, we are not concerned as to the manner of your death. For reasons which are merely sentimental we understand your crime, and pity you just enough to let you choose. If you like to be your own executioner, you shall be."

"Let us fight to the death, then," Maundeville said.

The admiral spluttered. "I won't fight you, and I'll allow no one else to do so. This is an execution, not a quarrel. You've forfeited your life three times over. But you may choose the means yourself."

Something seemed to snap inside Maundeville. He broke loose and cursed us all where we stood waiting round about him, even Lethredge rising to lean upon the chair's back.

"You sanctimonious ravens!" Maundeville hissed. "You vampires! I'm more alive than any of you. More of a man than any two of you. You haven't vitality enough to break your damned laws except all together. Your law's made by cowards to protect themselves against men."

No one answered him, and he became silent. I felt in my pocket and found my hypodermic syringe case.

"We all agree in the judgment and sentence," I said, "but no one is anxious to be executioner. To blot him out is all we want, is it not?"

"And quickly," the admiral added.

"I'm ready, if need be," young Steyne said. "I've done less than anyone."

The admiral raised a hand to him to be quiet and nodded for me to go on. I showed them the case.

"There's death here for twenty men," I said. "And no one better understands the working of it than Maundeville. He's prostituted his knowledge to evil purposes. Let him make good use of it now."

In reply Maundeville jeered at me as a sanctimonious hypocrite and a blabber. But I believe his only object was to taunt one or more of us into a fight—and in that he failed, and recognized it.

"Very well." He was abruptly calm. "There's nothing left worth wrangling about. 'All or naught' holds to the end."

I held out my pocket-case to him again, and he looked at us and saw, no doubt, that his time had come. He took the case and limped away silently toward the door leading to the bedroom.

"Is it safe?" the admiral asked softly.

"Let him be," Maxwell answered. A strange look came over his face and he said sharply, "I see his shroud to his lips..." He was shivering and put my hand on his shoulder. He clenched his jaw and was silent.

When Maundeville reached the bedroom door he turned and looked back at us. A more evil, more malignant face I never saw. In fact, for one strange moment I seemed to see the features of the Mummy superimposed over his own.

He stood there a moment, his lips silently writhing, though I'm sure it was not in prayer, then went through, shutting the door quietly behind him.

That was the last any man ever saw of Maundeville alive.

Days later, when Miss Hennessey begged me to tell her how I had managed to house the Mummy without harm to myself, I refused to say. But I honestly confessed that I owed my life to Maxwell's help at a critical moment.

When I mentioned his name, a shadow crossed her face. She told me that she and Mrs. Vavasour were soon to return to the States. I wished her good luck with all my heart. "You leave behind many admirers," I told her.

"Alas, admiration is not love," she replied.

I believe one of her admirers was Bird, who upon hearing she was leaving England, offered me his condolences on missing my opportunity. "Still, we can't hall be 'appy," he told me bracingly.

"How true," I said. "And how like you to point that out."

"After hall, you an' me an' the Captain are comfortable enough. 'E needs you an' you need me."

"Ah. And what do *you* need, Bird?"

But to this he only grinned and went off to finish cooking breakfast.

As for Maxwell, my favorite patient continued to improve and even thrive, although he insisted he needed to remain under my constant care lest he again fall into temptation.

(In private I couldn't help telling him that it was I who was forever falling into temptation when he was about.)

When he decided to move into the tall house on Park Lane left to him by Perceval, Bird and I went with him. I kept my old practice, however, and began to specialize in treating opium addiction. In fact, I began to build rather a name for myself in the fashionable world for my success in treating the disease. Now and then Bird tried to convince me to move my practice to Harley Street, but I was happy as I was.

More than happy.

There's only one thing more I will tell you. We found Nefertiabet in a steamer trunk in Maundeville's cellar. The following spring Maxwell and I took the Mummy back to Egypt ourselves, found her tomb, and buried her there.

As we dumped the last bit of earth from our spades, a blue-black beetle pushed through the soil and scuttled past the toe of Maxwell's boot.

Maxwell looked at me and said, "You don't think—?"

"No," I said. "I don't." And I kissed him there in the golden shade of the pyramids.

Some little while later he said, "We'll frighten the camels," and kissed me back.

For purely sentimental reasons I'd brought Methuselah, the tortoise, too, and we left him sunning himself in the desert sand outside the tomb.

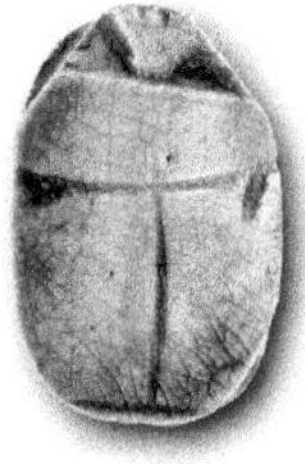

THE END

AUTHOR NOTES

What is a literary mash-up (also called "mashup" or "mashed-up novel") you ask? It's a work of fiction which combines a pre-existing text which has entered into public domain—very often a classic work of literature—with another genre to create an original single narrative.

One of the best-known examples of the genre is *Pride and Prejudice and Zombies: The Classic Regency Romance - Now with Ultraviolent Zombie Mayhem!* by Jane Austen and Seth Grahame-Smith.

The basis of *The Curse of the Blue Scarab* is the 1912 novel *The Mummy* by horror writer Riccardo Stephens. Sadly, little is known of Stephens, and *The Mummy* appears to be his final published work. This particular mash-up is an extra mashed mash-up for I've also included segments of the following books: *The Treatment of Opium Addiction* by Dr. J.B. Mattison, *The Opium Habit* by Horace B. Day and *Cupid, M.D.* by Augustus M. Swift.

Finally, I feel I should add a word of reassurance for the copyeditors in the audience. All those crazy hyphenated words and that elaborate, convoluted sentence structure is original. I did my best to preserve it intact, although I'm sure you wonder why!

ABOUT THE
(STILL LIVING) AUTHOR

Author of over sixty titles of classic Male/Male fiction featuring twisty mystery, kickass adventure, and unapologetic man-on-man romance, **JOSH LANYON**'s work has been translated into eleven languages. Her FBI thriller *Fair Game* was the first Male/Male title to be published by Harlequin Mondadori, then the largest romance publisher in Italy. *Stranger on the Shore* (Harper Collins Italia) was the first M/M title to be published in print. In 2016 *Fatal Shadows* placed #5 in Japan's annual Boy Love novel list (the first and only title by a foreign author to place on the list). The Adrien English series was awarded the All Time Favorite Couple by the Goodreads M/M Romance Group.

She is an Eppie Award winner, a four-time Lambda Literary Award finalist (twice for Gay Mystery), an Edgar nominee and the first ever recipient of the Goodreads All Time Favorite M/M Author award.

Josh is married and lives in Southern California.

Find other Josh Lanyon titles at www.joshlanyon.com, and follow her on Twitter, Facebook, Goodreads, Instagram and Tumblr.

For extras and other exclusives, please join Josh on Patreon at https://www.patreon.com/joshlanyon.

ALSO BY JOSH LANYON

NOVELS

The ADRIEN ENGLISH Mysteries

Fatal Shadows • *A Dangerous Thing* • *The Hell You Say*

Death of a Pirate King • *The Dark Tide*

So This is Christmas • *Stranger Things Have Happened*

The HOLMES & MORIARITY Mysteries

Somebody Killed His Editor • *All She Wrote*

The Boy with the Painful Tattoo • *In Other Words...Murder*

The ALL'S FAIR Series

Fair Game • *Fair Play* • *Fair Chance*

The ART OF MURDER Series

The Mermaid Murders •*The Monet Murders*

The Magician Murders • *The Monuments Men Murders*

OTHER NOVELS

The Ghost Wore Yellow Socks

Mexican Heat (with Laura Baumbach) • *Strange Fortune*

Come Unto These Yellow Sands • *This Rough Magic*

Stranger on the Shore • *Winter Kill* • *Murder in Pastel*

Jefferson Blythe, Esquire • *The Curse of the Blue Scarab*

Murder Takes the High Road • *Séance on a Summer's Night*

The Ghost Had an Early Check-Out

NOVELLAS

The DANGEROUS GROUND Series
Dangerous Ground • Old Poison • Blood Heat
Dead Run • Kick Start

The I SPY Series
I Spy Something Bloody • I Spy Something Wicked
I Spy Something Christmas

The IN A DARK WOOD Series
In a Dark Wood • The Parting Glass

The DARK HORSE Series
The Dark Horse • The White Knight

The DOYLE & SPAIN Series
Snowball in Hell

The HAUNTED HEART Series
Haunted Heart Winter

The XOXO FILES Series
Mummie Dearest

OTHER NOVELLAS

Cards on the Table • The Dark Farewell •The Darkling Thrush
The Dickens with Love • Don't Look Back • A Ghost of a Chance
Lovers and Other Strangers • Out of the Blue
A Vintage Affair • Lone Star (in Men Under the Mistletoe)
Green Glass Beads (in Irregulars) • Blood Red Butterfly
Everything I Know • Baby, It's Cold • A Case of Christmas
Murder Between the Pages • Slay Ride

SHORT STORIES

*A Limited Engagement • The French Have a Word for It
In Sunshine or In Shadow • Until We Meet Once More
Icecapade (in His for the Holidays) • Perfect Day
Heart Trouble • In Plain Sight • Wedding Favors
Wizard's Moon • Fade to Black • Night Watch
Plenty of Fish • The Boy Next Door
Halloween is Murder*

COLLECTIONS

*Stories (Vol. 1) • Sweet Spot (the Petit Morts)
Merry Christmas, Darling (Holiday Codas)
Christmas Waltz (Holiday Codas 2)
I Spy...Three Novellas
Point Blank (Five Dangerous Ground Novellas)
Dark Horse, White Knight (Two Novellas)
The Adrien English Mysteries
The Adrien English Mysteries 2*

www.ingramcontent.com/pod-product-compliance
Lightning Source LLC
Chambersburg PA
CBHW051003180726
48291CB00006B/1953